*For Every Woman
There Is a Season—
A Time To Find Love
And Make It Hers
Forever.*

Constance O'Day Flannery

SEASONS

WARNER BOOKS

A Time Warner Company

WARNER BOOKS EDITION

Cover design by Elaine Erch
Cover illustration by Michael Racz

Warner Books, Inc.
1271 Avenue of the Americas
New York, NY 10020

 A Time Warner Company

Printed in the United States of America

First Printing: February, 1995

10 9 8 7 6 5 4 3 2 1

Dedication

Adele Leone and Jay Acton . . . for making it happen

Acknowledgments

Leslie Esdaile . . . for her assistance and laughter. She made writing this book a pleasure.

Jeanne Tiedge, Mel Parker and Larry Kirshbaum . . . for their unwavering support.

Vernon Edwards . . . for teaching me how to play again, and still meet a deadline.

and

Ryan O'Day Flannery, my son . . . for his patience and his great sense of humor. Thanks.

Prologue

Once upon a time she had believed that you get back what you give out in this world, that there was such a thing as karmic justice; she had rejected that belief while living out the cold, wintry nightmare of her marriage. Now she knew once again it was true.

It was simply all in the timing.

The knowledge of that truth frightened her, for her own heart was stained. She was the kind of woman that prayed for the souls of dead animals on the side of the road. She'd been told that she was gracious, kind, and giving of her time and self. A pillar of strength in the community. So how could she sit in church with such hate in her heart?

Watching the priest go through the motions of the mass, she wondered why she was even there. Didn't her presence make her a hypocrite? If she was truly strong she should stand up and shout that it was all a lie. Nothing was real any more. Her friends, her family, her God ... everyone, everything, had let her down and forgiveness wasn't in her heart, though she silently played the

role everyone expected, while vowing to no longer participate in the farce. Not any more. She recalled the scenes
of horror, scenes she had lived out, scenes that would
haunt her for the rest of her life . . .

*It was far worse than any nightmare. Her face was
swollen with purple bruises. Her eyes puffy, yet dry, for
there were no more tears left to shed. Her clothes were
torn and the muscles in her body screamed in pain, a pain
that was all too familiar as she crawled away from him.
There was nowhere to hide. He was always there. He
would find her and kill her. Hadn't he promised to see her
dead?*

*She could sense him bending over her, his face a
grotesque mask of hatred and insanity. His breathing grew
heavy as her fear excited him.*

"You lying bitch. You'll never escape me!"

The strong, rank odor of whiskey surrounded him.

*"Please . . . please. Don't hurt me anymore." It was
what he wanted to hear, and she no longer had any pride.
Cowering, crouched into a corner of the kitchen, she
crossed her arms over her head to protect it from the inevitable blows.*

*"Please! I—I'm sorry!" She would say anything, do
anything, to make him stop, for there was no reasoning
with a madman.*

"Ginny? Are you okay?" The whisper was soft and familiar, and filled with love.

Nodding, she forced his image from her mind and
willed her heartbeat to return to normal.

She hated him . . . even in death.

Virginia Harrison sat up straight in the front pew of the church and stared at the priest, pretending to listen to the eulogy. Everyone was looking at her; she could feel their eyes, their pity, and the muscles between her shoulders tightened in defense. If only they knew . . .

But secrets must be kept.

Just concentrate on the priest, she told herself, refusing to look at the bronze casket before the altar. The long metal box containing the body of her husband was adorned with white lilies, the flowers of innocence, and she wanted to laugh out loud at someone's foolish gesture. Evan Harrison had been born evil. It wasn't enough that he had killed himself in a drunk driving accident—he had taken the life of a teenaged girl along with him. And now their friends and neighbors were pitying her, the wife of the district attorney who had fought so hard against drunk drivers and was now labeled one himself.

Poor Evan, they must be thinking. Poor Ginny. So tragic . . .

Little did they know that her nails were cutting into her palms in an effort to hold down the rising hysteria. She wanted to flee this tribute to the man who had made her life a living hell.

She was almost free. Almost.

If she could just manage to sit very still and play the part of the grieving widow for a few more hours, it would finally be over. It shouldn't be that hard; her six-year marriage had been one long, agonizing, acting stint. She had played the part of the attentive, proper wife of Burlington County's crusading district attorney. Evan had had long range political goals, and so Ginny had volunteered for the right charities, had attended numerous chicken din-

ners, clasped hundreds of palms and smiled into countless
faces. The press said she was gracious, yet distant enough
so that no one really knew her. How right they were. No
one knew she feared for her life every waking moment.
She was always worried that she might do the wrong
thing, say the wrong thing, and word would get back to
her husband. Not a single person gathered in this church
ever imagined that Evan Harrison had kept her in a state
of constant terror.

How could it be possible that she had loved him? Once,
so very long ago, they had laughed together and
loved . . . or had she only thought it was love? Was it only
her imagination that they had planned the perfect future together? It was so hard now to remember. When had the
good times turned so bad? When had the laughter become
anger? The love, hate? At first, in the beginning of the
marriage, she had thought it was her fault that he lost his
temper. Somehow she must be doing something wrong, always displeasing him. And so she had tried to change, had
allowed him to manipulate her life until she was little more
than a POW, terrified of her captor. He could be charming,
promising that he would never hit her again, that he would
get help, that he needed her . . . and for two years she had
believed him and his fervent apologies. Then she learned
how to survive. She learned that his drinking was a warning sign and she'd taken to locking herself in the bathroom, only to realize that it was no barrier against a
madman. When the beatings became more frequent, more
bizarre, she had tried to leave. It was then he had threatened to kill her. He would have done it eventually.

He'd laughed at her threats to expose him. In her mind,
she could still hear his laughter, that sarcastic snicker. As

district attorney, he'd boasted that he could count on the police and even the judges to support him, that he belonged to a male power elite she could never enter. He was so charming to the outside world, with many friends and acquaintances, yet none of them actually knew him. God help her, but she believed that he would have done anything to protect his reputation and his ambitions . . . even murder.

How many nights had she spent hating him, and hating herself? How many nights had she lain awake, wondering if she had the courage to kill him first? She despised the fear that had paralyzed her, the horrible statistics that had turned over and over in her mind: four women a day were killed by the men that lived with them, and sixty percent of those were killed after they finally left. Hopelessly trapped, she had believed that death would be the only way out.

She never thought it would be his. He had picked up a seventeen-year-old girl in a bar and driven his car into the Rancocas Creek.

And now the people who filled the church gazed at her with pity—the poor widow whose husband died in such a terrible public way. That's why she knew there really was karmic justice after all. They thought she was in shock, that she couldn't show emotion yet. If only they knew.

Inhaling deeply, Ginny glanced at her sisters, one on either side of her. Why hadn't they known? Why had no one ever suspected the nightmare she'd been living? Had she been that good an actress that even her own sisters had never suspected her clumsiness was too frequent, the bruises on her arms and legs too chronic? But then Allie and Nan had their own lives, their own problems.

As everyone knelt for the benediction, Ginny felt Allie's hand close over her own.

Allie smiled sympathetically and whispered, "It's almost over."

Ginny nodded and took another deep breath. It wouldn't be over until that bronze coffin was buried, until six feet of earth separated them. She would never feel at peace until the house was cleared of Evan's things, until she could physically wipe him out of her life. Then, only then, would she tell them about her plan.

She had spent years dreaming, fantasizing, about this day. How many nights had she cried herself to sleep, terrified it would never come? She had promised herself that if she ever found her way out of the nightmare, she would do something with her life, and the first thing she was going to do was sell that huge Tudor house. To her it was a prison, every room carrying a memory of horror.

It was almost here. Freedom. She could feel it in the current that ran through her body. Taste it in the air that she inhaled. Once it was hers, once she was totally free, there would be no going back.

She sat down with the others and waited as the priest said prayers over the coffin. The air filled with the strong scent of incense and Ginny almost gagged as it entered her throat. Only a few more minutes and they would leave for the cemetery. She could hold out that long. She had to, she told herself as the priest invited the congregation to join him in praying for the repose of Evan Harrison's soul.

Her lips refused to move. She wasn't even listening. Instead, she was silently talking to a presence that she had long believed to have deserted her. *If you really exist, then thank you . . . thank you for this chance. I can't pray for him. I can only say thank you for giving me back my life.* Only now, when her future awaited her, was she close to tears. She looked down to her hands, clasped tightly in the lap of her black gabardine coat. Her wedding band gleamed bright gold, and she couldn't wait to rip it from her finger. Wasn't it odd to be dressed in black, she thought. Black was the color of mourning.

Dear God, what was the color of joy?

Chapter 1

Four years later

Finally, it was spring.

It happened to her every year, but this particular season Ginny felt it with such force that she pulled the old VW convertible over to the shoulder of the road and deeply inhaled.

Turning her face up to the sun, she enjoyed the warmth as it entered her pores and burned away the last trace of winter from her mind. The scents of apple blossom and lilac filled her nostrils and she was suddenly seized with the crazy biological urge to mate. It was true spring fever, and she was reacting like any other animal.

She opened her eyes and looked at the new green leaves that were just beginning to unfurl and dress the naked limbs of the old oaks. Nature went on, year after year, renewing itself, multiplying. Why was it so hard for her?

A fat robin lighted onto a limb and stared down at her, its tiny feathered head cocked to one side, as though asking that very question. Ginny imagined he must be laughing, maybe even pitying her, and she deeply exhaled before whispering, "It ain't easy, my friend." Another robin landed a few branches above the other and Ginny had to chuckle. Even the birds were at it.

Couples. Mating. Reproducing.

It was everywhere . . . except in her life.

If nothing else could be said about her, Virginia Harrison could lay claim to being a realist. She was too short in a time when athletic women were admired. She was cursed with twenty miserable pounds that had attached themselves to her body like barnacles on the side of a boat in an era when health spas were sprouting up faster than crabgrass. Upon occasion, when she allowed a male, usually a client, to get close enough, she had been told that her eyes were pretty, an unusual hazel. She would admit that she was happy with her hair, straight dark blond hair that could catch the rays of the sun and swing back into place when she turned her head. And she did that fairly often, just to feel it brush against her shoulders and, truthfully, because she paid a small fortune to have it straightened, to chemically command the curly hair that she had fought with most of her life. And, to be honest, she also had it lightened every month. She had always felt out of proportion to her height. Her nose was too big, along with her breasts and her thighs . . . and her feet. One would think God could have at least played with the gene pool a bit and given her feet smaller than an eight and a half.

Reality. Recognizing and admitting it now was important. She had spent far too many years in denial.

Listening to the sounds of the birds, she realized that she didn't know one female who was happy with her body, and she felt that said something sad about the present culture. As much as she hated the double standard, of a man becoming distinguished and a woman merely aging, Ginny had to admit that she was as guilty as the next by trying to hold off the process. She'd aerobicized until her breasts ached and threatened to drop inches closer to her waist, before giving up. She had once allowed a facial peel, a body wrap, and acrylic nails to be attached to her own . . . all because she wasn't perfect. She simply didn't measure up to the image that the media and society were touting. Then it finally hit her: She never would. She would only make her life miserable by trying to be someone she wasn't. And hadn't she learned that lesson before? No more hypocrisy, no more pretending. Many years ago she had realized that she wasn't perfect, and that was okay.

But she was successful.

Harrison Real Estate was the number two brokerage firm in the county, and it was entirely owned by Ginny, started with the insurance money after Evan's death. She was a widow, a successful widow, and many a night she lay awake thanking God for making her one. That was another thing. She had come to a truce with God. She no longer thought of God as she'd been taught by the nuns. She was more comfortable with the notion of Higher Intelligence. All she had to do was look at the perfection of nature to know that man hadn't had a thing to do with it. Man didn't create, he screwed it up.

Glancing back up to the robins as they flew away, she wondered why some people were denied what so many others took for granted. Ever since Evan, she refused to believe that she would one day find a mate. The thought terrified her. Never again would she allow a man to control her. Prisoners of war don't willingly go back. Yet in the daydreams, the ones she was too old and too intelligent to be having, Ginny always saw herself standing in front of a man. They were both facing the same way and she couldn't see his features, but she could feel his arms, even his heart beating against her back. His gentle arms were around her shoulders, his breath soft upon her ear.

Dear God, why was it that she still wanted the dream? She should have learned that it didn't exist outside of fairy tales. She should be happy, find her own happiness in her success, in her life . . .

Damn spring. It always did this to her.

Throwing the red VW, her second car, her first act of independence as a widow, into first gear, she left the countryside and headed for her sister's home. She'd wasted enough time in introspection.

It was definitely time for the kids.

"Are you serious? You want to take them for the weekend?"

Grinning at her sister, Ginny nodded. "Why not? Why don't you join Dave? Isn't he in Washington?"

Allie lifted a basket of unfolded laundry from the sofa and dropped it to the floor. "I don't know," she said, sitting down and staring across the room. "Dave's there on business. He might not appreciate it if I just showed up, and—"

"Don't be silly," Ginny interrupted, picking up her nephew's undershirt and automatically folding it. "He's your husband. Go. When was the last time the two of you got away?"

Allie hesitated. "But Pat's going to the game this

evening and I promised Meghan we'd bake cookies. I told Nan I would call her tonight. You know how long it's been since we've seen her. Something's wrong there. And, besides, Bummer's been acting weird all morning . . ."

Looking at her older sister, Ginny smiled with affection as she listened to the litany of excuses. They weren't really excuses, for Allyson Barbera took her role of mother very seriously. She was, in fact, a terrific parent. Pat and Meghan were great kids, well adjusted and smart. But Allie wasn't a great housekeeper, nor was she much of an organizer. The Barbera house was in a very pleasant neighborhood and, from the outside, appeared no different from any other on the street. Inside was an agreeable clutter. It wasn't out of the ordinary to step over two years of National Geographic stacked in the foyer, or to come upon three dozen Zinnia seedlings on the dining room table because of the perfect southern exposure. Pots always seemed to be soaking in the kitchen sink. There were toys in every room, stacks of laundry that never seemed to find their way into drawers, and enough plants scattered about to suck the carbon dioxide from a small state. But there was also a lot of love present, and that's what kept drawing Ginny back.

Her sister was the quintessential earth mother.

"So Bummer's pregnant," Ginny said with a smile. "And, if I'm not mistaken, she's not due yet. I think she can get through a weekend without you. I also believe I'm perfectly capable of making cookies with your daughter. In fact, I think she likes my batter more than yours. Next objection?"

"I promised Nan that I would call. I don't know why, but I think something's up with her. Don't ask me. It's just a feeling. She keeps putting me off when I invite her for dinner."

Thinking of their younger sister, Ginny forced a smile. "Allie, just because you're the oldest doesn't mean you have to keep on mothering us. Nan's always been . . . distant. Family has never been a priority with her."

"I wish the two of you could get along better. You're both so much alike, and—"

Uncomfortable with the suggestion, Ginny interrupted. "I promise to call Nan tonight. Now what other excuses do we have to overcome?"

"Pat is going to the Federals game tonight with Billy Kehoe. I promised him, Ginny."

"He can still go. I don't see a problem."

"He won't be getting back until after eleven, and to ask Martin Kehoe to drive to your house is too much."

"I'll stay here. Next?"

Allie ran her fingers through her dark brown hair and roughly exhaled. "I have nothing to wear."

Ginny looked around her. "In all this you can't find something?"

Catching her sister's meaning, but obviously refusing to acknowledge it, Allie said, "I don't think the point of this getaway is to surprise Dave in my sweats."

"You can borrow something of mine. And, if this is your underwear," Ginny added, picking up white cotton underpants very similar to what they had worn in grade school, "then you need this weekend more than you know."

Grabbing the underwear, Allie nearly glared at her with annoyance. "This is crazy. I can't arrange everything in a matter of minutes. The kids are in school. I have to find something to wear." She threw her panties back into the laundry basket. "Maybe buy some new underwear. Pack. Get to the train station. It can't be done."

Ginny looked at her watch and stood up. "It's only one o'clock. We can do it. We'll go to my place first. While you find clothes for Washington, I'll pack a few things to bring back here. Then we'll head for the Mall." Ginny grinned. "What about Victoria's Secret?"

At the mention of the lingerie shop, Allie shook her head. "I can't, Ginny."

The meaning was clear. Weeks ago, Allie had confided to her that Dave's commission checks in the last few months had been less than expected. "My treat," Ginny stated. "I will not allow you to spend a romantic weekend with that Italian in cotton underwear."

Again, Allie shook her head with refusal. "You're always doing this," she protested. "I'm not a charity case. We aren't destitute."

"And how many times do I have to remind you that I get more pleasure out of this than you? Listen, Allie, we've gone over it before; let's not do it again. Evan . . . he left me . . ." God, even now, four years later, she still hated to talk about him. Would it never end, this tight feeling of outrage against her dead husband? "Between the insurance, the hidden accounts and his portfolio, there's more than enough for a couple of silk panties. Can we just do this?" she whispered. "Please?"

Allie smiled and a sweet understanding passed between them. It reminded Ginny of all the times, since childhood, that she and Allie had banded together.

"What about the kids? If we leave now, no one will be here when they get home."

Ginny returned her sister's smile with a wider one. "Let's pull 'em out of school."

Allie was horrified. "We can't do that!"

"Why not?"

"Because . . . because it wouldn't be right. What kind of an example would we be setting?"

Shaking her head, Ginny pulled Allie to her feet. She led her sister into the foyer and yanked jackets from a heavily burdened clothes tree. "They'll never forget the afternoon we pulled them out of school just for fun. It's called making memories. Who knows, future generations may speak kindly of us."

Exasperated, Allie thrust her arms into her jacket. "Why do I allow you to do this to me?"

"Because I shake up your life. You've become too predictable, Allie. You need me."

Allie stopped in the foyer and Ginny collided with her. Turning around, Allie said, "Excuse me? *I've* become too predictable with *my* life? This, coming from a woman who lives alone and whose life consists of working twelve hour days? You don't even have a pet." She zipped the jacket and raised her chin to make a point. "It's like you have a split personality. To the rest of the world you're Miss Organized Perfection, not a hair out of place or a nail chipped, while close your big deals. I think the only time you let your hair down is when you're here with me and the kids. Where's Ginny Sullivan? Where's that kid who loved to climb trees and make forts in the woods so we could play with our dolls? Do you ever play anymore?"

Ginny merely stared at her older sister. Allie had come too close to the truth, and she didn't know how to answer her. "I'm playing now," she whispered. "I took the afternoon off to see you."

"No," Allie corrected, with a hint of a smile. "You're playing a role. *Auntie Mame*. And when you're like this, there's no stopping you."

Ginny grinned. "Then surrender."

Allie reached up and messed Ginny's hair. "There. If you're going to be Auntie Mame, then look the part. Be a little daring yourself," she said, fishing for the house keys in a bowl that contained no less than twenty others. "And I have surrendered. Can't you tell?"

Okay, so she was allowing her younger sister to take over her life this weekend. Maybe Ginny was right about surprising Dave, but just as easily it could all backfire in her face. Dave was working, or he would have been home. He'd called Wednesday to say that he was very near to closing the leasing deal with his biggest account, and he'd been invited to a golf tournament Brack Trucks was sponsoring over the weekend. She'd agreed that it would have been foolish to drive up from Washington to Jersey on Sunday, only to make the return trip the next morning. But still . . . Could this be a mistake?

Running her fingertips over the silk bra, Allie stared at her reflection in the mirror. A dressing room at the mall was a hell of a place to realize that one's marriage had gone stale. She loved Dave. She was sure he loved her, but lately they were more like brother and sister than lovers. Lately? It felt like years since there had been any real desire between them. There was the house. The kids. The job. The list of life's essentials went on and on. When had they both decided that comfortable was easier than excitement? Was it a sign of age? Had they both become stagnant, afraid to disturb the calm for fear of what was beneath the surface? It was too scary to think about in Victoria's Secret, too scary to think about any—

"You must see this nightgown!"

Ginny's excited whisper broke off any further thought, and Allie gratefully opened the door to let Ginny and Meghan inside the large dressing room.

"Mommy, we . . . we picked this. Me'n Aunt Ginny."

Allie gazed into the sweet face of her six-year-old and smiled. Would she remember being abducted from first grade and taken to the mall? Already Ginny had bought the child a stuffed animal and Meghan reeked of perfume. Too much perfume. She looked to her sister. "What did she do? Apply every sample at Macy's?"

Allie watched as Ginny pretended not to notice that the dressing room was quickly filling with the strong mixture of scents. "We tried on all the hand lotions right here, didn't we, Megs?"

The child nodded and held out her arm for inspection. Allie leaned over and sniffed. "Very nice," she muttered.

"We decided on the Camellia," Ginny added with a straight face. "Very light bouquet, yet stirs the imagination."

"Right," Meghan agreed, while waiting for her mother's opinion.

Allie held her daughter's tiny hand and again inhaled. "Very good choice," she said and grinned down at Meghan's pleased expression.

"Try on the nightgown, Allie."

She looked at the silk and lace gown in her hands and immediately searched for the price tag.

"I asked them to remove it before I brought it in. You'll never know if it was five dollars or five hundred," Ginny stated with a sly grin. "Will you please just try it on?"

"Please, Mommy?"

Resigned, she slipped the gown over her head while saying, "It probably costs a small fortune. This bra is fifty-six dollars, and—"

"Mommy! You look beautiful!" Meghan's voice was filled with awe. Obviously, she had seen her mother in too many cotton nightshirts.

Gazing into the mirror, Allie suddenly felt shy. How could a gown, even this one of cream silk, make her feel so totally different? She felt pretty again. It didn't matter that she had found another cluster of gray hair amidst the dark brown last week, or that her stomach would never again be flat after delivering the children. Maybe if she tried some makeup to cover the fine lines around her eyes. Dave used to love her brown eyes, and her back.

She looked in the three-way mirror and saw how the gown was cut low below her shoulder blades. Dave had once said she had the sexiest back he'd ever seen. That was over fourteen years ago, but still . . . "I don't know. This has got to be really expensive."

"I agree with Meghan," Ginny said. "You're beautiful."

Allie looked at her younger sister holding her daughter. They were both gazing up at her with such love that Allie's throat constricted with emotion. Ginny looked like she could have been Meghan's mother. Both had the same odd hazel eyes that could turn gray or green, depending on their mood. Poor Ginny, Allie thought. She would have made a wonderful parent, and there was something special about Ginny, something that made both men and women want to know her. But Allie didn't envy her sister, for Ginny didn't allow many people to get close. Ever since Ginny's marriage, Allie had sensed a sadness about her. It had eased after Evan's death, but every once in a while the melancholy resurfaced. And that's when Ginny came to her and the children. She wasn't sure what they did for her, but Ginny always seemed to leave happier and calmer. Not like Nan. Nan could never stand to be around the children for longer than an hour.

"Well? You've been staring in the mirror long enough," Ginny said. "I think it's perfect. What do you think, Miss Meghan?"

The young child nodded several times and assumed a very proper voice. "Perfect," she announced.

"There you have it," Ginny concurred. "And I'm willing to wager that Dave will join us in agreement."

At the mention of her father's name, Meghan turned to look at her aunt. "Daddy'll like it, too."

Allie watched as Ginny hugged Meghan and then caught her gaze. "See? Daddy'll like it. Isn't that the point? How much more convincing will it take?"

Touching the long thin strap at her shoulder, Allie whispered, "Of course, it's beautiful, but it must be so expensive."

"That's it," Ginny interrupted, standing and carrying Meghan from the dressing room. "They already have a sales slip drawn up and are waiting for you. We did charge a few things, didn't we, Megs?"

The child nodded happily and Ginny laughed. "I love this kid's shopping instincts. A true female. Listen, why don't we find Pat and meet you at the food court?" She glanced at her watch. "You still have to pack, remember?"

Allie was at a loss for words. She knew there was a need inside Ginny to do this, but still— "Thanks, kid . . . for everything."

Shrugging, Ginny shifted her niece on her hip. "What are sisters for if they can't bully you once in a while? Fifteen minutes in front of the frozen yogurt stand, okay?"

Allie smiled, knowing further words of thanks were unnecessary. "Okay. Frozen yogurt. I'll be there."

Maybe all her marriage needed was a little excitement, something unexpected . . .

Chapter 2

They found him in the back of the store, watching a ball game. Ginny shook her head as she walked up to him. "Hey, I thought we were supposed to meet out front."

Patrick Barbera turned from the screen and smiled at his aunt. "It's the bottom of the ninth, and Atlanta's up. *Please,* Aunt Ginny?"

He looked back to the television and Ginny wondered how this child could have grown so quickly. It didn't seem all that long ago that she had helped diaper him, and now he stood looking her in the eye. Tall for thirteen. His voice was changing, two pimples marred his face, one on his nose, the other on his chin. His brown hair was precisely trimmed into a fade haircut, and his smile held a hint of innocent flirtation, as if it had worked on another female. She couldn't help wondering what he'd been asking for that time.

"Half an inning could take twenty minutes and we have to meet your mom in ten. Sorry, kid. Let's go."

"Aww, come on . . . Please?"

Meghan pulled on her hand, impatient to be gone, and

Ginny asked her nephew, "Aren't you going to the game tonight?"

"That's tonight. Atlanta's going to play the Federals next week and Billy's dad said he might take us again. His dad's company has season tickets."

She looked to the large screen. "How much of this can you take?"

He grinned at her again, that little boy, flirty smile. She was sure he thought it was devastating, one no female could resist.

"C'mon, Aunt Gin . . . I'm just checkin' out the competition for the guys."

She put her arm over his shoulder, as if she might be considering. "I don't know a whole lot about this game, but somewhere I remember hearing that most major league teams have regular scouting reports. If the Federals need your help that bad, Pat, I'm sure the phone will ring. Now, let's go get your mother."

"Barney!" Meghan tore away from Ginny and headed down the line of televisions to the one showing the huge purple dinosaur.

Ginny groaned as her packages fell to the floor. They were never going to meet Allie on time.

"I'll go get her," Pat said in a disappointed voice. "They were losing anyway."

When Pat returned with a rebellious Meghan in hand, Ginny led them out of the store and back into the mall. It was crowded for early afternoon. Perhaps many were of the same thought. The welcomed spring weather had brought them. Ginny felt it was cabin fever, being cooped up so long during the winter, that made everyone fling open the doors and get out. Winter in New Jersey wasn't the same as in New England or Colorado, where snow could be beautiful. Especially this past winter. They had been hit with one ice storm after another. Winter here meant gray skies and barren trees. It signified bitter cold, shoveling, accidents, an interrupted work week, and being stuck inside.

Winter was made for children, and Ginny hated to admit it . . . she was getting old. That had to be it. Even though she was only thirty-nine, her complaints sounded suspiciously like those she had heard as a child. It was shocking to realize that she was almost forty and turning into an old grouch. When did it happen? When did she slip into middle-aged disillusionment? Was Allie right? Had she forgotten how to play with anyone but her niece and nephew?

"I wanna go there!" Meghan pulled on her hand toward the toy shop. "Please, please, Aunt Ginny?"

Pat made an impatient sound with his mouth. "Cripes, Meghan! Didn't she say we have to meet Mom? You're such a baby." As if just noticing that he still held his sister's hand, Pat released it like some distasteful dropping he had accidentally picked up.

"I am not a baby!"

"Okay, you're a pain in the——"

"Knock it off," Ginny interrupted. She didn't know how Allie did it. This sibling competition went on all the time. "You will not talk to your sister like that," she said calmly.

"She's in love with Barney," Pat answered. "A goofy dinosaur. Have you heard those dumb songs? I can't stand them!"

Ginny had to bite the inside of her cheek not to laugh.

"I don't care. Stop teasing her or I'll be forced to return this box I've been carrying around." Seeing she had his attention, she added, "Does the name Don Ross mean anything to you?"

He stopped. "You mean DunRuss?" His expression became excited.

She opened the plastic bag and looked inside to the rather large box of baseball cards, Pat's current passion. Grinning, she said, "I believe you're right. DunRuss—"

"Holy Shit!"

"I'm telling mommy." Meghan sounded very pleased. "And you're in trouble."

Annoyed, Ginny looked up. She knew she should reprimand Pat, but something about his expression made her stop. He wasn't even looking at her and Meghan, but across the mall. He appeared speechless.

"What is it?" Ginny whispered and followed his line of vision. A small crowd was gathering around a tall man with a garment bag over his shoulder. He seemed vaguely familiar, but she was unable to place him.

"Who is it, Pat?" she asked, more out of a need to connect a name with a face.

"Cripes, that's Matt Lewellyn!" Her nephew didn't stop gawking at the man, but his voice told her that she was to be regarded as brain damaged for not knowing the retired third baseman for the Philadelphia Federals. "C'mon. I've never been this close to him before. I'm gonna ask for his autograph. Got any paper?" He started fidgeting in his pockets. "I can't believe it! He's here in the mall!"

Pat began pacing in front of her as she searched through her purse. "Hurry, before he leaves!" Impatient, he started to walk toward the other side of the mall as if the ballplayer might disappear before his eyes.

"Come on, Meghan," Ginny said in a tired voice. "This won't take long." Kids and a mall were a powerful and exhausting combination.

She caught up with her nephew at the edge of the crowd of adults. She was sure Pat thought he was fortunate to be the only kid playing hookey *and* running into a baseball legend on the same day. Memories . . . yeah. Maybe this would help Allie feel better about taking the kids out of school.

"Here's your paper," she whispered and had to touch his arm to get his attention. Glancing at his face, she had to smile. Pat's expression had been transformed by a look of pure joy as he tried to see his hero over the heads of the adults in front of him. Leaning closer to his ear, Ginny again whispered, "Just be polite. Excuse yourself and make your way up to him."

Paper in hand, Pat left her side and was soon swallowed up in the four-deep crowd of awe-struck fans. She and Meghan stood to one side and waited. She tried to see Pat and was finally successful. Her nephew stood right in front of the ballplayer.

Dispassionately, Ginny surveyed him. Even from a distance he was better looking than the pictures in the papers and magazines. Tall and lean, Matt Lewellyn's smile was his best feature. From thirty feet away she could see straight, white teeth flash from beneath a full, dark mustache. It was natural, not the celebrity smiles from the papers that seemed to hound him wherever he went, always in the company of beautiful young women.

Playboy. Jock. Unstable. Ginny's mind categorized him.

"Why can't we go to heaven?" Meghan asked, interrupting her thoughts.

"What?"

"Are there unicorns in heaven, Aunt Ginny? When you die?" Meghan clutched the stuffed animal to her chest.

Ginny smiled and reached down to brush back a curl from the young forehead. "I don't know, sweetie. But wouldn't it be great if there are?"

Meghan grinned, her loose front tooth slanting at an angle, and Ginny blew her a kiss before looking back to the crowd. She watched as Pat handed the man a piece of her notepaper from the real estate office. Lewellyn asked her nephew a question and Pat appeared confused before pointing across the increasing crowd. The tall man lifted his head and looked over the people surrounding him.

Right at her.

When their gazes met and held, Ginny tensed as a feeling of dread came over her. She glanced behind her to see if he were really looking at someone else. There was no one, and she slowly turned back.

Again, he smiled.

Shocked by the sudden wash of emotion, she tightened her hold on Meghan's hand and quickly looked away. As she stared at the rows of tulips planted in a precise design, she realized that she was falling back into the old familiar pattern of suspicion and fear. Something strange had happened when they stared at each other. She had experienced it a few times in her past—that scary feeling in the pit of her stomach that she knew this person, that they were *connected* somehow. Shaking off the unnatural feeling, Ginny looked back up and saw that the ex-ballplayer was talking to Pat. Then, as if he sensed that she was watching, he lifted his head.

Even from a distance, she could see that his eyes were friendly. She couldn't tell what color they were, but they immediately assessed her and, when he smiled, she actually found herself exhaling the breath she'd been unconsciously holding. She didn't return his smile, and was horrified to realize that she was incapable of the simple movement of her lips.

He returned his attention to her nephew and they spoke for what seemed like a long time, considering the others waiting to be recognized. Then Pat shook the man's hand and nearly skipped back to where she and Meghan waited.

"Aunt Ginny, you're never gonna believe this!" Pat skidded to a stop in front of her and Ginny swore she had never seen such a happy expression on anyone's face. His smile was almost beatific, like those of the saints on the holy cards she had collected as a child.

"What will I never believe?" Ginny asked, grateful that her voice sounded normal.

"Matt's gonna help with the play-by-play at the game tonight, and he said to come see him and he'd show us the locker room and stuff!"

"Us?" she managed to get in.

"Yeah, us . . . me, Billy and his dad. Cripes! Who'd believe it, huh?"

"That's terrific, Pat." Why in God's name was she disappointed that the second half of "us" was Billy Kehoe and his father? Her hand instinctively reached for the fine gold link chain at her neck. "Let's go, guys," she said in a quiet voice. "Your mom is probably worried."

She led Allie's children toward the food court and felt embarrassed for herself. Dear God, she really had been leading the life of a social recluse if something like this could make her adrenaline pump faster. Big deal. So some jock smiled at her. That wasn't any reason to act like some sports groupie. She was pathetic—it was *just* a smile. Why should she be filled with fear and anticipation? It was truly embarrassing, and made absolutely no sense.

"There's your mother," she pointed out. "Now let's hurry. We have to put her on a train in less than two hours."

"Hey, Mom," Pat yelled. "You're never gonna believe who I just met! Matt Lewellyn! Right here in the mall, like he was regular people. Wow! Some guy, huh, Aunt Gin?"

Ginny smiled into her sister's wide eyes. "Right. Some guy. You don't know what you missed."

As they left the mall she was mortified to find herself wondering if Lewellyn's eyes were brown or blue. And if there were lines from laughter or anger in the corners. As quickly as that thought came, she banished it from her mind.

Four years ago she had come to terms with her life. She had recognized its possibilities and its limits. She knew what to expect during her lifetime, and what was beyond her reach. She had, as she'd approached forty, finally grown up.

There would be no regressions. So she would never be June Cleaver.

Big deal. She'd live.

It was spring . . . somehow she'd get through this season.

* * *

She was supposed to love her.

As she listened to her sister's voice, Nancy Lynch found her jaw tightening and she ran her fingers through her short dark hair. Her whole body reacted to the sound on the telephone and Nan resented Ginny for making her feel like this . . . again.

"What do you mean, the dog is acting funny?" Nan tried to be patient with her older sister, but it was beyond her comprehension why Ginny would think she was interested in Allie's dog.

"She's pulling Allie's bedspread into a corner of the room. I've put up barriers to keep her in the kitchen, but she's acting really weird. You don't think Bummer's going to have puppies while I'm here, do you?"

"And how would I know? I'm not a vet." Nan knew she sounded bitchy, but she couldn't help it. Honestly, the way her two older sisters went on about such trivial things. "Call the vet if you're worried," she added to fill the hurt silence on the telephone line.

"Maybe I will," Ginny finally answered. "Well, as long as you're okay. Allie was worried."

And you're not, Nan thought. Typical. "Everything is fine. It's always fine. Why did Allie go to Washington in the first place? She'd know what to do. She has a rapport with children and animals. At least she's—"

"—Allie happens to be very gifted," Ginny interrupted a bit too defensively. "And she's in Washington to surprise Dave."

Nan couldn't help the sarcastic laugh. "I'll just bet she's accomplished her goal."

"What is that supposed to mean?"

Grabbing her purse from the chair, Nan sat down on her bed and emptied the contents onto the mattress. "Nothing. I hope they have a wonderful time. And I'm sorry I don't know anything about whelping dogs. What more can I say?"

"Nothing. I'd better be going. Meghan's in her bath. I shouldn't leave her."

She could hear the impatience in Ginny's voice and smiled with satisfaction. "Give her a kiss from me," Nan said while reaching for a small brown leather case.

"And you give my best to Robert."

Nan's eyes closed briefly as she shook her head. "I certainly will."

After she hung up, Nan very carefully filled the tiny silver spoon. What a cold, cold woman, she thought while raising the bowl of the spoon to her nose. As if Ginny ever cared. Virginia Sullivan Harrison had been a thorn in her side for most of her life. They had always fought, even as children.

The hit was immediate, entering her brain and traveling to every nerve ending, sending out a primary pleasure. Nan closed her eyes to shut out the world and savor the moment.

Give my best to Robert. Yeah, she thought as she brought the bowl to her other nostril, I'll certainly do just that when and if I see him. Within seconds, she wiped her nose and stood up ready for the evening. Throwing off her Donna Karan blouse, she giggled as she headed for the shower. Right. Robert Lynch had walked out of this apartment three weeks ago after delivering his ultimatum.

"Good riddance," she said aloud, thinking of her husband while adjusting the fine spray of water. Tonight she was meeting Tony Amato. Young, right out of college, and eager to make it in advertising. She would help him along the way . . . as long as he didn't disappoint her later this evening. Being an associate director at McKinley, Carter and Brown had its advantages.

She entered the shower and stood before the water, feeling it hit her skin like tiny pinpricks that made her flesh tingle with excitement. Letting the heat envelop her, Nan grinned with anticipation as she pictured the young Tony Amato without his Italian suit from Boyds and his designer shirt and tie. He wanted so much to succeed and to please her. He wanted to learn from the Lady with the Midas touch, the one who had brought more business into the company than any other ad exec, the one who had so many awards and plaques covering her office walls that she had been forced to take down her Impressionist paintings to make more room.

Pouring a luxuriously scented bath gel onto the sponge, Nan ran it gently over her body, kept model-thin by exercise. She had a feeling Tony would be an avid student.

The bathroom was more neat, more orderly, than her own at home. Allie imagined it was seldom that the Madison Hotel had to worry about a six-year-old painting with toothpaste on mirrors. She satisfied her feeling of inadequacy by noting that the staff of this distinguished hotel probably did not often deal with teenagers, who left more grime on the towels and floors than in the sink. And for the first time Allie realized that her husband was probably more comfortable here than at home.

Dave's toiletries, his brush and shaving cream, his

pewter shaver, his deodorant, were all lined up like sol-
diers against the sparkling white tiles. Even his toothbrush
was in a plastic holder. So clean. So precise. So unlike
their bathroom at home. Not for the first time Allie wondered why she was so disorganized. As the oldest child
she should have been just the opposite, but somehow,
Ginny and Nan acquired all the organizational skills.
Maybe life worked out such things for each person. She
had the children. They were both healthy and happy, and
perhaps that should be enough. But Dave wanted more.
Inside, where honesty was painful yet unavoidable, she
knew that her husband wanted someone with the perfection of Donna Reed to greet him when he came home at
night. He wanted a clean home, dinner on the table, happy
educated children, his socks rolled into neat little
pairs . . . in drawers, not laundry baskets. And, since com-
parisons were being made, she might as well admit that
the image of Lucy Ricardo sprang forth much too easily.
But at least her children were happy, and educated.

Sighing loudly, Allie slipped the silk nightgown over
her head and remembered how Dave had tried to act
pleased when he saw her in the hotel lobby. He *was*
pleased, she reminded herself. He'd been surprised, that's
all. And wasn't that the purpose? Just because he hadn't
seemed too happy about rearranging his dinner plans wasn't
cause to worry. But what continued to niggle at the back
of her brain was the actual dinner. She and Dave had met
with two people from Brack Trucks and over dinner in the
elegant dining room, Allie had begun to feel the full measure of her problem. It was so typical that she almost dismissed it, but one of her dinner companions was a
woman . . . a very lovely woman who reminded her of

Nan with her efficiency of manner. Denise Merkle was tall and thin and intimidating as hell in exquisite white silk. Only someone without children would dine in white silk.

The conversation began with niceties but soon, almost unconsciously, she was quietly excluded as the talk turned to leasing contracts and points and bonuses. Sitting there, unable to enter the conversation, she watched her husband react to Denise. His face was animated. He was interested . . . That's when the knot had formed in her belly, and it hadn't gone away.

Hating the doubts, she picked up her own toothbrush and started brushing her teeth. Of course Dave was faithful to her. She rinsed her mouth and looked at her reflection. Compared to Denise she looked exactly like who she was—a middle-aged housewife trying to be someone else. Determined, she picked up Dave's hair brush and bent over to pull it through her hair. When she straightened, she fluffed it with her fingers and then reached for the French perfume.

The exotic scent of sandalwood lingered on her skin where she dabbed it—behind her ears, between her breasts, behind her knees and, finally, between her legs. So what? Tonight she could pretend. Pretend it was just the two of them again. Before the children, the job, the house . . . before any of it had tamed them. Tonight she would show him that she hadn't forgotten, that it could be exciting.

She smiled, almost shyly, as he looked up when she left the bathroom. Dave was staring at her over his reading glasses as she glided toward him. She felt silly, yet sexy. The nightgown was obviously working.

"Where did you get that?"

Did she detect a note of annoyance in his voice? Smiling, Allie lifted the long skirt and climbed up onto the bed. Maybe she should somehow turn around now so he could see her back. Not wanting to appear obvious, she sat before him and asked quietly, "Do you like it?"

Dave gazed down to her breasts and then quickly looked back at her face. "It's pretty, but do you think we can afford it?"

She wanted to tell him that Ginny had paid for it, but she knew he wouldn't like the answer. Instead, she reached out and traced the line of his jaw with her finger. To some, Dave might have been ordinary, but that was just one of the many things she loved about him. He was a good man. Reliable. "Do you know how long it's been since we were alone, away from the children?"

He nodded, a little distracted, and then asked, "Is Pat still going to the Federals game tonight?"

This time Allie nodded, for once not wanting to talk about the kids. "We should do this more often, don't you think? Getting away?"

He raised his eyebrows and shrugged. "You do realize that if word gets back to the home office that you stayed with me, I'll have to pay for half this room."

"Why? I'm your wife." Why was he ignoring every overture she was making? It was as if he didn't want her there.

"Company policy. I'm working here, Allie. This isn't a vacation."

She stiffened. "I know that. I just thought it might be a good idea to join you. And, anyway, it's a stupid policy. I would think a sales force would be much happier if their spouses could join them on occasion."

Why did this man in front of her, this face she had

grown so familiar with over the last fifteen years, suddenly seem strange? The dark brown hair was the same. The brown eyes and crooked smile were identical to her husband's. So why was she this uncomfortable?

"It was just an idea," she said feebly, swallowing down the burning sensation in her throat.

He patted her arm. This *stranger* patted her arm and smiled like an indulgent father.

"And that, Allie, is why you're not head of sales."

He pulled the blanket up to his waist, as though showing her that he was ready for sleep, and she moved to make it easier even though she wanted to reach out and slap him.

"You forget that I have to be in Arlington by six-thirty. Brack's golf tournament." He quickly kissed her forehead. It was a chaste grazing of flesh, almost brotherly.

Then she knew. He wasn't going to make love to her.

"I didn't forget. Shall I leave a wake up call for us?" Her voice sounded so odd, so weak, as she tried to mask the pain and humiliation. She would not let him know that the knot in her stomach had tightened into a severe ache.

"I already called it in while you were in the bathroom," Dave said, settling his pillows and reaching toward the lamp. He looked over his shoulder to her. "Are you going to read, or can I turn this off?"

Not able to trust her voice, she shook her head. When the room was in darkness, she followed her husband under the covers and rested her cheek against the feather pillow. Waiting until her eyes adjusted to the dark, she was finally able to make out the doorway leading into the bathroom.

"There's no need for you to get up so early, Allie. It's

just a golf outing, and you know how much you hate golf. It's business. You could sightsee, if you'd like."

"I'll see," she said in a tiny whisper to his back.

There was a moment of silence.

"Suit yourself. Good night then."

She waited. She didn't move until she heard the deep rhythm of Dave's breathing that indicated he was asleep. It had been so hard to lie in the darkness and wait to escape . . . and that's what she wanted to do. She wanted to run home to her children, to her chaotic house, to the familiar. She didn't want to lie in this bed with a stranger. She had invaded his territory, and he resented her.

What was worse was that he didn't want her.

Slipping out of bed she quietly made her way to the bathroom. She waited until the door was closed before turning on the light. Slowly, almost afraid, she looked into the large mirror over the sink. For a second, a brief flash in time, she appeared young again before her brain registered the fear in her eyes.

Fear.

What had she just uncovered? Staring in the mirror she touched her cheek, her lips, her chin. Her fingers trailed down to her throat and settled, ever so lightly, on her breast beneath the cream silk. Her lips were quivering and her eyes burning from unshed tears.

This had been a mistake. *Oh, Ginny, you meant well.* It was like Pandora's box. As long as it wasn't opened it was all right. But now the lid had been lifted and she had peeked inside, and what she had found scared the hell out of her.

She was losing her husband.

It was that simple, and that frightening.

Sitting on the toilet seat, Allie buried her face in her

hands and finally let the tears come. When they threatened to become sobs, she grabbed a thick towel and bit on it. She would not let Dave hear her. Somehow, from somewhere, she was going to find the strength to fight. She sniffled and wiped her eyes with her palms. She came from a family of strong women. Survivors.

She could do it. She'd just have to change. She had always poured all her energy into her home and her family. Somewhere along the way she had forgotten about herself, or maybe she had merely put it off. But now it was her turn. It had to be her turn, or she would lose the only man she had ever loved. Again, she sniffled and reached for a tissue. She'd be okay. She would just have to take it one step at a time.

Allie took a deep shuddering breath and stood up. Now where the hell was she going to find a white silk suit?

Chapter 3

Ginny told herself that she was watching the news for the world report, the weather, the results of the game so she could discuss it with Pat when he came home. In truth she was just too tired to get up and clean the kitchen. Being a surrogate parent, even for the day, was exhausting and she again marveled that her sister did it and remained cheerful and loving and giving. It was too bad that God didn't only give children to people like Allie, people who never screamed or hit or ridiculed. But she knew from her own childhood that God didn't make those decisions. Mentally scolding herself for putting off a job, Ginny stood up and walked into the kitchen. It was a disaster. She and Meghan had baked chocolate chip cookies and the room looked like aliens had attacked it. Bowls, cookie sheets, and ingredients covered the counter. Normally she cleaned as she went along, but tonight she had been having too much fun with her niece to bother.

"How're you doing, Bummer?" she asked softly as she stepped over the gray shutter she had found in Allie's garage. She'd placed it sideways to create a barrier and confine the small black dog to the kitchen.

Large brown eyes stared back at her with a miserable expression.

Assuming the same look, Ginny frowned in sympathy and knelt in front of the animal. "Poor baby," she whispered while scratching behind Bummer's ear. "Please don't do anything. Don't have your babies while I'm here." She straightened and walked towards the counter, worrying about what she'd do if it actually happened. The dog heaved its bulky torso up and followed.

Ginny opened the dishwasher and began loading it while observing Bummer's behavior. The dog was restless, as if each position were uncomfortable. It whined at the shutter and then turned to go back to its box.

Shaking her head, Ginny watched the dog rearrange the old towels to its satisfaction. Bummer looked up, as if asking for help, before lowering her body back down. The animal continued to stare at Ginny and no words were necessary as she and Bummer communicated. Leaving the bowls in the sink, the empty cookie sheets lying on top of the stove, the flour smeared over the counter, Ginny sat down in front of the dog and softly brushed the silky hair away from its eyes.

Thinking of her call to the vet, she said, "I promise I will not insert a thermometer into any orifice of your body. What a hell of a way to tell if birth is imminent."

Bummer's ears flattened, as if she understood, and a small pink tongue appeared to softly lick Ginny's hand. She prided herself in staying with the animal even though she should be cleaning the kitchen. She should get up and just do it. Normally this kind of clutter would drive her nuts, but tonight there was something comforting in it. Glancing at the clock, she saw that it was eleven forty-five. Even with a tour, Pat should be getting home soon. Maybe she should have listened to all the news to find out if the Federals had won.

She sighed with fatigue and looked down to Allie's stained and ripped sweats that she had borrowed to make cookies with Meghan. The staff of Harrison Real Estate would be shocked if they could see her now, but it had been worth it. She and Megs had laughed and teased and had eaten more dough than they had baked. Maybe that's why she came over here and assumed Allie's place. For just a little while she could pretend that this was all hers . . . this messy kitchen where people cooked and then nourished each other with laughter, where the floor carried footprints of those who cared about one another. It was a family, the natural extension of love, and Allie was so lucky to be at its center. Her own home was spotless and silent. There were never any prints on her kitchen floor. It was sterile, just like her life.

Bummer made a noise deep in the throat and Ginny turned her attention back to the dog. "Poor thing. What happened, huh? Some big hairy schnauzer swagger across your path?" Her smile was truly sympathetic.

Those brown eyes stared back at her and Ginny thought she could see the pain reflected in them. Dear God, what if this dog really was in labor? Why had she nearly forced Allie from her own house? Nan was right. Allie would know what to do. Closing her eyelids, Ginny rested her head against the wall and thought back to the phone conversation with her younger sister. What was wrong with Nan? What was wrong with her? Why couldn't they get along? They hardly saw each other, so one would think that on the rare occasion when communication was necessary they could make the effort. But they didn't. Cold politeness. That was the only thing they shared now, besides Allie. Neither woman liked the other any more today than they had as teenagers. When had the dislike started? As the older of the two, Ginny should have remembered, but she didn't.

Except for her earliest memories, it seemed there was always a current of competition lying beneath the surface of their relationship. When Ginny had married it had gotten worse. Maybe all sisters went through this at some point. But it was different with Allie. There had never been any real friction between them. She and Allie had banded together after their parents' divorce to protect Nan. Nan had just wanted Allie's attention, and not hers. And who could blame her? Allie was love and patience, and she was happy with her life. She wasn't perfect and she didn't try to be. She was normal. Not like Nan, and certainly not like herself.

Depressed and tired of thinking, Ginny tried to summon the strength to leave the dog and get up off the kitchen floor.

Why was life so damned complicated?

His tongue traced a thin wet line up from her heel, over her calf and behind her knee. She didn't move so much as a muscle as his mouth made its way up her inner thigh. Lying face down in her bed, Nan felt more annoyed than excited. He wanted too much. Perhaps it was because he was so young that he thought quantity was more valued than quality. The first time was exciting, raw with the primordial energy of a new conquest. The fact that both of them were high only added to the exhilaration. The second time was satisfying and pleasant. Now she merely wanted to be left alone.

As his tongue continued on its course, Tony placed his hands under her thighs and lifted her off the mattress. She was about to tell him to stop, to go home, when the tip of his tongue slid into her.

A long sigh escaped her mouth. It felt so good, so soothing, after a frantic night of lovemaking that she allowed him to continue, allowed him to slowly stroke her until her breathing quickened, until she could feel that familiar cluster of desire building up inside of her again. Somewhere, in the far recesses of her brain, a thought occurred to her that he would expect something in return. And, even for a twenty-six year old, Tony would take too long. It was late. She didn't want him staying the night, and she didn't think she had the energy to wait him out.

And so the decision.

It took only a moment for her to make up her mind. As Tony's mouth worked its magic, licking her, nipping the tender flesh, Nan bit her bottom lip and clutched the pillow to her face. The sheets smelled of perfume and Bombay gin and the musk from their lovemaking. In her mind's eye there was nothing but images of Tony's mouth caressing her, making her arch back involuntarily as exquisite shocks of pleasure surged up inside of her. Too late. She wouldn't stop him. Not now. Not when in that dark place in her mind she was already soaring . . .

"I'll call you," she said later, stifling a yawn. "If you don't hear from me this weekend, I'll see you Monday in the office."

He looked hurt, as if just realizing that he had been

used. "How about going out sailing on the Delaware? My uncle has a forty footer docked at Riverton."

Holding open the door to her apartment, Nan smiled. His Italian heritage was coming to the surface, all that Mediterranean machismo, yet she didn't care. "It's late, Tony. I told you I'll call. Right now I just want to sleep."

"It's only a little after twelve. I could stay and—"

"No one ever stays," she interrupted. "My rule." Lightly taking his arm she walked him over her threshold. "As a matter of fact, I have to see my sister tomorrow. Some kind of family emergency. So I'll see you Monday, all right?"

Again his expression registered that mixture of hurt and anger. She was tired and wanted nothing more than to take a shower and sleep. As if to formally end the evening she kissed his cheek and then gave him the news he wanted. "I'll have you assigned to the Markey Foods account. You should do very well."

Tony's injured male ego was forgotten and replaced by ambition, as his face glowed with pleasure. He was almost as cunning as she, and would more than likely succeed in this business of public persuasion.

"Really? You think I can handle it?"

Now he was pushing it. Actually, she had wanted him to wait until Monday to get the news, but he had earned it. Her body felt sore, yet sated. Younger men were definitely better in bed, but they never seemed to know when to call it a night.

"It's my account. You'll be assisting me, and I believe we'll have to wait and see how well you handle that," Nan answered in a deceptively strong voice. "Tonight was a beginning," she added, just to let him know that she was still in charge, that sex hadn't made her vulnerable.

Power. It always came down to that factor.

She wasn't exactly proud of herself, yet she wasn't ashamed. Standing under the spray of water, Nan lathered herself with soap and deeply inhaled the delicate designer fragrance that matched her perfume. The image of her estranged husband flitted through her tired mind and she wondered who Robert was spending the night with, if anyone. He's probably alone, feeling self-righteous . . . and horny. Robert Lynch could never handle a real woman who knew what she wanted out of life, and who would take it by any means. It was all right, even accepted and admired, if a man used the same methods. And Nan had to admit that she felt a certain power to know that she could use an attractive young man like Tony Amato to do her bidding . . . that there were thousands of Tonys out there who understood how to get ahead. Power and control. It was a strong aphrodisiac, almost as good as cocaine.

It almost didn't matter that men found her attractive. She wouldn't let the Tonys of this world admire her body without making them appreciate her mind. She demanded that they engage in a conflict other than sex, a contest that included subtle bending of wills. It amused her to watch them try and take back some of the power by doing exactly as she told them. Sometimes men were so stupid. They thought if you could bring a woman to orgasm, she'd be so grateful that she would relinquish command.

Her laugh was low and cynical as she brought the sponge down her arm. Power. Control. It was exciting, and it was exactly what men had been doing for centuries.

Now it was her turn.

* * *

"Aunt Ginny?"

She felt a movement by her shoulder and blinked a few times, trying to awaken. Yet, when her eyes focused she refused to believe what she saw. Standing in front of her was Pat, his arm in a navy blue sling. Behind him was Billy Kehoe and his father, both smiling and looking embarrassed to find her asleep on the kitchen floor, next to a dog.

Trying to gather whatever dignity she could muster, Ginny pushed the hair out of her face and started to get up when she noticed an ox blood cordovan loafer step over the gray shutter and enter her sister's kitchen. Her gaze followed the extremely long line of tan slacks up to the forest green sweater.

And then, horrified, she saw the face.

His face.

The ballplayer. Ex-ballplayer.

And he looked amused.

"Oh, shit." She wasn't quite sure, but she thought she muttered the profanity out loud.

"You okay, Aunt Ginny?" Pat asked, a worried expression changing the features on his young face.

Desperately trying to bring some order to her confused mind, Ginny held on to the back of a kitchen chair while rising. This had to be a dream. She must still be asleep. That's it . . . this simply could not be happening to her! Again focusing on her nephew's arm, she suddenly found her voice.

"What happened to you? Are you all right?"

Pat looked pleased, proud of the sling around his neck and arm. "I'm okay."

"He had a little accident," Martin Kehoe announced from behind her nephew.

Ginny looked at Allie's neighbor. "What accident?" Oh, God, why now? Allie would never forgive herself for going to Washington.

Martin Kehoe glanced back at the ballplayer who, though taller than any of them, was standing behind them at the entrance to the kitchen.

"He tripped over some equipment in the locker room." The man's voice was low and deep, and attempting to be friendly.

She found herself nodding stupidly as she again pushed her hair back off her forehead. No one spoke and Ginny wondered if somebody was going to continue.

Martin Kehoe cleared his throat and said, "You see, Pat and Billy were told to wait until Matt came back for them but they couldn't, and—"

"We sneaked up to the locker room door to see the reporters and everything," Pat interrupted. "And when we heard somebody coming we ran back down the hallway and I fell . . . and . . . and that's when I hurt my arm. But it's okay." Pat touched his wrist. "Matt had Nate Weinstein take a look at it."

"A doctor?" Ginny asked.

Pat shook his head, obviously embarrassed by her lack of knowledge. "Nate's the Federals' trainer."

"But a doctor did look at it," Martin quickly interjected.

"Dr. Cramer. Harry Cramer," Lewellyn added. "He said it was just a minor sprain. It might be bruised, but it should be okay in a few days. I came home with Pat to assure you that he wasn't seriously hurt. I feel sort of responsible."

"The team was going to call or send a representative," Martin said. "But Matt insisted."

"It's not exactly out of my way. And I should have stayed with the boys."

"Isn't this great?" Billy asked. "Matt lives in Medford."

Ginny kept blinking. This had to be a dream. A nightmare.

"I drove home from Philly with him," Pat bragged. "In a Mercedes. What a car! The seat adjusts like nine different ways."

Acutely aware of her appearance, Ginny straightened the stained sweatshirt and looked at her nephew. "Wait till your mother hears about this. Did you at least apologize and—"

He suddenly came through the crowd of males with the agility of a dancer. Or an athlete. Brushing past everyone, he knelt at her feet. She was so amazed by his actions that she didn't even move when he looked up at her.

"I think this dog is about to have puppies."

Pandemonium broke out as everyone started talking at once.

"Puppies? No kidding," Billy Kehoe cried, while straining his neck to see Bummer.

Closer to the dog, Pat looked down and said, "This is going to be gross, isn't it?"

"Perhaps we'd better go," Billy's father suggested while nearly strong-arming his son out of the room. "Thanks for everything, Matt." He looked to Ginny. "Good luck. Ahh . . . let us know what happens."

She wasn't paying attention to anyone except the man who continued to kneel before her. "Puppies? Now?" Poor

Bummer was panting and staring up at her as though asking for help. "Are you sure?"

Shrugging, the ballplayer grinned. "I'm afraid so. I think this one's in labor. Got any newspaper?"

Thinking he must have walked over at least a two foot stack of it in the foyer, Ginny turned to her nephew. "Pat, get some newspaper and bring it in here." Seeing his sling, she amended, "Never mind. I'll get it. Do something else."

With the dexterity of a hurdler, Ginny leaped over the shutter and raced for the foyer. It took less than half a minute for her to return with an armful of newspapers. She stood like a soldier, waiting for her next order.

Lewellyn smiled. "Here. Let me help." He took the papers from her arms and placed them on the floor. "It would probably be best if we tore some of these into strips."

"How do you know this?" she asked, amazed that this man kneeling in her sister's kitchen was the same one that had been on television only hours ago.

Ripping up paper, he smiled before speaking with an easy confidence. It was a voice that held more than a hint of nostalgia. "I once helped my mother deliver our dog's puppies. I guess I was about Pat's age, maybe a little older, but I'll never forget it." His grin widened. "Quite an experience."

Pat pulled a chair out and sat down. "You didn't get sick?"

Lewellyn shook his head. "I was scared at first. But you get so involved you don't have time to think about it."

"Shouldn't we call a vet?"

Pat and the ballplayer looked at her and she wondered

when Martin Kehoe had left. Everything seemed so un-
real. "Well . . . don't vets make house calls?" she offered
in defense.

"Matt can handle it," Pat stated. "Can't you, Matt?"

Lewellyn appeared uncomfortable. "Mrs. Harrison?"

"Ginny. Virginia." Damn, why couldn't she even say
her name intelligently?

"Virginia. I don't know if your vet would make a house
call, but don't worry. Usually the dog does all the work.
You'll do fine."

Her eyes widened with shock. *"Me?* You aren't going
to leave, are you?" she heard herself asking. Was that
panic in her voice?

He petted Bummer's head and answered, "I really don't
know all that much about this, and it could take all night."

She realized then who he was and what she was asking.
Ginny wiped the sleep from the corner of her eye and took
a deep breath. "I'm really sorry. Of course I can't ask you
to stay. It's . . . it's just that right now I feel like Butterfly
McQueen." She shrugged her shoulders. " 'I don't know
nothin' . . . ' "

Laughing, he scratched behind the dog's ear and then
looked up at her. "So what's the name of this little lady?"

"Bummer. It's my sister's dog. I . . . ah, I'm babysitting
this weekend."

"Dad said Mom was crazy for getting a puppy after
Dandy died," Pat offered as an explanation. "Said it was a
real bummer after getting new rugs, or something. Anyway, the name kinda stuck." He got up from his chair and
headed for the refrigerator. "Hey, Matt. Want something to
eat?"

Ginny marveled that her nephew could behave so casually in front of his idol. Wasn't it only this afternoon that she had watched him nearly swoon over this man?

"Thanks, Pat. Maybe later."

Later? Ginny looked down at him. "You'll stay?" she asked hopefully.

He stared back at her for the longest time, as if searching her face for something. It took every ounce of willpower she possessed to allow him the scrutiny. Feminine instinct was screaming at her to run into the bathroom and wash her face, comb her hair, apply *some* makeup, and rip Allie's sweats from her body. Instead, she stood very still and looked back.

He had a tiny scar over his left eyebrow, a thin silver line on a lightly tanned face. A handsome face, she admitted, but not perfect. Rugged. What a dumb term, but it applied to him. His dark hair was thick and she could see that he was trying to tame a natural curl that fell over onto his forehead. His nose was straight and she could detect the slight movement of his nostrils as he breathed. His full moustache ended right at the corners of his bottom lip. And his chin was square and strong. How totally, totally, pathetic to be sizing up the man.

Slowly, he stood and extended his hand. "Hi. We haven't really been introduced. I'm Matt Lewellyn."

As if she didn't know that. Ginny swallowed and she saw herself reaching out to place her hand inside his large palm. "Ginny Harrison. And thanks."

He grinned. "Always wanted to be a hero."

She pulled her hand back, shocked by the warmth she felt within his palm. Maybe it was from stroking Bummer, or he was sick or hot-blooded or something. Determined to get control of herself, she straightened her shoulders.

"Would you like tea or coffee? A beer?" she hastily added, remembering that he was a jock. Didn't they all love beer?

"Tea would be fine. Thanks." He pulled his sweater over his head and she found herself staring at a broad chest behind the crisp cotton of his shirt and arm muscles that reminded her of young tree trunks. She had never, ever, thought of muscled men as attractive. A lean runner's body had always been more pleasing to her eye. Yet now, watching as he folded back his shirt sleeves, she found herself staring at the dark hair on those muscled forearms . . . those strong fingers. He was so healthy looking. So male. So threatening.

"I'll have a beer."

Ginny blinked and turned to stare at her thirteen-year-old nephew. "What?"

Pat grinned sheepishly. "Hey, it's an occasion. Matt Lewellyn's in my kitchen and Bummer's going to have puppies. Cripes. In *my* kitchen!" Pat's head bobbed up and down, as though not quite believing his good fortune.

Trying to regain her composure, Ginny said, "Pat, do something helpful, will you? Boil water. Find scissors. Do something. Help Matt with the papers. I'm going to check on Meghan," Ginny tossed out, though she really didn't care what either one of them thought. She simply had to get out of that kitchen.

She raced up the stairs and didn't stop until she was in the hallway. Collapsing onto a large clothes hamper, she clutched one of Meghan's undershirts and brought it up to her forehead. Wiping away a sudden eruption of sweat, Ginny whispered, "Cripes! Who'd believe it? Matt Lewellyn in Allie's kitchen . . ."

Realizing she sounded just like Pat, she leaned against the wall and closed her eyes, seeing Lewellyn once more as they had studied each other's face. What was it about him? If she believed in that weirdo stuff on TV, she would think they might have known each other in another life.

His eyes were brown, with tiny amber flecks. His lashes were long, far longer than any male's should have been. And at the corners were fine lines that told of laughter. Somehow she knew they would be there.

It was crazy. Irrational. Completely out of character for her.

Once more wiping her face with her niece's underwear, Ginny felt like crying. Why was she even thinking those thoughts? What did it matter? But it did, damn it! Why did he have to see her like this? This was not her. She didn't live like this. She had nice clean clothes, a charming, orderly house. He had found her asleep on the kitchen floor! With a dog!

She grabbed the front of the gray sweatshirt and brought it to her nose. A low groan escaped her lips. She even smelled like Bummer!

Dear God, how was she ever going to get through this night?

"Would you like more tea?"

Matt Lewellyn looked up from the pedestal mug and shook his head. "No, thanks." At least she wasn't nervous anymore. For the first hour that he was in the house, she'd acted like a frightened rabbit. He was used to people treating him different, but Virginia Harrison had really been frightened. He'd sensed that right away, even in the mall.

For the life of him he didn't know what he was doing sitting in her sister's kitchen waiting for this small dog to deliver puppies. He had a plane to catch for the West Coast in . . . he looked at his watch . . . less than four hours. He should be home. Packing. Sleeping. But not here. Not with this widow.

What had surprised and annoyed him was that when he had walked through the front door of this house he had found himself to be equally nervous. He had felt it under his rib cage this afternoon when he'd first seen her with the little girl at the mall, and it had returned when he'd stepped into this kitchen. There was something about her face, her eyes . . . He'd even been disappointed when Pat showed up without her after the game. He'd wanted to see her again. Just once, to put to rest the crazy, illogical notion of feeling connected to a total stranger. One with children around her, no less.

He wasn't exactly proud of the fact that he had steered the conversation around to Pat's aunt on the way home from the stadium. He had learned from the boy that she was widowed. Pat had easily supplied him with a brief family history, thus saving himself the guilt of having to pump the child for information. He liked the kid and didn't want to use him that way.

Watching her load the dishwasher, he mentally groaned. She was a widow, and he didn't know whether or not to be relieved. Widows weren't like women who'd been divorced. They were more like virgins . . . something to stay clear of, for both were filled with illusions and dreams. At the moment she was very interested in cleaning a large glass bowl, and he took the opportunity to study her more closely.

Earlier he had seen a scar under the bangs on her forehead. It looked like it might have been from chicken pox—tiny and interesting on an otherwise flawless complexion. Her cheeks were not quite as pale as when he'd first come in the house. Somehow, he doubted that the attractive blush could be attributed to his presence, and he hid a smile as he surmised that she must have used something, some makeup. It must have been when she'd escorted the very sleepy Pat to his bedroom.

Growing up with four older sisters had taught him something about women, but not about women like Virginia Harrison. His sisters were never frightened of men. Never in his life had he frightened a woman. This short, attractive female was nothing at all like the women he'd been attracted to in the past . . . which made the attraction all the more intriguing. She was neither tall nor thin. She was nervous, or at the very least shy, not exactly like the outgoing or confident women he'd known.

He couldn't find any reason to be sitting in this kitchen twenty minutes from his house, waiting to deliver puppies. There wasn't any reason, except that this woman touched something inside of him. It wasn't sexual. It wasn't even the normal attraction he felt for most women.

It was the damnedest thing.

He just wanted to know her.

She liked him. He wasn't as she had expected. Ginny rose from the table and filled the empty plate with more chocolate chip cookies. She relaxed as she slid back onto the chair opposite him.

"These really are great," he said for the third time. "Pecans, huh?"

She nodded, suddenly realizing that he was as nervous as she. It gave her a courage that she normally wouldn't have had. "Doesn't it ever bother you," she asked in a hesitant voice, "to be the object of so much attention?"

Grinning, he made an appreciative noise as he bit into the cookie. "Of course," he mumbled. After sipping his tea, he added, "It's totally misplaced. Kids should look up to someone like Nelson Mandella or Mother Theresa. But you want to know why they pick athletes?"

She raised her eyebrows in question.

He wiped his moustache with the flowered napkin that had been resting on his thigh. "Because most kids can't imagine growing up and changing the political system of a nation, or saving the underprivileged. But they lie awake at night, just as I did, knowing if they're serious, and with a tremendous amount of luck, they just might be able to play major league ball. That dream seems so accessible with TV and commercials, so if they see it enough times they're almost brainwashed into thinking it's admirable. Sometimes I wonder, if we did the same thing with healers and educators, what this world might be like."

He grinned at her surprised expression. "Yet any kid that's ever been to a ballpark and listened to the crowd dreams of making it one day. You can't believe how real the fantasy is to stand down there at home plate. I'm just one of the lucky ones, Ginny. And to get back to your original question . . . taking time with kids is an enjoyable price to pay for having been allowed to do something that I loved."

Ginny toyed with the handle of her cup. Without looking up, she said, "I didn't expect to be, but I'm impressed."

Lewellyn shocked her by laughing. "Don't be. Hell, lady, one of those kids took my job."

It was the giggle bubbling up from her throat that did him in. That, and the fact, for just a moment, her eyes lost that haunted look. She appeared young and happy, and without planning it he opened his mouth to say, "Next Saturday night there's a black tie dinner for the Child Guidance Clinic in Philadelphia. And, well, some of my old teammates have adopted this particular charity and we're expected to show." He felt awkward, almost like a teenager, yet he forced himself to finish. "It's just dinner and some dancing afterwards. Do you want . . . ? I mean, why don't you come with me? You might enjoy it."

Immediately he saw it was the worst thing he could have proposed. She tightened up on him, like a flower closing at dusk. He watched the color rise on her cheeks, saw her expression take on the guarded look he had first seen at the mall. What the hell had been done to her to make her so frightened?

She brushed a cookie crumb from the table and stuttered, "I . . . Ah . . . I don't think so, but thank you for asking."

The silence that followed was almost painful. Matt found that he was embarrassed, for both of them. He couldn't put his finger on what it was, but he had the unnatural urge to run, to put distance between himself and the woman across from him. Hating the abruptness of his actions, he glanced at his watch and quickly rose from the table.

"I hadn't realized it was this late. I have to catch a plane for L.A., and—"

"—Oh my God!"

He stopped speaking and followed her stare to the box in the corner of the room. The dog was sniffing a dark-purplish sac that was moving on the papers. And, once he really looked, the outline of tiny paws could be seen pressing against the membrane.

"Do something!" she nearly shrieked, while rising from her chair.

"The dog is supposed to do it. She should break it open, or something . . ." Why was she staring at him like that?

"Or something?" Her look turned from incredulous into disbelief. "I thought you said you knew all about this?"

There was certainly nothing shy or frightened about her now. He glanced back at the dog. "I'm telling you the dog should—you know—it's instinct."

"Well, my instinct is telling me Bummer's isn't working right now." She looked at him with a murderous expression. "Get that puppy out!"

He returned her stare with one of equal disbelief. "Me?"

She rushed past him while issuing orders. "Get me the towels. Hurry up. And bring those scissors that Pat boiled earlier. I'll get the thread."

He did as he was told and then watched as she knelt in front of the small black dog. Amazed, he stood behind her and listened as she talked out loud.

"Okay, Bummer. I don't think you've got the hang of this. You see, we're going to gently press down on this thing and . . . yes, there it is . . . Oh, God . . ."

He could hear her breathing heavily, as if to settle her stomach as the membrane broke under the pressure she applied with the towel.

"Well, I'll be damned." His voice was a soft whisper as he watched the tiny wet puppy open its mouth to receive life.

"Hand me the scissors," Ginny said in between gulps of her own labored breathing.

He did as he was asked.

"Now the thread. C'mere. Tie this off. Really tight."

"You have to make two knots," he said as the memory came back. "I remember now. You cut in between."

She looked over at him as he knelt by her side. The corner of her mouth lifted in the beginnings of a smile. "Glad to hear you're good for something, Lewellyn. I was beginning to get worried."

He grinned. "Hey, I resent that. I make a great salad. I can iron my own shirts and I batted .310 in my day. I'd also like to add that three golden gloves sit in my office. I'll have you know some people happen to think quite highly of me."

She cut the thin cord and watched as Bummer finally got around to taking an active interest and participating. Looking up at him, she finally broke into a wide grin.

"Will you look at this? We did it. .310, huh? Is that good?"

He shrugged, embarrassed now by stating his lifetime

batting average. "You don't know much about baseball, do you?"

She shook her head and looked back to the puppy squirming under Bummer's constant licking. "I guess I know as much about baseball as you know about birthing puppies." She sighed and wiped her forehead on her sleeve. "I come from a family of females. When we watched TV, it wasn't baseball. But I have heard of you. And Pat seems to think you're a living legend."

He had gotten over the urge to impress people with his stats after his second year in the majors. So why did he want to impress her with his last twenty years of achievements? Every batting title, MVP, Golden Glove; every All Star game he had started? He even wanted to tell her about the thrill, nineteen years ago, at being named Rookie of the Year—the way he had cried, all alone in a motel room in Atlanta when he'd first heard. Instead, he crushed the memories and returned his attention to the scene playing out in front of him.

"Hey, look. It's a male."

She gazed down to the tiny puppy. Shaking her head, she whispered, "How about that Lewellyn? We did it."

She didn't look up at him and he was glad. Chalk it up to fatigue, or emotions . . . he wasn't sure what was causing the thick lump in his throat. He only knew that for the first time since he retired from baseball, he felt connected to someone, part of something larger than himself, and it frightened him.

Swallowing down the emotion, he glanced over to Bummer and said, "Looks like we're about to do it again."

"But your flight . . . ?"

"Hell, I can sleep on the plane. This time I'm ready."

She raised her head and stared at him. In that moment he recognized what it was in her eyes that had struck such an intense chord inside of him.

She had the haunted, stricken look of a war veteran.

He knew it. He recognized it. He'd been there himself.

Chapter 4

I t would cost her at least thirty-five dollars, plus tip, to pay for the cab from the train station, and it was money that she didn't have to waste. She could have called Ginny to pick her up, probably should have, but she didn't. She needed this time, this peace, to adjust before facing the kids. Leaning her head against the cracked leather seat, Allie was grateful the cab driver didn't want to talk on the way to Jersey. Her mind was filled with images and snatches of conversation as she once more thought of the disastrous Washington visit. She had spent two hours dissecting it on the train ride back to Philly. Two hours of torture, and she still couldn't put it behind her.

Her husband had not appreciated her surprise visit.

And Allie continued to wonder exactly why.

Was it her? Marriage? Marriage to her? Why did he seem happier in Washington than he had at home in many months? What had those strangers given him that she and the children had not?

When the cab pulled into her driveway, Allie looked at her house with a dispassionate eye. The white and black colonial needed trim work. The shrubs were overgrown, weeds were clearly visible and the grass needed mowing. Meghan's doll carriage was lying on the sidewalk and Pat's bike appeared to have been thrown down on the front lawn.

This was what Dave saw when he came home.

This place, this home, looked unloved. Maybe that's just how Dave felt—unloved. She certainly did.

She and the house were alike. Each had been neglected and now needed attention. She felt as if she were waking up from a dream and seeing things as they truly were. How long had she been drifting, allowing everything to fall into disrepair? Well, now that her eyes were opened it was obvious she had her work cut out for her.

After paying for the cab, Allie drew in a deep determined breath. She would start right now.

"Mommy! You're home, you're home! And we have a surprise."

"Allie. How did you get here?"

She walked through her front door and was greeted by her sister and her youngest child. Leaving her bag in the foyer, she bent down and picked up Meghan. "I took a cab," Allie said after kissing her daughter. "Where's Pat?"

Ginny rose from the couch with a sleepy expression. "Pat? I think he's out back. Why did you take a cab? I said I'd pick you up." She smiled as she came closer. "How was Washington?"

Allie returned her daughter to the floor and answered, "Washington was hot, and it just seemed easier to take a cab. Meghan, I want you to go outside and pick up your doll carriage. How many times have I told you not to leave your toys outside?"

"But what did you bring me?"

Allie took a deep breath to control her patience. "I didn't bring you anything. I didn't have time. Now, do as I've asked."

"Mommy, you said—"

"Pick up the carriage, all right? We'll talk about it later."

Allie looked around her living room and shook her head. "Does anyone do anything around here? What a dump!"

Ginny returned to the couch and sat down while both women watched a teary-eyed Meghan look back at them.

"We won't tell you then. Will we, Aunt Gin?"

Allie raised her eyebrows. "The doll carriage? Now?"

"What's wrong with you, Allie?" asked Ginny.

Pulling off her jacket, Allie turned to her sister. "Nothing's wrong. What's Pat doing out back? It's about time the crown prince mowed the lawn." She pushed the hair away from her forehead with a quick, impatient motion. "It's beginning to look like we're growing soybeans out there."

"That might be a little difficult. At least for a few days."

She faced her younger sister. "What do you mean?"

Ginny looked hesitant, as though uneasy with her next words. "Well, you see, Pat sort of had an accident."

"An accident?" Her muscles tightened. "Where is he? Is he all right?"

"He's fine. Just a sprain. He's not even wearing the sling any more."

"A sling? What the hell happened here?" Without giving Ginny a chance to reply, she added, "I swear, Ginny, it's fine for you to play your Auntie Mame routine with me, but you need some responsibility if you intend to spend time around my children."

She watched as Ginny's mouth opened in shock while she sat upright. "I beg your pardon? I don't think I heard correctly."

"You heard right. Children are a responsibility. You aren't used to them, I understand, but—"

Ginny shot to her feet. "Wait a minute here. Your son got hurt at a ball game, something you arranged. He was seen by a doctor and it was nothing. I didn't call you because I didn't want to ruin your weekend—"

"Hi, Mom," Pat interrupted as he walked into the living room. "What's the matter?"

Both women turned to the young teenager. Allie spoke first.

"Nothing. How's the arm?"

Pat shrugged. "It's okay. Did Aunt Ginny tell you about Matt? And Bummer?"

Allie shook her head. "Matt?"

"Lewellyn."

"Matt Lewellyn and Bummer? I don't get it."

Pat grinned, obviously thrilled to be the one to break the news. "Matt brought me home from the game and stayed to deliver Bummer's puppies."

"Wait a minute," Allie demanded. "Bummer had puppies?" Why did she feel like she stepped into someone else's life? "Matt Lewellyn was here?"

Pat nodded and grinned to his aunt. "We helped him with the puppies, didn't we?"

Ginny smiled back at the boy. "Oh, yes. We helped

him. C'mon, Allie. Take a look at the new additions to your family."

Allie allowed herself to be led into the kitchen. In the corner was a large box and inside lay Bummer with tiny black puppies asleep by her stomach. Very slowly, Allie knelt down by the dog and ran her hand over its soft head. Tears welled up as she looked at the puppies and she whispered, "What a weekend. I even missed this."

"We took care of it," Pat announced, as he stood behind her. "Right, Aunt Gin?"

Ginny nodded. "I have to admit I'm glad to see your mother, though. My midwife days are over."

Allie glanced up to her sister. "You really delivered these?"

She watched as her sister gazed down to the litter with pride and affection. "I delivered the first out of necessity. Bummer didn't have any idea what to do. I couldn't believe it. The big one, over on the right, came first. He was pushing at the wall of the sac, trying to get out, and Bummer was just staring at it." She shrugged again. "I had to do something."

"Then tell her about Matt," Pat demanded in an excited voice. "You said he helped, too."

Ginny looked toward Pat and nodded. "He helped with the second, the other male, but we really didn't have all that much to do. Instinct kicked in and Bummer took over. She completely handled the delivery of the last one, the little female."

"The runt," Pat proclaimed. "That's what they call the littlest one, Billy said. But can you believe it, Mom? Matt Lewellyn. Had to be the best day of my life."

Allie stood up and took a deep breath. "Do you mean to

tell me that Matt Lewellyn was in my house? In my kitchen? And it looked like this?"

Ginny stared back at her, and suddenly Allie felt frazzled and angry. She knew she should have been happy about the puppies, but she just couldn't muster the energy at the moment.

"We handled it," Ginny said in a soft voice.

"Oh, I can see how you handled it," Allie countered, giving her kitchen a disgusted look.

Ginny seemed to take notice of the clutter. It was the same mess that had been there two days ago when she'd left for Washington.

Her sister walked over to the counter and closed a bread wrapper while saying, "Pat, why don't you go outside and help Meghan with her carriage. I want to talk to your mother."

Pat looked at both of them and shrugged. It was obvious he didn't want to be included in the forthcoming conversation.

Before he hit the screen door, Allie called after him, "And get the lawn mower out. There's no excuse for the lawn looking the way it does. Everything's going to change, and we're going to start now!"

"Welcome home, Mom." The door slammed behind him, causing Bummer to become startled and her puppies to begin rooting again for nourishment.

"That little brat." Allie started to go after her son when Ginny stopped her.

"Leave him, Allie."

She spun around to her sister. "He's my son. I'll handle him."

"Like you're handling everything else? All right, what

happened? Why are you ready to jump down everyone's throat? This isn't like you."

Allie ran her fingers through her hair and took a deep breath. "Nothing happened. I'm just seeing this place with clear eyes. It's a dump."

"No, it isn't," Ginny insisted. "It's the same place you left two days ago." Obviously struggling with annoyance, she added, "You're what's different, Allie. Something has changed you."

"How would you know? You come from your perfect little house to spend a few days with Pat and Meghan. You walk in with your grand plans . . . let's pull the kids out of school. Let's send Allie on a train to Washington—"

"Wait," Ginny interrupted. "What happened in Washington?"

"We're not talking about Washington," Allie said in a defensive voice. "We're talking about here. My home."

"All right. So what's so wrong with your home?" Ginny asked, while looking around.

"After the great Auntie Mame leaves, I have to listen to how wonderful Aunt Ginny is, how she buys them everything they want, and why can't I be more like Aunt Ginny. It's so great to be mommy for a few days and then go back to your perfect tidy little world."

"That's not fair, Al. I'm only trying to help. And if the condition of your house bothers you, then you should clean it up. Every time I babysit I usually try to pick up a bit for you, but because your dog had a medical emergency, I couldn't. And now you're pissed at me? I had my hands full this weekend."

Bummer rose from her box and began a low growl deep in her throat, but it didn't stop Allie. Once she had begun, nothing could deter her. All the old resentments rose to the surface and demanded recognition.

"Well, try having your hands full like this twenty-four-seven. I don't just worry about the house being clean. It's not just that. I can't be you and give these kids everything they want. I have to worry about winter coats, soccer camps, doctors' and dentists' appointments, let alone saving for college. Do you have any idea how I feel when I have to say no, and then listen to how Aunt Ginny would do it for them?"

Ginny shook her head. "I never thought . . . I just did—"

"Of course you didn't think. You're always ready to sweep everyone along with your spur-of-the-moment plans. You don't think about the consequences. I wasn't ready to go to Washington. You pushed me into it, and now I've come home to a disaster—"

"Wait just one moment," Ginny interrupted. "You can rip me to pieces, but where's the disaster?"

Breathing heavily, Allie stared back at her sister. "Pat was injured."

"Taken care of. I've explained that."

"Bummer and the puppies."

"Safe and sound."

"Matt Lewellyn here. In my kitchen. Like this."

Ginny stared back at her with an angry expression. "Your fault. It's your kitchen. If it bothers you so much, then clean it once in a while."

Her sister's words stung her, like a slap in the face.

Needing to strike back, Allie said, "You're the most anal-retentive person I've ever met. I've actually seen you walk into a room and change the position of an ash tray at least seven times. In your home, everything has to be perfect. Nothing else is good enough."

"That's not true," Ginny shot back. "And, anyway, what's that got to do with this?"

The tension in the room was almost palpable. "Everything," Allie returned. "We're totally different. You have—"

"Well, well. Trouble in familial paradise?"

Ginny and Allie turned to the doorway and saw Nan, dressed in an olive green silk pant suit. She looked polished and pretty and snug. Holding Meghan's hand, she smiled down to her niece. "Meghan brought me in. We met outside, didn't we, darling?"

Meghan stared back up at her glamorous aunt and nodded. The child seemed to be in awe. Nan rarely paid any attention to the children.

"See the puppies?" A small finger pointed the way.

Ginny watched as Nan looked to the box in the corner of the kitchen. Her sister's smile appeared less than enthusiastic. It might be because Bummer was growling with a canine's intuition.

"How cute," Nan remarked. "So she had them. I see you did manage, Ginny."

"How are you, Nan?" It took a great deal of willpower to swallow her anger and pretend everything was fine. "You look well."

Nan smiled. "So do you," she said in a voice that clearly stated otherwise. "I thought I would pop over and see if you needed help. You sounded so . . . so desperate on the phone."

"I wasn't desperate," Ginny quickly answered. "I just didn't know anything about delivering puppies. We did all right."

"How are you, Nan? Really?" Allie asked, concern in her voice.

How easily she forgets her anger, Ginny noted, while watching her older sister hold out a kitchen chair for Nan.

"I'm fine."

Letting go of Meghan's hand, Nan walked over to the table. She sat down and smiled at her sisters. "I might as well tell you before you hear of it elsewhere." She drew a deep breath and said plainly, "Robert has moved out."

"Out?" Allie sat down next to her and touched her shoulder. "Oh, Nan, I'm so sorry . . . When?"

Ginny watched as Nan pulled away ever so slightly. It was a small gesture of nervousness.

"A few weeks ago."

"A few weeks ago! Why didn't you tell us?" Allie sounded shocked.

Ginny knelt down in front of her very interested niece. "Meghan, why don't you take Bummer out back? She looks like she could use a break from the puppies."

Not too young to notice that she was being politely excused, Meghan looked decidedly disappointed as she called to the dog. Ginny watched as the two of them went out the kitchen door. She heard the hum of the lawn mower and wanted to go outside and hug Pat, explain that his mother wasn't herself, and that they should all be patient. But she didn't feel patient. She felt angry. Allie had attacked her and now she was acting like nothing was more important than Nan's announcement.

A moment of shame passed over her. Nan's marriage was over, and she should be sorry. But it seemed like re-cycled news. Robert Lynch had not appeared happy with her sister for the last three years. She was surprised he had stayed this long. Secretly, she wished her brother-in-law happiness, for Robert was far too nice to be trapped in an unhappy marriage.

"Enough about me," Nan said in a hurried voice, "What did I walk into? Allie, I've never seen you like that be-fore. What did Ginny do?"

"Never mind," Ginny answered before Allie had a chance. "It hardly seems important after your announce-ment." Ginny immediately recognized the look of amusement and satisfaction on Nan's face. It tore into her stomach, making her cross her arms over her ab-domen in protection. This had been going on for years. Too many years. It was a question of control and power, of divide and conquer. Nan saw the opportunity to come between her two older sisters, and she was taking advan-tage of it. What Nan would never know was that Ginny felt as if she were losing a lover, someone with whom she had shared nearly all of life's intimacies. She and Allie had been more than sisters, and Nan had always re-sented that bond. Perhaps it was understandable. Nan. The baby. The one they had always protected. The one who always got everything she wanted. Nan, who al-ways wanted Allie all to herself, looked like she was about to get her wish.

"Men!" Allie stated in a heated tone of voice. "You would think, we, of all women, would have a handle on this. I mean, considering Daddy—"

Ginny put her hand up to stop her sister. "Please," she interrupted. "Let's not go through it again. We've all made mistakes, too."

"Why do you continue to defend him?" Nan demanded. "I was just a child when he walked out on us, but I can still recognize a bastard. How many times did he try and see us? You tell me."

Ginny looked at Allie, not Nan, and shrugged. "A few."

"In nearly thirty years, that man didn't see us more than five times. Now that he's dead, he can rot in hell for all I care," Nan said. Her voice was vehement with resentment.

"I'm going home." Ginny pushed her hair out of her eyes and added, "I'm sorry about Robert. He was a good man."

"And I'm not a good woman?" Nan's eyes narrowed with anger. "Is that what your statement was supposed to imply?"

Shaking her head, Ginny answered, "I'm not going to argue with you. I'm sorry about your marriage, all right?" She looked at Allie. "I'm leaving. Give the kids a kiss for me."

Within five minutes she had her things together and was fishing for her car keys in the bowl on the foyer table when she heard Allie's voice.

"How can you leave like this? Can't you see she's in pain? Her marriage has just ended, and you can't even try to get along with her."

Angry, hurt, and more than a little tired, Ginny turned

on her older sister. "Look, you take care of it. If you ask me, she's relieved. Now it won't be considered adultery when she cheats on him."

"Ginny!"

"Wake up, Allie. You love to talk to hear your own voice spouting out advice. Go back into Nan and give her some of it. Watch her laugh in your face. Or, better yet, why don't the two of you have one of your famous talks about how our father and our mother's boyfriends have screwed us up with men? Or how we're all afraid of turning into tramps like our mother? And isn't Nan fortunate not to have any children? That way she doesn't have to worry about touchy introductions. Why don't you two figure out how many 'uncles' we had? How many spent the night, or stayed for months? Jesus, why don't the two of you dissect it to death and be done with it. Just leave me out. My life is messed up enough without going through that again."

Ginny watched as Allie's jaw muscle moved beneath her cheekbone, as if she were clenching her back teeth in anger. It took no more than five seconds for her to whisper, "I think you're right. It's time for you to go home."

Ginny stared at her, refusing to give into the tears that threatened to spill over. This wasn't an ordinary fight or disagreement. This was serious. She was about to apologize, to tell Allie that nothing was worth losing her friendship, when she spied Nan coming out of the kitchen. From the look on her face, she could tell Nan had overheard their conversation. She felt violated. She watched as her younger sister walked up to Allie and placed her hand on

Allie's shoulder. It was an act of possession, of victory, and suddenly Ginny was too tired for the fight.

"I'll leave," she whispered back. "With pleasure."

She pulled the robe tighter about her and then pushed the wet strands of hair away from her forehead. She hoped it wasn't Allie or Nan at the door, for all she had wanted was to take a hot bath and go to bed. No more discussions. No more tears. This weekend was proving to be a true test of her stamina . . . and her patience.

"Who is it?" Ginny called through the heavy wooden front door of her home.

"Delivery."

She frowned. It was Sunday. Who made deliveries on Sunday?

"Who?" she repeated, feeling her shampooed hair dampening her robe. This was the one part of living alone she dreaded. Anyone could be on the other side.

"Courier Delivery."

She stood on tiptoe and looked out the small peephole. A man was standing on the other side. He was dressed in a dark blue uniform, and appeared to be from a delivery service.

"Who is it from?" she asked as a precaution.

The man looked down to the small package wrapped in brown paper. It took him a few seconds to answer. "Uhhh . . . It says M. A. Lewellyn."

She stood in front of the door and breathed heavily. Matt Lewellyn? What in the world would he be sending her? Curiosity got the better of her and she unlocked the door. Not able to stop the silly grin from appearing on her lips, Ginny accepted the package in a state of wonder. Matt Lewellyn? Wasn't he in California, or someplace? After thanking the man, she shut the door and carried the package back upstairs to her bedroom. Laying it down on her comforter, she stood back and stared at it.

What was inside that brown paper? For two days she had thought of that night she had spent in Allie's kitchen. It was like a dream, something very precious to take out and enjoy, for nights like that seldom happened to ordinary people.

What did he want with her?

Unable to stand the suspense anymore, she climbed up onto her four poster bed and ripped the paper away from the box. Inside, wrapped in black and white dotted tissue, were three tiny white dog collars and, attached to each, were miniature bronze discs. Ginny smiled as she read the engraved names.

Rhett. Ashley. Scarlett.

She made a noise of appreciation as she picked up the folded white paper. His handwriting was bold and dark, as though he had written it in a hurry.

Thursday night. Charity dinner. Four Seasons Hotel. I'll pick you up at six. Please, you can't say no to a fellow midwife. Don't make me fly solo.

Her mouth opened in shock. How could he do this? How did he get her address? Was it on the paper Pat had given him to sign?

She read the note again, hoping she had misunderstood. The wording was plain and direct. He was coming.

Despite the shower, she felt a thin sheen of sweat break

out on her forehead, as panic and fear rushed in on her. A man was trying to control her again.

This couldn't be happening. There was no telephone number, no address. In four days he would show up at her door, and she had no way of stopping him.

Not again, God. Please. Not again.

Chapter 5

D addy! You're home. Bummer's had her puppies!"
Allie heard Meghan's excited greeting as she gave the bathroom a quick last check. Grabbing up Pat's undershirt and *Sports Illustrated* from the floor, she stuffed both in the hamper and hurried to the living room. There was a mixture of fear and anger inside of her, churning together and eating at her stomach. He had to notice. He had to be impressed. She had worked like a woman possessed to clean the house, and had even dragged her kids, kicking and screaming, into the process. But she had been determined that when Dave came home the house would be orderly.

"Hi," she said in an even voice, as she brushed back a strand of hair from her forehead.

Dave was holding his daughter on his hip as he looked over to her. "What's wrong with Meghan? She says you've been mean to everybody."

Allie stared at him. No hello? No, the house looks great, the lawn's been mowed? "Excuse me, I don't even rate a hello?"

She watched as he placed Meghan back on the floor

78

and handed the child his briefcase. Waiting until Meghan skipped off to the family room, he took a deep breath and said, "Hello. Now what's wrong with Meghan?"

It took every ounce of willpower not to yell at him for ignoring their efforts. Instead, she steadied herself and said, "Meghan's trying to adjust to the changes around here. So's Pat. We'll all have to adjust," she added, leveling him with her gaze.

He loosened his tie and brushed past her to the kitchen. "What changes?" he asked in a bored voice. "So you finally got around to cleaning the house?"

She turned and followed him, observing him rummaging through the refrigerator for a Snapple. She listened to the loud pop of the vacuum seal being broken before she spoke. That's exactly how her nerves felt, like they would snap at any moment, she thought as she watched Dave bend over the box of puppies and pet Bummer.

"Then you did notice the work we did in the last two days. You know, Dave, I think if your secretary had done as much in your office, you would have complimented her. Why is it that you treat us worse than the people you work with? We're your family."

He held his hand up, as though dismissing her comment, while standing and leaving the dogs. "Look, I just walked in the door. I don't need this. Keeping the place together was supposed to be your job. And now that you've finally done something around here, you want me to start handing out office achievement plaques? The place looks good. Is that what you wanted to hear?"

Tears of frustration formed at her eyes as she looked back at him. It didn't make any difference. It wasn't the house, or the clutter. It wasn't the stacks of magazines in the foyer or the seedlings in the dining room, or the piles of laundry.

It was her.

Swallowing down the tightness in her throat, she managed to say, "No, that's not what I wanted to hear."

He slammed down the bottle of juice onto the counter, spilling a little on the cleaned formica. "Then what is it?" he asked with impatience. "And why the tears? God, don't tell me you're pregnant again?"

"Hardly," she whispered as his words formed a knot of resentment in her stomach. "When was the last time you touched me? It would have to be an immaculate conception."

He let out a long, weary breath. "I really don't need this. I just got home from a difficult trip," he said as he walked past her. "I'm gonna take a shower. Since you've turned into Suzy Homemaker, let me know when dinner's ready."

She spun around, all thoughts of control vanishing. The vacuum seal on her emotions broke and her voice escalated. "Just stop right where you are," she demanded. Her hands clenched at her sides with anger. "A moment ago you said you wanted to know what was wrong. Well, let me tell you," she added, drawing each word out for emphasis.

She felt a small measure of satisfaction when she saw the startled look on Dave's face. She had never used that tone with him before.

"A difficult trip, Dave? Playing golf with your cronies, and flirting with the other sales reps? Let me tell you what was difficult about that trip. For me, it was dealing with the humiliation of realizing that all I had was cotton underwear, and having my sister buy me silk ones because every dollar I spend is put back into the house or the kids. Difficult was how I'd describe agonizing over how you'd react to me showing up at your hotel. What was more difficult was that my worst fears were realized. When we were in that hotel room alone and you made it perfectly clear you didn't want me there."

She refused to cry, even though the sobs were practically choking her. If she didn't get it all out now, he'd walk away and she'd lose her nerve. "But let me tell you what I thought was the most difficult part of that trip— watching my husband admiring a woman at dinner and ignoring me. It was then I realized that I had spent almost fifteen years devoting myself to this man, his children and this house, only to find out that it wasn't appreciated. I couldn't help wondering if Miss White Silk Suit would have been as interesting to you if she had done the same. I don't think so."

He appeared shocked by her statement, maybe even embarrassed to have been caught in mental philandering. Trying to recover, he said, "What are you saying? You want out of this? After fifteen years—"

"No," she hotly interrupted. "Here's the deal, Mr. Businessman, since you so obviously respect women's opinions when they're outside this home. Number one, this house stays clean. And since it's not such a hard job, we all won't mind cooperating, will we? Number two, now that Meghan is in school, I'm getting a job. Since your commission checks are down, we can use the extra cash and I want my own pocket money, not house money. My days of cotton panties are over. Even if you don't appreciate the difference, I do."

"Is this all because we didn't make love in Washington? God, women are so—"

"Hold it," she interrupted, raising her hand as if stopping traffic. "I'm not through. This has nothing to do with whether or not we made love in Washington. Washington just opened my eyes. The final thing I want to discuss is your cooperation. The last two days were tough on the kids. I realized how spoiled they were. I'm not going to be the bad guy in this. We're both going to parent our children. That means you sit them down and talk to them, and back me up a hundred percent. Things have changed in this house." She held it together for as long as she thought she could, before adding, "Now go take your shower."

"What're you two doing? Fighting? She's been yellin' at everybody."

They both turned and saw Pat standing in the doorway, one shoulder leaning against the molding and that too familiar, teenaged disgust on his face.

Allie seized Dave with a glare of challenge, defying him not to handle this one.

"Pat," Dave said in a stern voice. "Knock it off and set the table for dinner."

Her son pushed himself away from the wall. "Oh, what? She's yelling at you, too? And now I take the heat? Why do I have to set the table?"

Allie didn't say a word. This was her husband's fight. She'd had enough. More than enough.

"Watch your mouth," Dave answered in a more authoritative voice. "Set the table and then go up to your room. I'll talk to you later."

Pat glowered at both of them before sulking over to the

cabinet and flinging it open. Taking out four plates, he slid them out on the table like he was dealing a deck of cards.

"Keep it up, Pat," Dave said, "and you'll be grounded for a week."

"Cripes! What's wrong with this house? Welcome home, Dad."

The sarcasm was clear in their son's voice, yet both of them ignored it. Dave left the kitchen and Allie escaped outside into her garden.

It was the only place that never got cluttered. For years she had tended the neat little rows with tender care, ensuring that weeds and insects stayed out of her little patch of peace. Standing before the rows of newly planted seedlings, Allie finally gave into a good cry. Sorrow and frustration settled heavily on her heart. After all her hard work, her husband didn't even appreciate it. It wasn't that he didn't notice the difference in the house. He didn't care. An old emotion rekindled itself inside her as she said the words aloud.

"He doesn't care."

Fear wrapped itself around her. What did he want? What wasn't she doing right? More importantly, what could she do about it? Would getting a job make him appreciate her more? She wiped the tears from her cheeks and sighed. They used to talk about everything from politics to music. They used to laugh so much, being able to play off each other's quirky sense of humor. They used to sit up until the wee hours of the morning, dreaming and planning their future. And they used to make spontaneous, uncontrolled love. She covered her mouth as her desperate grief forced a sob from her lips.

God Almighty, was her husband having an affair?

* * *

Nan tightened her grip on the pen to stop her fingers from shaking. She told herself it was frustration. Seven o'clock and they were still at it with the Markey account. Seated at the long conference table, she tried to concentrate on what Tony was presenting to the group of disgruntled execs from their client's marketing department. She had worked with these guys for three years, developing great campaigns for them, and now they thought she was a little stale and they'd turned on her. In the last four hours they had given thumbs down on every story board that had been presented. And one of them even had the nerve to suggest that maybe it was time to switch agencies . . . after she had pulled their sorry butts up from a Mom and Pop grocery into a respected chain of supermarkets. She was sure it was just a negotiating tactic, but it was one that pissed her off nonetheless.

Feeling jittery, she abruptly stood up and adjourned the meeting. "Look, gentlemen, we've been at this for hours. It's late and we're not getting anywhere. This is Tuesday. Why don't you give us until Thursday to come up with some new ideas. I'm sure everyone's tired and wants to go home."

Tony, who had been stopped in the midst of his presentation, stood by his easel with a look of silent horror on his face. She ignored him. Joe Carter, president of McKinley, Carter and Brown, and her superior, appeared stunned but maintained a cool facade. He'd get over it. The clients pushed back chairs and stood up, almost in unison.

"Fine," Pete Delancy agreed. "Nothing's being accomplished here." The threat in his tone was implicit, yet Nan refused to dignify his comment.

She forced a smile. "Then we'll see you on Thursday? We'll knock your socks off."

They didn't answer, but began clicking shut briefcases and zippering portfolios before quietly walking out with Joe Carter in attendance. The breach of protocol disturbed her. Markey was her account. She should have been the one to escort them out, and she didn't like the confidential low buzz that went on between her clients and her boss.

"I don't understand," Tony said in a tense whisper when they were alone. "I didn't even finish the presentation."

Grabbing her purse, she summarily dismissed him with a wave of her hand. "Hey, it wasn't working. Nothing we gave them today would have pleased them."

"But these were all your ideas," he challenged back. "You wouldn't let me try out any of mine."

She stared at him for more than a few seconds. Did he dare assume that his rookie garbage could compete with her work? "Tony, I told you before. If you can't run with the big dogs, stay on the porch."

Turning on her heel, she left him in the conference room and hurried into the bathroom. Once inside the stall, she frantically searched through her purse. They were all turning on her. There was nothing wrong with her ideas. Markey was just being difficult, acting like they were General Foods or something. They probably wanted to renegotiate their contract. Cheap bastards. It wasn't the first time she had taken a small account into the major leagues, dragged them is more like it, and they were used to paying small time rates. Now they resented the cost for a multimedia campaign. What do they think they're going to pay if they have to go to New York to find an ad agency? It would almost serve them right to go up there, get their pockets turned inside out and be sent back to Philadelphia with their tail between their legs.

Nan almost laughed as she unscrewed the top of the vial. Where was that damned spoon? Unable to find it, she pulled out a new twenty-dollar bill and folded it in half, lengthwise. Shaking the white powder out and into the fold of the bill, she closed the top of the vial with one hand and dropped it back into her purse. They had till Thursday. That was enough time to come up with something. They might even use Tony's old stuff. She wasn't worried. Markey was such a hick account, they'd probably reconsider by Thursday. No problem.

Bringing the bill up to her nose, she held one nostril shut with her finger and inhaled quickly. She licked her thumb and wiped away any powder from her nose and then licked her thumb again, to taste the bittersweet numbing substance. Waste not, want not, she giggled to herself, as she shook the remaining powder in the bill toward the edge of the fold. Taking another quick hit, she ran a damp finger down the crease of the bill and then rubbed her bottom gum.

She felt an immediate rush of self-confidence return. Her senses were acute once more, and that awful, dragging fatigue had vanished. Instantly, the thought crossed her mind that she wished the guys from Markey hadn't left. She could have handled them now.

Looking at the creased face of Andrew Jackson on the bill, she folded it width wise and dropped it into her purse. If money could buy this feeling, it was worth the late charge on her condo payment. Those bloodsuckers could wait until next week when she got paid. And how was she supposed to handle everything now that her husband had walked out? They hadn't even discussed financial arrangements. Did he expect her to carry everything, just because her salary exceeded his measly college professor earnings? Well, she'd handle that one, too. Hadn't she always handled everything? Right now, she needed to get out of this office and buy some more powdered adrenaline. She had a tough project to navigate a rookie through, and only two days to do it.

Leaving the ladies room, she heard Joe Carter call out to her. "Nan, I need a few minutes."

She smiled instantly. "Sure. I know you're wondering what I'm doing with Markey, but I've got it covered."

Joe looked at her for a few minutes in silence. Finally, he said, "I'm concerned. They were not happy when they left here."

"Oh, Joe, c'mon. You know they're trying to play hardball. There was nothing wrong with that presentation."

"Nan, I have seen you do better."

She returned his steady gaze, and laughed. "Pardon my strategy. Let's make them think they're paying for hard work. If we gave them our best shot right off, they'd start taking us for granted and think they were paying too much. Now they think they have half of our staff at their disposal and in a minor uproar in order to please them. They want to know we're working hard for their money, Joe. And we'll show them Thursday."

Joe put his hands in his pockets and jangled some change. "Don't pull my chain on this one. It's too important."

Nan brushed an imaginary speck of lint from his lapel

and smiled seductively. "Hey, Joe, have I ever pulled your chain? The work's already done."

The president of McKinley, Carter and Brown smiled back at her. "I knew you must have had something up your sleeve. Sorry for doubting you, Nan."

Smile still in place, she nodded and turned toward her office. "No offense taken. Good night, Joe."

Nan slipped into her office and let the door close quietly. Her heart was racing so fast that her ears were beginning to ring. All she needed was a moment to pull it together. How long would it take them to find out she was an imposter? She'd made it through that one. Joe had bought her bluff, thank God. But how many plates did she still have spinning in the air? Sooner or later one of them was going to crash. Right now she'd just have to make sure it wasn't Markey Foods.

Absently throwing Tony's proposal into her briefcase, she shut it and stood up to get her raincoat. She felt trapped by the confining office. Ten hours in this place was enough. Running her fingers through her hair, she figured she'd catch a cab and beep her connection. Tonight she'd buy extra weight. Surely that would guarantee a priority house call.

Exhilarated, Nan left her office, confident that she could handle it all. Hadn't she always?

Chapter 6

S he promised herself that she would not look at the clock again. It was ridiculous. No man was going to come into her life and disrupt it. To ensure that, she had arranged a six o'clock appointment with the Caldwells, a wealthy couple who were interested in finding a home near Randall Cunningham. That area in Moorestown would mean a price tag starting at a million, and a commission from that sale could keep the firm comfortable for a few more months. With a staff of eighteen agents and office personnel, Harrison Real Estate was still holding its own, despite the economy. A sale to the Caldwells would put her ahead of the spring projections.

And Mr. Matt Lewellyn could use his machismo charm on someone else.

Ginny didn't care if it was the night of the dinner dance, and if he showed up at her house in tux and tails. He had not consulted her first, therefore leaving himself open for disappointment, and an empty, dark house.

She had business to conduct.

"Ginny, here's the printout for the multiple listings in Moorestown."

She looked up and smiled at Jim Hudson, a young, eager junior agent that she had just hired. "Thanks," she murmured as she took the computer printout.

"I did the range from houses that start at eight hundred and fifty thou, up to 1.5 mil. Should I go higher? There were only a couple up for sale in this locale."

She quickly scanned the sheet and shook her head. "This is enough to begin. They may even want to find a lot and build if nothing suits them. I'll get on the phone with the owners and see if I can arrange a showing. It would be great if I could take them through a house after I meet with them tonight."

Looking back up, she added, "Jim, see if you can find some nice lots, just in case. You know, something pastoral. Farm, trees, horses . . . they're coming from New York City and are convinced that this is farm country."

"You're kidding," Jim grinned back at her.

"No. That's what Mr. Caldwell said on the phone. He'd heard that this county was bucolic, and had easy access to the turnpike and 295. I almost asked him why he didn't just buy in Connecticut, but who'd want to lose a sale like this? They must have their reasons. Maybe the guy likes to drive," she said with a shrug.

Jim backed out of her office, saying, "Anybody who would drive ninety miles on the turnpike every day has to be crazy."

"Different strokes for different folks," she muttered, already looking back to the multiple listing. Selling real estate came natural to her. It was strange that she had been afraid to take the risk of opening her own agency. Her success was due to simplicity. Get to know the client. Match people. Match houses. And good instinct helped.

After a few minutes she found herself checking her desk clock again, and almost groaned with frustration. Why should she even feel guilty about standing up a man who didn't have the decency to call and confirm? It was so presumptuous, as if poor little Ginny Harrison would just jump at the opportunity to attach herself to the arm of a celebrity ex-jock. Men. Okay, so the puppy collars were a cute gesture, but she had told him no in Allie's kitchen. The fact that he ignored her wishes made her nervous, very nervous.

She had seen what power and authority could do to certain men. They'd always start off as charmingly assertive, but then the thin border between assertiveness and aggression would become blurred. It was a slow process, one she knew well, and one she had vowed never again to witness.

Her secretary buzzed her and she picked up the phone.

"What is it, Carol?"

"Richard Caldwell on line one. Do you want to take it?"

"Absolutely. Put him through," Ginny said, this time glancing at the clock with concern. He should have been on the road by now.

"Hello, Mr. Caldwell. Virginia Harrison."

"Look, we ran into a problem here. We're not going to make it tonight."

Ginny felt her shoulders sag with disappointment. "I'm sorry. I hope everything's all right."

There was a slight pause. "Fine. When can we reschedule?"

"What's your availability? I'll make myself open to your schedule." Even though the man was abrupt, she could sense he liked her attitude.

"I'll have to check my calendar and get back to you. My secretary will contact yours in a day or two."

She let out her breath in a silent, slow exhale. "Then I'll wait to hear from you. I have in front of me several listings that I'm anxious to show you."

"As I said, we'll be in touch."

After she hung up the phone, Ginny threw the printout on top of her mail tray. Carol buzzed again, and she snatched up the receiver. "Yes?" Her voice was preoccupied, and she added, "I'm sorry, Carol. What's up?"

"Your sister, Allie, called while you were on the line. She said she was in Philly and couldn't wait, but was on her way to your house with some great news and she'd meet you there by five-thirty."

"What?" Ginny started to panic. "She was in Philadelphia? Did she leave a number where I could reach her? I'm not going home . . ."

Carol's voice became concerned. "Gee, she said she was at a pay phone and was leaving for your house. I thought you'd rearranged your schedule and hadn't told me. It'd be such a shame to miss her. She sounded so excited."

Shaking her head with exasperation, Ginny got off the line and sat back in her chair. What the hell was Allie doing? She *couldn't* meet her at the house. Not with Matt Lewellyn planning to show up in black tie at six. She quickly pushed herself up from her chair and began pacing in front of her long antique desk. This could not be happening. If only Allie had talked to her first. What was wrong with people? Didn't anyone confirm anymore?

She drew her hand through her hair, as if the act might bring rational thought back into her brain. She needed a plan. As long as she had a plan, she could deal. Allie would get there around five-thirty. Matt would probably show up around six. It was ten after five now, which meant she had approximately twenty minutes to rush home, head her sister off and get her away from her house before Lewellyn rang her bell.

Could she do it?

Hell, she didn't have a choice.

Grabbing up her purse and her gabardine coat, she headed for the door. Whatever Allie's news was, it had better be good.

Sisters.

She'd beaten Allie to her house and had hidden her car in the garage. Pacing in the foyer, she looked out the side panel window every time a car came into the development, willing the beat up station wagon to appear. Where *was* she? Ginny looked at her wristwatch and silently cursed again. Twenty of six. Allie was always late for everything and had no sense of urgency. She ran her life like she ran her house, with absolutely no organization. She had said five-thirty!

Here she was, hiding in her own home, because her harebrained sister had called at the eleventh hour, fifty-ninth minute, with some cryptic message about good news. And this after Allie had nearly thrown her out of her house on Saturday. She had better not be pregnant again. Only Allie would think that being forty and pregnant was great news.

She heard a car and hurried back to the window, only to see a neighbor driving home from work. "Allie, where are you?" she whispered, knowing she was either going to have to leave, or hide upstairs in her bedroom, because

Matt Lewellyn was about to show up on her doorstep in a matter of minutes.

This was stupid, she thought while nervously chewing on her bottom lip. She was a grown woman and she was acting like a teenager. She paced the green and white marble floor and thought of several ways to wring her sister's neck for putting her in this position. She hated losing control of a situation, of not being given a choice or having others disregard her decisions, for then the old fears resurfaced with a vengeance. She had worked too hard and too long to find a place of calm in her life for anyone to threaten her peace. She just wanted to be left alone to live her life quietly.

Her doorbell rang and Ginny froze as she stared at the entry to her house. Who was on the other side? Was it her sister? Or the Jock, who couldn't seem to take no for an answer? In an instant she realized she'd have to open it. If it was Lewellyn, she couldn't leave him standing at her door when Allie drove up. Her sister would probably make him break it down, for fear something had happened to her.

So, tonight she would just have to be a grown up and handle everything like an adult. She would just explain—

The bell rang again and Ginny rushed forward to open it.

"Oh, thank God. It's you!" Ginny let her breath out in a rush before grabbing Allie's coat and pulling her inside. "Get in here and shut up."

"What?" Allie allowed herself to be dragged into the foyer before turning around. "Are you crazy?"

"Am I crazy?" Ginny demanded in an angry, though low voice. "I'm not the one who calls up leaving their schedules, just to show up a half hour late. Couldn't this be handled on the phone?" She spun around to the window. "Oh, my God, where's your car? Get it out of the driveway!"

"Where was I supposed to park it? What's wrong with you?"

"Okay, we've got to get out of here," Ginny ordered, while picking up her purse and grabbing Allie's coat sleeve.

Allie jerked her arm back and didn't move. "I'm not going anywhere until you tell me what's going on. You really are acting weird all of a sudden."

"I don't want to be here," Ginny said in a barely controlled voice. "I have to leave. Are you coming with me?"

"Tell me why."

"I'm not one of your kids, Allie. I don't have to listen to you. I'm leaving."

"Then I won't tell you my news. I wanted you to be the first to hear."

Ginny closed her eyes and shook her head, feeling as if she were dealing with a foreigner, someone who spoke a different language. "What? You're pregnant again? Fine. Congratulations. Let's go out and celebrate."

"I got a job."

Hand on the doorknob, Ginny stopped and looked over her shoulder. "You got a job? Where?"

"Philadelphia. At a woman's center. I'm going to be processing women in and—"

"We'll talk about it in the car. C'mon. Oh, no . . . please God, this isn't happening to me . . ." Hearing the motor of an expensive engine, Ginny peeked through the side window and groaned.

"Who are you hiding from?" Allie demanded, startling her sister even more by coming up behind her and looking out the window. "Who is that?"

Ginny leaned her head against the door and clamped her eyes shut. "Matt Lewellyn."

"The sports guy? The one Pat met? What's he doing here? Hold on a minute . . . He's all dressed up. In a tux!" Allie hit her on the shoulder. "Is this an overdressed client coming for a business meeting, or is he coming here for you?"

Ginny pushed herself away from the door and pulled Allie into the living room. "We're not answering it, do you hear me? I want you to shut up and not make a move," she commanded in a threatening whisper.

"*What?* Are you having a nervous breakdown, or something?"

"Be quiet!"

The doorbell rang, and the two sisters stared at each other, until Allie's mouth started to twitch with barely controlled laughter.

"This reminds me," she whispered, "of the time we were teenagers and hid from the Jehovah's Witnesses, and Nan starting laughing so hard she wet her pants."

"Shut up," Ginny whispered back, while watching Allie cover her mouth with her hand to stop her giggles.

"I can't . . ." Allie gasped and laughed out loud. "This . . . this is so dumb. You can't leave the man out there like that." She broke away from Ginny and raced for the door.

Ginny backed up into the room while frantically trying to wave her sister away from her mission. "Please, Allie," she called out. "Don't . . ."

She watched in horror as events spun out of control before her. Nobody heard what she said, nobody listened. Why weren't her words enough? Didn't no mean no? What was it about her that made certain people feel as though they could run her life? As Allie opened the door, Ginny felt a cold sweat break out over her body. It was fear. She didn't know this man, or what he was capable of. He was physically strong, well known and respected. What if he was cruel? What if he was Evan?

Don't cry, she told herself. Don't do this to yourself again. Be strong. He isn't your husband.

She heard Allie introducing herself. "Matt, my son told me all about you. I'm Pat Barbera's mom, Allie."

They shook hands, and he came further into her home.

"Nice to meet you. Sorry about the accident. How's Pat's arm? That's quite a kid you've got."

Allie nearly preened before the man. "Oh, he's just fine. Of course, he's been bragging to everyone who would listen about having Matt Lewellyn in his house to deliver puppies, no less. I should really thank you. Those puppies are now celebrities, and I have homes already lined up."

Matt laughed. "Your sister did all the work. She saved the first one." He turned his head and looked into the living room.

Ginny didn't even know what to do. She couldn't even smile.

His smile widened. "Hi," he said with a boyish enthusiasm. "Did you get the collars?"

She merely nodded.

"What collars?" Allie asked.

Ginny pushed herself forward. "Rhett, Scarlet and Ashley."

"What?" Allie again asked. "Am I missing something?"

Matt chuckled. "My co-midwife here said 'she didn't know nothin' about birthin' no puppies', so I sent the collars as a little memento of her success."

Allie was shaking her head. "I can not imagine the two of you down on my dirty floor helping out Bummer. I wish Pat would have gotten it on video. I know I'd want to see it."

Matt's gaze shifted nervously between Ginny and Allie. "Am I interrupting something? Do you need more time to get dressed?"

Ginny didn't know what to say, and Allie rushed in to fill the awkward silence.

"Oh, she's just running late. Actually I was the one that made her late," Allie announced while pulling Ginny toward the stairs. "I came over here to tell her about my new job and we started gabbing and lost track of time. It's a Sullivan trait. You'll get used to it." They were at the stairs. "She'll be ready in a few minutes."

"Is there a problem?" Matt asked, looking at the sisters.

Allie pushed her up the steps. "No, not at all. Just make yourself at home. We'll be right back."

It seemed to Ginny like the only escape at the moment and she hurried into her bedroom. When Allie shut the door behind her. Ginny turned on her.

"How dare you? I am not going anywhere with that man. Neither one of you really listens to me. I told him I wouldn't go and then he sends those collars and a note that he'd pick me up for this charity dinner thing. I told you I wanted to get out of here, and not to open my door.

And what do you do? What! Invite the man in. Tell him I'm going, and offer him free range of my house. What about me? What about what *I* want?"

Allie's voice held a note of patient empathy. She came up to Ginny and placed a hand on her arm to quiet her. "Listen, Gin, I know you're scared. It's been four years now since Evan passed, but you have to start getting back into the world. You're too young and too full of love to not have somebody in your life. This man seems nice. God, Matt Lewellyn! You could do a lot worse for a first date. Not a bad way to get back into the swing of things."

Ginny shook her head with disbelief. "You still don't get it, do you? I am back into the world. I have a business and a life."

Allie ignored her as she walked over to the double closet and flung open the doors. "And now you've got a date. Ain't life grand?"

"I'm not going," Ginny protested, as she watched Allie rummage through her clothes.

"God, look at this one," Allie said, holding up a dark blue sleeveless gown with bugle beads at the high collar. "The last time I had on anything this dressy, I was twenty and in Georgia Moss' wedding party. Remember her? I wonder if she's still married."

Ginny walked closer to her sister. "See? You're still not listening to me. I'm not going."

"And *this* . . . this is the one you should wear." Bringing out a cream-colored sheath, Allie held it up against herself. "I love this one. Feel the fabric."

"I haven't worn that in five years," Ginny said and grabbed it from Allie to place it back in the closet. "If you have trouble listening, then read my lips. *I am not going.*

And, since you're the one that invited that man into my house, then you can go down there and tell him to leave."

Still in her coat, Allie jammed her hands into her pockets. "How long is this going to go on? You live like a nun, and it's not healthy. You came into my house a week ago and told me to clean up my act and I did what you wanted. It may not have been comfortable, or even what I wanted to hear, but it was necessary. And you were right, Gin. I needed to get out of the house and that protective bubble I was living in. You know what? It was scary, but I did it."

Ginny watched her sister straighten her shoulders and come closer.

"I learned a few things down there in Washington," she murmured. "And it forced me to deal with some issues that I was unconsciously sweeping under the rug. But I realized those things wouldn't go away. They would just mount up, like the rest of the clutter in my house until they became so big you couldn't ignore them. Wait until you see my house, Ginny. It's clean. Maybe not immaculate, but really pulled together."

Sighing, Ginny ran her fingers through her hair. "I know you're trying to help, Allie, but I'm just not ready for this. I don't know if I ever will be. I like my life. I want to be alone. Stop being a matchmaker, because we wouldn't be good together."

"This isn't a lifelong commitment. It's just a date to a charity dinner. It's not even candlelight for two. This is a public function. I know he's not Evan, but he seems like a really nice man. Don't make that man, dressed like that, walk out of here alone."

He's not Evan. The words rang inside Ginny's brain. Intellectually, she knew she shouldn't compare every man with her dead husband. Not all men were cruel and abusive and violent. But she was terrified to take the risk.

"Look, we've been up here for ten minutes now. You get dressed, and I'll go down and keep him company until you're ready. It'll be okay. Don't you think I was terrified when I went for that interview today? But I pushed myself and I got through it. And I got the job."

Ginny walked over and wrapped her older sister in her arms. "I'm so sorry that I ruined your good news with all this. What in the world made you go out and get a job?"

Allie pulled back a little and the two of them stared at each other. "It's a long story and a man is waiting downstairs."

"Let him wait. Tell me."

"This is a new beginning for both of us. My whole life is changed. Now get dressed. How about lunch tomorrow? I want to hear about this date."

Ginny hugged her quickly before Allie pulled away. "All right. Lunch tomorrow. Twelve-thirty, and *don't* be late. And this is not a date. I'm only going because it's for a charity." She walked into her closet and brought out a black raw silk suit with a mid calf length skirt. Then she grabbed a black shell with a sheer chiffon yoke.

Allie covered her mouth, as if shocked. "You cannot be serious. With all those beautiful colors and clothes, all those beads and sequins, you pick out a depressing black suit."

Ginny laid the clothing on her bed. "Those others were from my life with Evan. He always thought that beads and sequins were classy and fit the image of a politician's wife on the chicken circuit. If you want them, you can have them. This is something I picked out after he was gone. It's my taste, not his. And if I have to go to this thing, I don't want any memories of Evan."

"Don't you have anything that's a little bit sexy that *you* picked out?"

Ginny flipped back the front panel of the skirt. "See, there's a slit up to the knee that's not immediately noticeable. Understated. Elegant. And even sexy. Now, get out of here so I can get dressed."

When Allie left, Ginny pulled off her coat and threw it onto the bed. How in the hell did she allow this to happen? She didn't know who she was more angry with— Matt for being so presumptuous, Allie for being so bossy, or herself for losing control of the situation.

It was for a charity to benefit needy kids, and at this point, she'd might as well make the best of it. But Mr. Matt Lewellyn would never pull this on her again. Before this evening was over, she'd let him know it.

Chapter 7

The orange-rose blush of early evening reflected off to the Philadelphia skyline as they left New Jersey behind and crossed the Delaware river into the city.

"You're very quiet. Are you okay?"

Ginny inhaled deeply, again smelling the scents of spring. "I'm fine," she said softly, "but there is something that I have to get off my chest."

"Go ahead," he said, making the approach onto the interstate, "What is it?"

She hesitated, not sure of how to begin, but needing to state her position. "When you first mentioned this dinner, I thought I had made it clear that I wasn't able to attend. But you sent the dog collars, with a note, disregarding what I told you earlier. I have to say, Matt, that I was a bit taken aback to see you at my door without confirming first."

She watched him glance in her direction, and he appeared a little embarrassed.

"You're right. I should've called you first. I guess I just thought that if I did, you'd turn me down flat."

Surprised by his honesty, she concentrated on the long lines of traffic before them. He was actually nervous. She wasn't ready to change her opinion of him, but she found it interesting that the ex-jock was unsure of himself. "Look, we're going to go to this dinner together, but I just needed to clear the air. I have a real problem when people don't listen to what I'm saying."

"I'm sorry," he apologized with a smile. "But if I had called, you would have backed out. Right?"

Ginny returned his smile cautiously. "I wouldn't have been backing out, since I never really accepted."

"Touché. I'm sorry if you thought I was a little under-handed, but I am glad that you came."

Wanting to change the subject, Ginny took a deep breath and said, "This is so remarkable. Here we are stuck in traffic and we haven't even hit the city yet, and it still smells like the country. I don't know—there's something about this spring."

Matt hesitated and glanced at her. "It might have something to do with the lilacs lying on the floor in the back."

Ginny stared at him. "You're kidding. There are lilacs back there?"

Matt shrugged as he passed a slow moving car. "It's going to sound stupid, but when I was leaving, I thought maybe I should have brought you flowers. I went over to the lilac bush in front of the house and broke off a few branches." Settling back into the middle lane, he added, "But the closer I got to your place, the more foolish I felt. So I just left them there."

Ginny immediately tried to turn and get the flowers from the back, forgetting that she was harnessed in tightly by the seat belt. They both laughed as Matt reached behind to get them.

Ginny gathered the fragile blossoms in her arms and lowered her face to capture the exquisite fragrance. She inhaled deeply then exhaled slowly, allowing the tension to leave her body along with her breath. It really was sweet of him, and she admitted to herself that the act of him picking the lilacs meant more than if he had showed up on her doorstep with a florist's bouquet.

"Thank you, Matt," she whispered shyly, "it was really nice of you to do this."

Matt again shrugged as he concentrated on the heavy traffic leading into the city. "I know it may seem corny, a little old-fashioned—"

"It's perfect," she interrupted, realizing that he was as nervous as she. "I love lilacs." Ginny looked out over the rooftops of the old Philadelphia row homes. A rush of nostalgia captured her as she breathed in the essence of the lilacs. "You know, the last time anyone brought me flowers was a boyfriend in college. It was my birthday, and he was taking me to an Earth, Wind, and Fire concert."

Matt perked up and grinned. "You like Earth, Wind, and Fire?"

Suddenly feeling young, Ginny let out a chuckle. "Are you kidding! And how about Creedance Clearwater, or Chicago, The Doors, George Benson . . . ".

"Or the Commodores," Matt cut in enthusiastically. "I have all of those oldies on CD."

"In the car?"

"Yeah, look in the glove compartment."

Ginny reached into the glove compartment and pulled

out The Best of Earth, Wind, and Fire CD. She removed the classical disc and replaced it with her choice. Soon the car filled with the melodic strains of her youth, and she sat back and leaned against the headrest. Closing her eyes, she listened to the music as it took her back to a carefree time before her marriage, before the horror.

A time of innocence.

Suddenly, another chuckle escaped her lips.

Matt grinned at her. "What? What are you thinking?"

Shaking her head, Ginny laughed. "I was just thinking about how silly I must have looked. I had my hair permed into a blonde afro. And clogs! Matt, I have to ask, did you ever have clogs or earth shoes?"

He let out a hearty laugh. "I must confess that I gave clogs serious consideration, but decided against them after I found out what a turned ankle could do to my career. But earth shoes did win out."

"You know all of that stuff is back in style now? Can you believe it?"

"No. I had hoped that those clothes would never come back, and that perhaps they would stay trapped in the time capsule that NASA shot into space in the seventies. It had to be the ugliest fashion period in the history of man."

"Well, when you go to the mall again, you'll see that it's back with a vengeance, at least for women. It's a good thing that aliens never found that capsule, or they'd be convinced that there really wasn't any intelligent life down here."

They both laughed and settled into a comfortable silence as they listened to the music. Ten minutes later, Matt maneuvered the car into a line of limousines in front of the Four Seasons Hotel. As she looked out of the window, Ginny felt the old tension return. There were several news minivans across the street from the hotel, and directly in front of its entrance, standing behind a roped off VIP aisle, were eager reporters and fans clamoring for attention.

"Oh, God. Do we have to go through this to get in?" she murmured, clasping the lilacs closer to her chest.

"Don't worry about it," Matt said reassuringly. "We just have to smile, wave, and walk in."

The scene was too familiar to her. She had gone through the same thing when Evan campaigned. Putting on a practiced facade of calmness, she allowed the curbside valet to help her out of the car and nervously waited for Matt to join her. Brushing tiny lavender blossoms off her suit, she reminded herself that she could make it past the flashing cameras, bright lights, intrusive mini-cams and microphones, if she just concentrated hard enough. Ginny felt her face tense as she pasted on a pleasant smile and began walking down the long aisle, holding on to Matt's arm for support.

"Over here, Matt. Can we do a short interview?"

"Can you give us a minute? Sports Update wants a quick profile."

"C'mon, Matt, 610AM Sports Radio here. We just need a few comments."

Appearing oblivious to her distress, he waved and stopped every few feet to shake an outstretched hand, or to give an acquaintance a hearty slap on the back. It was odd, but Matt now seemed more like a politician than an ex-athlete. The parallel was unnerving.

"Yo, Matt, what'dya think of that new kid, DeWayne Henderson, that the Federals brought up to play third base? They said he's as good as you were, maybe even better," a reporter called out.

Matt hesitated, and said over his shoulder, "Ask me that when he's thirty-five."

A woman standing behind the rope with three young boys waved a piece of paper and a pen frantically. "Please, Matt. My boys loved you!"

Matt turned to Ginny and shrugged. "I'm sorry about all of this," he muttered before walking over to the woman.

Ginny stood alone, uncertain amid the chaos, when she heard one of the reporters ask another, "So, who's the new broad with Lewellyn? She's certainly a lot older than the Barbies he usually shows up with."

Another male voice answered. "Maybe the Federals' legendary playboy is gettin' long in the tooth and can't keep up with the young babes any more. Who knows?"

"Damn shame, though. I'm gonna miss the spandex and those long legs."

"Excuse me, Miss, who are you?"

Ginny slowly turned and stared at the two middle-aged reporters with disdain until they looked away and cast their attention to a more willing subject. Julius Erving and his wife exited from a dark Mercedes sedan, and the men immediately forgot about her. In those brief moments, they had stripped her of all self confidence. How foolish to believe that a few old songs and some stupid flowers could give her back the innocence she'd lost. She was a middle-aged woman, forced to endure an evening with a man who dated Barbie dolls. What the hell was she doing here, putting herself in the position to

be humiliated again? She should have followed her instincts.

This was all Allie's fault.

He glanced at the woman sitting so stiffly, so properly
next to him. What was wrong with her? What had happened between the car and sitting down at the table? She
made polite small talk with those around them, yet
avoided looking in his direction entirely. He'd thought
they'd made some progress in the car. For the life of him,
he didn't even know why all of this was bothering him so
much. Why did he want to be with this woman? She certainly wasn't his type. But he had to admit that it was refreshing to be with someone his own age and to share
common experiences, rather than listening to a rambling
discourse on Rap and Alternative Rock. He appreciated
the fact that she was dressed very stylishly and, for once,
he didn't have to cringe at the youthful misinterpretation
of class. Why was it that some women felt that push-up
bras, spandex minidresses, two pounds of makeup, and
over-teased hair was the prerequisite for an evening out?

Matt noticed the way Ginny held her wine glass. Her
nails were natural, with only clear polish, and she wore no
jewelry save for a gold watch. He couldn't remember the
last time he'd been out with a woman who didn't have
long, fake, red talons. The realization hit him like a ton of
bricks as he looked around the room. The elegant ballroom was filled with sports and entertainment personalities. Some of the men appeared to be with their wives, but
all too often, an aging, out-of-shape male was accompa-

nied by an overdone armpiece half his age. His stomach muscles clenched with fear. Was that his future?

With renewed determination, he tried to initiate another conversation with Ginny. "I hate these things too. But it is for a good cause. I've been to a few of the children's shelters, and they're pretty dismal. I guess that's why I can put up with this hoopla for a couple of hours, knowing that some kids who are really in need will benefit." He sounded like he was trying to raise money.

Ginny simply nodded. "A couple of hours won't kill anyone, and that's probably why I agreed to come and help out."

"That's the only reason?" he asked hesitantly, hoping that she might have come for more than just the benefit. What the hell was wrong with him? If she didn't want to come, why had he nearly forced her into this evening?

Not looking up at him, she merely shrugged. "As you said, it's for a good cause."

Somewhat deflated, Matt took a sip of his wine and picked at the standard chicken fare on his plate. "I must confess, though, I've had enough broiled chicken at these kinds of events to lay eggs. I wonder why the people who organize these affairs can't be more inventive?" Great dinner conversation! He felt as if he were trying to converse with his high school English teacher . . . and failing miserably.

Her smile was reluctant.

"I know exactly what you mean. I was on the chicken circuit myself some years back."

"You were?"

She hesitated for a few seconds before answering. "My husband was in politics."

"Really? Would I have heard of him?"

She shook her head. "I don't think so. He was just a District Attorney with ambitions."

Matt ran his thumb up the stem of the wine glass as he stared down into his plate. Key pieces just didn't fit. He had thought her initial reluctance toward him was because she was still grieving. What about the flowers in the car? She said she hadn't received flowers since college. Didn't her husband ever give her flowers? Pat had told her his aunt had been a widow for four years. Was she still grieving for the man? And, for a moment, her comment about the chicken circuit made him wonder if going to a charity benefit would bring back painful memories of the loss. Perhaps that's why she had been so quiet after they'd passed the press. But yet, something in the tone of her voice when she spoke of her husband didn't fit the image of a grieving widow. It was only there for an instant, but he had recognized it.

Maybe she wasn't grieving at all?

He watched Ginny Harrison intently. She had the poise of a politician's wife—the mask of someone enjoying herself when she clearly wasn't. This was a woman of many layers, and she had perfected the subtle art of illusion, of giving others exactly what they expected.

He should know. He had been doing it himself for twenty years.

Not yet willing to go down that road, he saw couples abandoning their tables and rising to go to the dance floor. Taking a deep breath he turned to her. "If I get them to play some Earth, Wind, and Fire, will you dance with me?"

The tension left her shoulders as she laughed and

looked at the formal orchestra before them. "If you can get these guys to play Earth, Wind, and Fire, I'll dance with you."

Matt gulped the rest of his white wine and pushed his chair back. "Excuse me," he said in a quiet, confident voice, as he got up from the table and headed across the dance floor.

Ginny's mouth dropped open in astonishment. The man was a lunatic! She watched in horror as Matt talked to the conductor and reached into his pocket for money. He couldn't be doing this. Her brain refused to function as she saw the conductor nod several times and Matt's expression held a satisfied look of triumph as he caught her gaze and held it while walking back to the table.

He stood before her and extended his hand. "May I have this dance?"

With the attention of everyone at the table centered on them, she knew there was no graceful way to decline. She gave him a feeble smile and accepted his hand as he led her to the floor. She had to give him his due. After all, she was the one who had thrown out the joking remark, and he had unfortunately interpreted it as a dare.

The band had transitioned into the melodic Earth, Wind, and Fire ballad "That's the Way of the World," each chord pulling her toward the dance floor along with the pleasant memories that blended in with the music. Grateful to see other couples beginning to fill the empty space around them, Ginny relaxed a bit, and walked into Matt's arms.

"I can't believe you actually got them to play this," she said after a moment, trying to get used to being so close to him.

"Actually, it wasn't that hard at all. The band leader said they love to play this kind of stuff, but didn't think it was appropriate for the crowd. It was almost as if they were waiting for an excuse to play something contemporary. The guy kept thanking me over and over again. It was really pretty funny. I think they might be enjoying this as much as I am."

Ginny didn't respond. She just allowed herself to sway to the easy strands of the music and, for the first time since she had left her house this evening, she admitted that she might even be enjoying Matt Lewellyn's company.

The hand at her back was sure, yet gentle. She could sense that he was giving her room as they moved around the floor in time to the music, and she appreciated the non-threatening way he held her. It amazed her that there wasn't the typical awkwardness of trying to adjust to each other's rhythm. Matt Lewellyn was a good dancer. She hadn't been on the dance floor in many years, and had forgotten how much she enjoyed it. There were so many of life's pleasures that she had buried, even long before Evan died. It seemed to her that everyone took such simple things for granted, like dancing, laughing, and receiving flowers. How had she allowed someone to rob her of all this? And why had she been too frightened to stop him? The memory of her marriage threatened to take away even this small moment, and she stiffened with resentment.

"Are you okay?"

Ginny glanced up and realized that her body must have been echoing her thoughts. She was embarrassed and, looking toward the orchestra, she muttered, "I'm sorry. I guess I was just thinking about how long it's been since I've been out dancing."

"Well, you're doing just fine." His smile was immediate and warm. "How long has it been?"

"Years."

"Then we'll have to make up for that tonight."

She returned his smile and searched for something to say. "You're a pretty good dancer yourself." God, she hated this small talk, always struggling for something witty. Being with politicians was much easier. All she'd ever had to do was ask their opinion on a current issue and they'd talk through the entire dance. This was so different. Matt didn't talk about himself very much. He seemed more interested in her, and it unnerved her. She carried too many secrets, too many lies, for anyone to go poking around in her past.

"I liked your sister," he said, interrupting her thoughts. "She's funny."

Ginny smiled. "Allie is the perennial Earth Mother. She nurtures every living thing in her path, be it people, or plants, or animals." As she spoke about her sister, Ginny found herself relaxing.

"There's just the two of you? Any brothers?"

She shook her head. "I have another sister, Nan. She's the youngest."

Matt smiled and turned her neatly in the dance. "Three girls, huh? It must have been fun growing up."

She stared at him for a few seconds. "Yes . . . yes, it was." Blinking, Ginny felt the muscles at his shoulder move and she concentrated on the texture of his suit jacket. Fun? Was that another lie about her past, to add to the many others? There had been good times when they were little girls, before their father left, but most of her childhood memories had been repressed and replaced by those created in her marriage. Who thought about childhood anymore? Who had time?

Except Nan. Nan liked to blame every bad thing in her life on her lousy childhood. Nan was the youngest, the baby. The one she and Allie had always protected.

"You're tense again."

Looking up at the man holding her in his arms, Ginny forced herself to relax and smile at him. "I'm sorry. I was just thinking about my sisters."

"I'll bet you're all close, aren't you?"

She merely continued to smile. No sense adding any more lies. There were enough already.

"I couldn't have heard correctly. You did *what?*"

Allie wiped the Animal Cracker crumbs from the kitchen table and placed four dinner plates on it. "There's nothing wrong with your hearing, Dave. I got a job." There. She said it again, and it felt good. More real.

"Where? Why?" Dave sat at the head of the table and stared at her as if she'd just said she was taking up Flamenco dancing with Jose Greco. "How could you do this without discussing it with me first?"

She put out the knives and forks and folded the paper napkins. "Let's see . . . I'm starting at the Woman's Center in Philadelphia on Monday morning. As to the why portion of your question . . . because it's time, and I need to get out of this house." She opened a cabinet and pulled out four glasses. "And the reason I didn't discuss it with you is because I knew I would get this reaction. Every time I've tried, you've talked me out of it."

"Because you're needed at home. What about your children? What about Meghan? She's too little not to have her mother here full time."

"Don't try and make me feel guilty, Dave," Allie said, finally sitting opposite him. The casserole was in the oven and wouldn't be ready for ten minutes. Enough time to have this discussion. Already she felt stronger. Being hired by someone who believed that she had worth gave her the courage to continue. "Meghan is in school now, and she'll go into the after-school program. Most of her friends are in it already. She'll be happy."

Her husband shook his head. "After school program, like we're on welfare, or something. Like I couldn't afford to get proper care for my child."

"Stop it," she chided, as if he were her teenaged son and not her husband. "No one's going to think that. And, since you brought up the subject, another income right now would help. Besides—"

"What's that supposed to mean?" he interrupted. "Are you saying I can't support my family."

"No, not at all. It's just that things are a little tight right now and maybe I could help out." She tried smiling. It didn't work. His ego was bruised.

Taking a deep breath, Allie tried again. "Listen, this has more to do with me than anything else. I need to feel useful again, and—"

"You are useful. Right here in this house. Your place is here until the kids are old enough for you to leave them."

"Hey, we both know I'm not the greatest housekeeper

in the world. If we all cooperate, we can clean the house on weekends and—"

"Weekends? I work all week, and you expect me to give up the weekend to clean this house? Tell me again how all this is supposed to make our lives easier."

Dave's look of horror almost made her laugh. But she didn't. She needed to make him understand before they called in the kids for dinner.

"We can work together and have this place clean before noon. Then the rest of the weekend is free. Anyway, it isn't the house that's bothering you. It's the kids. Pat'll be fine. Just don't make it sound as though I'm leaving Meghan all alone. She'll be with her friends for two hours at the most. Really, Dave. This is a dream job for a working mother. The hours are from nine-thirty to four-thirty, so I can pick up Meghan on my way home and then we can all sit down and have dinner together and talk about our day."

"Jesus, Allie, you make it sound like some dumb sitcom on TV. We're all going to discuss our busy and fulfilled lives . . . real life's tougher than that. What happens when one of them is sick and has to stay home from school? Who's going to take care of them?"

It was the one thing Allie hadn't yet worked out. "I suppose their parents," she said in a quiet voice.

"Their parents?" Dave repeated. "You mean me?"

"They do have two parents," she answered defensively. "Your job is sales and you could rearrange your work time better than I could. We'll work something out. I just need some cooperation and—"

"Mom, is dinner ready yet?" Pat demanded as the back door slammed behind him. He reached into the large box that sat by the door and picked up a puppy. Snuggling it close to his chest, he added, "I'm not pushing her on that swing any more. Every time she swings back, she tries to put her feet on me. She's such a pain. I swear I can't stand her anymore."

"She's your sister," Allie answered, pushing back her chair and standing. "Put the puppy down and call in Meghan. And then both of you wash up for dinner." Why was it that every conversation she tried to have in this house was constantly interrupted?

"Meghan! Get in here!"

"I could have done that, Pat. Now go out and get her."

"Cripes, why couldn't I have gotten a brother? At least I could have taught him something, like baseball. She still likes Barney." He turned to his parents before walking out the door. "Do either one of you know how embarrassing that is? She started singing that crap in front of Billy yesterday when he came to see the puppies."

"Go get your sister," Dave ordered, ignoring Pat's outburst.

As soon as Pat left the room, her husband asked, "How much does this job pay?"

"Fifteen dollars an hour." Allie kept her voice steady, even though she wanted to yell that she was entitled to a life, too. That she wanted to feel useful and appreciated. She wanted to dress up and be with grownups. She had spent fifteen years at home. Where was it written that her life was supposed to be all sacrifice and his was to go on undisturbed? When she entered the marriage, she knew Dave wanted her home. She had wanted it, too. But she had never counted on seeing her husband look at a woman outside the home with more interest than he did toward the one within his own. It was a rude awakening.

"Is it full time?"

She could see the mental calculation taking place in his brain. "At least until the summer."

"How did you get a job like that so fast?"

The implication was obvious to her. Why couldn't he just give her credit for the accomplishment, without trying to take away from it? "It was in the paper."

She wouldn't give him the satisfaction of telling him that Marge Harmon had told her at Shop Rite that her agency was looking to hire an intake coordinator. Nor would she admit that the position had been in the paper for two months, and Marge had said that they preferred to hire an employee-recommended candidate. Okay, so she had an inside connection, but she still got the job. Marge may have helped her get in, yet she still had to prove herself. It was no guarantee.

The back door opened and the usual commotion followed as the kids washed up under protest and took their places at the table. Allie didn't even listen to their clatter. She kept wondering why Dave couldn't have put his arms around her and been more supportive.

As her family dug into the casserole, Allie looked at the man across from her and remembered a time when they were so in love. It seemed so long ago. She never expected the euphoria to last, and was prepared for the hills and valleys that was an inevitable part of spending your life with another. Just like everything, there were seasons in a relationship. Yet why was it that this long winter of her marriage seemed so lonely?

* * *

The car came to a stop at her driveway, and Ginny watched as Matt opened his door and came around to her side. She was still smiling from their conversation on the way home about how once the band had played Earth, Wind, and Fire, they couldn't seem to get back to the ballroom mentality. It was as if they had transformed into a group of funky middle-aged men having a good time. They had played everything from Motown to the Rolling Stones and the guests had loved it. She had to admit that her feet hurt from dancing, and that it had been years since she'd enjoyed herself this much. And she even liked the company. Matt had taken her around from one interesting cluster of people to another, and introduced her to the most fascinating individuals from the worlds of art, sports, music and the media. It had, all in all, been quite an evening.

"And did you see Jim Garwood from KYW doing the bump?" Matt asked with a laugh. "I swear I thought he was going to throw his back out."

Ginny giggled as she got out of the car. "I don't think I'll ever be able to watch him anchor the six o'clock news again without laughing. Everybody seemed to have a good time."

"Well, you started it," he answered, touching her elbow as he led her up to the front door.

"What do you mean? I didn't start anything . . . "

"If memory serves me correctly, a certain somebody dared me to get the orchestra to play Earth, Wind, and Fire. They were never the same afterward."

She chuckled and conceded with a nod. "Okay, but I wasn't the one that kept going back with requests."

"I had to do something to keep you dancing with me."

She didn't know how to answer.

"You did have a good time, didn't you?"

She could hear the eagerness in his voice. "Yes, Matt. I had a great time. Thanks for coaxing me out."

"Then I hope you'll let me coax you out again some-time soon."

Before she could say anything, he cut in, "And I promise that I'll ask with plenty of lead time, wait for and listen to your reply, and I'll also be sure to confirm in advance. Deal?"

Ginny had to smile. He had heard her.

"Thanks," she murmured as they approached her door. She took her key out of her purse and inserted it in the lock. She didn't want to look up. She didn't want to see his face. She wasn't ready to deal with this awkward end-of-evening ritual. Why couldn't it end right now while they were still laughing? She couldn't invite him in and she wasn't ready to kiss him. What was she supposed to do?

Forcing her gaze to meet his, she tried to take the tension out of her smile as she said, "Again, thank you for a great evening, Matt."

Searching for something to gently let him know that the evening was over, Ginny was surprised to see him bend down to place a kiss on her forehead. "I had a great time. I'll call you soon."

Not knowing how to respond, she merely nodded before entering the house. Once on the other side of the door, she locked it and found herself leaning up against the heavy wood, unable to control her smile.

It had been the most surprising evening. What she had started out dreading had turned into real enjoyment, and she couldn't remember the last time she had felt like this. Matt was funny and kind and gentle and understanding. Not at all the playboy jock she had imagined. He had understood her unspoken wishes when they'd said goodnight, and he hadn't pressed the issue.

The knock on the other side of the panel startled her, and she jumped away from the door. Ginny could feel herself tensing with apprehension as her fingers slid to the lock. How could she have forgotten that she was a lousy judge of character?

She opened the door ready to defend her point, when she was stopped by the sight of Matt holding a huge bouquet of wilting lilacs.

"I'm sorry to be back at your door so soon, but we forgot these in the car." He stretched out his hands and offered her the flowers with a nervous smile. "You'd better get these in water or they'll be gone by morning."

Matt didn't wait for her to answer as she accepted the lilacs, but turned and walked down the steps, looking back once to wave goodbye again. She returned his wave shyly and slipped back into the house. Maybe she wasn't such a bad judge of character after all. Maybe she just had to start looking at things differently.

Chapter 8

Damn it, nothing was coming.

Nan leaned her elbows on the desk and rubbed her eyes, then cursed as the combination of mascara and lack of sleep made them burn and itch. It was past one a.m., and still she hadn't come up with a new campaign for Markey Foods. What was she going to tell those old farts in the morning?

She took another sip of Diet Pepsi, and stared down at the array of papers strewn before her. Where the hell was Quincy? She had beeped him two hours ago, and he was late as usual with her delivery. God, all she wanted was a lousy quarter key of coke. That much would last her for more than a month, so she wouldn't have to go through this again. Damn him. He promised she'd be one of his first stops. But then again, that wasn't the weight that he was used to dealing. Normally, he only carried the small stuff, a couple of eighths, even as small as a twenty dollar bag. Still, if she treated her steady accounts the way Quincy treated her, she would've been out of advertising a long time ago.

Tired of looking at the papers that held no answer, she

got up and started pacing in front of the window. She pulled the sheer curtain back and stared down at the nearly empty street. Running her fingers through her hair, she knew that she had to come up with a new story board before morning. Tap dancing for time, she'd told Joe Carter she had something dynamite up her sleeve, and he'd made it clear that her ass was on the line—after all she'd done for them. She had brought Markey Foods into the firm, along with countless other blue chip clients. Hadn't Joe called her the girl with the Midas Touch? And now, just because she was going through a little slump, there wasn't an ounce of sympathy to be had.

One-thirty.

Her head started pounding, and she walked into the kitchen to find the Tylenol. Bringing the glass of water to her mouth, she saw that her hand trembled as she took a sip and swallowed the pills. She set the glass down on the counter quickly, in an attempt to deny what she'd seen. All she needed was an idea and sleep, and for Quincy to get his butt up here. As though her thoughts had summoned him, the phone rang. Startled, she jumped at the sound, and then ran to buzz open the lobby door without even checking the intercom to see who it was.

She stood at her open door, staring down the hall at the elevator. Her fists were jammed in her pockets as she impatiently watched the digital display slowly move through the floor numbers. When the doors opened, Quincy strolled out, as if he were taking a lazy walk through the park.

"Hey, Babe," he called out before he reached her door.

"Where have you been?" she whispered back, aware

that it was late for company. "You said before one. It's going on two."

"Yo, I had business to transact. I got what you need, so why're you hasslin' me?"

"C'mon. Get in here," she urged, looking at her neighbors' doors. All they needed to see was this tall skinny man decked out in flamboyant leather and wearing more jewelry than Paloma Picasso.

He flipped a stray dirty blonde lock of hair behind his ear and smiled. "You're okay, baby. I'm here and my product's always on time."

Nan didn't respond, just locked the door quickly behind him. She couldn't afford to piss him off, especially since Quincy was known for skimping on weight if you hassled him. She just wanted to get what she needed, then to get him out of there. Having him around, even if it was only for a few moments, made her skin crawl. His very presence felt like it turned her luxury condo into a seamy backstreet, and he always wanted a drink for the special deliveries.

"Wanna taste test this first?" he asked, sitting down on her white damask sofa and pulling out a large plastic bag filled with white powder.

"Sure," she said, fighting to keep her voice under control. As much as she wanted the stuff, she hated the sight of him even sitting on her couch.

Pulling out another plastic bag, Quincy grinned. "This hit is on the house. Private label. Practically uncut. It came from the top of the key."

Nan took a fresh twenty from the wad of bills in her pocket and rolled it up into a straw. She eagerly dipped it into the bag and quickly inhaled. Immediately she felt a rush of energy as her eyes watered and the back of her throat began to numb. He was right. It was good. Wiping her nose on her sleeve, she returned the bag to Quincy and said, "This is really good stuff. I hope what you're selling me is as good."

"I told ya a long time ago, babe, if you'd just be nicer to me, you wouldn't have to pay retail. You're too fine to have to pay for this shit. Why don't ya let ol' Quincy set you up right?" he said leaning closer. "What's this joint run you a month anyway?"

Her brain recoiled from the idea of being one of Quincy's strung-out girls who eventually *catered* to his high-roller customers.

"I can still afford to pay retail, thanks. I just want to be sure that I'm getting what I paid for."

Quincy took a hit and then shoved the bag into his jacket. "You're always so suspicious," he said leaning back. "I wouldn't pull a bait and switch on one of my best customers. Relax. Go get me a drink, baby. Got any tequila?"

Nan dropped the wad of money on the coffee table and walked into the kitchen. She felt as if her world was being invaded, yet she knew she couldn't tell him to get the hell out. The time would always come when the coke was gone. She poured the Cuervo into a short glass and walked it back to him. Knowing how he loved to socialize after completing a deal, she handed him the drink and said, "I guess you've got a lot of other stops to make, and I've got this project—"

"You ain't trying to give me the bum's rush now are

you, sweet thing?" he asked before taking the shot. "Why don't you join me?"

"I told you, I have work to do." She jammed her hands back into her pants pockets and walked over to the window. How the hell had she ever let this happen, or let this sleaze into her life? But then again, the mother sleaze of them all had introduced her to it five years ago. At that time, she had been so afraid of life. Her marriage had been in trouble. She had been moving up in the ranks professionally and scared to death of the challenges. Someone she trusted, someone who was successful, dynamic, and beyond reproach, had made the whole thing feel safe. He'd told her that after one hit, she'd feel like she could conquer the world. He had been right about that part, but had never told her that the time would come when she'd need it just to make it through the day, or that someone like Quincy would be sitting in her living room.

"If you're gonna work, and do all this tonight, how 'bout some V's? Or maybe I can do something else to help you relax?"

His breath came over her shoulder smelling of tequila, while his hand suggestively moved across her back. Jumping away from his touch, she answered, "I don't want valium. I told you I have work to do, and I've got a meeting in the morning."

"What'ya pullin' away for? Can't be your old man. He moved out, right?"

"That's none of your business. Look, Quincy, I told you, I have work to do. Thanks for bringing my package. That's all I need tonight."

He slowly closed the space between them, and she

fought the urge to back away. "Well, now, maybe all your needs haven't been met." Quincy reached out and ran his hands through her hair. "Usually I like broads with long hair, but this suits you."

Nan pulled her head back and smoothed her hair into place. "I told you I have to work. Please leave." A sudden fear ran through her. From the beginning, Quincy had made it clear that he found her attractive, but he had never been this aggressive. What if he pressed the issue? What was she going to do? The police were not an option. Not with a quarter kilo and a couple thousand dollars lying on her coffee table. She'd have to handle this herself.

Feeling like a cornered animal, she stared into his eyes and mentally pleaded with him to leave her alone. The feeling of being stalked was too frightening, too familiar. Suddenly Quincy smiled and, in that moment, she knew he understood exactly how she felt. It was all a question of power.

"Well, I got people waitin' on me. Next time. I gotta go make some money. The night's young yet," he said as he turned and walked toward the coffee table. Picking up the bills, he counted them and stuffed them into his pocket while heading for the door. When he opened it, he turned back to her and said, "Don't work too hard now," then brought two fingers up to his lips and blew her a kiss before leaving.

She rushed over to it and slipped the chain lock into place. Shaken, she headed toward the bag on the coffee table and took another hit, vowing to never put herself through this nightmare again. She would have to find another connection.

As the drug took effect, she felt her fists clench with anger. She hated that feeling of powerlessness. Why didn't she just tell that creep to get the hell out of her house? She was going to have to find a way to protect herself, she thought, jumping up and walking over to her desk. But she wouldn't think about that right now. She had to find a solution to the problem with the Markey account.

Once seated in her chair, she organized the papers in front of her and said aloud, "I'm back." Confidence surged through her veins. This was her account, and she had every intention of giving them a show for their money tomorrow.

Her gaze fell upon Tony's portfolio, and she threw her head back and laughed.

There was always a way out.

"You say this property is on the same street as Randall Cunningham's house?"

Ginny instinctively disliked the man. People like Richard Caldwell, who always flaunted their power, made her skin crawl. "Yes, it is," she said evenly, pasting on a businesslike smile. "The homes were all built by Gary Gartner. They're all exquisite, as you can see from the photos."

She looked to the man's wife, and again smiled, but more genuinely. "What do you think, Joan? Is this the style you had in mind?"

The woman appeared startled, and quickly looked to her husband then down at the pictures of the home. "It seems lovely, but then, Richard knows more about this," she said in a hesitant voice.

Ginny couldn't figure it out. In the last four years she'd matched hundreds of people with homes, and the women were always more enthusiastic. She knew from experience that once the wife was excited about the property, the deal was more than half done, especially if you were talking about spending a million and a half to acquire a dream home. But something was amiss here. It was almost as if Joan Caldwell was afraid to voice her opinion. And something was a little off about their body language. Maybe they had a fight on the way down. This was not her business. Her business was to get them interested in this property and sell the house.

"As you can see, there's a twenty square foot foyer, with a magnificent central staircase that branches off to the right and to the left. I believe to the right, it would take you to the master suite. If I remember correctly, to the left are four bedrooms, all with bathrooms en suite." Getting no response, Ginny searched for something spectacular to spark more interest. "At the top of the stairs, there's a railing, and you can look down on the family room from the second level." Still no reaction. "Didn't you say you had a daughter?"

Joan Caldwell brightened and lifted her head. "Yes, Sarah."

Immediately Richard Caldwell stiffened, and said "What difference does that make? She's not buying the house."

Although taken back by the man's bluntness, she also noticed his wife once again retreating into her shell.

"I was about to point out that there's a lovely playroom right off the kitchen and, for you, Mr. Caldwell, you mentioned that it was important to have space for your office. There's an exquisite rosewood paneled study with a fireplace right off the family room. I've already called this morning and made a tentative appointment. If you like what you see in the pictures, we can drive over and look at the house."

Ginny watched as Joan Caldwell glanced at her husband from the corner of her eye.

"Well, we've driven ninety miles to get down here. We might as well see something," he said standing up and grabbing his cashmere overcoat. His wife quickly followed suit, never uttering a word.

"Great." Ginny gathered up the portfolio on the house and slipped it into her briefcase. If there was one thing she'd learned in this business it was that you can never tell a book from its cover. The Caldwells were wealthy, young, and blue blooded. They appeared to have every advantage. Yet they definitely weren't happy. The icy distance that prevailed between them was too painfully familiar, and only confirmed her belief that the state of matrimony just didn't work.

Shrugging off the unpleasant thought, Ginny picked up the telephone and buzzed her assistant. "Carol, would you please call the Brandywine Glen property and let them know that I'll be over with the Caldwells? We should get there in about fifteen minutes."

Richard Caldwell helped his wife into her designer coat. "By the way, I saw your picture in the newspaper with Matt Lewellyn. Since I'm a sports agent, and if I should decide to relocate here, I'd need to begin to network with local sports figures. Would you arrange an introduction?"

Startled, Ginny merely stared at the man. It was her supreme embarrassment that a photo of she and Matt entering the benefit had appeared in the local Philadelphia papers. The only way Caldwell could have seen it was if he was getting Philadelphia papers sent to him in New York. She supposed that made sense if he was moving. Richard Caldwell had contacted her about his plans to relocate long before she even met Matt Lewellyn. But now it became clear that he'd use the leverage of the possible $1.6 million dollar house sale to force a meeting with Matt. His request was clearly an ultimatum. It was in the way he stared back at her with the slightest trace of a smile. Instinct told her to run from the deal, to run from this man, but in this economy no realtor could afford to back off something this big. With nearly twenty employees, she had to think of more than herself.

Taking a deep breath, she forced a smile as she picked up her briefcase and purse. "I'll see what I can do. My car is the green Oldsmobile." How in the hell could she call Matt and ask for this favor? Why did people prey on each other like this? It went against everything she believed in, and left a bitter taste in her mouth to know that she was now a part of the cycle. This wasn't the way she normally did business, and she most definitely didn't use her friends.

She could tell by the way he was studying her that it had now become a test of wills.

"That's all right. We'll follow you."

She had called it right. If this was a game, Caldwell

knew he had the advantage. Ginny had to admit that she was relieved that they'd be taking separate cars. Richard Caldwell was not an easy man to like.

Allie could barely contain herself as she waited for Ginny to arrive at the restaurant. For once in her life she was early, and she anxiously watched the door for a sign of her sister. She couldn't wait to get Ginny's reaction, for she had spent the morning transforming herself from a housewife to a professional career woman. She'd had her hair dyed and cut to a manageable shoulder length. Her eyebrows had been waxed, and she even allowed Cindy to show her how to apply make up that would camouflage any imperfections. She looked down to her hands and admired the French manicure. She couldn't wait to start work on Monday.

All of a sudden, she noticed two men at a far table staring at her. To her surprise one smiled, and she quickly picked up her glass of Chardonnay. It was the most amazing thing. It was as if she had spent the last fifteen years in a cocoon and only now had emerged as a butterfly. She couldn't wait to see Dave's reaction.

Ginny entered the restaurant and hesitated a moment, as recognition turned into surprise. Her sister's expression was once more transformed into a wide smile as she made her way to the table.

"Look at you!" Ginny exclaimed as she sat down.

"You like it?" Allie asked shyly, truly appreciative of her sister's reaction.

"Like it? I absolutely love it. What made you do this?"

"I'm starting a new job, and so I needed a change. You really like it? It's not too much?"

Ginny laughed. "Oh stop being so insecure. You look ten years younger. Has Dave seen it? What did he say?"

"No. He hasn't seen it yet. But it doesn't matter anyway. *I* like it."

"Are you and Dave okay? Is something wrong?"

"Oh, he's fine. He's just a little upset that he'll have to pitch in around the house, and I won't be there to wait on everybody hand and foot like I used to. We're okay."

Afraid her sister would sense the real trouble in her marriage, Allie quickly changed the subject. "Listen, Gin, before we talk about anything else, I want to apologize to you for flipping out when I came home from Washington. It wasn't you, or the kids. It was me. I'm sorry."

"You're okay?"

"Do I look okay?" So it was an evasive question. She wasn't about to bring up her insecurities again. "Hey, I couldn't believe it this morning when Dave showed me the picture of you and Matt Lewellyn in the paper. God, that must be so exciting."

Ginny deeply exhaled as the waiter filled their water glasses. "You couldn't believe it? I didn't even know it until I walked into work and three of the agents had copies of it."

Allie leaned forward excitedly. "But you looked great. You were right in choosing that black suit. It made you seem like a celebrity—so sophisticated."

Ginny covered her eyes with her hand and shook her head. "I was mortified. You know what a private person I am. No one asked for my permission to splash my face all over the newspapers. I even have a client who is politely blackmailing me because of it."

"What? Blackmailing? You're so paranoid."

"Forget it. Enough about me. So tell me about this job. A women's center? Where? How did you hear about it? How did you get it?"

Allie moved in closer and leaned her elbows on the table. "It was the strangest thing, Gin. I was over at ShopRite talking to Marge Harmon—you know, she's committee chairman of this year's Athletic Association dinner . . . Anyway, she's a social worker, and I was talking about how to re-enter the job market after all these years. She asked me about my background, you know, college, any jobs I might have had before the kids came. And she told me that her agency was looking for somebody to do client intakes, and maybe even teach a life skills class. At first, I tried to tell her that I didn't have any life skills, and Marge almost went ballistic right there in front of the frozen foods. She said that her agency dealt with abused women, people who were getting back on track after substance abuse, and teen mothers. She told me that they had just received a grant to try to teach them how to budget, do healthy meal planning, parenting skills, household organization, and how to network with other mothers for support. Gin, I'll tell you, when she really started describing this, I knew I could do it. After fifteen years of managing our home on a tight budget, clipping coupons, being chief cook and bottle washer, not to mention social activities coordinator, this was something I didn't have to go back to school for. Hell, I have my doctorate in this."

Ginny laughed and leaned forward to squeeze her hands. "I am so happy for you. Oh, Allie, this is perfect and you'd be fantastic at it."

Hearing her sister's words, Allie began to fill up. "Ginny, it's been so long since anybody appreciated what I do. You know? When I stood in that market and had someone like Marge Harmon, a person I've always admired, say that I had something of value to offer—that I wasn't just some housewife who couldn't cut it in the *real* world—I almost cried. She let me know that what I was doing was indeed the invisible and, unfortunately, unappreciated fabric of this society. Here was somebody who was out in the workforce, who saw all of the problems that we hear about on the news daily, and she was telling me that I had made a major contribution. She made me feel good about the years I had put in, trying to raise healthy, decent human beings, and for the twenty-four-hour, seven-day-a-week job that I did have—without vacations or pay. Ginny, when that woman started telling me some of the horror stories about how children are being abandoned and abused, I knew I had something of worth to teach and share with these women."

"So where is it? In Philly?"

"Yeah, right in center city, not far from City Hall."

"I'm so proud of you, Allie. When do you start?"

"Monday. Can you believe it? Me, with a job."

"Did they give you an idea of what you'll be doing?"

"The Center Director said that the first day will be orientation to the program, then I'll start off with doing client intake before the social workers are paired with the mothers. After that, as soon as another seminar series is run in the area, I'll be scheduled for a one- or two-day class on controlled substances and how to look for signs of child abuse. From what I understand, then I'll follow another teacher and be her shadow for about a week. After that, I'll get my own group to lead for a six-week class. I still can't believe it. It just feels so good to be given the chance again."

"This is great, Allie. Maybe I can come into the city sometime and we can meet for lunch. I'm so excited for you. I feel as if I'm starting with you on Monday. What did Nan say?"

"I left a message on her machine, but I haven't been able to catch up to her. Frankly, I'm still worried about Nan."

"Now why are you worried about her? Did she say something?" Ginny asked with a sigh of exasperation.

"No, not exactly. She's just been so distant. It's as if she doesn't even want to get in touch with me. Even when she came over that Saturday, every time I asked her about what happened with Robert, she evaded the question. He absolutely adored her. Why do you think he left?"

Ginny shrugged her shoulders. "I don't know. You know how she is. Living with Nan would seem difficult to me, and Robert is so easygoing. Maybe he just got tired of trying to please someone who constantly demands attention."

Not wanting to get in between her two sisters again, Allie decided to drop the subject. She was tired of playing peacemaker, she thought, as the waiter came for their order.

"All right, forget Nan. I'll catch up with her this weekend. So tell me all about this date."

"It wasn't a date."

"Oh, please. Will you stop. I was there, remember? I witnessed it. We even have a picture in the damned paper. It was a date. So what happened?"

Ginny laughed. "Okay, all right. It was sort of a date."

"And . . . ?"

"And, we went to the benefit, he drove me home, we said good night, and he drove himself home."

Allie stared at her sister, issuing a silent warning to not skip over the good parts.

After taking a sip of iced tea and setting the glass down hard, Ginny finally acknowledged the stare. "What?"

"Don't give me that. What happened? What's he like?"

"Nothing happened, but he turned out to be nice."

"Are you going to see him again?"

"I don't know, but I'll probably have to talk to him again. Remember I told you someone was blackmailing me? Well, this client saw the picture and wants to meet him."

"I don't care about a business meeting, I want to know about you and Matt Lewellyn. What is he like?"

"Just nice. You know. Nice."

Realizing that she was going to have to perform root canal to get to the juicy part of the story, Allie began a series of questions designed to make Ginny talk.

"Is he funny? Is he charming? Was he easy to talk to? What did you guys talk about on the way to the benefit?"

She heard her sister sigh with exasperation, or possibly defeat.

"Oh, I don't know. We talked about things we had in common."

"Like?"

"Like, the seventies, and music. He is pretty funny," Ginny admitted. "He wasn't anything like I had imagined."

Allie could feel her smile widen. "So you do like him?"

"He's okay. He's a very nice man, but don't go reading anything into this. I know how you are."

"I'm just optimistic. So what else? How was the benefit? Did you guys dance?"

"The benefit was a typical fundraiser. What can I say? It was all right."

"But did you two dance?"

"Yes we danced."

"You danced. Actually danced with him!" Allie exclaimed, feeling more positive about her initial hunch.

"Keep your voice down," Ginny ordered, looking down to her plate.

"Was it a slow song?"

"One slow dance, that's it."

"Oh, my God!"

"Allie!"

"Well, I was right, wasn't I?"

"Right about what? That I could dance? That he could dance? Let's just change the subject."

Feeling triumphant, Allie speared some of her salad with her fork. "Isn't this great? Things are finally turning around for you."

Allie immediately noticed her sister's posture stiffen.

"Things have turned around for me, Allie. I have my

own company, my own home, my own life. I don't need any confusion. Matt Lewellyn and I had a decent time together, but I don't expect it to go any further. And you shouldn't either. So drop the plans for a lawn wedding, okay?"

Still smiling, Allie raised her glass. "All right. Let's just toast to my new job and to your possibilities."

Allie was a firm believer in fate, and something instinctively told her that big changes were in store for all the Sullivan girls.

It was time.

Chapter 9

The telephone sat before her as a menacing instrument, threatening her privacy as she attempted to make the call to Matt. God, she hated this. Usually, the phone was a comforting barrier between herself and people that she didn't want to interact with face to face. Now, it was a bridge or a connection to a person that she had decided not to deal with. Ginny knew if she called, it would send the wrong message, almost an open invitation into her life. She picked up the receiver, then quickly replaced it. She would not do this. It was nothing more than blackmail, and everything inside of her rebelled against it.

Standing, she stretched out the tight cords in her back and walked over to her file cabinet. Who in the hell did Richard Caldwell think he was, insisting on an introduction so he could do business? She would have never been so presumptuous—even in a situation where she had the advantage. It was just plain tacky, and she would not create havoc in her life to accommodate him. He was typical of the old cliche: money—no class.

The knock on the door startled her, yet she was grateful

for the interruption. Jim Hudson stood in her doorway hesitantly, and she could tell by the way he held the papers in his hand that he was not bearing good news.

"I've pulled this month's sales report for you," he said quietly, "and it's about the same as last month's. Nothing's moving out there."

Ginny crossed the room and took the report, looking over the numbers as she went back to her desk. "I know, Jim. We haven't closed on a property in the last two months."

"There's a lot of people still looking, but nobody's committing. Everything's dragging. Even the Monsarati deal is still pending," he said nervously, moving into her office and standing expectantly by her desk.

Ginny blew out a deep breath of frustration and ran her fingers through her hair. "We're supposed to be in a recovery, but it looks like people are still afraid to do anything yet. What about the Whittaker property? Isn't that near closing?"

Jim looked down and fiddled with the pen in his shirt pocket. "I don't think it's going to close. Not anytime soon, anyway. The buyers are shaky with the financing, and the owner can't drop the price because of the remaining mortgage balance on the house. At least that's what Sam said last night."

Ginny tried to force her voice to remain calm. "Well, isn't anything going to turn over this month?" It wasn't Jim's fault, or any of her agents' fault that the properties weren't selling. It was no secret that all the real estate firms were having trouble, and even though she was the second largest firm in the county, it still didn't exempt her from the sluggish economy.

"I can ask them again," he said quietly, "but they all seemed pretty sure about their forecast."

Slipping the report into her top drawer, she shook her head and looked at Jim. "No, that's okay. I know it must be tough asking for numbers from a bunch of frustrated agents and then having to be the bearer of bad news. Thanks a lot for the report. I'll talk to everybody as the month progresses."

Jim seemed relieved as he left her office and closed the door behind him. He was a devoted employee, and she knew this had been a difficult task. In fact, all of her staff people were excellent, and over the years they had become more like a close knit little family than a group of co-workers. But the sad reality was, if revenue didn't start pouring in soon she would have to consider staff cuts. She couldn't bear to think what it would do to these people's lives and their families.

Ginny shook off the unpleasant thought with a shiver. She panicked whenever she was reminded of poverty. The dread and anxiety sprang from her childhood experiences, but that was a long time ago. She was safe now. Secure. In control. It would never be like it was before. Never.

She looked at the telephone again and flipped her rolodex over to the L's. She could do it. This was not just about her. This was about ensuring that every member on her staff could keep his or her job if the deals dragged on until early summer. She knew the Caldwells loved the house. She could see it in Joan Caldwell's barely contained excitement as she went from room to room. Even Richard Caldwell was impressed by the study. Instinct told her that this deal could close within the week. Granted, the Caldwells would be spending a great deal of money. And if they bought the house, she was prepared to show her appreciation by giving them special attention. Richard Caldwell's request went well beyond the bounds of normal professional courtesy, and although it wouldn't bother some, it did her.

Again she thought of the dismal sales report and eyed the telephone with a sense of foreboding. As she punched in the number, she closed her eyes and took a deep breath, counting the rings in her mind.

"Hello, Lewellyn."

Ginny hesitated a moment before speaking. It was foolish, but she liked the upbeat confidence that came through in his voice. He seemed to be in a decent mood.

"Hello?"

"Oh, ahh, hi," she stammered, trying to grapple with an appropriate way to begin the conversation. She almost cursed at herself for how stupid she must have sounded.

"Ginny?"

Dear God, he recognized her voice.

"Yes. Hello, Matt. Am I catching you at a bad time?" There. That sounded normal.

"No. Not at all. Don't be silly. It's a pleasure to hear from you. How've you been?"

"Oh, okay, I guess. I really feel awkward about calling you like this, but something has come up, and . . ."

"Is everything all right? You sound like something's wrong."

Ginny could feel her stomach lurch with anxiety. It was pure torture. Forcing her voice to sound more cheerful, she took a quick breath before she spoke. "Everything is fine. It's just that I have this real pompous, arrogant client who saw our picture in the newspaper."

"Really? You looked wonderful."

Despite her feelings about having her privacy invaded, Matt's compliment pulled at her. "Thank you, Matt, and thank you for the evening," she said quietly. "But I do dislike everything being so public. That's how this client found out that I knew you, and he's angling for an introduction. I'm sorry. This is so embarrassing, because now I'm invading your privacy."

To her surprise, Matt laughed. "Is that what all of this hedging is about? Because you didn't want to ask me to meet one of your clients? Ginny, it's okay. No big deal."

She let out an audible sigh. "Matt, I wouldn't have imposed on you like this. You've got to believe me when I tell you that I just don't go around doing things like this. But this guy is virtually blackmailing me."

"Blackmailing you? I see," he chuckled. "Well, I'm not proud. If I had to wait for an extortionist to make you call, I'm still glad you did. I was beginning to get nervous, and wondered if I might ever hear from you."

She tried not to let him hear her swallow. Her mouth was dry and a cord of tension was running laterally across her shoulders. "I really appreciate this. Richard Caldwell is a pretty substantial client, and it would mean a lot to the firm. I'm so sorry to drag you into this mess."

There, she had said it—without addressing Matt's reference to seeing each other again.

"Well, it couldn't be any messier than delivering puppies," he said warmly. "I'd be glad to do it, Ginny. So tell me about this Caldwell guy. What's he like? What's he do? I guess, most importantly, what does he want?"

Ginny quickly arranged the barrage of questions in her mind. "Matt, I'm not exactly sure of what he wants. And you are not under any obligation here. He's definitely the very pushy type. I don't even want to consider that he might try to take advantage of your time, but he probably would. In fact, the more I think about this, the more I'm sure that it's a bad idea, and you shouldn't do it. Forget it. It's not worth it."

"C'mon, Gin. I'm a big boy and can handle myself. So what's this character do?"

He called her Gin, just like Allie, just like anyone who had known her for a long time. "He's a sports agent who's relocating from New York City down to the area, and he wants to meet you. He'll probably hit you up for some contacts or something. Oh God, I can't stand people like this."

Matt was laughing. "I get it now. This jerk is buying a house, so he sees us in the paper, then lords the sale over your head until you agree to an introduction. Then he thinks that because the two of us are dating, or something, he thinks I'll help him out to help you out. Right?"

Matt's accurate assessment of the situation nauseated her. Hearing the words said out loud made the whole thing sound even more seamy. Dragging Matt Lewellyn into this was like living out a nightmare, and the fact that he was being such a good sport about it was even worse.

"Well, am I right?" Matt asked again.

"Unfortunately, yes," Ginny said quietly, feeling near tears for some strange reason.

"Ginny," Matt said in a gentle voice. "It's really okay. I'll take care of this character. We'll have a few beers, talk some sports stuff. I'll tell him I'll see what I can do, then send him on his way. An hour or two won't kill me. I'm used to dealing with his type, and trust me, Gin, after a stint in pro sports, I've seen his kind before. It'll be like water off a duck's back for me. No problem."

This time when Ginny sighed, it was one of relief. "Thanks, Matt. I really appreciate this."

"Consider it done. Just give him my number, and I'll get together with him soon. I'll let you know how I made out, if it will make you feel any better. Okay?"

"Okay," she said, truly grateful.

"I'll call you in a couple of days . . . if that's all right?"

"That's fine, Matt, and thanks. I'll talk to you soon. Bye."

When Ginny hung up the telephone, she let her body slump in the chair for a few moments, savoring the quiet. What had she just done? It seemed like a week ago her life was planned, orderly, and in control. No thrills, but no big surprises either. Just a calmness that she could depend on. Now it seemed as though everything around her was changing. Perhaps it was just spring, or a full moon. Whatever it was, she'd have to pull it together and get off this roller coaster.

Taking a deep breath, she steadied herself and flipped her rolodex over to the C's.

Allie was so nervous that it was all she could do to keep breathing as the elevator of the tall Center City high rise slowly ascended to the sixteenth floor. Day one. Now she knew what Pat and Meghan must have felt like on their first day of school. She wanted to laugh and cry at the same time, and she kept smoothing her new hair style in the mirrored doors while she waited for the car to come to her floor.

Everyone else in the tightly packed space around her seemed so normal, so blasé about going to work. They all had briefcases and cups of coffee in their hands, or newspapers under their arms. She wanted to know what each and every one of them did, how long they had been doing it, did they like it, were they good at it . . .

When the elevator finally came to her stop, she politely edged her way out and stood in front of the door to the office suites of her new job. *Her* job. Allie almost giggled. It was insane, but in the next instant, she seriously considered pushing the down button and going home. Pulling herself together, she took a deep breath and went in. The secretary was already there, even though Allie was early, and the place had a mild hum of pleasant activity that she hadn't expected.

"Uh, hello. My name is Allyson Barbera, and this is my first day. I'm the new coordinator."

The woman seated behind the little window stood and, to Allie's relief, smiled broadly. "Oh, hi," she exclaimed. "I'm Betty. Welcome to The Women's Center. Boy, do we need you!"

Allie wanted to throw herself at the older woman's feet. They cared, and wanted her, actually needed her. Returning the smile, Allie extended her hand through the window. "Thank you for the warm welcome. I'm so excited and can't wait to get started."

The short brown woman gave her hand a hearty shake and left her desk to walk to the small lobby area where Allie stood. "Let me show you around before it gets too busy in here, darlin'. They'll be driving me crazy soon, 'specially these phones, in about a half an hour. Now, see that cabinet over there?" she said motioning to a large gray metal file. "That's where all the office supplies and forms are kept. I distribute them for everybody, 'cause I don't like folks messin' up my system. If you need anything, just ask. It works better that way."

Allie nodded and followed behind the kindly drill sergeant, attempting to match her pace. She couldn't wipe the smile off of her face as Betty, correction, *Miss* Betty, escorted her through the corridors, pointing out with authority each office and classroom.

"Now, over here, this is the Executive Director's office, and that one next to it is the Director's, your boss. Don't pay the Executive Director no mind, though. She gets her panties in a bunch all the time over the grants. The Director is the one who can get things done—you know what I mean?"

The two exchanged a silent understanding along with their smiles. Allie knew instinctively that she was getting an insider's tour, not just a perfunctory one. It was nice. Really nice. In just five minutes, she had made a friend.

"Miss Betty," she asked timidly. "Is there a rule book or a job description for each position? I really want to do well. I mean, I don't want to do anything that will cause a problem."

The older lady patted her arm as they turned the corner to Allie's new office and chuckled. It was obvious from her patient smile that she liked the special designation of "Miss" in front of her name that Allie had accidentally let slip out. Pulling herself up a bit taller, the authority in her tone softened. "Oh, darlin', I'm gonna like you. Chile, there's job descriptions all right, but nobody follows them. There's more work to do in here than bodies to do it. So we kinda all pitch in where necessary. Now, when the state auditors come, we all get real proper-like, and follow the book for a day or so. But after they leave," she said with a whoop, "pull*eeze*. All hell breaks loose, and we start scurrying around here tryin' to help all these folks that come through our doors needin' it. Hope you're used to chaos."

This time Allie let out a belly laugh. "Are you kidding? This will be just like home."

"Know whatcha mean!" Betty grinned. "You got kids?"

"A little girl and a boy—five and thirteen," Allie said with emphasis.

"Then you'll be right at home," Betty said warmly, pointing her toward a tiny cubicle. "Well, this is it," she said sucking her teeth with a click. "It ain't much, but we're a non-profit, and ain't got much space. Don't have no IBM budget, but we get the job done."

Allie looked around the small cubicle and beamed. "It's perfect! Thank you so much."

"I filled up your desk with pads and pencils—don't tell nobody I gave you some extras, okay? Gotta hoard stuff around here. Your phone extension is 5670, and there's some brand new pendaflexes and manila folders in there for you, too."

Blinking away sudden tears of gratitude, Allie just nodded and murmured another, "Thank you."

"Wished everybody'd come in here so grateful to be working," the older woman said. "Listen, you get settled down and put your things around. Bring in some pictures and plants from home to cozy it up for yourself, then it won't feel so strange. In about an hour the Human Resources Director, Mrs. Jones, will be in. She'll take you through the forms, give you a little orientation, and then you'll meet the Center Director who'll give you your marchin' orders."

Allie was speechless. The whole process was so overwhelming, and she felt so brand spanking new. As she sat her purse down on the desk, Betty gave her arm another reassuring squeeze.

"Now, the ladies' room key is on a hook by my desk. Gotta deal with security, since this is Center City, you know. Don't leave it around. And, Lordy, where are my manners? There's a fresh pot of coffee on, brewing in the back. Your first week's free. After that, we all chip in two dollars a week to the coffee fund. Also, you can put your lunch, if you bring it from home, in the employees' fridge. But if you leave it past Friday, I throw everything out, Tupperware and all."

Betty gave her a wink and efficiently began pacing back down the hall. "All right, all right! Hold your horses!" she fussed good-naturedly. "These phones start lightin' up as soon as I get away from the board for five minutes. Gets on my nerves."

Once alone, Allie stared at the new blotter/calendar that was still wrapped in plastic. On her desk was a welcoming card from the staff, a new pencil holder with seven newly sharpened instruments, two pens, and a yellow highlighter. When she opened the drawer, there was a militarily ordered row of office supplies; a box of paper clips, white out, rubber bands, and in the small attached short file were the pendaflexes and folders that Betty had promised. Her little area even smelled new, and it was all she could do to restrain herself from the urge to call Dave. She wanted to tell him about every nuance of her first moments at work. How she felt, how nice the reception had been, how needed she felt, everything. She surveyed the environment carefully, determined not to forget a crack in the wall so she could tell her family about the entire experience.

Allie almost jumped out of her skin, however, when she wheeled her chair around to the opening of her cube. Looming in the entranceway was a tall amiable-looking fellow, with a mass of black hair and intensely curious brown eyes.

"First day, huh?" he said smiling and extending his hand. "You and I will be doing a lot of client work together. The name's Jason Levy. I'm the local-yokel attorney around here, and do the advocacy work for the agency."

An attorney? *She'd* be working with an attorney? Finding her voice, Allie cleared her throat and spoke cautiously. "I'm Allyson Barbera. But I don't know anything about law. They didn't tell me I'd have to."

Jason Levy seemed to already be paces ahead of her confusion. Smiling, he popped into her office and casually sat on the edge of her desk, a gesture that oddly put her at ease. "You know about people, or they wouldn't have hired you, right?"

Allie shrugged and looked down. He seemed so sure of himself, yet he had a gentleness in his tone that made her comfortable.

"This is my first real position in a long time. I hope I won't disappoint anyone."

"Nonsense," he said with confidence, while pushing up his sleeves. "We need more people who care enough to work on behalf of the community. You'll see the clients first for intake. You'd be surprised at how much people will tell you when they trust you—and you, Ms. Barbera, have a kind demeanor about you. I'm sure that they'll begin to bond with you after a while, and that's when you can really begin to help."

She was perplexed. How could bonding with people really help, other than making them feel better? As though reading her facial expression again, he went on.

"Look, it's simple. Some of these folks have serious problems that need to be sorted out legally. For example, a low-life landlord who's trying to cast them out into the street in the dead of winter. Or a kid who has gotten in trouble with the police. Or a husband that's beating them up. When women come into this agency, the instructors and coordinators become more than teachers of the three R's. Talk to Betty, she'll tell you. Even she does her fair share of listening to client problems. She's like everybody's mom around here. After a while, all of us hopefully turn into friends, a shoulder to cry on, an arm of support—or the long arm of the law, a resource bank to refer them for help, you name it. You won't just be teaching, then packing up your briefcase to go home at night. You'll be making a real difference."

Allie was awed. Never in a million years would she have expected an attorney to be sitting on the edge of her desk, with his shirt sleeves rolled up, picking at the worn sole of his penny loafer, telling her that she'd be making a significant impact on somebody's life. It was as if she'd stepped into the Twilight Zone vortex, and everything that she once understood had changed. Maybe she'd changed, and it had happened so subtly that it had gone unnoticed until this very moment.

Again, searching for her voice, she paused before she

spoke. "This is a serious responsibility. What if I make a mistake?" She no longer cared about making a good impression. This was too important.

"If you care, you can't mess up. Our clients can detect fraud a mile away. They can also detect genuine concern, too. And they're so starved for it, that even if you do mess up a little, you'll find that they're very forgiving and will work with you." Standing, he gave her a reassuring smile. "Listen, I've got a hundred client files on my desk that need attention. Besides, I don't want to get too deep and dramatic on your first day. It's a real pleasure to see someone with such commitment come in here—not everybody can hack it. You'll be great. It's in your eyes. I can tell. And you're no fraud, lady. I'm sure we'll be a fantastic team."

Just as soon as he appeared, the Jason Levy dynamo disappeared, leaving Allie to her thoughts, her clean, orderly desk, and something very serious to ponder.

Matt took a deep breath and entered the center city restaurant. He hated this crap. He was already sure that he wasn't going to like Richard Caldwell, especially after the way he tried to back Ginny into a corner. In his opinion, any man that would use a woman to get ahead was scum, and he kept that mental picture before him as he searched through the crowd at Houlihan's to find Caldwell.

Almost immediately, he saw a very well dressed man motioning him toward a table. It had to be Caldwell. But who was the woman sitting with him? Caldwell never mentioned that there would be anyone else joining them. Taking a deep breath to preserve his patience, Matt approached the table, swallowing away his growing agitation.

Richard Caldwell was standing when he neared the couple, extending his hand to perform the standard business greeting.

"Matt Lewellyn. It's a pleasure to finally meet you. I thought that Virginia Harrison would be accompanying you?"

Matt shook the man's hand and looked at the woman seated in the chair next to where Caldwell stood. "No. Virginia had another obligation and was unable to make this meeting. However, she told me all about you." He couldn't resist the inadvertent cut that slipped out. Ginny was right. This guy was a pompous ass.

"Figures," Caldwell said with a hint of annoyance, and clearly oblivious to the double entendre. "Well, in any event, let me introduce you to my wife, Joan."

Matt ignored the irritating inflection of Caldwell's voice and smiled at Joan Caldwell. "I'm sure Virginia will be disappointed that she missed the opportunity to have dinner with you. It's a pleasure to meet you."

The compliment was directed at the shy woman who smiled briefly before looking down, not toward Richard Caldwell.

"Well, if I had known that Ms. Harrison would be otherwise detained, Joan need not have joined us."

There was something about the tone of the man's voice that grated on him. Richard Caldwell had openly disrespected his wife in front of a virtual stranger, and she didn't even blink an eyelash. Watching the two carefully as he sat down, Matt didn't know if the woman had even taken a breath when Caldwell spoke. Almost reflexively, he found himself strangely coming to her defense.

"Whether Virginia was able to attend, or not, I'm pleased to meet you both. Mrs. Caldwell, I hear you have been looking for houses in the area. Have you chosen one you like?"

Matt wasn't sure what it was that made her blanch, but she nearly choked and sputtered on the sip of water that she was taking before he asked the question. He'd only wanted to let Richard Caldwell know, diplomatically, that his wife's presence was not a problem, then to change the subject to a more benign topic. That was it. Simple. But her expression was one of panic. No, sheer terror. And a basic question directed toward her shouldn't have caused such a strong reaction.

Dabbing her mouth with the napkin on her lap, Joan Caldwell looked at her husband quickly, as if for approval before speaking. Matt's gaze focused on Richard Caldwell, not the wife. He was used to reading people, and could tell that the tension that hung in the air went well beyond a little marital spat. What had he walked into?

"We have seen some lovely properties in this area, but Richard will make the final decision. He's so much better at handling these things than I am," Mrs. Caldwell finally responded.

After Joan spoke, she immediately retreated and looked down, but not before giving her husband another sideways glance. Her husband's posture seemed rigid, and his eyes appeared to smolder with resentment. Something was wrong. This woman was definitely frightened.

"Yes," Caldwell sneered as he adjusted himself in his

seat, "if I were to leave it to her, she'd choose a house based upon the window treatments alone."

Matt was at a loss. The man spoke as if his wife wasn't even in the room. He didn't know whether to stand and leave, or to punch Caldwell out. Never in his life had he watched a woman treated like this, and without her giving as much as a flicker of resistance. It wasn't what he said, but how he said it, and the way that she seemed to beg for his permission with her eyes before she spoke. This was the nineties, but the scene was right out of the sixteenth century or something. His mind raced and rebelled against the eerie familiarity of the couple's brief interaction. For the love of Pete, he *had* seen this type of fear in a woman's eyes before. Recently. It was mirrored in Ginny Harrison's too-controlled expression the first time he met her. The parallel unnerved him momentarily, and he shook the odd feeling as he tried to garner some control over his thoughts.

There must have been an incredulous look on his face, since Richard Caldwell smiled and put his arm around his wife's shoulders. "But then, she is the decorator in the family," he said in a falsely upbeat tone, clearly designed to put him at ease.

Matt returned a strained smile but made no comment as he placed his napkin in his lap. Too many questions pummeled his mind at one time, and he was grateful that a waitress came over to take their drink orders. After putting in his request for a beer, he decided to try another subject. Maybe this time he'd pick one that wasn't loaded and ready to detonate.

"So, Virginia tells me that you're a sports agent," Matt commented dryly as he waited for his order to come. He used Ginny's formal name on purpose. He didn't even want to think about Caldwell being around Ginny.

Richard Caldwell beamed, and this time the smile appeared to be more genuine. "I can see Ms. Harrison doesn't waste any time getting to the bottom line. I like that. Yes, in fact, that's why I insisted you and I meet. I am probably going to relocate to this area—that is, if I can get connected."

Matt hated the thinly veiled threat. It was clear that this man was going to make getting to his sports connections a contingency to doing the house deal with Ginny. Okay, so he'd throw him a few bones, but he'd make him work for them during this interminable dinner. He always liked a good game of poker.

"It's a tough business, Richard. You've got to put a lot on the line to woo the high stakes clients. Who do you have in your portfolio now?"

Caldwell took a sip from his glass of Zinfandel, and Matt took a sip from his beer. The two never lost eye contact.

"I've got a decent stable of NBA and NFL players on the New York and Connecticut benches. But it's time to expand and get some of the baseball players in this area, especially if I'm going to acquire this dream house. I assumed that you might be able to set up a formal introduction."

"Possibly. If an introduction is in order. Speaking of ordering, are you two hungry yet?" Matt was almost sure that he saw the trace of a smile cross Joan Caldwell's mouth before instantly vanishing. Maybe she didn't like the man either.

Matt picked up his menu and refused to look at Richard Caldwell. The bastard could wait. He could tell Caldwell was impatiently making small talk as they went on and on about local sports news and, during their meal, Matt took extreme pleasure in giving him all the statistics and run-of-the-mill, boring information that anyone could glean from the newspapers. His goal was to make Caldwell sweat in order to get what he wanted. He was obviously used to pushing people around, but Matt wouldn't stand for it. Were it not for his affinity for Virginia Harrison, he wouldn't have even stayed to finish the beer.

Without much room for evasion left, Matt steered the conversation back to the issue at hand. He had had enough, and couldn't wait to get away.

"So you want to meet the key players in the Delaware Valley? Okay. I'll see what I can do. Maybe there's still a few names in my phone book that are up for contract renewals, and I can call them."

Caldwell's expression was even, and it was obvious that the man was not pleased by the lukewarm offer.

"What about that kid the Federals just brought up to play third? DeWayne Henderson. I know for a fact he isn't properly represented. Somebody like him would be enough for a start."

Now it was Matt's turn to blanch. No way in hell would he throw a starry-eyed rookie in this piranha's path. A guy like Richard Caldwell would rob the kid blind, then abandon him. It was out of the question.

"I don't know him on a personal basis. I'll try a few veterans that already have a track record."

"I'm not interested in has-been's who are locked into lengthy contracts. I'm looking for new blood. Somebody who hasn't signed yet."

New blood, hell! Matt repeated the words mentally, and

forced a casual demeanor. "Yeah, well, like I said, I don't know the kid."

Caldwell took another sip of wine and leveled his gaze at him. "But you could probably get a meeting set up with him, right? I'm sure you're probably one of his heroes. They say he could play third as well as you did."

If there wasn't a woman seated with them, and this wasn't for Ginny . . .

"I'll need to give the kid a call and feel him out first. No promises."

"I'm sure you can be persuasive, Matt," Caldwell said, smiling with triumph. "Let me know in a few days. I need to get back to Ms. Harrison soon."

On that note, Matt stood up. "Mrs. Caldwell, it has been a pleasure. Richard," he said stoically, extending his hand by rote, "I'll be in touch."

"You have to go so soon?" Caldwell said calmly, rubbing in the definitive win. "You can't stay for dinner?"

"Yeah, well, I've got to go. I've got another appointment."

"Tell Virginia we said hello," Caldwell called behind him as a parting shot.

Matt refused to dignify the comment. It was all he could do to get out of the restaurant without exploding. Yeah, he'd talk to the kid, and tell him what a slimeball Richard Caldwell was. He'd use Caldwell as an example of who not to get involved with.

Shit! How could she have forgotten about the meeting with the Delaware Valley Ford Dealership account yesterday? She'd tell those old farts something or other. Nan pushed herself away from her desk with irritation. Drumming her fingernails on the arm of her chair, she rummaged through her mind for a good excuse to tell her boss. She was sick of him hounding her. It seemed as though everybody was on her back lately, and out to get her. And, damn it, she needed a manicure. When was the last time she had kept her appointment for a fill-in?

Nan turned her hands over and studied them. The polish was starting to erode away from the cuticle line, leaving an ugly, telltale gap between her real nail surface and the acrylic. Men didn't have to deal with this crap. So what if she wasn't picture perfect today? She was a pro, and that should be enough, but she made a mental note to get her hair trimmed and her nails done. It would have to wait until next week, though. She had too much catching up to do.

When her secretary buzzed the inter-office console, the sound of the telephone jarred her nerves. Snatching the receiver off the hook, Nan responded to the annoyance with impatience.

"What the hell is it? I said *no* interruptions!"

The voice on the other end responded timidly. "Ms. Lynch, your two o'clock is here, and they seem a little upset. They said you owed them the story board a week before this meeting today, but I wasn't sure of what to tell them. I sent them into the conference room for you."

It was a nightmare. Nan snatched her daytimer from her desk and flipped through it furiously. God Damn! How had she overlooked this meeting? Standing quickly, she snapped back a hasty response. "Tell them I can't make it today. Tell them I'm not even here. Give it to Amato."

"But Ms. Lynch, they're all here, and already quite perturbed, and—"

Nan felt her voice escalating beyond her control. "I don't have their fucking story boards! What do these people want from me? I can't make shit up on a dime. They'll just have to reschedule!"

Nan didn't even wait for her secretary to respond before slamming down the receiver. She had to get out of here. The walls of her office were closing in on her. As she reached for her coat, a button popped off of her Seville suit. Rather than picking it up, she kicked the small black bead across the floor. Details. To hell with the details. She was outta here. Halfway to the door, she stopped. Her purse. Shit! She needed her purse. As she reached across her desk to grab it, her knee collided with the edge of the furniture, opening up a long, ugly, run in her silk stocking. If it wasn't so infuriating, she would have laughed.

Freaking details!

Chapter 10

Ginny cringed as she held the receiver to her ear and listened to Matt's blow by blow account of the Caldwell dinner. Asking him to participate in this travesty was definitely a bad decision, especially since it seemed that things were getting more tangled by Caldwell's insistence on meeting one of Matt's contacts. Didn't the man ever give up, she wondered as her fingers tensed around the telephone receiver.

"And get this, Gin, the guy nearly threatened me."

"Threatened you? No! How?"

"Oh, just by a not-too-subtle reference to your house deal if he couldn't find a big-time rookie to pull into his stable."

Ginny groaned, and felt her stomach lurch with pure humiliation.

"Hey, it's not your fault. It doesn't take a rocket scientist to figure out that Caldwell is a sleaze. Take for example how he treats his wife. The man talked about that poor woman just like she wasn't even in the room. But the worst part of it was how scared of him she looked. For real, Ginny, the woman looked terrified. It was almost like

163

she was afraid that he might punch her out or something if she said the least little thing wrong."

"I know what you mean, Matt," she said nervously, wanting to end this part of the conversation, yet oddly compelled to complete her train of thought. "I noticed it when they came to my office. He treated her just like you described, and she was most definitely afraid of him."

"Maybe we're making a mountain out of a molehill, though. Those kind of people settle things between very well-paid attorneys," he said chuckling. "But I don't think divorce is in the picture if they're looking for a new house. Hell, maybe she's afraid that he'll sue her for half of her trust fund if she leaves him."

Ginny could feel the bile come up from her liver, and a sudden flash of fury overtook her. "Just because they're wealthy does not mean he can't be an abuser. Everybody always thinks that kind of thing only happens in poor neighborhoods, where the blue-collar husband kicks the door in on a Friday night after having one too many at the corner bar. You'd be surprised, Matt."

Immediately shame and fear engulfed her, and she took deep breaths to regain her control. She had revealed too much, way too much, and her delicately balanced house of cards was in jeopardy of being toppled.

"Look, you're right. I'm sorry. It is no laughing matter. Certainly, if something like that is going on, the lady needs help. I guess you really think I'm a Neanderthal now?"

Ginny took a moment to respond. Perhaps she was safe, and Matt just thought she was a raving feminist. He could believe whatever he needed, as long as he didn't come close to the truth. After a pause, followed by another deep breath, she answered him.

"No, I don't think you're a bad person. But that kind of attitude is what keeps the police, and even neighbors, from responding to domestic violence every day of the week. Did you know that battering by a spouse or lover is the number one killer of women—not cancer?"

"No, I didn't," he said quietly, and sounded confused. "All I meant was that maybe they just have a bad marriage, and that it's not quite as dramatic as we're making it out to be. I'm sure the fact that we both despise Caldwell doesn't help."

"Maybe," she said grudgingly. "Let's just drop it."

"Good," he answered, yet still sounding worried. "But let's not end one of our few conversations on a down note. How about if I make it up to you?"

"Oh, really, Matt, I'm the one that owes you." She knew this was coming, and there was no polite escape. All she could do was pray for a diplomatic way out.

"Then make me feel better by agreeing to a dinner with a Neanderthal Man," he chuckled. "Please?"

What could she say? Not only was she painted into a corner, but the wistful tone of Matt's voice had cornered her as well.

"Sure," she finally said in a quiet voice.

"I don't want you to feel blackmailed, though. I know how much you hate extortionists."

Ginny laughed. There was something about Matt Lewellyn that defied all of her attempts to build a barrier between them. "When?" she asked.

"How about Friday night? However, I've gotta tell you

that I'm a little nervous about making a date so far away. Promise you won't cancel?"

"I promise," she said cheerfully, feeling better as she said it.

"Okay, then I'll pick you up at seven o'clock—without minicams and reporters this time."

She smiled. "That would be most appreciated."

"Absolutely. See ya, Gin. I can't believe I have to wait until the weekend."

"Bye," she said shyly, then hung up.

Ginny allowed her gaze to linger on the telephone for a few moments. He had called her Gin again. Like one of her sisters. Like someone who had been in her life long enough to use the shortened endearment. So much was changing and whirling out of control before her. But this time, she wasn't sure if she was being swept up in a maelstrom, or if this was just something wonderful like fairy dust. Why couldn't she just be excited and flattered like normal women? She was so used to being guarded, remote, and intense about everything. As she sat staring at the phone, it hit her. Allie was right—she had forgotten how to play. What she remembered was that the last time she had played, she fell down and got hurt badly.

The somber thoughts returned with a vengeance, and quickly evaporated the few seconds of elation that she had allowed herself to experience. How long would this go on? How long would she have to protect herself? "As long as there are people in the world like Richard Caldwell," she murmured as she stood and stretched, making a mental note to call Allie to find out how she was doing on her new job.

* * *

"I was thinking maybe for this commercial we could use my granddaughter. I already promised her anyway, and she's told all the kids at school that she was going to be on T.V. with her grandpop."

Nan couldn't take it. The more she sat across from the group of idiots at the conference table, the more she wanted to scream. Her head was pounding, her skin itched and their stupid banter grated on her nerves. To make matters worse, Joe Carter had just slipped into the room like an intrusive hall monitor, obviously to watch how the negotiations were going. It was an insult that she wouldn't tolerate.

"Look, Bob, I've been in this business a long time, and trust me, that isn't going to work."

Nan ignored the startled expression on Joe Carter's face. Hell, if he wanted to see her in action, she hoped he would like the side show.

"Well, why not? Most of my competitors appear in their own commercials, and they seem to be doing all right."

Nan groaned with exasperation. "Do you want to be perceived in the industry as a joke? Or do you want to be regarded as a professional dealership that can be counted on to deliver quality cars and great service? We've all seen those other commercials. If that's what you want, then you'd might as well go stand in your car lot and get your wife to hold the camcorder while you and your granddaughter put on clown suits and stick stuffed animals on top of cars! Who do you think the customers are? You're not selling to kids, you're selling to the kids' parents. If you want to do a tacky, local-yokel spot, then we're not the firm for you. I'd rather lose your business than our firm's professional reputation."

Nan watched Bob Jegnes and his staff sit back and bristle with indignation. She heard Joe Carter audibly inhale, yet she wasn't going to break eye contact with her quarry. She meant business and the truth was the truth. Sometimes the truth hurt.

"So, Ms. Lynch, since we're talking professionalism," Jegnes began, "I take it that rescheduling a client three times, being late on every proposal, and not returning phone calls is now the new standard of professional conduct here. Or, to use your own words, is it just the *tacky* way that your firm does business?"

Nan could see the smug satisfaction in his flunky entourage. As her fingers tightened around the folder in her hand, she knew she couldn't let that one go. An attack done in front of Joe Carter, the head of the firm, was more than just business. It was personal now. She was not about to let this two-bit, four-wheel-drive selling, snake-oil hick tell her her business. She was the lady with the Midas Touch, and Joe knew it.

She sat back in her chair, pretending to be unruffled by the exchange. "Look. Let me be real honest with you fellas. You're simply not a major account. You may help keep the lights on and pay the cleaning service, but a Markey Foods you're not. If you want to move up to the majors, you've got to leave your rookie mentality behind."

Men. She was tired of having to prove herself to every damned one of them.

Bob Jegnes stood quickly. "Then maybe I oughta take my minor league money to a firm that would appreciate it."

Joe Carter immediately rose and held out his hands in a

conciliatory manner. "Wait a minute, gentlemen. Emotions are running high, and we are getting way off the subject here." Joe shot a stern warning glare in Nan's direction. "It has always been our policy to treat all of our clients with respect and professionalism, regardless of the size of their advertising budgets. Why don't we all sit down again and try to incorporate the various ideas that will help you reach your objective—to sell more cars."

Nan could feel herself trembling with rage. How dare Joe Carter come in like the U.N. peacekeeping forces and wrest control of the situation from her? She hated the way they deferred to him, as though he were some patient father figure, but not as much as she hated the return of their smug expressions.

"I've been at this for over an hour, Joe. You boys amuse yourselves and go over the story boards that we've examined at least fifty times. I'm going to the ladies room." Fixing her glare on Joe Carter, she added, "And maybe when I get back you fellas will have come up with something that the firm can stomach."

Without waiting for a response, Nan turned on her heels and left the conference room, heading down the hallway to her office. All she needed was her purse, and a few moments away from the claustrophobic atmosphere around the male tribal fire—formally known as a meeting.

Snatching her bag off her desk, Nan continued her breakneck pace down the corridor to the ladies' room. Once safely closed away in a stall, she began to relax. Control would soon be hers, and it came in a tiny vial of white powder.

Her hands were shaking as she scooped the substance up using her pinky fingernail. Inhaling deeply, she allowed the shot of self-confidence to race through her system like adrenaline. She took another stinging sniff, and leaned her head against the cold steel of the stall. She felt better already. A couple more hits, and she'd go back in there and blow the doors off of that damned conference room. They couldn't hold a candle to the Golden Girl. Not even Joe Carter.

When she opened the doors to the meeting, she stood in the archway for a few moments for dramatic effect. She loved to make a grand entrance and was glad that she'd worn her red Ann Klein suit. The only problem was that those buffoons were still sulking, and hadn't looked up. Men . . . they were so childish.

"Well, gentlemen, any great ideas while I was gone?"

"Only one," Bob Jegnes said in a surly voice, "I refuse to work with someone like you." Turning his attention to Joe Carter, Bob went on in an excited, angry voice, "I'd rather deal with that new *rookie* of yours—what's his name? Amato?—than this arrogant, hot shot, *professional.* We may be a small business, but at least we know how to treat all of our customers."

"What!" Nan couldn't control the volume of her voice. "Who the hell—"

"Nan," Joe Carter again interrupted, standing and cutting her off with a severe tone. "This is not the time or place. We'll discuss this in your office later. In the interim, please tell Eleanor to send Tony in. Thank you."

"Tell him yourself!" she nearly screamed before allowing the door to slam loudly behind her. They were all against her, and Joe was obviously out of his mind if he thought she was going to help him slit her own throat.

She could feel the air rushing around her as she strode

down the hall. She hated them all. Her vision was beginning to blur from the rage, and a slight buzzing had begun in her ears. She'd get even. Nan brought her hands up to her face as she walked, and her cheeks felt flushed. Anger and humiliation tore through her surface exterior in the form of tears. Fury overtook reason as she bitterly wiped them away and turned into her office, but not before she saw Tony Amato exiting his cubicle and heading toward the conference room. Bastard. It was an insufferable indignity. She'd never stand for it.

This was war.

Allie pored over the manuals before her, getting even more overwhelmed as she tried to absorb the massive amount of red tape and procedures outlined in the documents. She had no idea that she'd have to become a walking textbook of rules and regulations. Any mistake on any form could mean that a client would be kicked out of the system, or that their benefits would be delayed. The responsibility seemed enormous. How did they expect the people who came in, some without even the ability to read, to wade through this information, if college grads were having trouble with it? There were amendments to the amendments, and time-dated materials were stapled and pushed into the ragged binders like an unending labyrinth of bureaucracy.

"So this is The System," she muttered to herself as she studied the four part intake forms for the hundredth time.

The phone at her elbow suddenly rang and she jumped with a mixture of excitement and fear. This was her first phone call. What if she didn't know the answers to the client's questions? What if she sounded like the truly confused, overwhelmed woman that she had become? Instantly, she thought of her home, her kitchen, her family, everything familiar, and wondered if she was up for this challenge.

"You can do this," she muttered to the empty office, as the phone rang for the third time. "If you don't know the answer, you can . . . " She shrugged, knowing she sounded like an idiot talking to herself. ". . . you can get help."

Taking a deep breath, she steadied herself and reached for the receiver to answer the call. "Hello, Philadelphia Women's Center. May I help you?"

"Al?"

"Gin? Oh, thank God!"

Allie collapsed back into the chair as relief swept through her body.

"Are you okay, Allie? Is everything going all right? Remember, I said I would call."

"I'm okay. I'm just a little rattled. You would not believe the paperwork involved in this job. I don't know if I'll ever learn it."

"Well, give yourself a break. It's only your first week."

"Ginny, I didn't realize that people's lives would be depending on me. If I fill out the wrong box, or enter the wrong code, some poor woman's benefits will get hung up in the system. Maybe I bit off more than I can chew."

"Oh, will you stop it? Everybody's insecure when starting a new job. I'll give you a month, and by then you'll be too busy to speak to me."

Allie let her fingernail run over the thick binder of instructions. "I don't know, Ginny. All of a sudden, carpools and trips to ShopRite seem pretty appealing."

She heard her sister laugh before saying, "You've been out of the work force for fifteen years. Just wait until you get your first check. Then you'll feel better."

Allie conceded grudgingly. "You're probably right. But enough about me. What's new with you?"

She could hear her sister let out a long sigh.

"I've been backed into a dinner with Matt."

"What? That's wonderful! How'd it all come about?"

"I was stupid enough to rope him into meeting one of my clients. So to return the favor, I had to agree to meet him for dinner Friday night."

"That's great."

"It's not great. It's terrible."

"Ginny, why do you fight everything so much? Why don't you just let go a little and have fun?"

There wasn't an immediate answer, and Allie smiled. Maybe she was finally breaking through.

After Ginny let out another breath, she heard her sister begin again, this time sounding annoyed.

"Al, I'm trying to tell you it's not that simple. I *had* to ask Matt to meet with this horrible client of mine, Richard Caldwell. The man is a sports agent, a . . . a bloodsucker, and after seeing Matt and me in the paper, he virtually blackmailed me into setting up an introduction for him. If I didn't, then he wouldn't close the house deal. I hated the whole thing, but the firm really needs the business."

"Still, what's so terrible? Okay, so your client is a sleaze. But through him, you were forced to call a person who really likes you and ask him for a favor, which I'm sure he didn't mind doing. Because of that, you now have a chance to go out with Matt again. And maybe, just maybe, you'll have another great night out with a handsome eligible man. I'm glad Caldwell forced your hand. Somebody sure had to."

"I don't need, or want, anybody to force me to do anything. Why is that so hard for everyone to understand? And don't go making Richard Caldwell out to be a heroic Cupid of some sort. He's the worst kind of individual that you can imagine. If you saw how he treated his wife, you'd understand exactly what I mean. Even Matt saw that much."

Allie was silent for a few moments. She could tell that Ginny was really upset and, as usual, that hadn't been her intention. Curiosity pulled at her, but she didn't want to end the conversation on a bad note.

Hesitating, she cautiously began, skillfully changing the subject. "Gin, what did this guy do to his wife that was so bad? I mean if Matt saw it, it must have been pretty blatant."

Her sister took another long pause before responding. "I'm not exactly sure of how to describe it, but the woman seems terrified of him, and has no self esteem whatsoever. Every time I asked her opinion about some feature of the house, she'd look at her husband nervously, then defer to him. And he took almost sadistic pleasure in cutting her down in front of me at every opportunity. It was horrible. Finally, I just stopped asking her questions, not because I didn't think she had an opinion, but because I didn't want to put her in an awkward position."

"He did that in front of Matt too?"

"Yes, and Matt was so angry he wanted to hit the man. I

can't believe I got him involved in such a horrendous evening."

Allie's brain was racing, but her focus was not on Ginny this time. "Listen, Matt's a grown man and can handle himself. If he was angry, or felt put upon, then he wouldn't have asked to see you again. But Mrs. Caldwell sounds like she obviously needs some help or something."

"Maybe she's just in a bad marriage," her sister said in a tight voice.

"Or maybe he beats her. Listen, Gin, I'm going through all these courses, and it's unbelievable. I'm learning how to recognize the signs. You'd be surprised at how often this happens, and from all walks of life."

There was a long silence on the other end of the phone and she could tell that Ginny was grappling with what she just said.

"I don't know," Ginny nearly whispered. "We can't just go around accusing people of things. You have to have proof, don't you?"

"If you're even considering that as a possibility, then it's serious enough to talk to her."

There was another long pause. "Allie, what would I say to her? You can't just walk up to someone and ask them if their husband is beating them. God, I don't want to get involved in this."

In that instant, Allie knew why she was hired. She did know people. She did know how to get people to trust her. She did have value.

Taking her time, she carefully formed the words. "Ginny, when someone is in crisis and frightened, you have to first let them know that they're safe talking to you."

"How in the world do you begin to do that?"

Allie thought for a moment. It was so difficult to try to put into words what she had known how to do intuitively all her life.

"I think," Allie began slowly, "you have to help her understand that you've noticed something unusual." Allie paused for a moment to collect her thoughts before continuing. "But not in a judgmental way. You have to let the person know that you've seen them being hurt—at least by the words. You tell Mrs. Caldwell that you want her to know that you care about what's happening to her, regardless of whether they decide to buy the house or not, and that if she ever needs to talk, you'll be there." Allie let out a sigh. "I suppose, then you try to make her know that she isn't the only one in the world that this has happened to, and that it's not because there's something wrong with her—but rather, something's wrong with the person who's abusing her. Nobody deserves to be treated that way, even if it's only words. Perhaps once she knows that she has an ally, she'll start to reveal a little more, and you can go from there."

Another silent moment passed as her sister absorbed her answer. "Allie, what if she does start to tell me something really horrific? What can anybody really do?"

"You tell her where she can seek help, and give her examples of others from all walks of life that have gone through the same terrible problems. But most importantly, you talk to her about how they triumphed and got out of those bad situations. Gin, the reason most people stay in these toxic relationships is because they are afraid of what awaits them on the other side."

"I don't think so, Allie. How can that be? I don't think

it's fear of what's outside. It's fear of who's inside, and re-taliation. Aren't they just afraid of the abuser?"

"No. The abuser is familiar. He's a known quantity. They've spent a lifetime learning how to read his moods and emotions to tell when the abuse is going to happen or not. Also, their self esteem has been so damaged, that they think they can't make it alone, that no one will believe or help them—all the trash that the abuser has put in their head. Most times, it isn't until they see a way out, a light at the end of the tunnel so to speak, with the knowledge that there are people who care to help them through the dark part of it until they can get out. Only then will they even consider attempting it."

The pauses were long and almost painful. She didn't know why this woman meant so much to her sister. It sounded like more than just trying to complete a house sale.

"Where did you learn this stuff?" Ginny finally asked. "In one week you couldn't have picked all this up. I have to say I'm impressed."

For the first time in her life, Allie heard a sense of awe in Ginny's voice. It was both an exhilarating and hum-bling experience all at once.

"No, Gin. I didn't learn this in a week. Remember, I majored in psychology. But I suppose I've spent my entire life feeling like I wanted to help anyone who was down and out. Maybe because I saw so much of that when we were kids."

Neither of them said anything for a few moments, then they both spoke at once, their words colliding together and making them laugh.

"Okay, you go first."

"No, you."

"All right," Allie said. "Listen, whatever's going on, that woman needs a friend. I'll see what I can find out here about where she could stay, what her legal rights are, and stuff like that. If she does confide in you, at least you'll be armed. Sound fair enough?"

"Fair enough."

"Now, what were you going to say?"

"It wasn't important. I suppose I just wanted to say thanks for listening. Hey, I've already taken up enough of your time on the new job. So I'm going to go now, and I'll let you know if I ever have the opportunity to speak with Joan Caldwell. Honestly, I don't know if I can do it."

"Give it your best shot, Ginny. Nobody deserves to be left without support. But enough doom and gloom for now. I hope we're making this out to be more than it is. Anyway, you have a date on Friday."

Ginny laughed. "I'm saying goodbye now before you can get started on that subject again. Bye. Say hi to Dave and the kids for me."

"I know when I'm beat. I'll give them all a big kiss from their Aunt Ginny. You take care, and *try* to have fun, okay? See ya."

When she hung up the telephone, Allie just stared at it for a few moments. Suddenly the manuals didn't seem nearly so threatening. All they represented were the unnecessarily complex bureaucracy that had been layered over her real job. She'd done it all of her life. And she wasn't about to let a little paperwork get in her way.

*   *   *

Nan began angrily throwing files into her briefcase. She was determined to get the hell out of there. Never in her career had anyone undermined her like that, and to have it done by Joe Carter, her friend and mentor, was unforgivable. Her head was again pounding, as though a vice was tightening over her temples. It felt as if there was no room in her skull for her eyes to stay in their sockets. It was one of the worst headaches that she'd ever experienced. There was no point in staying in this place where she wasn't appreciated or respected. Nothing seemed more inviting than soaking in a warm tub and then climbing into bed.

It had not been a good day.

She was clicking the lid on her attache case closed when Joe Carter walked into her office.

Nan sat back in her chair and glared at the man, ready to do battle. "How dare you treat me like that in front of a client."

"It was exactly because of the client that I had to stop you," he said, closing the door behind him. "You and I need to talk."

She began rubbing her temple and inhaled, trying to gather the strength for one more battle. "Okay, Joe, you're the boss. What do you want to talk about? The fact that you undermined me in front of the client? Or perhaps, the Tony thing? No—maybe we can discuss how this firm is going to come off after doing a home video commercial for Grandpop Jegnes in there?"

Joe Carter sat down opposite her. "No, Nan. I don't want to talk about any of that," he said.

Her instinct told her this was not going to be about office policy, and her insides began clenching with apprehension. He was staring at her without anger or compromise.

"Okay, so if it's not about the client, then what do you want to talk about?"

"I want to talk about you."

"Me?"

"What's wrong with you? What's happening? This isn't the first grievance I've heard about you. But this is the first one I've witnessed, and I've gotta tell you, Nan, I was appalled."

"So that's why you came in there, to check up on me like an eighth grade safety to make sure I was behaving myself?"

Joe sat back in his chair and laced his hands over his stomach. "Nan, Tony Amato has talked to me about a sexual harassment suit against you."

"What?"

He remained calm, and a feeling of dread passed through her. She didn't know what was happening. Her brain was on overload.

"Tony told me about the Markey presentation. He said you stole it, and that you threatened his job if he came to me. That you forced him into a sexual liaison that he didn't want, but that he didn't intend to lose his job."

Nan bolted upright and clutched the edge of her desk with fury. "That son of a bitch! I don't believe this!"

Joe put his hand out as though motioning her. "Sit down, Nan. I may be old but I'm not stupid. I didn't believe that part either. You're an attractive woman, and I see the way he looks at you when you walk into a room. I'm sure if you two were together, then it was mutually beneficial. He's definitely a young pup trying to scratch his way to the top—almost as hungry as you were at that age. And I also don't think you're above using the advantage of taking someone who's hungry under your wing. Truth be told, I did that a few times myself along the way. But you know what, Nan? Times are changing, and you can't have your cake and eat it any longer. It's far too risky. The stakes are too high, and now the law's involved. Nobody snickers at sexual harassment any more . . . for either gender."

Nan sat down, still incredulous. "But, Joe, I don't understand. If you know this guy is lying about being *forced* into a relationship, then what's this all about? What can I do to protect myself?"

"I said I knew he was lying about being forced to sleep with you. But I'm disturbed about his accusations regarding the Markey account."

Nan's eyes widened. "I don't see what the problem is. We were working on that project together. He was my assistant. He—"

"Give it up, Nan," Joe interrupted. "I don't know if it's because you and Robert have split. I don't know what's going on in your life, but I do know that you stole the kid's work because you couldn't cut it."

"That's a lie," she snapped back. "He stole it from me and is trying to pass it off as his to move up. The kid doesn't want to pay his dues, Joe. It's as simple as that."

"I don't think it's quite that simple, Nan. Look, don't bullshit a professional bullshitter. I'm the one who taught *you.* The kid showed me the time date stamp on his computer. Then I had Eleanor fire yours up. Guess what? No proposal."

Stunned, she could only stare back at this man who had once been her friend.

"You've lost control, Nan. You need to pull yourself together. As your friend, I'm telling you to get some professional help. As your boss, I'm telling you to check yourself into rehab."

"Rehab? Where did that come from?"

Joe put his head back, glanced out the window and sighed, and then turned his riveting attention back to her. "Look, I'm not going to go through the litany of signs. When Tony told me that you'd offered him some coke every time the two of you were together, everything in the last couple of months fell into place. You're losing it, Nan, and you're losing it because you're strung out."

"That lying bastard! He's trying to ruin me! The guy's after my job and you're falling for it."

"I didn't believe it when he first told me, but prove me wrong and take a urine analysis test."

"I'm not taking any goddamned piss test! Tell Amato to take one."

"I didn't have to. He volunteered."

She felt like a cornered animal. The walls were closing in around her, taking away her breath and her reason. She didn't know if she could find a way out. But she had to . . . her credibility was on the line. This could not be happening. Not now. How could she have read Tony so wrong? Of course he would volunteer. If he hadn't done anything, it wouldn't be in his system any longer. But what was she going to do? Her only option was to keep bluffing.

"I will not subject myself to that humiliation. I can't believe you're asking me to do something like that."

Joe held her in a predatory gaze, the same deadly negotiating tactic that had always been his hallmark. He didn't
waver as he leaned forward and captured her with steely
determination. "I'm not asking you, Nan. I'm presenting
two very clear options to you. Either you take the test and
prove me wrong, or you check yourself into rehab and recover." He took a deep breath and began again slowly.
"As much as I hate to say this, you check into rehab, or
you check out of here."

She was stunned. "You would fire me?"

Even to her own ears her voice sounded tiny, pathetic,
almost like a child's.

"I don't have a choice, Nan. I care about you, and I
won't watch you destroy yourself . . . or this firm's reputation."

It was as if an invisible hand reached inside of her and
twisted her stomach into a painful knot, cutting off her
ability to breathe clearly. With a sense of fear, she realized
his words mirrored the exact same thing her husband had
said when he'd walked out of her life two months ago.

Chapter 11

*A*llie stood in the front doorway and stared at the madhouse that she had left ten hours ago. There were clusters of children holding puppies in her living room, amid clothing, school books, and toys. MTV blared from the television and Meghan's Fisher-Price recorder was loudly competing for playing time with her favorite Barney tape. There was a half-eaten bag of cookies spilled over the rug, which one puppy was noisily enjoying while Bummer barked incessantly from the kitchen enclosure. Plastic juice cups littered the table tops, and one was laying on its side on the floor next to a large purplish sticky stain. The whole melee was almost too much to bear as Allie steadied herself, took a deep breath, and announced that she was home.

Pat looked up and gave her a nonchalant, "Hi." Meghan reluctantly left her friends and came over to give her a hug. Allie immediately grabbed her daughter's sticky hands before they could soil her work clothes and bent down to kiss Meghan's forehead. Even though she wanted to scream to clear everyone out, she forced herself to evacuate the band of kids calmly.

"Okay, everybody. It's seven-thirty and it's a school night. I want all of you to help clean this mess up, then it's time to go home. Patrick, turn the T.V. off and put those puppies back in the kitchen. Meghan, pick up the popcorn and put away your toys. I'll get the juice cups."

She dropped her purse onto the hall table, and picked her way through the clutter telling herself over and over again not to lose her temper. She hadn't seen her children since breakfast, and she didn't want to come through the door like the wicked witch of the East. But it was a struggle. How could they be so thoughtless? Where was Dave? Where was the parental authority? In all her fifteen years, she had never let him walk into such chaos after a hard day at work. Why should it always be like this on her late nights?

Bringing the half-empty plastic cups into the kitchen, she stopped at the shutter they were still using to keep Bummer and the puppies out of the rest of the house. She surveyed the wake of destruction that had been left in her kitchen. Hardened, crusty food still clung to dishes on the table. A half-eaten casserole was cold and dried out on the edge of the counter. Soiled newspapers from the puppies were lying on the floor, and Bummer was up in one chair licking the remains from a dinner plate.

Where was Dave?

A sudden rush of fury pulsed through her veins and she started barking out orders to the children. "Pat, when you're finished with that, I want you in the living room. Somebody spilled juice out there and I want it cleaned up, *now!* Go find the spray bottle of rug cleaner under the kitchen sink—and use a rag and a brush. I want it done. I'm not cleaning this up. Meghan, get every one of those toys put in your room and go find your pajamas. You need a bath. Have you done your homework yet?"

Allie heard their disgruntled "No's," and became even angrier. "You haven't? Why not?"

"Relax, Mom," Pat said in a blasé voice. "Dad said we could do it after dinner. I don't see why you have to get all bent out of shape every time you come home late from work."

She felt her voice escalate beyond her control. "Is that what you were doing out there? Since when does listening to MTV and playing with puppies with half the neighborhood kids become homework? Get that stuff cleaned up, then go to your room. And do it now! Not twenty minutes from now when I have to ask again. Where is your father?"

"Outside," she heard Meghan say in a tiny voice.

Allie was too angry to deal with them, and turned toward the door leading to the deck. Dave was sitting in a lounge chair reading the paper. He barely looked up as she shut the door behind her.

"So you're finally home," he said in a disinterested voice, going back to whatever article held his attention.

Allie stood before him, trembling with repressed rage. "How can you be sitting out here, when the entire house is in chaos?"

"I fed the kids," he answered, still not looking at her.

Incredulous, she merely shook her head in disbelief. "That's it? You fed the kids and that's the end of your responsibility? There's total chaos in there. Meghan hasn't even done her homework. Dave, she's five years old. In a half hour, she isn't going to be able to keep her eyes open. And the kitchen—everybody just gets up and leaves everything where it is? Who's supposed to clean that up? I found Bummer eating at the table. But at least it's nice to know that the dog ate. I didn't. Would it have been so damned hard to put a cover over the casserole to keep it fresh so I could eat? Did I ever do that to you? Huh? Ever?"

He lowered the paper slowly and stared at her. "Then maybe you should've gotten home earlier so you could eat with your family."

It was unbelievable. Something inside her snapped as her tightly held control vanished.

"Don't you dare try and use guilt on me. For fifteen years, I've supported you in whatever decisions you've made. I tried to have homework done, and a hot meal waiting for you so that you'd never have to walk into this. I respected that you put in a hard day at work, and all I'm asking for is the same consideration. This isn't going to work if we both don't cooperate."

"If it's too hard for you, then quit," he said evenly, picking up the paper again.

"That's what this is all about, isn't it? You're trying to make me quit. You're sabotaging me."

Dave put down the paper with obvious annoyance. "Look, you spend all of your time trying to help strangers, and your own house is falling apart around you—and you blame me? Maybe if you put half your energy into pulling it together around here, all of *this*, as you say, wouldn't be happening."

She hated the triumphant tone in his voice. "If you did your job as a father tonight, *this* wouldn't have happened! Where is it written that everything has to fall on me? You may not have noticed, but my job isn't from nine to five.

Dave, I work two jobs now, one outside of the house, and one inside the house. Despite the fact that I have to drive to Philly and work during the day, when I come home, it's like pulling a second shift."

She ran her fingers through her hair with frustration. Why couldn't she make him understand? "Kids have to be fed, homework has to be done, laundry has to be done, the house has to be cleaned, oh, and let us not forget, the next day's meal has to be prepared and lunches packed, and to do that, food has to be bought. The list goes on and on. But everybody thinks that this stuff just happens by magic! Well, let me tell you, it doesn't—and it's not fair. All I asked you to do was to pick up a little slack, and to do three things today since I had to take class tonight. One, heat up a casserole that was already made and feed your children. Two, go to the bank since it's in Jersey, so we can pay the mortgage. And three, pick up Meghan from after school care and oversee the kids' homework. Was that so hard?"

"Well, if it's so tough, why don't you just quit?"

"What if I don't want to quit? What if I can't quit? Did you go to the bank today? That ought to tell you why we need this job."

She knew by the way he stared back at her with the same guilty expression Pat had whenever he hadn't taken out the garbage that her husband had neglected more than their children's homework. "You didn't go to the bank today, did you?"

Dave sat up straight and became defensive. "You soon forget that I too have a job. I can't be running to the bank in the middle of the day, like—"

"Like I used to do, Dave?" she hotly interrupted. "I

work in Philadelphia. You're ten minutes from the bank and could've gone on your lunch hour. How in the name of God are we going to pay the mortgage in three days if you didn't go and withdraw the money from Pat's college fund?"

Too angry to sit in one of the lawn chairs, Allie began pacing. "We've already spent half of our son's money in the last two years. Money we were saving for his college tuition. In September, he'll be a freshman in high school. In four years, he'll need it for school, and we won't have it. But, now that I'm working, we can replenish his fund and pay the mortgage without having to continually dip into savings so much to just get by. My God, I don't know why you can't see this. Whether you know it, or accept it, we're in this together. This isn't about you against me, or vice versa. This is about trying to make it, Dave. This is about survival and reality."

"Oh, so it's all my fault? And, I suppose you'll find a way to blame me for pushing us into a higher tax bracket now that you're working? That's reality, Al. The economy will pick up and people will start buying again."

"You can't depend on that. That's supposition, conjecture. We've got a smart kid in there, but one who may not be smart enough to get a scholarship. I'm working so our children can get an education."

"Oh, and I can't take care of my family?"

Allie sighed with exasperation. "You are not getting this. We've got to declare a state of truce and cooperate. I'm doing all I can, Dave. I'd need to be another person to do more. When I work late, you've got to accept that you have to step in and take over. And you've got to do it because you know it's right, and fair, and not do it with resentment."

"So now you want me to be the happy camper because you've gone on a crusade to save the family?"

"Why can't you understand that this is a family, and that the family is taking a new direction now? You're acting as though I have nothing to contribute, and that my salary is more of an annoyance than a help. When I go out of here every morning, it's to contribute, Dave. Basic, plain, and simple. I wish it were different, but it's not. That's life."

"I bet you wish it was different, and that you could be like your rich sisters who throw away money on clothes and have high-faluting husbands. Like, how much did that getup run you, Al?" he said with a sneer, motioning toward her outfit with his hand. "Is that part of Pat's college fund? Or did Ginny buy it for you?"

It was a low blow, and Allie felt her stomach muscles clench with resentment. How dare he attack Ginny, who had helped them out so many times in the past? This time Dave Barbera had gone too far.

"Listen, I go out of here to work to contribute, but I also go for me. I go because when I get there, people respect me, they treat me like an adult, and listen to my opinion without this kind of malicious attitude that I get from you. And yes, damn it, I spent some of the money I earned on new *clothes* because I looked like a frump in my old outfits and I couldn't wear them on the job. It's called an expense for doing business. Did I ever deny you a suit, especially knowing that you couldn't feel good about yourself or be accepted going to work in jeans?"

It wasn't until Pat poked his head through the door that

Allie realized they had been yelling. She could still feel the blood rushing to her temples and the veins standing out in her neck.

"Mom, didn't you guys hear the phone ring? Aunt Nan is holding on for you," Pat said in a worried voice as he looked from one parent to the other. He let out a sigh of disgust before allowing the screen door to slam shut.

"Yeah, that's right, go talk some more to your sister about how to make money in the business world. I'm sure Nan knows all the tricks of the trade," Dave said bitterly, then snatched up his fallen newspaper.

Without answering him, Allie turned and headed toward the door to get the phone. But she was jerked abruptly to a halt as her heel caught between the wooden slats of deck flooring and snapped it off at the base. Near tears, she shook off her broken shoe and stooped down to pry the trapped heel. She could feel the wood picking at her nylons and stifled a curse.

But what she could not believe was the sound of her husband's sarcastic laughter. Picking up the shoe she stared at him once before turning toward the house. It was as if she were married to a stranger. The Body Snatchers had come some time during the last month and replaced the man she loved with this alien creature.

She picked up the phone, sat down heavily on a kitchen chair and stared at the congealed and hardened mess of chicken, noodles, and vegetables. "Hi, Nan. What's up?"

"Hey, Allie, are you sitting down?" Nan's voice sounded falsely cheerful.

Allie sighed. "As a matter of fact, I am."

"Well, listen. I don't know how to tell you this, so I

might as well say it straight out. I've checked myself in to Hanson House, in Mt. Laurel."

"Wait. What?" Allie's brain clicked off one family crisis and turned on another. Hanson House was a private psychiatric hospital that specialized in depression and substance abuse! "Nan, what happened? What's wrong? You didn't even seem upset about Robert leaving. This can't be real. You're joking, right?"

"Wish I was, but I'm not."

"My God, why didn't you talk to me? It's Robert, isn't it? I knew you still loved him. You can work it out. You can—"

"Allie!" Nan interrupted. "This isn't about Robert. This is about me. I'm not here for depression."

"Well, then what? I don't get it."

Nan let out a long sigh. "It's all a conspiracy, Al. I used coke a couple of times at work, and this guy tried to set me up by telling my boss. I had a pain-in-the-ass client who I had to set straight, and Joe Carter accused me of freaking out on the man. So he gave me an ultimatum. Either check in to rehab, or lose my job. Like I said, it's all a conspiracy. I don't care, though. I'll use this as a month-long vacation then get the hell out of here."

Stunned, Allie sat staring at the soiled newspapers littering her kitchen floor. "I don't understand, Nan. Why would you ever use cocaine?"

"Look, I can't discuss this now. Part of this madhouse program is that they have these crazy rules. You only get five minutes to use this hall phone each day, and I've used up four already. I've got three lunatics staring down my throat as we speak, waiting to use it. It's pathetic. *A hall phone.* Anyway, I hope you don't mind that I put you down as my closest relative. I'm sure some social worker, or case worker, will be calling to dredge up more dirt on me, but don't worry about it. This is a real pain in the ass. But they're not going to beat me, Al. I'm a fighter. When I get out, I'm gonna sue that son of a bitch Amato. Trust me."

Allie was almost too shocked to respond. Finding her voice she said hesitantly, "Nan, if you were in trouble, why didn't you call me? I knew something was wrong. Why didn't you tell me?"

" 'Cause I'm not in trouble. I'm just going along with this crap because I got backed into a corner. I put too many years into that firm to start all over. Look, Allie, I gotta go. In ten minutes I have to be with the rest of the inmates while we watch some film called *Clean and Sober,* and three of 'em are staring at me right now and they don't look too happy. I'll call you tomorrow. Bye."

Allie heard the line disconnect and stared at the receiver in her hand with disbelief.

"Mommy, Pat won't let me in the bathroom so I can have my bath," Meghan whined, as she burst into the kitchen in tears. "Make him stop teasing me!"

Allie hung up the phone, still in a daze. "Tell him I said to let you in, or I'm coming up there," she said in a distant voice, not looking in her child's direction.

She stood up slowly and climbed the stairs toward the bathroom door. Banging on it loudly, she yelled at Pat to let his sister in, then went into her bedroom, shut the door and locked it. Without thinking about it, she climbed into the unmade bed, and pulled the covers up around her. What was happening to her family? Sobs finally broke through, choking her as her mind careened from one issue to the next. But there was no time to cry now. Soon she would have to clean up the kitchen, help her children finish their homework, make dinner and lunches for the next day, lay out school clothes, study her own homework, and press something for herself to wear to work. And then there was the thing to do that she dreaded most. Call Ginny.

Inexpensive champagne flowed freely into plastic cups as the staff of Harrison Realty toasted the closing of the Caldwell deal. The selling of the house, settling at 1.1 million, meant the pressure was off, and a six percent commission would cover everyone's paycheck until the economy recovered and people started buying middle-income housing again. For Ginny, the victory wasn't as sweet as she had thought it might be. Too many things about this deal bothered her. Somehow, she felt her integrity had been challenged, and she wasn't comfortable with the thought.

Settlement had been a nightmare, with Richard Caldwell making last minute demands that she'd had to smooth over with the seller. At one point she had wanted to reach across the conference table, grab him by his expensive tie and strangle him. But those impulses had been stopped each time she saw the look of fear on his wife's face. Nothing except instinct told her Joan Caldwell was being abused, but she couldn't shake the thought. It stayed with her like a fever, draining her enthusiasm and making her shiver with alarm. It kept her from enjoying this celebration. She tried to smile at all the right times, to gracefully accept congratulations from her staff. Nothing worked. Joan Caldwell's pleading eyes during the last negotiation haunted her. The woman seemed to be saying, *Please don't anger him. I'll pay for it later.*

What was she going to do? What could she do? She had wanted to grab Joan by the arm, drag her from the table and urge her to get away. She had wanted to tell her that nothing, not even security, was worth living that nightmare . . . that the house she was buying would only become her prison. But she hadn't, and now guilty feelings washed through her.

"Ginny, your sister's on the phone. When I told her about the party she said it was important, that she had been trying to reach you at home." Her assistant took the tray of plastic wine glasses from her and nodded toward the back offices. "She sounded worried."

"Was it Allie or Nan?"

"Sorry," Carol said, placing the tray on a desk. "It's Allie. I don't think I've ever spoken to your other sister."

Tired, more tired than anyone not yet forty should feel, Ginny answered, "Okay, I'll take it in my office. See if you can wrap this thing up in the next half hour."

"Don't worry. When the booze runs out, so will they."

Forcing a smile, Ginny nodded and turned to walk away from the noise and what felt like a hollow celebration.

She could tell from the sound of her sister's voice that something was wrong. Closing the door of her office, Ginny moved around the corner of her desk and sat down, trying to absorb what Allie said.

"Now slow down, Al. You're not making sense."

"Ginny, I don't really know what's going on. But she's checked herself into Hanson House to save her job, or something. It's all too incredible to take in. Dave and I were out on the deck having a discussion . . . well, an argument. Pat ran in and said Nan was on the phone. She only had five minutes to talk, but told me that her boss had found out she was using cocaine—"

"What? What are you talking about?"

"And he threatened to fire her if she didn't seek help. Ginny, what are we going to do? Why didn't she come to us first?"

Ginny felt her body go numb. "Cocaine? A hospital? Nan?"

"Yes," Allie blurted out, sounding near tears. "Our sister is in a rehab facility, and we didn't even know that she was depressed, or . . . or even had a problem! This is the kind of thing that you only hear about on the talk shows. But when it happens in your own family . . ."

As her sister's voice dissolved into sobs, Ginny searched her mind for a solution to the twofold problem before her. First she had to get Allie to calm down so that they could figure out what to do next, then they had to somehow figure out what that was.

"Allie, honey, don't cry. Listen, we have to be strong for Nan and come up with a way to help her. If we both get hysterical, then what good will we be to her?"

"I know, I know," Allie sniffled. "But I love her so much, and she's our baby sister."

"She's also a grown woman," Ginny interjected a little more harshly than intended.

"Look, I know you and Nan have had *your* differences, but now's not the time, Ginny. She's *our* sister!"

Slightly taken back by the rarely authoritative tone in Allie's voice, Ginny fell silent for a moment. It wasn't that she wasn't worried about Nan, or that she didn't love her, but in truth, she was sick of the family always running to Nan's rescue to bail her out of a mess. As she thought about it more, the feeling of worry began to transform into resentment. Why was it that everyone always forgave and covered up for the infamous Nan Sullivan? Why was she always able to do the unspeakable, and yet family and friends just passed off these transgressions as Nan's style? It was appalling. She'd lived in her own personal hell, her marriage, for six years and no one had come to her rescue.

Immediately ashamed, Ginny asked, "What are we going to do?"

"I've already called over there and visiting hours are twice daily. Neither one of us can go tomorrow during the day, and they said she'd be in testing tomorrow anyway. So the best we can do is get over there tomorrow night. I'll pick you up at six-thirty after work, and we'll ride over together. Okay?"

Still stunned, Ginny murmured, "That's fine. God, Allie. How could this have happened? Does Robert know?"

"No, I don't think so. She said they only let her make one call, and she called me. It sounds like a jail. God, I don't know what to do. What do you think Nan would want?"

"She probably doesn't want him to know."

"But he is still her husband. Maybe this had something to do with the split."

"Listen, Allie, why don't we leave it till tomorrow after we talk to her?"

"I just don't know. Poor Nan. She's had enough to deal

with. Her marriage breaking up and now this. I just don't want to cause her any more problems, but I don't want to avoid helping her if we can in some way."

The old resentment refueled itself as Ginny listened to Allie's words. "Look, nobody forced her to use cocaine. Everything that's happened to Nan has happened because of her own choices. So let's not go in there with—"

"Stop it," Allie yelled, cutting her off angrily. "For once, can't you stop being so self righteous and have a little pity for your sister? It's gone far enough between you two."

Ginny sighed with exasperation. "This is part of her problem, Allie. She takes no responsibility for what she does to herself, or to others. It's always somebody else's fault. And you aid and abet her in all of her trials and tribulations."

"Aid and abet her?"

"Yes, Allie. You're the one in the social services. Haven't you ever heard of co-dependency? Well, I refuse to support her in this escapade. She was snorting coke at work!"

"This isn't an escapade, Ginny. Our sister is addicted to cocaine."

"Correct. And I'll help her kick the habit by following whatever the doctors prescribe as treatment. But allow her to blame everybody around her for her troubles, or allow her to wallow in self pity? No. I won't do that."

"Well, I can see who will be the one once again to have to step in and help out. You never did, not since we all grew up, and I don't see why I even expected you to do any differently now."

"Hold it, Allie. I'm always there to support everybody

in this family. Just because I don't condone what goes on doesn't mean I won't help or don't care."

"When did you get so cold? You weren't like this as a kid. Sometimes people need more than just your money, Ginny. Try a little warmth and compassion. That's what Nan needs now."

Ginny was speechless. Allie's accusation cut to the quick, and she felt tears of rage and hurt filling her eyes. "I have given more than you'll ever know, Allie. So don't you dare judge me! Nan's not the only one who's had problems."

"I can see this is going nowhere. Look, I'll be over at six-thirty. We'll talk about it on the way to the hospital, and hopefully you'll have found a little compassion in your heart before we have to face Nan."

She couldn't even dignify the comment, for fear that her voice would give way to sobs of anger. All Ginny could do was to whisper, "Fine," and hang up. Why did some people get away with murder while others had to put up with their lies, dalliances, and stupidity? Why was it so wrong to call a person on their game when it was finally revealed? Did that make one self righteous, or mean? Ginny had lived a life of lies and secrecy, and she refused to go back. Not now. Not any more.

Her hands were shaking as she tried to gather up her files and shove them into her purse. Allie was the one who sounded self righteous, not her. Yet, if she truly believed that, then why was it always so hard to stand up for that belief? It seemed like she was being punished by Allie for speaking the truth about Nan. Obviously Allie viewed her as an ice queen, and poor, sweet, baby sister Nan, as the victim. Neither one of her sisters knew what it really was to be victimized, to have one's personal power stripped from her. Ginny found it impossible to tolerate their false sense of powerlessness. Rage dried her tears and gave her the momentum to stand.

She had to get out of there. The celebration, as always, was over much too soon, but she didn't care. Unlike her sisters, she was a realist, and had accepted long ago that life just wasn't fair.

Propped up in the narrow twin bed, Nan ignored the stack of papers in her hand and stared at the dull, green, undecorated wall in front of her. After bolting from the screening of *Clean and Sober*, she had gone straight to her room in an effort to escape the din of fellow inmates who hung about wanting to socialize. Disbelief engulfed her as she glanced at the half-inch thick stack of rules and regulations for being a member of this nut house. How the hell had this happened? What she had thought was going to be a month long sabbatical of rest and relaxation was turning into a nightmare.

Some of the patients had a medicated dazed stare that seemed to look right through her, while others appeared menacing and aggressive. They frightened her, but perhaps the ones that scared her the most were those who looked perfectly normal. What was their story? She didn't want to know.

Deciding she had made a mistake, she planned to spend the night, then she would sign herself out tomorrow. Simple. She wasn't going to put herself through this hell. Not even for her career. She would just have to start again.

She had thought a place this exclusive would be more

like a spa. But Hanson House was nothing more than a private jail. Every moment was filled with some asinine activity. Group therapy, movies, reading, private therapy sessions, homework, meals, talks . . . and she hadn't even begun the program! Her arms ached from the blood work that she had undergone earlier in the day and, now, all she could do was think about tomorrow, when she would be free.

Turning her head, she looked at the vacant bed across from her. She hadn't known she would have to share a room when she signed in. She still hadn't even met her roommate, but she hoped that she'd get one of the passive, quiet, medicated zombies that she'd seen patrolling the halls, and not a chatty, intrusive zealot on a recovery quest. She didn't feel like discussing mutual dependencies and shitty childhood memories. Her sole objective had been to go along with the program, appease Joe Carter and the hospital staff, fake it till she made it, then get the hell out.

Nan allowed her line of vision to peruse the barren room once again. There was no television, except in the large social room, nor was there anything to read but a bunch of damned recovery manuals and books. At least there was a bouquet of flowers on the dresser. Unfortunately, they weren't for her, but they did brighten the room a little.

When the door opened, she almost jumped out of her skin. She still couldn't get used to the idea of sleeping in a foreign place with virtually no privacy. Nan cautiously surveyed the young woman who stood in the doorway of her dorm room. She almost groaned when she saw how young her roomie appeared to be. She'd be sharing the tiny place with a teenager! Christ.

Without waiting for her permission, the young girl entered the room and flopped down on the bed, dropping a duffel bag of clothes on the floor. Her dark brown face was serious, and her eyes seemed wary.

"The name's Camille. I don't steal. My parents have money. Oh, and I won't cut your throat in your sleep either. If you want a white roommate, say so now, and you can move out. I've been here before and know the drill."

Nan was stunned, yet curious. Never before had anyone sized her up so quickly and been so brutally honest. There was something about this young woman that reminded her of her own youth. She was direct, forceful, and obviously didn't like to play games.

"I've paid for the room, and will be gone tomorrow," Nan said, trying to remain calm.

"Yeah, well, that's what you think," Camille answered, not looking at her as she sorted through her clothes. "Your first day, huh?"

"Yes. It's my first day, and my last day," Nan muttered in a worried voice, but not wanting to give in to her fears.

"You may be gone soon, but at least not for seventy-two hours."

Nan stared at the young woman sitting yoga style across from her. "What do you mean, not for seventy-two hours?"

The young girl smiled but didn't look up. "Haven't read your homework, huh? House rules. Can't go nowhere for three days. So make the best of it and chill out."

Nan was standing now. "I'll see about this!" she nearly

yelled, her voice escalating beyond her control. "I'm not in prison, so I'll leave when I want to."

"Well, knock yourself out," Camille said in a blasé tone. "But I've known some people with a lot more money than you've obviously got, with bigger titles, who couldn't get out. Some senator's kids, a mayor's wife. *Pulleeese,* give it a rest."

Nan began to pace and her mind reeled with this new information. "How do you know who I am? And how do you know what my connections are?"

For the first time since she began unpacking, Camille glanced up. Offering Nan a sigh of indifference, she looked her straight in the eyes. "You don't think my father would let me room with some lowlife, do you? He's connected, and got a brief rundown on who you are, why you were here. A cokehead. But not violent. That's the only way I agreed to come back to this joint in the first place. I wasn't about to room with some nut. I've done that before. A burnt-out executive I can deal with. But, truthfully, I didn't have to ask Daddy dearest. I could've talked to one of the inmates. You gotta have your own network to function around here, you know? Now I suggest you cool out, or they'll put you down with elephant tranquilizer—thorazine."

A mixture of fury, embarrassment, and defiance engulfed Nan as she stood looking at this teenager who dissected her life so nonchalantly. She'd sue this fucking hospital for releasing her chart to a stranger! She'd sue the state! Thorazine? She was outta here.

Grabbing her purse from the top of a dresser, Nan rushed down the hall toward the nurses' station. She wasn't about to let them perform a routine lobotomy on her without a fight. To hell with tomorrow—she was leaving tonight!

Thirty-five minutes later, Nan walked back into her room, shell-shocked from her encounter with Nurse Rachett. None of her negotiating skills or bullying tactics worked. They had obviously seen and heard it all in here, and when they showed her the entrance paperwork in black and white, she knew she was trapped. She should have paid more attention when she signed that damned form upon admittance. She had to wait three days to get out. She felt as though she were a hostage on some alien planet where the mother ship forgot to beam her aboard.

Camille glanced up from her lotus position on the bed and smiled with triumph. "Like I said, chill out, girlfriend. You'll get used to it."

For the first time in years a tiny prayer formed in her mind. God help her, for she had descended straight into hell.

Chapter 12

Allie turned her car into her sister's driveway and blew the horn twice. She was not looking forward to the inevitable confrontation with Ginny, and was sure that the sooner they got to the hospital the better. It had been impossible to ignore on the phone the deep resentment that broke through Ginny's normal surface calm, and now all she could pray for was that her sister had collected herself during the night. Somehow, they had to make the visit to see Nan as uneventful and as pleasant as possible.

When she saw Ginny's blonde figure at the doorway, she could tell from the look on her sister's face and the rigidness of her carriage that nothing had been forgotten and a probable exchange of words would ensue. Bracing herself, Allie leaned over and unlocked the passenger side of the car and waited for Ginny to hop in. Why did it feel like she was fighting with everyone near and dear to her? First Dave, now Ginny. Why was all this happening?

"Ready?" she said in a stern voice, hoping to ward off a verbal assault before it began.

"No," Ginny said tersely, settling herself and pulling on

the seatbelt. "How can anyone be ready to visit a sister in . . . in a rehabilitation facility?"

Allie refused to respond, and simply put the car into gear to begin the long drive to Hanson House.

"What did Dave say?"

Again, Allie didn't respond immediately. It was the one question that she'd hoped Ginny wouldn't ask. How could she tell her sister that she and Dave were barely speaking after their earlier confrontation, and that he'd been less than supportive when she told him about Nan?

"He's worried like the two of us are," she finally said, hoping that her cryptic response would be enough. She wasn't about to repeat the nasty things Dave said about Nan. It would only reinforce Ginny's position.

"Well, I don't know if you meant that sarcastically, but I am worried," Ginny returned, sounding annoyed. "It's just that ever since she was little, Nan has always gotten herself in trouble and everyone has always pulled her butt out of the fire. This time, she'll have to deal with the consequences of her own actions."

Feeling the old anger resurface, Allie snapped back, "Well, at least we can be supportive. No—we *have* to be supportive."

"Being supportive is one thing, Allie. Allowing her to continue this destructive behavior is another."

Allie could see they weren't going to get anywhere like this and abruptly changed the subject. "I brought a care package with some toiletries, a couple of books, just a few things that she might not have thought about when she checked in." Pulling onto the interstate she shook her head. "I can't believe that a member of our family needs to be in a place like that."

She could feel the tension in the air again rise as Ginny turned in her seat.

"Think about our childhood. We had two abusive, alcoholic parents . . . After our father left, our mother ran men in and out of that house until we could get out. The fact that any of us is a functioning, responsible adult is a minor miracle."

"Why do you choose now to go back to our childhood?"

"Just because I don't like to talk about it, or wallow in it as an excuse, doesn't mean that I'm not aware of what went on. Face it—we were a dysfunctional family."

Allie let out a long sigh of exasperation. "Every family has its problems, Gin."

"The way any of us was brought up is dysfunctional by definition. I'm just saying that Nan's problems go back a lot farther than this episode with cocaine."

"She hasn't been a drug addict all of her life. Drugs never had anything to do with our family!" She was appalled by Ginny's reference and couldn't let her concepts go unchallenged.

"Right again, Al. The drug of choice in our family was alcohol. Look, you've been covering this stuff up since we were little. Nan would do something totally off the wall, and everybody would rush in, fix her problem, then sweep the event under the rug. Well, now she's a big girl, and her scrapes are more serious. This time wall-to-wall carpeting won't cover it up. She is caught, and she'll have to deal with it. Maybe if she'd been found out a long time ago, her problems wouldn't have gone this far." Ginny turned away and stared out of the window.

Allie concentrated on her driving. There was nothing to say. She wondered what had gone wrong? What had happened to Ginny that made her unable to give an inch in this situation? She was a woman with a heart of gold to everyone except her younger sister. All Allie could do was silently pray that it wouldn't get ugly at the hospital. After all, this was family.

As they pulled into the hospital parking lot, Allie made one last attempt to mollify her sister. "Listen, Gin, Nan is our sister and she's in trouble. I don't care why she's done this, but I do know that I love her. And she needs us."

Ginny stared back at her with an unfaltering gaze. "Allie, I love her too. More than you'll probably ever understand. I love her enough to make her face herself this time, because I know what damage lying can do. Trust me."

Nan was seated in the visitor's lounge, staring at the unbreakable, wired-glass security doors that led to the outside world. It had been one hell of a day, and she just hoped that she could get through the visit with Allie. She felt like she had a really bad case of the flu. Her joints ached, her head pounded, her eyes felt scratchy, and she was nauseated, yet she couldn't sleep. She felt jittery, and her entire being craved the stuff she had hidden away in her apartment. It was impossible to believe that she had to feel like this for two more days before she could get out and get relief.

A man in a bathrobe startled her as he sat down on the

couch next to her. She recognized him from one of the therapy groups she had attended earlier—the ones where she'd silently sat refusing to participate. Moving away from him to put more physical distance between them on the sofa, Nan turned her head slowly in his direction, and bored through him with her eyes, issuing a penetrating stare that dared him to speak.

But typical crazy person that he was, the man was oblivious to the death ray that she'd given him, and began to chatter incessantly about some nonsensical topic. She thought she would gag, or at least slap the fool. Crossing her arms before her tightly, she fought the temptation to strike the man.

". . . If you don't know how to play, I can teach you," he went on, still ignoring her expression.

"I said, I don't play cards. Not gin rummy, not bridge, not anything. Especially not now," she nearly hissed, her voice escalating beyond her control as she stood.

"First day, huh? Yeah, the first forty-eight to seventy-two are rough when you're trying to get that monkey off your back. But it does get better. Cards will help take your mind off how miserable you feel."

"Go to hell. I've got one more day of this shit then I'm outta here. I'm signing myself out day after tomorrow. I don't belong here. I'm not an addict."

The man simply shook his head and smiled at her as he stood up, stoking her fury to fever pitch. "Yeah, that's what everybody says. If you didn't have a problem, you wouldn't be here. So let's cut the bullshit. Cards, a walk, scrabble, name your poison. That's the only thing you're allowed to get you through the DT's."

Drawing herself up stiffly, she spun on her intruder. "I'm not going through withdrawal. I'm just sick of being in here with crazies. It's like *One Flew Over The Cuckoo's Nest*. One sane person amongst this crowd would make anybody freak out. So why don't you go find a fellow in-mate and get off my back!"

"Nan?"

Thinking things couldn't get worse, she jerked around at the sound of her sister's voice, only to be confronted with both Allie *and* Ginny. If she didn't feel so rotten, she would have laughed out loud. Things had definitely taken a turn in the southern direction. Ginny was there.

Allie immediately enveloped her in a tight hug. "Are you okay, Nan? I'm so sorry. What can I do?"

Nan suppressed the urge to scream. Her sister, Mother Earth, had obviously rounded up the troops to save her and it was sickening. What the hell did Allie have to be sorry for? She had a plan. It was all a front, and she'd be signing herself out in a couple of days. Allie looked like she was about to cry, and had obviously brought the Chief Inquisitor along for support. It was definitely a mistake to have called her.

Pulling on one of her familiar masks, Nan smiled. "I told you not to worry. I'm out of here in a day or so, and that should satisfy Joe Carter. No problem."

"*No problem*? Upsetting Allie like this, sending the family into a panic is no problem? This is too much. How do you just sign yourself in one day, then get out the next?" Ginny said, sounding thoroughly annoyed.

"Well, hello to you too, sister dear," Nan answered in a

flippant tone that had been designed through the years to get under Ginny's skin.

Allie jumped in between them. "Why don't we all find a place and sit down so we can talk?"

Grudgingly, they followed Allie over to a vacant seating area and sat down. Nan smiled triumphantly at Ginny from her vantage point across the conversational area. Big sister Allie was good for something.

Filling in the awkward silence, Allie leaned closer and spoke in a confidential tone. "Nan, we brought you books and toiletries to make you feel better, but they took them away from us at the door. I couldn't believe it. Why would they do that?"

Nan shook her head in disgust. "Al, I told you this was like a private prison. They take perfume because it has alcohol in it and they're afraid the inmates might drink it. And they don't want you reading anything that isn't related to recovery. You should see the homework they give you."

"Allie told me about what happened at your firm, and I think it took a lot of courage to check yourself in." Ginny said. "But, let's get back to the issue at hand. It's not toiletries and books. What did the doctors say about checking yourself out so soon?" Ginny asked, returning the conversation to its original, unpleasant track.

Nan leveled her older sister with a glare. "I don't give a damn what they say. I'm checking out as soon as humanly possible."

"You've got a serious problem here, and this is one thing you can't run from, Nan," Ginny answered back sternly, not flinching from her glare. "If you check yourself out of here, it won't do you any good. You can't keep running from yourself or your problems, and we are not about to keep cleaning up behind you. So it's time to deal with it. Right here and right now."

"Ginny, will you give her a break? Can't you see that she's confused and in pain?" Allie blurted out, trying to avoid the unavoidable.

"No, I can't give her a break, Allie. That's the root of the problem here," Ginny said, her voice rising. Turning her focus to Nan, she cut through her with a scowl of her own. "Nan, you're my sister, and I love you. But I'm tired of your facades, your lies, your games. Either you clean yourself up, or you don't. It's your life. I'll support you in an earnest effort, but not in a game."

"Ginny, let it rest," Allie cut in. "We have to—"

"We have to what?" Ginny demanded, interrupting her. "Go on pretending that there's nothing wrong here? This isn't Nan getting caught smoking a cigarette in the girls' room by a nun! This is serious!"

"That's right, Ginny. We *all* have to stop pretending, don't we?" Nan interjected, her expression narrowing to a threatening glare. What would the prim and proper Virginia Harrison say if she just blurted out that she knew her husband had been an adulterer and a wife beater? They'd probably have to shoot Ginny up with 500mg of Thorazine and put her in a straitjacket. Well, at least they were in the right place for it. The thought formed a smile on her face. "Well, Gin, now it's true that we all have our little secrets. So I'll assume that mine is safe with my sisters."

It was the best hand of poker she had played in weeks,

and with no small measure of satisfaction she watched Ginny retreat. Damn right. She knew how to defend herself. That's the one thing Ginny never learned. Too bad. She should know better than to corner a trapped animal.

Turning her attention to Allie, she almost shook her head in pity. Her poor older sister was twisting her hands nervously and looked near tears. Allie was the gentle one and, for an instant, she almost felt sorry that she'd been dragged into this unnecessarily. But Allie was also a glutton for punishment who didn't know how to set limits. It almost served her right that everybody used her for a doormat. Maybe she'd learn one day. For now, she had her own problems to contend with, and Allie would have to figure out hers on her own.

The three sisters sat without speaking, allowing the intense quiet to engulf them. As expected, Allie finally broke the standoff and began to talk in a conciliatory tone.

"Look, we all love you, Nan," she said, sending a fierce look in Ginny's direction before continuing. "If there is anything we can do to help, you have but to ask. That's why we came. To let you know that."

Ginny sat silently, staring back in her direction. Allie looked from one sister to the other nervously, as though hoping for a truce. Nan pushed back in her chair and folded her arms over her chest.

"Does Robert know about this?" Ginny finally said in a voice that was all too calm.

Damn it. Maybe the good Virginia Harrison had learned to protect herself. She was obviously going for the jugular now.

"No," Nan responded abruptly, trying to sound confident to ward off the attack. "There's no reason for him to know."

Ginny sat forward in her chair, taking what appeared to be an aggressive posture. "Maybe he needs to know."

"Don't even think about it," Nan shot back.

"Why not?" Allie interjected in an annoyingly compassionate voice. "Maybe this is what really caused your problems. Maybe if he knew that you were seeking help, that you really—"

"I said no!" She could not believe how stupid her older sister could be at times. "Have you lost your mind? We didn't have an Ozzie and Harriet relationship like you and Dave pretend to have. So give it a rest, and stay out of my disaster that was a marriage."

She hadn't meant to yell at Allie, or go for her Achilles heel, but she could tell by the helpful glint in her sister's eyes that she'd tell Robert if her wishes weren't made crystal clear. Glaring at Ginny for bringing up the unthinkable, Nan rose to her feet. This family therapy session was over. She'd had enough. Ginny had made her point. Allie had done her good deed for the day. She had gone through her obligatory family ordeal. Enough was enough.

"Well, listen," Nan said in a weary voice. "I do appreciate you coming up here to see me, like I said, I'll be home soon. It'll all work out." Turning to her older sister who still registered the hurt on her face from the earlier comment, she gave her a hug. "Al, I'm sorry. I'm just a little out of sorts in here. I'll be back to my old self soon, you'll see. How about if I meet you in Center City for lunch and you can tell me all about your new job?"

Allie returned a tearful smile. "I'd like that, Nan," she murmured, hugging her back.

Looking over Allie's shoulder, she stared at Ginny. "You take care of yourself, Gin. Thanks for riding up here with Allie." It was an intentional dig, one designed to pass through Allie's radar undetected, but to make a point with Ginny.

"You too," Ginny said quietly. "I hope you take this time to do some soul searching."

She refused to be baited in again. Her sisters were too close to leaving to start up at this point. But unable to let the return salvo go totally unchallenged, she sent a small one back in Ginny's direction. "You too, Sis. We've all got a lot to think about."

Walking them to the locked doors that led to freedom, Nan knew she was almost rid of her sisters. Only a few feet more and the knot in her stomach would ease. They'd be on the interstate, and she could go back to her room and relax—as long as her militant teenage roommate wasn't around. Yet, as they passed the nurses station she heard a voice that made her blood turn cold. Coming down the hall in her direction was her assigned therapist.

"Nan, I'm glad I caught you and your family." The small, gray haired woman extended her hand in Allie's direction first. "I'm Doctor Alberts. Mary. Call me Mary. I'm Nan's therapist. As she's probably told you, Nan is determined to check out early. We have a policy here that requires at least one family therapy session prior to a patient's release." Returning her focus to Nan, she continued. "How is tomorrow night at about six-thirty?"

"Family therapy?" Nan repeated, stunned. "Look, we

just had a session in the visiting area, and you missed it. It wasn't fun. I'm out of here the day after tomorrow."

Seeming nonplussed, Dr. Alberts spoke calmly, but with authority. "If you want to check yourself out before the end of the month, we need to set up a session. Since you're leaving in two days, then the only time is the evening before your scheduled release. I thought an evening would be better, since I assume that your family members are working."

Resentment curdled in Nan's stomach as she stood glaring at her therapist.

"That would be fine for me, Nan. It's no problem at all, if you think it would help." Leave it to Allie to pipe up.

Ginny stood by silently. Her intent was implicit. She was going to make her ask her to come. What a bitch.

Turning to Ginny, Nan finally gave in. "Would you come so I can get the hell out of here?"

Ginny didn't move a muscle and appeared to be deciding her fate. She hated the way her sister just let her twist on the vine, and how she had to wait for Ms. High Society to make up her mind.

"I'll come Nan. But only if you take the session seriously."

Without waiting for the doctor's reply, Nan turned away from the small group and blurted out angrily, "Good. Satisfied? Now pull together my damned paperwork, so there's no last-minute hassle when I check out of this joint."

She had to get away from them. All of them.

*   *   *

When Evan had died and she'd moved into this house, Ginny found that it wasn't frightening to sleep alone. She had welcomed it. The fears she had harbored in her marriage were far stronger than any she might face from a stranger. But she had felt unloved, unwanted. There was a need inside of her to be held in a secure embrace. Maybe it was childish, but she had improvised. Six pillows were on her queen size bed and every night she performed a loving ritual. She used them to form a cocoon of softness around her. Sometimes, it was just relaxing to lie in bed with the stress relieved from all the pressure points on her body. At other times, she pretended that it was a man, a lover, someone who cherished her . . . someone who knew all the ugly secrets of her past and loved her anyway. If she were lying on her side, then the pillow behind her was the chest of a man, a good man, a man of character, someone who valued her. She had a vivid imagination, yet she couldn't place a face on this person. Perhaps because he didn't exist.

Tonight she would give almost anything to make it real, to have someone she could talk to about the terrible confusion that was keeping her from sleep. What did Nan mean when she said it was time for all of them to stop pretending? There was something almost frightening in her sister's expression, as if she knew all about Evan. She couldn't! No one knew. And, if she somehow did, why hadn't she ever said anything before?

She thought about Nan and Evan. At family gatherings, usually at Allie's house, the two of them had been friendly. Evan seemed to like Nan's aggressive attitude toward life, and he had allowed his sister-in-law to say things to him that he would have beaten his wife for even whispering. Evan never would have told anyone, especially her sister, that he was terrorizing her. Then why did she have this horrible feeling that Nan knew? Could that be why Nan disliked her so? Because she despised weakness, just like Evan?

Ginny turned in bed as her stomach clenched with fear. It could not be unraveling now. She had spent too many years protecting herself for it to all fall apart. She wouldn't let it. She would go to this family therapy session and keep her barriers intact.

What exactly was Nan implying? Did she know about Evan? How could she do this, how could she talk about the past? And why now, after all these years?

Allie sat quietly in her bedroom chair and stared out of the window. Kicking off her slippers, she allowed her feet to feel the soft pile of the rug beneath her feet. What was happening to her family and the life she fought so hard to control? She had once thought that if she didn't talk about the ugliness, didn't acknowledge the pain, then perhaps by some miracle it would go away. Now she was being forced to face it, confront it, before a professional. More importantly, she had to open up the old wounds in front of her sisters who wouldn't allow her to put pretty wrapping paper on it. She didn't want to go back. She didn't want to remember her childhood. It was over. Finished. What was the point of dragging up that mess?

She had opened the lid of Pandora's Box in Washington, and now she was living with the results. She far preferred pretending because it served its purpose. When she was young, she had pretended to be an adult while her mother pretended to be a teenager. She took on the role of responsible caretaker for her sisters. She had done the cleaning, saw that they had school clothes to wear. She always made sure that there was more than liquor in the house to consume and, even if it was just peanut butter sandwiches, she saw that her sisters ate. On more than one occasion, she had taken the money from her mother's purse and walked down to the gas and electric company to pay part of the bill, enough to keep the lights and heat on. When Nan got in trouble in school, she was the one to talk to the nuns. Allie knew she had taken on this role of protector for most of her life, and now she didn't know anything else. The possibility that she had done something wrong in raising two sisters who were not much younger than herself gnawed at her.

She had also been pretending when she'd married Dave. He was a good provider, didn't drink, didn't hit her like the men in her mother's life, and he loved his children. Before Ginny made her go to Washington, that was enough. She had been happy in her world of make-believe. She had wanted so much to live a normal life, like the ones she had seen played out on television. As a young girl, she had clung to those T.V. families. She envied their peace and tranquility—their wonderful marriages with happy, healthy, children whose problems were resolved within a half hour.

Deep within her soul she had always known there had to be something better, and she had tried hard to make that happen for her family. Nan was right. She was playing at

Ozzie and Harriet. She wanted a life that was moderate, normal and fulfilling.

Staring out at the darkness, Allie stopped mid-thought. Her life with Dave wasn't idyllic or fulfilling any longer. She needed something more. Something that made her feel special and valued. Ever since her trip to Washington, she'd prayed to God that she wasn't becoming like her mother—a dissatisfied woman who sacrificed even her children in search of selfish fulfillment. She had promised herself that she would never let her own needs get in the way of taking care of her family, or jeopardize their happiness. But, recently, she had begun to wonder if anyone would ever care about her that unconditionally. Would anyone ever consider her desires, her need to feel loved?

In the television shows of her youth, the wives didn't have to ask for anyone to consider them. Because those women were wholesome, good, kind, and fair, the husbands automatically respected and cherished them. Their children appreciated every little act of kindness bestowed upon them by their good mothers, and thanked them often. While she never expected perfect children, or a perfect husband, at the core of her she had correlated being good with being rewarded by love and appreciation. Why was that so wrong? What was so unfair about asking for her turn?

Allie looked up when she heard Dave enter the room. He had taken a shower, and wore only his robe. There was a time when just the sight of him standing before her damp and nearly naked would make her muscles tighten with anticipation. Now they tensed with worry and leftover resentment. He didn't even look at her as he pulled on his pajama pants and dropped his robe on the floor beside the bed. She didn't move or speak for a moment. She needed time to form the words to make him understand without creating another explosion.

Finding her voice, she spoke to him calmly. "Dave, listen. We have to go to a family therapy session tomorrow night with Nan. It's part of the recovery program, and her therapist said that we have to do this in order for her to get released."

Dave still didn't look at her. He simply turned over in bed and turned off the lamp that stood on the night table beside him. "Figures. Your family . . . I just hope you don't expect me to go to the crazy house with you."

Allie stilled the rage inside of her. "No. You don't have to go. Dr. Alberts only wants to see Ginny and me, but that means I'll be out late again tomorrow night. Our appointment is for six-thirty, and I plan to pick up Ginny right after work so we can drive over together."

"Oh, that's just great. Your sister gets her ass in a sling and the rest of us have to pay for it. Isn't that typical. What if I had something to do tomorrow night? Christ. Another night of babysitting."

She refused to dignify his response. Tension crept up her spine and congealed into the beginnings of a headache. At that moment, she wanted to go over to the bed and rip the soft down comforter from him. She wanted to scream, and yell, and stomp her feet, or to even slap his face. Emotions swept through her like a torrent and, for the first time in her life, she frightened herself. Sitting in the dark, Allie allowed the tears to stream down her face without wiping them away. She would not go down that path. She would not become an out-of-control woman like her mother, who screamed and yelled and cursed.

Never. Not even Dave Barbera could take her there.

Matt's thumb felt sore from holding down the button on the remote control. What the hell was wrong with him tonight? Normally he could lose himself in a game, but even ESPN was disappointing him by showing bungee jumping. Now that was an intelligent sport. As he watched some free spirit throw himself from a bridge, Matt felt his stomach muscles tighten involuntarily . . . just like they did every time he thought of Ginny Harrison. And, by damn, he was doing that often. Often? She was taking over his thoughts day *and* night. He couldn't stop thinking about her, wondering what she was doing, who she was with . . . It was scary, like he was becoming obsessed. Or possessed. Sometimes he wanted to be with her so bad that his body actually ached for her presence. He could hear her voice saying his name, as if taking hold of his mind. Then he wanted to call her again to make sure she wasn't backing out of their date. How many times had he picked up the phone tonight, only to quickly replace it? Damn! It reminded him of those old vampire movies he had seen as a kid where the bitten victim is helpless to resist the supernatural pull. And he hadn't even been bitten yet! Hell, they really hadn't even kissed! So why did he want to rush over to her house, yank his shirt collar to the side, and willingly expose his neck?

What *was* it with this woman that messed him up so much? Something about her eyes . . . There was a story reflected in them, and he felt as if he had just started to read a mesmerizing book that he simply couldn't put down. He was fascinated, intrigued, and captivated. The trouble was he couldn't even peek at the ending to see how it all turned out.

Glancing at the clock, he again picked up the cordless phone. It was twelve thirty-seven.

Nah . . . it was too late.

Chapter 13

Ginny gripped the formica kitchen counter with determination and stared at the remnant crumbs from the dry toast she had forced down with tea. She had already decided that the horrible events from the evening before would not enter her new day. Not for one moment would she allow her mind to rake back through Nan's situation or Allie's overzealous, misdirected protection. It was settled. She had no family who she could confide in, no one who would clean up her life, and she would have to rely on herself. That's the way it had always been. That was all there was to this whole ugly world.

Cupping her hand at the counter's edge, she hurriedly swiped at the mess, gathering up the hard, browned particles of toast. Crumbs. That's all she ever got in her relationships. The leftovers, the dregs . . . and when would that change?

Even Matt Lewellyn probably had a long, sordid story that she didn't want to hear. But how did he suddenly enter her brain? Especially now? It was obvious that she was losing it. Was she so depressed and lonely that her mind could take this foolish turn in the face of such total disaster?

Impatient with herself, Ginny took a final swig of tea, draining the cup, and dumped a handful of crumbs into the trash. Quickening her pace, she slipped on her pumps and unplugged the toaster. She'd get into the office, manage her business, and lose herself in her work. There was plenty to do that required her full attention. At the firm she was needed. There she was in control. She had built a safe haven in that space where nothing could penetrate her being.

Although the sound of the phone momentarily jolted her from her thoughts, Ginny had already decided not to answer as she continued to prepare to leave the house. No. She'd just wait for the message to play, then ignore Allie's voice until she hung up. Simple. But there was no way that she could have been prepared for the deep, familiar male greeting that forced its way through the speaker. Frozen in midstep, Ginny tried to calm herself. In a brief few moments an entire range of emotions swept through her, leaving her almost weak. All at once she was excited, then frightened, then annoyed, but wanted to connect with him, yet unsure of whether or not her voice would betray her. It was terrible, but wonderful, and all too unsettling. He was calling her at home, personalizing their contact even more. What was so urgent that they had to talk outside of their offices? It was clear from his incoming message that he wanted to speak with her, and not about business.

"Hi, Ginny. Sorry I missed you before you left for work. Just wanted to check in with you to see how you were doing . . . I'm rambling aren't I? Well, just wanted to let you know I had to do a few errands, but should be in this afternoon if you want to give me a buzz back. Ahh, well, or maybe I'll try you later. Take care. Oh, yeah. It's Matt."

Was he finally calling in his marker for the Caldwell disaster? Probably. If so, why was she so electrified by the sound of his damned voice? Especially today of all days. Jesus, would this feeling ever end? Would there ever be just a constant predictable calm that prevailed, one that she could count on?

Ginny let out her breath when Matt's message ended. She knew he would probably try her at work next. That would be the logical place for him to contact her now. However, she wouldn't give in to his little game. She'd just change her route and let Carol screen his call. Looking at the massive pen and ink drawing that still leaned against her kitchen wall, Ginny quickly decided that it was high time to drop off the housewarming gift to her client.

If God cared anything about her sanity, Joan Caldwell would be home this morning.

Grudgingly, Nan pulled herself upright and swung her feet over the side of the bed. The initial contact with cold tile flooring jolted her senses, but she refused to give in to the ache that ran through her body. Only twenty-four more hours and she'd be free. No way in the world would she mess up now and give them another reason to keep her incarcerated. Her plan was working perfectly, even though Dr. Alberts had thrown her a curve ball by suggesting a family therapy session. But what the hell? Ginny would be too afraid to challenge her in front of a stranger, and poor Allie would probably be consumed with tears as usual. She would therefore orchestrate the event and strategically manipulate her own release. Everything was a matter of careful negotiation.

Although fatigue had doubled her body weight, Nan finally propelled herself from the edge of the bed to stand. It felt as if all of her blood had suddenly rushed from her head down to the soles of her feet. Immediately, she took a deep breath to stave off the consistent, irritating nausea that plagued her. "Just twenty-four hours," she repeated to herself quietly, summoning the will to wash her face and brush her teeth.

When she finally emerged from the room, it was well after breakfast. The thought of food turned her stomach. All she really wanted was a cup of coffee. Black coffee. A strong one. Espresso would have been heaven. But, like everything else, they didn't provide decent coffee in prison. Muttering to herself in disgust as she slowly strolled down the hall to the ten o'clock group session, she no longer felt threatened by the other inmates. At this point, she felt so rotten and so angry, fear was the last thing on her mind. Hell, if one of them even tried her, it'd be their last mistake, she thought sullenly as she entered the room and took her seat amongst the semicircle of metal folding chairs.

Eventually, more people filled in and found their seats, but Nan kept her gaze cast down to the ugly linoleum floor. That's it—she could count floor tiles while the other poor slobs went on with their incessant rhetoric. Who gave a damn anyway? What did their problems have to do with her? The whole process of unveiling one's deepest, darkest problems before a room full of strangers was ludicrous. It was probably the hospital's way of saving a buck. Instead of giving people real one-on-one counseling, they opted to sling a whole parcel of wackos in a room together and called it treatment. What a scam.

Mentally reviewing her itinerary for the day, she ticked through the schedule as though it were a bothersome laundry list. From ten to eleven she had group therapy. From eleven till noon she had individual counseling. What a crock. From noon until one o'clock she could have lunch. After lunch, there were two hours of additional testing and evaluation to make sure she hadn't gotten any drugs into her system from some source overnight. Art therapy for crazies followed. At three o'clock there was some bullshit workshop on how to live a drug-free existence once you re-entered the world and went back to your job and family. Then at four-thirty, she'd have to endure another short film. At five-fifteen she could eat the Godforsaken crap they called food, and they'd give out more evening reading at the end of dinner in the dining room. Of course they couldn't let you just sit and try to digest the lousy meal!

Nan felt her eyebrows knitting together with indignation, and she smoothed her hands over her forehead, then her cheeks, to ward off the headache that would not go away. Letting out a sigh of exasperation, she thought about the six-thirty family therapy session with Ginny and Allie. Christ. She wouldn't have five minutes to herself before those two descended upon her—all sweetness and light, with misguided beliefs about how to help their dear, sick, addicted sister. It was a nightmare.

"That's the most we've heard from you since you've been here, Nan."

Startled, Nan looked up and scanned the group. She

hadn't been paying attention to a word that had been said, and for a brief moment, she felt like a guilty high-schooler that had been caught daydreaming by one of the nuns.

"I didn't say anything," she answered in a hostile voice, now able to collect herself and focus her attention on Dr. Alberts.

"The sigh said it all," another patient interjected.

Glowering at the young man who had spoken, Nan's mind raced for a cutting reply. "Then I hope it told you to leave me the hell alone. Hey, I'm just here for the duration. I have to come to these stupid sessions to get paroled, then I'm gone. Okay? Satisfied?"

"You're not here to satisfy us, Nan," Dr. Alberts interrupted. "You're here to get better, and part of getting better is getting past the denial that you do indeed have a problem."

Nan refused to dignify the comment. She hated the self assured, smug, clinical tone in the doctor's voice.

"I hate the bitch too, Nan."

Again caught off guard, Nan's eyes searched the semicircle to find where the familiar voice came from. Spotting her roommate, she smiled. At least she had an ally in the group—even though it was an unexpected one.

"You know, these people who've never lived a day in hell think they can tell you all about it from some textbook they read in college. But if they got thrown into the same shit we had to deal with, I'd bet that heifer would be sittin' on a grate in Center City babblin' to herself."

Nan stared at the bold, fearless, young woman who was smiling back at her. It was an odd expression, one where the mouth and face seemed to be sparkling with mischief, but her eyes held an intense, unwavering anger. The com-

bination caused an eerie cognitive dissonace, but Nan
knew the expression well. The sly smirk on the girl's face
spelled triumph and, once again, her roommate had accu-
rately read her thoughts.

Shaking her head yes, Nan let a wider smirk play across
her own face, She loved the way the others sat silently appalled, and the way Dr. Alberts tried to keep from
bristling. Maybe this could be fun. Nodding at her roommate, Nan shrugged her shoulders. "Or at the very least,
she'd be on Prozac."

"Too true, girlfriend," Camille laughed, throwing her
head back and snapping her fingers twice for emphasis.
"Word."

It had happened so quickly but, in that instant, a bond
had been formed. Some unspoken pact, or at least a certain level of respect had been exchanged.

"Do you think she could hold a candle to either one of
us?" Nan asked, gaining defiant courage with her newfound partner.

"Pulleeese, spare me!" Camille shot back, motioning a
high five across the room at Nan who returned it.

"I am not the issue," Dr. Alberts said calmly. Too
calmly. "Your recovery is."

Immediately challenged, Camille took the offensive.
"Look, you white bitch. You don't know shit about me,
okay? So you can get off of the Dr. Freud trip."

Unprepared for the sudden violent exchange, Nan
looked between both combatants nervously. But she knew
this was her time to prove her loyalty to Camille. She
couldn't back down now, and somehow she felt like she
owed the girl a little defense from the rear.

"Why don't you get off of her case, Alberts? She's right. You don't know anything about any of us."

Although still nervous, Nan felt victorious. Somehow it was easier to fight for Camille's position than her own at this moment.

"Well, that's why we're all here, Nan. To understand each other better. To learn about the issues that have contributed to your addiction. It's important to—"

"To stop the bullshit, Doc," Camille sliced in, holding the therapist in a lethal gaze. "What can you tell me? You probably think that I'm some ghetto kid that had a hard time in the projects, so I take drugs. No, wait. Let's see . . . maybe you think that my drug dealer boyfriend, who wears a beeper, got me hooked, like *Boyz In The Hood*? After all, you know those *minorities*. Give me a break."

Nan was speechless. Guilt consumed her and, for a split second, she wasn't sure why. Perhaps it was because that *was* her initial perception of Camille. The person who had come to her defense was bitterly angry about the doctor categorizing her and yet she herself was no better than Dr. Alberts. In fact, she knew she was much worse. As thoughts bombarded Nan, she watched the exchange between the two carefully. Intuition told her to never give away her position, and to remain in Camille's corner. Like any delicate negotiation, she'd just have to play this one out very close to the vest.

"Well, how can anyone know anything about you if you aren't honest about why you're here?"

The condescending tone in Dr. Alberts' voice grated on Nan's frayed nerves. "Maybe she doesn't want to tell you why she's here. Maybe it's none of your godamned business." The retaliatory comment had flown from her mouth before she'd had a chance to develop a strategy. What in God's name was happening!

Camille had folded her arms over her breasts, and Nan was sure that the additional glisten in her roommate's eyes had to be from withheld tears of anger. How many times had she been there herself? The unfair thing about it was that this kid was just a minor, therefore forced to put up with the whims of adults. At least when she broke out of this asylum, she'd be an adult—her own boss making her own rules. Camille wouldn't. She'd still be trapped by somebody else's game until she reached the age of majority, and how long that would take could be anybody's guess.

A surge of rage ran through Nan's body. She remembered what it was like to be trapped in her mother's house, trapped by the violent, drunken men in her mother's life. She also knew what a life sentence felt like at fifteen years old, and how trapped one could really be, even without bars. She could remember feeling so powerless, so frightened, when they crept into her room at night . . . how no one, especially not her pathetic, alcoholic mother believed her. Clenching her fists in her lap, she vowed not to let her mind go down that dark alley— just as she had vowed when she was fifteen that she'd never be powerless again.

"Did you hear me, Nan?" Dr. Alberts asked patiently. "It *is* my business. That's why I'm here."

"Fuck you! I don't have to take this," Camille shrieked, standing up. "You won't believe me any more than they did. They've got money and power and will buy your stinking job to cover it up like they did with the last therapist. That's all any of them understand. Power. Complete, ruthless, selfish power!"

Nan stared at the scene from a distant place in her mind. It felt like a total out-of-body experience, and she couldn't react, just sit stunned.

"What wouldn't I believe, Camille?" Dr. Alberts' voice was almost hypnotic. "What do people with power do to people without it?"

"They spend their summers in the south of France and their winters skiing in Vale! They leave you at home with housekeepers and lawn boys, or pool hands who take you because nobody is there to stop them! Then they send you away to expensive boarding schools so they don't have to fucking deal with you. They send a goddamned *servant* to your school plays, or your recitals, and pray that one of your schoolmates will invite you to their home for spring break. Then they try to buy your affection back a few times a year—your birthday, Christmas is the big one, anything so you don't interrupt their precious, booked life schedule of events and soirées. Then they cringe when you tell them the truth, and put you in therapy for being a liar. That's what the fuck they do to you, Dr. Alberts. So don't you tell me what they can't do, or how they will give a shit about my well-being. Or that they're concerned, responsible parents. They're self-absorbed assholes who just want to sweep my existence under the rug and I won't let them! That's why the hell I'm here!"

Camille was trembling as she stood, her arms clasped about her body protectively. Rivulets of tears streamed down her face, yet she wasn't sobbing. You could have heard a pin drop in the room, except for the young girl's labored breathing. Nan watched the scene, no longer able to stay remote and detached. Her own tears coursed down her face, and without thinking she stood and wiped them away with the back of her hand.

"C'mon. You don't have to stay and take this crap." Feeling suddenly protective, Nan advanced toward the door and held it open. "This is such bullshit. You unearth this stuff from people, without a clue as to how to put them back together again afterward. What freakin' impact can you have on this girl's life? Correction, young woman. This so-called kid is more woman than any of you lousy bastards will ever be. Trust me. I know."

Camille walked through the door and their gazes met, transmitting a silent understanding as they both left the room. They walked down the hall side by side, neither woman speaking, neither woman looking at the other, just cloaked in their own painful experiences. When they got back to the room, Nan hesitated before putting an arm around Camille's shoulder. She knew too well how she would have reacted to pity. Camille was injured, but she was still strong, and undoubtedly hated weakness. The poor girl was probably mortified by her own outburst, which told too much of her hidden trauma. And the fact that she had allowed herself to cry in public was probably her greatest humiliation.

Thinking fast, Nan forced herself to chuckle. "Well you sure told that old biddy." It was the only thing that she could think of to allow her fellow inmate to save face.

Wiping her nose with the back of her hand, Camille smiled slowly without looking up. "Yeah. I don't take no shit from nobody. Not anymore."

New tears were beginning to form in Nan's eyes, and she immediately needed space, distance, anything to get her away from looking at the mirror of her youth sitting on the bed wiping her face.

As she moved to the door, Camille lifted her head and spoke softly. "Hey, girlfriend. Thanks for taking my back."

"Don't mention it. Never let the bastards get you down," Nan returned in a falsely confident voice. Swallowing away the tears that almost closed her throat, she turned to face her roommate once more before she shut the door behind her. "Never," she repeated more quietly, searching Camille's face with her gaze. "You've got too much life to live in front of you."

Pacing down the hall quickly, she felt like a trapped animal under hot pursuit. Her fast gait turned into a flat-out run as she neared the garden area off the visiting room. "I have to get outside for a minute," she demanded to the nurse at the station. "Let me out, *now!*"

Patiently, the nurse began a litany of schedules and rules, but Nan refused to listen. "I said I want to walk outside, you stupid bitch, and I am going now!"

As the altercation escalated, Dr. Alberts came out into the hall. Taking one look at Nan, she interceded. "Let her take a walk. She's just come out of group and she needs some air."

Relief swept through Nan as the nurse scowled at her and pressed the buzzer that opened the door to the terrace area. Once outside she basked in the quiet and, turning her back to the large picture window, she faced the trees. Wrapping her arms around herself for support, she was thankful to be alone. Alone enough to let the tears come without censure. Alone enough to sob until her throat hurt. Alone enough to acknowledge the suffering that she had denied for so long.

How could God let so many people be abused? And why would He torture her now, after all of these years, with a beautiful, intelligent, dark, teenage replica of herself?

She stood at the massive double oak doors and shifted the weight of the pen and ink drawing from one hand to another. Ginny always made it a point to bring her clients a gift after they had moved in to thank them for the business. Normally, it was flowers or fruit, but the closing of this deal required something special. She had wrestled for hours trying to think of the perfect gift for the Caldwells. After all, the deal had ensured her company's financial health for at least another quarter. Hopefully by the summer, home buying would pick up.

She knocked again, only this time a little more loudly. Her arms ached from holding the large drawing in the heavy wooden frame and, to be truthful, she wasn't exactly comfortable making this visit. Not wanting to run into Robert Caldwell, she had timed it for when she hoped he would be at work.

The door slowly opened and Ginny plastered a smile on her face. "Hi, Joan. I hope it's okay that I just stopped by. I wanted to drop off this gift and . . ." Her words trailed off as she saw sunglasses and concealer attempting to hide an ugly purple bruise under Joan's eye. "I'm sorry," she started again. "Maybe this is a bad time. I contacted the architect to get a copy of the pen and ink drawing that was done when the house was first built. I thought you might like it, and I wanted to leave you with just a little token of appreciation." She held out the drawing and Joan Caldwell moved stiffly to accept it.

"Thank you, Ginny," she said just above a whisper. "It's so thoughtful. Then, you've always been kind."

A silent understanding passed between the two women. For the first time Ginny's hunches were confirmed. She knew beyond the shadow of a doubt what Joan Caldwell had been aware of when she'd backed off of Richard Caldwell in her office. It was almost as though the woman's eyes had pleaded with her not to anger him, for she would be the unfortunate victim when they were alone. And Ginny had responded, understanding from her own experiences the terror that had been reflected in Joan's eyes. Now, as the two stood for a moment in silence, Joan again had thanked her for that small, but precious gift of understanding.

Suddenly, emotions that had been buried for years rushed up at her. There were so many things that she wanted to say to Joan, but she knew she couldn't. She didn't have the right. Knowing how Joan must be embarrassed, she offered her another gift—her dignity.

Hastily collecting herself, Ginny smiled warmly and placed her hand over Joan's. "Listen, I know that you've got a million things to do, having just moved in. I'll let you get back to organizing your new home. Take care, Joan."

Joan Caldwell returned her smile. "Thank you, Ginny. I knew you would understand," she stammered. "It's lovely."

Without thinking before she spoke, Ginny felt another wave of emotion wash over her. "You deserve it, Joan.

And if you ever need anything, just call. I'm not just your realtor, okay?"

Mrs. Caldwell didn't look up, nor did she answer. She just nodded her head as she shut the door, but not before Ginny noticed a tear splash onto the back of her hand.

Sitting in her car, she turned on the ignition and stared at the expensive, lush, shrubbery surrounding the house. To anyone passing by, it looked like the occupants had found the pot of gold at the end of a rainbow—someplace where dreams came true.

Her past slammed into her with the force of a Mack truck. Memories she had buried with her husband reached up from the grave and confronted her. This time there was no fear. This time there was no hurt. This time there was only anger.

Hell, no!

Maybe she didn't fight for herself all those years ago. Maybe there had been no one to turn to. But now she could fight for someone else. This was not going to happen again. Not without a fight! Not without Joan Caldwell at least knowing that there'd be someone to help her, someone to give a damn about her.

Fury propelled Ginny from the car. The speed with which she hurried up the walkway to the house felt like a burst of adrenaline had just rushed through her veins. With her car keys clenched in one hand, and her purse clasped tightly in the other, she knocked on the door loudly, and said a silent prayer for the right words to say. She had to calm down. She had to force her heart to stop pounding. But most of all, she couldn't allow her outrage to affront a woman who had already been brutalized enough.

Steadying herself, Ginny took a deep breath as she heard Joan Caldwell's light footsteps cross the marble foyer. As the lock turned, and Joan peeked out, Ginny could no longer force a smile. Nor could she stop a tear of pent up anger from flowing down her face. She took a deep breath and began to speak.

"Joan, I've been where you are right now. My husband was powerful, connected, had a legal background and a brilliant political career ahead of him. He was the county District Attorney. He also beat me every time I tried to act or think for myself, until I no longer acted or thought, but just reacted. I want you to know that you're not alone in this anymore, and you don't have to live like this."

Hearing her own admission said aloud for the first time in her life, Ginny stood shaking as she stared at Joan Caldwell. It was almost surreal, as if someone else were speaking instead of her. Yet, from somewhere, she felt a surge of righteous anger, and her words became more forceful. "You don't have to live like this, Joan. No one does."

As though she had crossed an invisible barrier of secrecy, Joan opened the door wider and slowly took off her sunglasses. The timid, yet courageous act, revealed a purplish, swollen eye that was now only open to a slit. The sight of it horrified Ginny, yet only made her more firm in her conviction. Joan Caldwell had issued her a silent invitation. It was a form of honor, an acknowledgement of respect that didn't require words—something to be held with the highest regard.

Joan allowed tears to spill over her face freely without wiping them away. "Ginny, I don't even know where to begin," she whispered.

Ginny crossed over the threshold and wiped the tears from her own eyes. "You're more courageous than I was, Joan. And you've just started to change things. Admitting to someone else that it's taking place is the beginning. C'mon—let's talk."

She took a sip of her coffee and looked around the deli nervously. There was no particular reason to feel guilty about going to lunch with a co-worker, but for some strange reason she did. Jason Levy was, after all, the staff attorney and they did have client business to discuss. It was true that they were both so booked with meetings, and that interruptions in the office made it impossible to talk. She was, however, married. But what did that have to do with it? This was just lunch. A business lunch.

Allie let her gaze roam over the crowded restaurant, and ignored the subtle excitement that coursed through her. Maybe it was the way Jason looked at her when she spoke to him. Nobody had looked at her like that in a long time. He had a way of making her feel as though he was really hearing and considering her point of view. He didn't act as if she was boring him, or as if he had better things to do with his time than hear what she had to say. When he spoke it was with insight and intelligence. Yet he wasn't a nerd or a know-it-all—and he could have been, given his education and credentials. Jason Levy had a sarcastic wit, but he also had warmth and a deep caring about people that could almost be compared to passion.

When he entered the deli, Allie unconsciously drew a deep breath. What was wrong with her? She was behaving like a foolish teenager sitting in a diner and mooning over some guy while she sipped a malt. It was pathetic. Had it been so long since she had a conversation with a man, that now she was . . .

"Hey, sorry I'm late. Shouldn't have taken that last call on my way out the door. Everybody always swears it'll only be a minute. But that means a half hour to forty-five minutes, of course."

Allie smiled as he slid into the wooden chair across from her. She was glad that he had stopped her inappropriate thoughts, and was grateful that he'd been late. It had given her a chance to pull it together.

"No, problem. I needed a minute to unwind after that last class."

"Pretty tough group in there this time. I saw them," he said fiddling with the packs of sugar on the table. "Maybe we oughta hold classes in the Women's Correctional Facility out in Homesburg, P.A."

Allie laughed. Jason Levy always made her laugh. "So what's good here? I haven't really gone out in Center City much. Usually I bring my lunch."

"Are you a vegetarian?"

The comment didn't make sense, and she cocked an eyebrow in confusion. "No, I'm not," she answered carefully.

"Great!" he announced, startling her and making her giggle. "Then you can indulge yourself in a four-inch-thick, New York style pastrami on rye, with chopped chicken liver and dark mustard."

"Sounds like it'll give you a heart attack even if you aren't a vegetarian."

"Live a little," he said, smiling cheerfully. "You've gotta learn to take risks."

For some strange reason, his comment pulled at her. "I'm learning to do that more every day," she said.

"Good. Then after you master a poor diet, I'll see what else I can do to corrupt you."

Standing, Jason went over to the counter window to place their order. As he walked away from their table, Allie found herself assessing him physically. Chastising herself, she rummaged in her purse for money, any diversion possible. She could not think this, even if it was for just a brief second. This wasn't like watching Tom Selleck on old Magnum P.I. reruns while the kids were in school and she folded laundry. That was an acceptable fantasy for any woman. It was also impossible, and very, very, safe.

This wasn't.

Jason returned within minutes, carrying a large plastic tray piled with food. Rising to help him, Allie lifted off a platter that contained a heaping sandwich with enough meat on it to feed a family of four, surrounded by coleslaw and huge pickles.

"I'll have to go back for the drinks," he said, still devastating her with his smile.

"No, that's okay. I'll go get them."

"I wouldn't hear of it. I do have a bit of chivalry left in these old bones, even though it's not popular in the nineties," he chuckled over his shoulder, as he left to go get the iced teas.

Allie sat down slowly. What the hell was she doing here? She couldn't remember the last time anyone had waited on her and been happy to do so. She wanted to laugh and cry at the same time. Since Jason returned quickly, she opted to laugh and eyed her overstuffed sandwich suspiciously. "How does one even begin to eat this?"

Jason smiled at her, but this time there was an intensity in his eyes that didn't match his mouth. Picking up one half of his sandwich, he stared at her without looking at the food in his hands. "Slowly—very slowly . . . and one bite at a time."

There was no doubt about it. Allie knew she was in trouble. Deep trouble.

Chapter 14

N an nervously surveyed the comfortable furnishings in Dr. Alberts' office as she waited for the doctor and her sisters to arrive. This time, when she was ushered in and asked to wait, their exchange didn't have the same rancor and animosity that always accompanied their meetings. Something had changed. Nan had changed. Closing her eyes as she lingered impatiently for Dr. Alberts to join her, she thought back on the last twenty-four hours. What was so different . . . ?

Without warning, tears threatened her composure and she opened her eyes, sat up straight, and stared out the window. When her gaze met the line of trees that edged the visitors terrace, it hit her. Camille's outburst of emotion had been too close to her own repressed feelings to shrug off. Again, from some deep reservoir of memory, her roommate's trauma brought back flashes of pain from her own childhood horrors. Even distanced from Camille, even with her eyes opened and her will reinforced, it hurt. The young girl's agony had seeped through the stone barrier around her heart, forcing her to deal with a life long forgotten. Camille's rage had become her rage. They shared the same demons that had made them build high protective walls around their emotions. The only trouble was Nan knew that she had been at it longer than her teenage roommate. Now the question: once one passed the moat, scaled the wall, and rode over the drawbridge, what was behind all of the fortressing that had been erected?

That question terrified her. What if there was only a shallow, petty, mean-spirited person behind the facade? What if she had become her mother?

Using her most effective defense against pain, Nan summoned rage. Why shouldn't she be angry? Why did she have to unearth this shit? What good would it do anyway? All of the key players were dead and buried. What the hell were they going to do about it now? Have a seance?

Nan bristled with anger as she heard the doctor's voice and two lower female murmurs that she identified as her sisters. After the day she'd already had, how could she deal with this?

The door opened and immediately Allie rushed in to embrace her. "Are you okay? You look tired."

Nan touched her own face briefly and stared back at Allie, realizing that she hadn't put on any makeup since that morning. She was sure that she must have cried it off already, and figured that she looked horrible. Trying to muster enthusiasm, she forced a smile and said, "I'm okay," then looked at Ginny and added, "Thanks for coming." The comment was issued with the first real hint of concern that she'd felt for Ginny in a long time. Something was obviously wrong with her older sister, and she could tell that Ginny was also anxious about the possible outcome of the session.

Dr. Alberts seated her sisters on a long couch, and Nan straightened in the overstuffed chair as if to take possession of it.

"Allie and Ginny, thank you for coming tonight. I know this feels a little awkward right now, but I sensed strong family ties and I really do feel this meeting will help Nan."

Both sisters nodded in agreement as Allie spoke. "She's our sister. We'll do anything to help. But I'm just not sure where to start, or what caused this problem in the first place."

Nan bristled as Allie spoke about her *problem* as if she weren't in the room. As Dr. Alberts' gaze shifted from Allie and Ginny to her, she could feel her own internal line of defense reinforce itself. They were not getting in. She wouldn't allow it. Not tonight. She'd already been through enough emotional drama for one day.

"Your concern and willingness to be here is the first step. How about if we start this session by talking about when the problem, or symptoms of the real issue, first became noticeable? Perhaps Nan would like to share when she first started using a controlled substance."

Nan crossed her arms over her chest and leveled her gaze at Dr. Alberts. "No."

"No, what, Nan? No that you don't want to share when you began using cocaine, or no, you aren't sure what made you begin using it?"

The hair on the back of Nan's neck almost stood up. Now everyone in the room was staring at her, waiting for an answer, an answer that she didn't want to give to either question. Narrowing her focus on Dr. Alberts, she issued the most lethal non-verbal warning she could. How dare she jump right in like that, allowing her no time to warm up or figure out what she wanted to say? Alberts was a sneaky one, all right. A real bitch.

"Well?" Dr. Alberts continued, not letting up. "Look, this is the time to share and be honest with those who care enough to support you. If you can't be honest with them, then how can you even begin to be honest with yourself? You have to start somewhere, Nan."

Turning her attention to Ginny, Dr. Alberts sought support for her position. "Virginia, how does it make you feel to come all this way and have your sister refuse to open up about a problem?"

It was a low blow, going to the one shaky ally she had—the one who would probably turn her in.

"It feels like it always does," Ginny said, adjusting herself to sit up straighter.

"And how's that?" the doctor questioned calmly, looking at each face in the room as she spoke.

"Like she's going to manipulate us to get what she wants, and never get to the bottom of this. I don't know if she wants help. Maybe this is just a waste of time."

Before Nan could speak, Allie rushed in to defend her. "Ginny! How can you say such a thing? Nan obviously wanted help, or she wouldn't have signed herself into this facility."

"Wrong! She did this because she got caught and she had no alternative. When will you learn, Allie? She's been playing this game since she was a kid."

Ginny was nearly trembling as she spoke, and it momentarily unnerved Nan to see her sister react so strongly. Perhaps what was more unnerving was the fact that Ginny had her pegged.

Marshalling her own self defense, Nan interjected bitterly. "Oh, yeah, right. I forgot. Little Miss Perfect over there can't stand lies, betrayals, secrets, or fuck-ups. She doesn't have any of her own. Noooo. She's above all that. Above the rest of us poor wretched souls!"

The whole scene was once again becoming surreal. Allie withdrew and clasped her hands in her lap and looked like she was on the verge of tears. Ginny had retreated grudgingly, but was still obviously armed. But Dr. Alberts . . . her expression was a mixture of amused observation, fascination, and excitement. It was clear that this was just what she wanted. Inadvertently, they had played right into her hands, and Nan could tell that her steely, analytical mind was looking for a new way in. Had they been at a boardroom table, she wouldn't have given that bitch an inch. But this was new territory, and she hadn't yet mastered the game. She was, however, learning quickly.

"Nan, you and Ginny seem to have a lot of tension between you just under the surface. Has it always been this way?"

Nan just stared at the doctor.

"They've always fought like this, ever since we were little. I don't know why. I'm sorry," Allie said quietly, her voice wavering.

"And why are you sorry, Allie? You don't have to be the peacemaker here. You didn't start this outburst, your sisters did. I want to hear from one of them directly, not through a translator or mediator, about why they have this tension. So, one of you, Ginny or Nan, let's discuss this tonight."

Nan hated to admit it, but she was good. Real good.

Deciding that it was in her own best interest to launch the offensive, Nan spoke first.

"Ginny and I have always had this tension, as you put it, since we were children. I was the baby and she was my older sister. Sibling rivalry isn't all that unusual, is it?"

Dr. Alberts sat back in her chair and laced her fingers together over her ample lap. "But you don't seem to have the same rivalry with Allie? Why's that?"

Nan looked at her oldest sister and found her lips forming into a smile of affection. "Allie . . . she was the one that kept us together. You see, adult parenting in our house was almost nonexistent. You want to probe into our past? You want to find out all the ugly secrets that make up who we are today? If you want that, you have to start with our parents."

"Oh, please," Ginny moaned. "Why is it every time something goes wrong, you and Allie constantly go back to our childhood and blame them? Yes. We were dysfunctional. But plenty of people have come from worse and survived. We didn't grow up in a ghetto. We had a roof over our heads. We got an education, and we did something with that as adults. Maybe we have to take some of the blame for what went wrong in our lives ourselves."

Nan could feel the old fire burning in her belly, that urge to slice Ginny down to size. Before she could stop herself, she said, "Oh, like you did with Evan? The man was a fucking bastard, and you pretended that he was the next Republican candidate for governor. All those politically correct functions and charities—who were you kidding? The guy went out, picked up jailbait, and then killed himself."

"Nan! Stop it," Allie demanded in a shocked voice.

Dr. Alberts calmly interjected, "Stay out of it, Allie. This isn't about you."

Nan saw Ginny's stricken expression, yet she couldn't muster any sympathy. Too many emotions were swirling about inside of her to channel any one of them toward mercy. "You want me to say I'm sorry, but I'm not. In fact, I feel a hell of a lot better to have said what I was thinking for years. The man was a rotten son of a bitch, even worse than our father, and you're better off without him. Fact is, Gin, you married your father. How about that, Dr. Alberts? Let's hear some psychobabble about my sister marrying an asshole like her father to get the love and approval she never got as a child."

Silence filled the small room until Dr. Alberts turned her attention to Ginny. "How do you feel about what Nan just said?"

Obviously fighting back tears, Ginny took a deep breath and Nan waited to have the arrows returned in her direction.

"Do you think that I don't know what Evan was?" Ginny's voice had become metallic and strident, yet she delivered each word with deadly control. "You've spent so much time feeling sorry for yourself, and moaning and wailing about your past, that you think it can excuse everything. Unless you've walked a mile in my shoes, don't you dare compare yourself to me or give me advice."

Nan sat back and glared at her sister. As usual, Ginny had said a lot without clarifying anything. Her sister had a knack for speaking without exposing herself. Ginny probably considered it diplomacy; to Nan it was fraud.

"Oh, and you've had such tough shoes to wear? Gimme

a break. When I was stuck in the house with Mom's lech-
erous lays of the week, you'd always cajole Allie to leave
and the two of you would escape. But did you ever think
about what was happening to me when the two of you
were gone? No, you were too concerned about your own
welfare and couldn't have given a damn about mine! So,
save your I-was-trapped-in-a-bad-marriage speech for
somebody who cares. I don't."

Appearing confused, Allie broke into the fray despite
the doctor's stern look. "Nan, what happened while we
were gone? No . . . no! Please, God, tell me nothing terrible happened to you. They didn't . . ." Allie's voice trailed
off and an expression of terror engulfed her face.

"You never wanted to know, Allie," Nan said softly,
fighting back the horrible faces, the large sweaty hands
from her childhood nightmares. "No, I take that back, you
just never needed to know." For some strange reason she
wasn't angry with Allie for abandoning her. Even though
she was younger than Allie, inherently she always knew
that her older sister couldn't have handled what was happening. Allie was indeed a gentle soul, unlike herself.
Allie had tried her best to be both mother and father, and
for that valiant effort she had tried to shield her sister
from an ugly reality that would have tortured her for life.
Ginny, on the other hand, was another subject entirely.
Ginny was the one that would always make the plans to
escape, which would leave her at home, alone, and
trapped in hell.

Dr. Alberts didn't speak as she handed Allie a tissue.
Nan watched her eldest sister dissolve into tears while
Ginny sat stoically looking down at her hands in her lap,

while shaking her head and repeating over and over again, "My God, this can't be real. It can't . . . It can't . . ."

Rage consumed Nan. How could Ginny be so distant, so above it all and removed? It was just like when they were kids. But tonight, the Ice Princess was going down.

"Al, listen, whatever happened wasn't your fault. If you had known, I know you never would've left me. I wish I could say the same for Ginny. She and Mother were the ones that taught me to look out for number one."

"What the hell does that mean?" Ginny no longer appeared to be near tears. She now looked armed and ready to do battle.

"Let's stop talking in circles, Gin. You know the kind of drunken slobs that came into the house. Remember Uncle Joe? He was the first of many. You also know what they'd try to do, if they could, to a thirteen-year-old, well-developed girl. But rather than stay, you'd coax Allie out with you. If you hadn't gone, maybe somebody would've been there to protect me."

Ginny leaned forward and looked at her closely. "You know very well that Mom was the one who always insisted we couldn't go out until our chores were done. We ran that house, not her. But she took all the credit. Allie and I would finish our jobs so we could get out. You, on the other hand, would always shirk your responsibilities and *have* to stay home. It was almost like you sabotaged yourself, doing stupid stuff that you knew would get you grounded. And you also know that we never had any idea of what was happening to you when we left. You never said anything, not to either of us. I'm telling you, Nan, if I had known I would have killed the first sonofabitch that put his hands on you, but I didn't know! Why do you keep making me pay for something I had no knowledge of? I'm sorry that this happened to you. I wish I could wipe it from your memory. I wish to God that it hadn't happened, but you are not laying this crap at my feet."

She wanted to rip her sister's vocal cords from her throat. "You selfish, cold, bitch! How can you put this back on me? Were you this cold with Evan? Is that why he cheated on you, trying to find a woman with real feelings to warm his bed?"

"You've always got to find a way to throw off your problems onto somebody else. So what is this Evan crap all about? Is it that you just want to find any way you can to turn the knife in my stomach, or pour salt into an open wound? Does it make you feel better to hurt me, Nan—because in your sick, petty little mind you can get back at me for some perceived childhood slight! Remember, I was a kid too when this happened. I was in pain too. I was afraid, just like you were. The difference is I followed the rules so that I could get the hell out of there. You didn't. That was your choice, even as a kid. And about my husband, you don't know a damned thing about Evan! Maybe if you had spent more time taking care of your marriage instead of sleeping around with any man that would give your depraved ego attention, Robert, who is still alive, wouldn't have walked out on you. I can't blame him. Who could stand it?"

The gloves were off now. It was down and dirty with no limits. Nan felt her legs propel her to a standing position, and when she rose from her chair, Ginny was up on her own feet in seconds.

"I know a lot about Evan," she said, hearing her voice sounding like a growl and not caring. She was fighting for her life here. "More than you'd ever guess. I know that he liked it rough. I know that he did coke before he could get it up. And I also know that he could land a punch like a heavyweight champ. Yeah, I know your fucking, dead-bastard husband."

Nan felt her face sting from the lightning quick slap that Ginny had issued. Before her brain could send the signal, she had returned it, making Ginny take two steps back to regain her balance. Were it not for Allie jumping between them with such pain in her eyes, she would have torn Ginny's hair out by the roots.

"Stop it, stop it!" Allie pleaded. She turned to Dr. Alberts, her voice begging for understanding. "How is this supposed to help? Tell me!" she demanded between sobs. "We're supposed to be here to heal the family, not tear it apart. Why are you letting them do this?"

"Because, Allie, this anger has been under the surface for a long time. It's like a cancer that was eating away at their relationship, each woman, and eating away at you while you tried to bring peace without resolution—an impossible task." Standing, Dr. Alberts looked at both combatants. "Nan, did I hear you correctly when you alluded to sleeping with your sister's husband, or was that just a snipe designed to hurt her?"

Nan's focus narrowed, and she stepped back from Ginny out of concern for what might happen if she didn't. "Yes, I slept with him!" she nearly screamed. "I did drugs with him. In fact, he was the one who turned me on to the stuff. And when I wouldn't sleep with him anymore, he beat me up and threatened to kill me, just like he always beat Ginny when she did something that pissed him off.

So, no, this wasn't idle rhetoric designed to hurt Ginny. It's the truth, and sometimes the truth hurts."

She watched the expression on her sister's face change. Apparently, Ginny hadn't realized what she really meant until the doctor made her clarify. It was ironic that initially her sister had been the one to talk in circles, and now, even in the heat of anger, she hadn't been able to just spit it out and confront Ginny with this nasty reality. An odd mixture of fury, relief, and remorse pressed the air from her lungs, paralyzing her vocal cords. Tears brimmed in her eyes and fell in large splotches on her shirt. She didn't care any longer. The ugly truth was out, and a burden had been lifted from her heart, yet the pain was unbearable.

Wrapping her arms around her body, Nan sought protection as she watched her sister's horror-filled face. Allie stepped away from her, and touched Ginny's shoulder, only to have her hand pushed away. But their stance was clear. The battle lines had been drawn and she'd crossed some invisible demarcation. Ginny and Allie were now inseparable allies, leaving her alone once again to face the world.

No words were exchanged. Ginny simply grabbed her purse and headed for the door. Dr. Alberts didn't stop her, and Allie was right behind her. She could hear their voices in the office foyer as Ginny made a hasty exit. Allie was obviously pleading with Ginny, and Ginny's voice was unmistakably authoritative. Her middle sister was going it alone, and she probably wouldn't accept Allie's shoulder to cry on. She knew Ginny better than that. Ginny was a loner. She'd retreat and then close them all out forever.

When Allie returned, she just stared at Nan. Her expression held a level of shock and disillusionment that she had never seen reflected from her sister's eyes before. "How could you? How could you do that to her?"

Nan just shook her head, feeling all strength dissipate. "Al, listen, it's not—"

"No! You listen, Nan. There are no words for this. There is no excuse for this. You don't even know the damage you've done." Allie wiped at her own tears and then crossed her arms over her stomach while slowly shaking her head. "Ginny was right. You're selfish and irresponsible and you hurt people without a conscience. Ginny's not to blame for what happened to you. Neither of us knew what was going on. We would have taken you with us, but we couldn't. You stayed in trouble and on perpetual grounding, so when we asked Mom, she always said no. Ginny was not the cause. She loved you, and you don't even remember. When you were born, Ginny was the one who took care of you. She was the one who would make you little dolls, read you stories, and let you climb in bed with her when you had bad dreams. Sure, I was the one who made lunches, and gave you your bath, and stuff like that, but that was only because I was older and could do those things unsupervised. Do you hear me, Nan? Ginny and I were a *team*. We worked together to take care of all three of us. She loved you. And it was only when we got bigger, and you got jealous of the relationship she and I had, that you tried to drive a wedge between us at every opportunity. And because she is a strong person, and wouldn't take it, you hated her. If I had been the same way, you probably would've hated me, too. Well, this time there are no excuses left. There is no one to take the blame, to smooth it over, to clean up your mess. Until you make this right with *our* sister, you've lost both of us. You've done a lot of stuff in the past that I've taken issue with, Nan. But this? This is so low that I don't even want to look at you."

Allie turned her focus toward Dr. Alberts. "I'm sorry, but I can't come back here. My sister is on her own." Snatching her purse from the sofa, Allie turned on her heels and left.

The complete isolation fell over her like an icy wave of separation. She had been banished, excommunicated, for an unforgivable act. The look in Allie's eyes had said it all. She was contemptible. How could she ever right this? How could she ever live with herself now?

"What are you feeling, Nan?" Dr. Alberts' voice sounded far away, and for a few moments it was hard to concentrate on her question.

"How do you think I feel?" she snapped back, trying to throw off the creeping dread, using her old anger. "I feel like shit."

Dr. Alberts just nodded in agreement as Nan's mind raced away from the room toward her childhood. Mentally she could see Ginny braiding her hair, breaking off half and sharing her popsicles, sneaking an extra piece of candy into her lunch, reading her *The Velveteen Rabbit*. God Almighty, why hadn't she remembered all that before? Stifled sobs began to constrict her throat, and she felt the immediate need for fresh air.

"Nan, what are you going to do about this? You know that drugs are only a temporary solution, something that you've been using to medicate away the pain."

As she opened her mouth to deliver a testy answer, her voice wavered and cracked. Somewhere deep inside of her the final dam broke, allowing a torrent of sobs to replace any verbal answer that she could have given. Dropping her head in her hands, she covered her face. She didn't want to look at herself, nor could she bear the thought of anyone else looking at her. What had she done? What had she become? Guilt threaded its way through her veins until she was too weak to stand, and she allowed her body to collapse in the overstuffed chair.

"Oh, God. Oh, dear, God." Her wail sounded like the cry of a small child even to her own ears. Had jealousy done this? She had gone beyond the protective barriers around her heart, and her worst nightmare was realized. Inside, she had found a small, mean-spirited, self-centered person. She had found her mother.

"Nan, we are all victims of victims. There are reasons for what we have become. You do have to take responsibility for what you've done, but think about this: you didn't start off where you are now. Before those men attacked you, there was a happy, beautiful little girl, wasn't there?"

Still sobbing, Nan nodded her head yes.

"And that little girl had an open heart and an innocent soul. We'll find her again, Nan. Let us help you find her." The doctor's voice was low and soothing. "You've taken the first step, this is just one layer of the onion skin that we've peeled back tonight. Don't leave here believing in only the worst part of yourself. Let's find the best part of Nan Sullivan before you go."

Nan lifted her head and wiped her nose on the back of her hand. Her voice was still shaky as she spoke, but she didn't care. She'd do anything to stop this torture and, for the first time in her life, she knew that she couldn't do it alone. "But what if this is all there is? What if this is my best? That little girl died inside of me a long time ago, and I don't know how to find her . . ." Her words trailed off in another wave of sobs as the doctor stood and came around from behind her desk to place a supportive arm around her shoulders.

"We'll find her, Nan. But you've got to give us a chance."

Clasping the doctor's hand for support, she looked up into the patient woman's eyes. "Help me," she whispered. "Please, help me. I can't go on like this."

Chapter 15

A llie sat in her driveway and looked at her house in the dark. She hadn't the slightest idea how she came to be there. Nothing seemed real anymore. Everything she loved was falling apart. Her home. Her marriage. Her family. Life had turned it all upside down and had left chaos. What was she supposed to do now? She remembered driving by Ginny's house, but it had been dark and her sister hadn't answered her knocks at the front door. Somehow she ended up here, in front of her own house, yet she didn't want to go in. There would be no comfort there. Dave would take satisfaction in hearing how miserable the Sullivan girls were at handling a crisis, and she knew she couldn't bear that. She might even throw him out tonight if he looked at her sideways. Where was she supposed to go to find comfort? Men went to bars or holed up in front of the tube to watch a basketball game and shut everyone out. Women always went to each other for comfort and advice. It was a sign of honor to confide in another woman, yet her best friends were her sisters and she was now isolated from both.

Moving as though she were a robot, Allie turned off the

ignition and got out of the car. Each step toward the house made her legs feel weighted, yet she pushed on, steeling herself before she turned the key in the lock. She felt like a stranger, and surveyed the now unfamiliar terrain with trepidation. She couldn't stand another altercation. Not now. Not for a long time.

Although everything was in its usual place—scattered everywhere—and the normal routine for that time of the evening was underway, she realized that something very important was different. She had changed. The fragile balance of her life, her sisters' lives, and by proximity, her family's lives, had changed. Gruesome realities had been unearthed, and there was no longer any way to pretend that they didn't exist.

As she passed the family room, she could see Pat lying on the floor while he did his homework, and Dave's attention appeared to be equally divided between a television program and the newspaper. Meghan was probably in bed. Allie never took her purse from her shoulder, nor did she fully enter the room. Peeking her head in, she murmured, "Did you guys eat?"

"Hi, Mom. Yeah, we had ravioli. Dad left some on the stove for you after we cleaned up the kitchen."

Allie looked at the expression on her son's face. He seemed to be waiting for praise that she was not in the mood to give. She had fought so hard for such a simple act of consideration, and now that they had conceded to be fair, she didn't care. Their earlier resistance had lessened the impact of something that she would have been thrilled about before. It was too little and too late. "Thanks," she finally uttered in a monotone voice. "Good night, guys."

To her surprise, Dave looked up from his paper to speak to her. "What's the matter? How'd it go tonight?"

She considered her words carefully before she spoke. Had this been six months earlier, she would have thrown herself into his arms and had a good cry. But such an act required trust. He had to be considered a friend, worthy of the honor of sharing. Looking at the man who had hurt her, shut her out, made her feel like she had no worth . . . he could no longer be considered a friend.

"It could have gone better," she mumbled, exiting the room without even looking at him. When she heard Dave rise from the couch and his footsteps behind her, she didn't turn around. She just hung up her coat, dropped her purse on the table, and headed for the stairs.

"You don't look so hot. Do you want some tea, or something? Maybe we can talk about this, Al. I mean, you look like a zombie."

"No, thank you. I'm fine. I'm always fine," she answered.

"Aren't you going to eat dinner? I know how you hate to walk into the kitchen with it all messed up. We cleaned it, so it's safe to go back there now."

As she ascended the stairs, Allie ignored the pleasantness of his voice and the hint of a smile that she heard in it. Yet she couldn't turn around, because she didn't want to trust that there had been some miraculous change in her husband's attitude. Too many illusions had already been shattered tonight. She wasn't about to rake through any more carnage at the moment. "I'm not hungry," she said over her shoulder when she got to the landing. "Thanks, but good night."

"Al? I've been thinking about us . . . About all those

things you said, and maybe you were right. I . . . I've been worried about the job, about the kids. About us, I guess. You working . . . I mean, God, it came out of nowhere. Everything seems upside down in our lives right now, and I'm not handling it well."

She heard his words, yet they couldn't seem to reach her. She *could not* comfort another soul tonight, not when hers and Ginny's were so wounded. Where was she supposed to find the energy, when all she wanted to do was get into bed and pull the cover up over her head? "I'm exhausted, Dave," she muttered. "We'll have to do this later." She refused to say she was sorry.

Closing the door to her bedroom, she stared at the telephone. Where was Ginny? Panic constricted the veins around her heart, and she said a silent prayer before reaching for the cordless unit. She hoped to God that her sister hadn't done anything rash. After the third ring, she heard the connection and started to speak immediately, only to be disappointed by Ginny's answering machine.

Impatiently waiting for the message to complete, then the beep, she spoke quickly. "Listen, Ginny. You're scaring me. If you want to be alone, I can understand why. But, please, just let me know that you're okay. Just pick up the phone and say that you're all right, and I'll leave you alone tonight. I went back into the session after you left, and I confronted Nan about this. I feel what she did was unforgivable, and I want you to know that I'm there for you—to support *you*. You were right. No more excuses. No more pretending. We've all made mistakes along the way, but please, don't shut me out. We're all we've got now, and I'm here for you."

Allie held the phone to her ear until the machine

beeped again and disconnected the call. She had hoped that Ginny would have heard the message, considered her words, then at least picked up. But she also knew that Ginny was now in some unreachable place, a place that was insular and protected from the hurtful world that had damaged her.

New tears formed in her eyes as she slipped off her shoes and began to undress. Evan had beat her sister? Her other sister had become a drug addict and had slept with one of their husbands? Damn Evan Harrison for what he'd done to both of her sisters. She had tried so hard to hold everything together, ever since she was a little girl. Now it was all crumbling. Even her marriage was falling apart.

Allowing her clothes to drop at her feet, she didn't make an effort to collect them and hang them up. She just stepped over the pile and climbed into bed with her underwear on. Sensing a presence in the room, she closed her eyes and adjusted the covers up around her shoulders and neck, tucking the ends under her fists protectively.

"Al? Hon, are you okay? I haven't seen you like this in a long time, and I'm getting a little worried."

She could hear Dave's voice from the doorway, but refused to answer. Shutting her eyes more tightly, she found her legs drawing up under her, forming her body into a fetal position. Not trusting her voice immediately, she just shook her head no.

When Dave crossed the room and sat down on the edge of the bed, his weight forced her to roll near his warmth, but she fought the invasion of his comfort. He had pushed her away so many nights when she needed him, denying her emotionally, sexually, refusing to validate her existence. Now he expected her to instantly trust him again

with the most painful crisis she'd experienced since childhood? He was mad.

When he reached out to place his hand on her covered
shoulder, she jerked and rolled over facing away from
him. "Don't," she said quietly, stifling the urge to get up
and run screaming out into the night. "Let's not pretend
any more, Dave. Let's just not pretend."

Ginny knelt by the side of the bed and clung to the comforter as a long wail of anguish escaped from her mouth.
Somehow when she was getting undressed she had sunk to
the rug in a kneeling position. It reminded her of all the
times as a child that she and Allie and Nan had gathered
around Allie's bed, and prayed to God for their parents to
stop arguing. But this time the pain was so sharp, so dis-
abling, that she couldn't rise. Even dead, he continued to
torture her. What Evan had done was even worse than his
beatings. This time he had taken away her family.

Evan and Nan.

Sudden nausea made her stomach lurch once more with
revulsion. How could they? The betrayal sliced through
her, overwhelmed her, taking away her ability to function.

The pain crushed down on her, paralyzing her, as she
listened to Allie's message. She couldn't even reach over
to pick up the phone, for fear that if she let go of the bedspread, she would simply slip away into that dark comforting place of peace where no thoughts, no decisions
existed. Yet Allie's voice pulled at her. It was a connection to ground her, almost like throwing out a life pre-
server to someone drowning. If she could just reach over
and pick up the receiver.

Too late she heard the phone disconnect and the beep signaling the end of the call. She had to call her back, or Allie would marshal the troops and the entire Barbera family would show up on her doorstep. Summoning the strength, she focused her concentration on the motor skills necessary to reach the phone and punch in her sister's number.

Allie picked up on the first ring and Ginny forced her mouth to form the words. "Allie, I just need some time to myself right now. I know it's not going to do any good to say this, but don't worry. I just want to be left alone."

"That's all I want to know," Allie whispered. "And to tell you that I love you, Gin."

"I can't talk about this now," Ginny said, fighting the tears that were finally breaking through. "I don't know when . . . look, I'll call you tomorrow."

"But if you do need to talk, I don't care what time it is, promise to call me anyway?"

The phone clicked and the familiar sound of call-waiting interrupted Allie's sentence. "Look, Al, that's my line. I've got to go. I'll call you tomorrow."

Taking a deep breath, she disconnected her call with Allie, relieved to get her sister off the phone. It had been her intention to let the answering machine pick up the next call, but after a series of clicks, she heard a man's voice.

"Anybody there? Hello, hello . . ."

Giving in, she took the call. Whichever client this was would have to understand that she'd deal with his problem tomorrow. Garnering strength, she acknowledged the person on the other end of the line. "Hello," she repeated without enthusiasm.

"Ginny? I'm so glad I got you. I have to tell you what's happened. That bloodsucker Caldwell is going to make me go to jail for assault and battery, I promise you. He went after DeWayne Henderson without my consent and used my name as an intro! Can you believe it? What balls."

Her brain scrambled, trying to take in all of the information at once. First she had recognized Matt's voice, then she had to put together the sketchy story, then figure out a way to appease him and get him off the phone. She knew she owed the man the courtesy of hearing him out, especially since she had been the one to throw him into an untenable position with Caldwell. But why tonight? Christ!

"I don't understand," she finally said, using the back of her hand to wipe away the sniffles. "What?"

"Look, I'll tell you about it when I get there. I'm too pissed off right now to handle this on the phone. I just left the kid's house in Philly and I'm calling from my car. It'll only take a minute, but I really need to just blow off some steam. Maybe the drive over will help."

Matt coming to her house? Now? The nightmare continued. Searching her mind quickly, she tried to think of a plausible excuse. But before she could speak, he was ending the call.

"I know this is spur of the moment, but I just found out about it. I don't want to do anything that will jeopardize your relationship with your client, so I need your advice—and I probably need to calm down. But, Gin, I gotta tell you, this guy slays me."

"I know, Matt. But—" The connection crackled with

static as she searched for the right words to delay him. They were losing contact.

"We're breaking up. Damn this phone. Okay, I'll see you in twenty minutes. Thanks a lot, Ginny. I really appreciate it."

In seconds he was gone and she listened to the dead air on the line before the dial tone came back. She stared at the receiver as if it were a meteor that had fallen from the sky into her hand. How was she going to make it through this? Her facade had never been so challenged before. She had always been able to hide until she was ready to emerge and face the world again. Now, she was a prisoner in her own home, having to put on a happy face and problem solve. Impossible.

Fear jettisoned her into a standing position. Snatching up her discarded clothes from the floor, she shoved them into the hamper and threw open the closet doors. Rifling through the hangers like a mad woman, she jerked down an oversized tee-shirt and began rummaging through her dresser for a pair of leggings. As her gaze caught her own image in the mirror, she literally shrieked at the sight. Mascara had formed black pools under her eyes and her lips were dry and white from crying. She had become a nightmare. For a few seconds, she turned around in the same spot on the floor, trying to get her bearings and decide what to do next.

Visine and a little make-up. Why was this happening tonight?

Grabbing her makeup bag, she made a beeline for the bathroom mirror. In the fluorescent light, the sight was even more frightening. Blush. Concealer. No mascara. Lipstick. She had pulled the contents out of the case and laid them on the vanity as though she were a surgeon going in to do a major operation. Tilting her head back, she squeezed a few drops of Visine into each eye, then snatched a tissue from the holder and tried to clean up the running makeup. Once the black had been removed, she reached for the concealer and liberally applied it under her eyes. It was then she made the connection between her reflection and herself. Her eyes stared back at her with a mixture of fear and pain. The sudden realization broke through her panic, and what little reserve of strength she had drained from her body, forcing her to sit on the edge of the tub. She couldn't handle this. Not now.

It was too much for one soul to bear in one night. Somehow, she had to make him understand that she could not solve anyone's problems tonight—not even her own.

Ten minutes later, she was sitting on the steps in her foyer, staring at the front door and waiting for the bell to ring. At that moment, she no longer cared what she looked like. She didn't care if he sensed something was wrong. It was. She had been traumatized for over half her life, but had skillfully hidden it. She had also spent her entire life trying to follow all the rules, to be the good girl, the good student, the good wife, the good sister . . . but it wasn't enough to chase away the ghosts of her past. They continued to haunt her. Her parents. Her husband. "I hate you, Evan Harrison," she whispered into the darkness and clenched her fists against her eyes to stop fresh tears. It was too much for one soul to bear; she wasn't able to hide behind a facade of strength any longer.

She rose slowly when she heard his car pull into her driveway. Standing in the opened doorway, she watched Matt jump out of his car and take her front steps two at a time. His face was flushed and he was breathing deeply when he greeted her.

"Ginny, I'm sorry for barging in on you like this."

His gaze was direct and unwavering, and the intensity of it made her step back to allow him entry into her home. Walking ahead of her in long strides, Matt went right into her living room, but didn't sit down. Instead, he paced like a caged tiger and shoved his hands in his pockets as he spoke.

"That son-of-a-bitch called Henderson and told him I'd said to set up a meeting. Then he coaxed him over to their new house, Caldwell Manor, insinuating that I'd be there. Once the poor kid got there, Caldwell made up some flimsy excuse about how I had to leave, but that I'd reviewed some contracts, etcetera, and tried to get the kid to sign with him! Can you just freakin' believe it?"

Ginny had to sit down. Matt's fury seemed to drain any energy she had left so she took a seat on the end of the sofa. He had only glanced at her while he railed on, still pacing and looking around the room as though searching for something to kick.

"And what's worse, that kid walked out of there with contracts in hand because he believed that I thought it was a good idea. Had I not called him, he probably would have signed up with the bastard! It was sheer happenstance that I connected with his mother and she told me where he was. So I drove over to South Philly and waited on his steps for forty-five minutes for him to get back home. That's when I found out the whole story and told the kid to trash the papers, and to never speak to Caldwell without me or an attorney present. What a scum bag."

Matt finally sat down and slumped on the other end of

the sofa. Running his hands through his hair, he looked down at the floor as he spoke, shaking his head in utter disbelief. "Ginny, I don't know how to handle this without getting you caught in the middle. Under normal circumstances, I would've driven over to Caldwell's house, cursed him out, then punched him out. Maybe that's why I came here first—to have you talk me out of doing something foolish."

In the midst of the emotional fray, Ginny tried to summon reason. Somehow, Matt's anger and confusion had temporarily cauterized her own wounds to permit thought, if not feeling. This man had respected her enough, in a crisis situation, to act in her behalf. He could have followed his first impulse, but something had stopped him. Concern for her. It was admirable, and appreciated, in a time in her life when no one around her seemed to possess honor.

Finding her voice, she spoke quietly. "Look, Matt—I am so sorry I got you involved in this. What Caldwell did was underhanded and unforgivable. I don't care what you do to the man at this point, but I do care that you don't hurt yourself in the process. If you hit him, he will most definitely sue you, and he's not worth that."

"I know, Gin," he murmured, sounding defeated. "But people like that should get what's coming to them, you know?"

"Yes, I know. But not at the expense of your own life."

Matt let out a long sigh of disgust. Rubbing his face in his hands, his voice held sheer contempt. "The kid told me that they had a sick Addams Family situation going on around there. Caldwell forced his wife to meet him, that was obvious, because the woman came downstairs wearing sunglasses at seven o'clock in the evening. The kid said it looked as if she'd been in a damned prize fight! That's what tipped him off not to sign anything until he talked to me. That's the only reason the kid brought the papers home. Jesus. We were right. He even beats his wife."

An icy chill ran through her body at Matt's words, and for the first time since he'd come in, Matt really looked at her.

"Did you hear me, Gin? He beats her."

Fury replaced fear and strangled all inhibitions. Her voice was unwavering now, and she clenched her fists to keep from crying out. "I know, Matt. I saw her earlier today and talked to her about it."

"You did?"

"Yes, and she's scared to death of him. But I refuse to just walk away and forget it. The woman needs protection, a way out."

She felt the intensity of Matt's gaze as it roamed over her face.

"God, you're pretty involved in this, aren't you? And you look like you've seen a ghost. I haven't stopped long enough to find out what was going on with you."

She almost didn't wait for him to finish speaking before she jumped in. It didn't matter any longer. The truth was screaming to get out now. There was no need to hide anymore. It was already out in the open. Nan knew. She'd known for years. And now Allie. "I am involved," she said bluntly, returning his direct gaze. "I *have* seen a ghost today. A lot of ghosts."

"What happened?" Matt's voice had lost all tenor of any anger. Now it held concern, if not fear.

"Let's just say that seeing Joan Caldwell like that brought back a lot of bad memories for me. But she doesn't have to be like me, terrified to confront the issues, thinking that there's no way out, humiliated by helplessness. I may have been incapable of helping myself, but perhaps I can help her."

She watched Matt's expression closely. Shock enveloped his face, yet there was no judgment, only concern in it.

"I knew there was something about you when we met," he whispered. "Something that I couldn't quite put my finger on. There was a fear in your eyes, or a quiet terror just under the surface, something that I'd only seen in battle."

"In battle?" The analogy was correct, but it didn't make sense to her.

"Ginny, you have that POW look in your eyes. It's a look that you can't describe to anybody who hasn't faced near-death. But once you've been there, you can spot it a mile away."

She didn't respond, but stood and walked over to the fireplace. Matt's assessment had hit too close to home. He was right—that's what had initially drawn her to Joan Caldwell. She had spotted another POW from a mile away.

"When did you learn how to see through a person? When did you get your veteran's status?" she murmured. The question had been designed to take the focus off of her own trauma. She needed immediate distance, if only for a moment.

Matt stood and walked over to her. Standing behind her, he spoke softly, but his voice was firm. "I did a stint in

Vietnam that almost cost me my sanity. I hated to talk about it, because I thought that I could make it all go away by ignoring it. But I was still sleeping with a knife under my pillow two years after I got home. I was afraid of the dark, and couldn't fall asleep without the lights on. I couldn't stand sudden movements or strange noises. Ginny, if somebody walked up behind me quietly, I'd freak. Then I finally started to get some help and little by little the nightmares went away. But it took a long time to get rid of that trauma. And it took an even longer time before I could relate to anybody, or have a relationship . . . make love, or do anything normal. I felt robbed. Utterly violated and held hostage by fear."

Once again, his words were too accurate to cope with immediately. She felt her body trembling so she wrapped her arms around herself. With her back still facing him, she tried to let a little of the pain seep out in a controlled dose.

"Evan beat me, too. I could never say that to anyone before, because I felt so afraid and weak and stupid for allowing it to happen. But it was also very familiar. I knew how to handle his violent episodes, just like I had learned to handle my mother's and father's arguments. I thought that if I just followed the rules, made myself as inconspicuous as possible, then it would be over soon. And when he died, I thought the terror would be over . . . but it's not. He's been gone for four years and he still haunts me from the grave. I found out tonight that he even attacked my sister and got her involved with drugs. But to the world, he was Mr. Community, Mr. D.A."

The open admission forced a violent sob to escape from her depths. How could she have poured this out into a near stranger's lap? But through his own admission, Matt had become more than a stranger, he had become a fellow inmate. She was thankful that he didn't reach for her right away. He seemed to understand that she couldn't handle any encroachment into her personal space, yet. Instead, he stood behind her, allowing her to sob, before asking permission to hold her.

"Ginny, I've been there," he said quietly, gently resting both of his hands on the outer edges of her shoulders.

The warmth of his touch radiated down her arms, soon making her crave to be enfolded totally by the protection that he offered. As though sensing her readiness to let him in, Matt slowly turned her around to face him and encircled her with his arms.

"I'm not going to let anyone hurt you, Virginia. I won't hurt you. It's over."

As he spoke, his breath sent a soothing current against her cheek. Burying her face in his shoulder, she let go of the tightly contained tears that had been bottled up inside of her for years. She could feel his hand at her back as he rocked her gently, smoothing away the pain and leaving a trail of warmth behind it. So many years had gone by since she'd felt such safety or comfort. She had denied herself the most basic human need of touch for so long that her skin ached for contact. Each tender stroke almost made her cry out, and she clung to him for support as the tears racked her body.

"Shh, shh, it's okay now," he murmured. "It's okay. No one's ever going to hurt you like that again."

The sound of his heart beating beneath his chest gently lulled her into a state of calm, and his constant, steady, breaths into her hairline were hypnotic.

"Tell me what happened tonight," he whispered, once her tears had subsided and her breathing had returned to near normal.

Held safely within his arms, she felt she could vent the words that were strangling her. "My sister, Nan, signed herself into Hanson House after she got caught using cocaine on the job. Allie and I . . . we went over tonight for a family therapy session." A hollow laugh escaped as she pressed on with her story. "Nan and I have never been close, but I didn't realize until tonight how much she hates me."

"Are you sure she hates you, or was it withdrawal talking? I mean, she is your sister."

Ginny felt her carriage stiffen within Matt's hold. "There's just no other answer for it. My sister slept with my husband."

She almost smiled when she felt Matt's posture straighten. It was shocking. Bizarre. Matt had to be affected.

"Slept with your husband?"

"Yes."

"Was she doing drugs, then? Did she do it because she was an addict?"

"Yes and no. I take it that they had an affair, and during the course of it, he introduced her to drugs. I don't even want to know the details."

"Wait a minute," Matt said, not hiding his shock or confusion, "He was on drugs too? Didn't you know he was using?"

Ginny measured her words cautiously. For a moment, she began to retreat, sensing that perhaps Matt would now start to blame her. Extricating herself from his hold, she tried to step away from him.

"Wait. No, don't do that. I'm not judging you, Ginny," he said, gentling her with his voice. "Don't run away from me now. I've known plenty of people in the pros who fooled even the doctors because they hid their addiction well. It was a stupid question."

Feeling more at ease, she settled back into his embrace. "No, I didn't know. I've never done drugs. But from what I'm learning, it obviously affected him and probably created some of the horrible mood swings that led to my beatings. But Nan sleeping with him, or doing drugs, wasn't the worst part of what I heard tonight."

She could almost sense Matt holding his breath. "What could be worse, Ginny? Dear God."

"Finding out that one of your sisters knew all along that you were being abused, but didn't care enough about you to intervene and help you."

They stood quietly holding each other for a long time without saying anything. Finally, Matt spoke to her carefully. "Gin, you said earlier that he attacked your sister. Maybe she was just as terrified of him as you were?"

She let the comment enter her brain slowly. The thought had never occurred to her. She had been so stricken by the immediate pain of Nan's confession that she hadn't processed the information at all.

Matt took a deep breath. "Maybe she started out partying with him, you know, doing drugs, drinking, and what not. Then, after they slept together, I would think that your sister would be mortified and vow never to let it happen again. In my mind, that would trigger an attack. Your husband was probably afraid that she'd come to you, as sisters would, and confess. That would totally make him lose control over you. Consider it, Ginny. I'm not trying to make excuses for her, or smooth it over. What happened was unspeakable, but you've got to eventually find a way to come to terms with this. If you don't, it'll haunt you forever. Maybe he held her in the same kind of terror that had trapped you."

Matt's words blanketed her, giving some solace to her tortured soul. If she could cling to that belief, if only for tonight, maybe she could make it through. She looked up at the kind face above her, and reached out to caress his cheek. He had given her so much in that instant to grasp onto. Protection, warmth, hope . . . oh God, what did it matter any longer? Too many years had passed without understanding or tenderness. To be held tonight, just one night out of hundreds . . . how could it be wrong?

"Thank you, Matt," she whispered, brushing his mouth with her own. Tears blurred her vision and she closed her eyes to deepen the kiss with gratitude. Holding him tightly, she parted her lips to accept his mouth more fully, and trembled as his body responded to hers.

"Ginny," he murmured softly, taking her face between both of his hands. "I want to be with you, more than you'll ever know. But . . . not like this. Not when you're this vulnerable. I don't want you to regret it later."

Matt's breath was becoming shallow as they stood inches apart staring at each other. Although he had stepped back, and their bodies no longer touched, the heat that emanated from the small space between them was charged. Looking into his eyes, every nerve ending came alive. Her body had craved this warmth for years. Not just since Evan's death, but from the beginning of her marriage. Need soon replaced shame, and she covered Matt's hands with her own.

Staring back at him, the intensity of his gaze made her shut her eyes briefly and, when she opened them, her lids felt heavy. "Matt," she whispered, finding it difficult to breathe. "I need you to make love to me tonight. I haven't in five of the seven years I was married. I haven't in the four since Evan died. Even if you don't care about me . . ." Tears choked off her words. As soon as she had said them, she felt the sting of humiliation. How pathetic had she become, to beg a man to be with her? Perhaps she was having a nervous breakdown. Never in her life had she behaved so wantonly.

Kissing the tears from her face, Matt nuzzled her cheeks with his own. "Oh, Ginny. You have no idea how I feel about you, do you?" His voice had become low and strained with emotion. "I've wanted you since the moment we sat on the kitchen floor, helping that crazy dog have puppies. I just don't ever want you to . . . well, hate me. To think of me as someone who would take advantage of you or abuse you."

The simplicity of his words could only be answered with a kiss. As she took his mouth, she wrapped herself in the honesty of his heart. His response was immediate, yet she could tell that he was holding himself back, trying to remain gentle, trying to give her time to adjust to his touch.

"Matt, I'll never hate you. Not after what you've given me tonight." Her voice had become throaty, and her body swayed with an avalanche of emotions as he brought his hands over her breasts. Closing her eyes to the exquisite sensation, she allowed a deep breath to escape from her mouth.

"What we've given each other," he repeated, landing tiny kisses along the bridge of her nose. Tracing her face with his forefinger, he stopped at the small scar above her eyebrow, and replaced it with a deep kiss. "You are so beautiful. Let me take away the pain, Ginny. Give it to me."

She nearly wept as he led her to the sofa and sat down next to her. He wrapped his arms around her and pulled her into another long, intense, kiss. His tongue slipped into her mouth, exploring it as his hands did the same to her body. She wouldn't think about how many years it had been, or allow her inexperience to rob her of this moment. She didn't care how she would feel tomorrow, or the fact that she had only been in his company a few times. She could only focus on the ribbons of pleasure rippling through her body begging for release. His lips left her mouth and trailed down her neck, tracing her collar bone before descending to her breasts. The soft brush of his mustache grazed her skin and sent tiny shocks of desire through her. She nearly arched against him when he slid a hand under the soft fabric of her tee-shirt, exposing the sensitive tip of her breast to the warmth of his palm.

Long forgotten sensations bombarded her, and she leaned back against the sofa, allowing him freedom with her body. There was no awkwardness or hesitation. Both moved in sync in an erotic dance. Almost reading her thoughts, Matt pushed up her tee-shirt and unhooked the center clasp of her bra.

"My God, you are so beautiful," he murmured. His warm breath sent shivers along her skin, and when his

mouth covered her exposed breast, she gasped with pleasure.

Winding her fingers through his hair, she closed her
eyes and reveled in the searing naked contact. Her body
felt liquid as he began a slow descent down her belly,
pulling off her leggings and panties in one easy motion.
Opening herself to him, she tried to pull him to her, but
felt a subtle resistance.

"Not yet," he whispered, as his head lowered to her ab-
domen and began yet another trail of sensual excitement.

She experienced a moment of surprise when she realized he didn't intend to enter her yet. Instead his mouth
caressed her, sending shock waves of heated torment
through her body. The intensity of the contact burned her,
releasing spasms of pleasure as his moist, wet, mouth ten-
derly consumed her. There was nothing now. There was
no betrayal. There was no pain. There was no tomorrow.
The exquisite sensation had banished the hurt, and was
begging for release.

Suddenly it consumed her. The explosion began low
and radiated throughout her body until it entered her mind
and settled there. Yet he continued to torture her as wave
after wave of unbelievable pleasure washed over her.

"Oh, my God . . ."

Instead of being satiated, her need now became almost
primal. She had to feel him inside of her, filling the empty
void within her, connecting her at long last to a loving
human being. Reaching to pull him to her, she again felt a
resistance.

"Please, Matt," she murmured, "I need you."

His expression was pained as he brought her close and
held her tightly against his chest. Wrapping his fingers

through her hair, he whispered raggedly against her ear. "Honey, I can't. Not unless you have something to protect yourself in the house. And I hope to God you do."

She forced her brain to work in order to comprehend what he was saying. "Do you mean condoms?" In the intensity of the moment it sounded so stupid, and she felt like such a novice.

"Yes," he said between deep breaths, allowing a low chuckle to escape.

"Oh, Lord. I don't. I never thought—it's been years— I've never bought them. What do we do?"

Matt held her even tighter, and she suddenly felt his chest move with suppressed laughter. "Is there a Seven-Eleven around here? Anything to keep me from having to take a very cold shower?"

She wanted to laugh and cry at the same time. Her body was in abject torment, yet her mind could not deny the sanity of his words. "I don't know what to do," she whispered. "I'm so sorry. I feel terrible about this."

"Don't you ever feel bad about anything like this, especially this," he murmured, squeezing her again. "It's all right. We'll have a chance to finish another time."

Hoping to give him some sort of comfort, she began stroking his back. Nuzzling his neck, she spoke low against his skin and could feel his breathing becoming stilted again. "Matt, neither one of us were prepared. Who could know that this would have started?"

It seemed as though each word sent a tremor through his body. "Ginny, honey, please. Your touch—I can't . . . Look, I have to stop now, or I'll give in."

"I'm sorry."

"Nope," he said with a smile, brushing her lips and

standing quickly. "No apologies, okay? Just promise that we'll get together soon."

"I promise," she answered, suddenly feeling shy as she gathered up her clothes and fought down the creeping embarrassment of the moment. Feeling like a young girl, she started giggling as she struggled to untangle her panties from the stretch leggings and get them on again.

"Dinner? Tomorrow?" he said, joining her laughter and giving her a devastatingly sexy smile as he watched her pull on her pants. "I can't watch you do this. It's doing something to the rational side of my brain."

His sly comment was flattering, and for the first time in years, she actually felt her face flush with excitement. The sound of his voice, combined with his unspoken intentions, sent a tremor of anticipation through her. Finally accomplishing the task of getting dressed, she looked up at him, only to meet his intense gaze. Matt's eyes held a raw hunger that made her body ache with renewed desire. The way he assessed her body and drew a deep breath through his nose when she stood before him made her want to throw caution to the wind. The man wanted her. Actually wanted her.

Timidly approaching him, she touched his shoulders. "Can I have one small kiss before you go?" Now she was flirting! It was horrible and wonderful at the same time.

Lowering his head, Matt gave her a brief kiss. Then almost as though his libido had gotten the better of him, he swept her into a full passionate embrace before parting from her abruptly with a groan. "I've gotta go. I'm losing this internal battle quickly."

He felt so good that it was hard to focus on the right thing to do, but she knew she had to stop torturing the man. Hell, she had to stop tormenting herself. Smiling at him as she ushered him to the door, she tapped Matt's shoulder for one last kiss. "Maybe we could do lunch? Dinner seems so far away."

What had come over her? In a tumultuous twenty minutes she had become Mae West!

"Yeah," he said in a deep murmur, brushing her mouth with another kiss. "How about if I pick something up— lunch, some wine, anything else we might need, and I'll meet you here at one o'clock."

The thought nearly made her shiver. "We could have a picnic on my living room floor. I'll open the windows, bring in some flowers, find some nice music . . ."

"I've gotta go. I'll tell you what, let's do dinner instead. If we meet for lunch, you won't make it back to work."

Looking at the almost painful expression on his face, she suppressed another giggle. It was obvious that her description of a possible lunch had been too enticing. The mere thought of what would happen during dessert gnawed at their resolve, and she hurried to open the door before Matt lost sense of his gentlemanly decorum.

"Matt, I don't know how to thank you for turning one of the worst nights of my life into one of the best. I was ready to curl up and die before you came. Good night," she whispered, touching his back as he left. When he turned to peck her on the forehead, she almost pulled him back inside the door, and had to fight against begging him to stay.

Smiling, he reached out and pushed a strand of hair behind her ear. "Remind me to tell you the story about the basket of peas tomorrow at dinner. Good night, Ginny," he said, taking another deep breath.

Ginny closed the door behind him and let her body sink down on the steps in the foyer, as the memory from their lovemaking played over again in her mind. The evening was beyond belief. Only three hours earlier, she had been fighting for her sanity, and now she felt like a young girl again, excited and dreamy, with a date scheduled for the next evening.

Hearing Matt's car pull out of the driveway, Ginny knew that somebody must be watching out for her, that someone had sent him to her tonight. Closing her eyes, she said a prayer of thanks. Someone, that night, had saved her life.

Chapter 16

N an rolled over and cringed at the intensity of the sun beaming down through the small, wired, dormitory windows. It had taken forever to fall asleep the night before, and when she had finally slipped into that forgetful cloak of darkness, she remembered her last prayer had been to make things better in the morning. Well, morning was here, and nothing had changed. She was still prisoner in an institution, only this time she had requested to extend her own stay.

"Rough night, huh?"

Nan peered at her roommate through a squint, trying to focus on the bright and chipper person speaking to her from across the room. "The pits," she finally muttered, trying to turn over and block her face from the sun.

"Those family sessions are a bitch. But, at least it's over."

Obviously Camille wasn't going to let her rest. That much she had learned from the short stay with her roommate. Once the kid was up, and she saw any sign of life in your body, Camille wanted company. Although she was in no mood to open the subject, Nan forced herself to respond and swung her legs over the side of the bed. Rubbing her face with both hands, she stared at the floor.

"Thought you were breaking out of here today? Change your mind?"

This woman-child had a way of slicing right through the garbage to get to the immediate point. Heaving herself up to a standing position, Nan just shrugged while looking around for her toothbrush. Everything seemed foggy, and her movements felt as if she were operating in slow motion.

"You know, I bet it can't be any worse than the first couple of sessions I had with my folks. My mother slapped my face, and I hit her back. Then Dad jumped in it and I tried to kick his butt. Whoop, there it is!" Camille said, chuckling at the memory and falling back on her pillows.

The sight of Camille's elfin expression, twinkling with mischief while she told this horrendous story, coaxed a smile onto Nan's face. This teenager was wild, and the similarity of their personalities was frighteningly ironic.

"Well, we exchanged a few blows ourselves last night," Nan uttered, becoming exhausted from the sheer memory of the incident.

"Get out! You did not! Miss High Society?" Camille was nearly doubled over with laughter, and she hung from the side of the bed as she hooted.

"Who, me? Miss High Society? With my mouth? Nah, my sister Ginny's the one with the blue blood. Or, at least she acts like it."

"So you got into a fight with your sister? What did Doc Alberts say? She must've loved that one!"

Sitting back on her own bed, Nan fumbled through her

makeup case, looking for contact lens solution. "It was really bad, Camille," she said, becoming suddenly serious and tearful. "I really hurt my sister, and she didn't deserve what I did. You know, sometimes you can be angry at somebody and it's not their fault. Maybe you just need somewhere to direct the rage, 'cause you're so damn mad at life, and loved ones get hurt in the process."

Oddly, Camille sat up and stared at her, this time with no levity in her voice. "Look, Nan, we've all done some pretty slimy shit, or we wouldn't be here. Right? Not to make excuses or anything, but we've also had some pretty terrible things happen to us. Now, I'm not saying that makes everything okay, but when you're fighting for your life or your sanity, you'll pull everyone down with you just to keep from drowning. It's like a law of nature ... instinct. That's why they tell people to never try to save a drowning person by jumping in the water with them. They say throw an object for them to cling to first, 'cause, unless you're a professional, they'll take you down and you'll both drown."

Nan just stared at the girl for a few moments. "Where in God's name did you learn that?"

"What's wrong? Don't believe me?"

"No. It's not that. But, jeez, for a kid to come up with something so deep, and so true ... I mean—"

"I know. I just blew your mind," she chuckled again, the merriment returning to her dark eyes. "No, seriously. I learned it in Annapolis, yachting classes when Dad bought his dream boat. But it makes sense for other crap too, you know? I may be young, but I'm not stupid."

Nan nodded in fervent agreement. "Touché! What you

said makes a lot of sense." Looking at her teenage friend directly, she formulated the words for the question that had burned in her brain all night long. Even though this kid was half her age, it felt like she was talking to a peer. Taking a deep breath, she let the words form themselves, watching Camille's facial expressions closely as she spoke.

"Okay. Here's a hypothetical question. Say you've done something really low life to your sister, but that she didn't know about it for years. When you did it, you were pissed at her . . . and high . . . and thought she deserved it. But then, the second you got done, you hated yourself and wanted to kill the other person that helped you hurt her. But that person blackmailed you not to tell. Then, say, the blackmailer died, and you thought you could sweep the whole nasty, ugly thing under the rug. But then, you come in here, and somehow, the truth comes out. Now, the sister you've hurt has totally banished you, and the other one is so disappointed and so . . . mortified, that she won't speak to you either. Some shit can't be redeemed, right?"

A slight smile formed at the corners of Camille's mouth. Nan felt herself holding her breath, not sure of which direction this mercurial girl's temperament might take the conversation. Yet, she held out the thin hope that at least her roommate would be gentle when she called her a whore.

"So . . ." Camille said, lacing her fingers together around her bent knees. "You were partying, right? Getting high, real high. Then you get horny, screw your sister's husband, because at that time, you think, hell, the bitch deserves it. Right?"

Nan blanched at the simplicity of Camille's assessment, not to mention how she had cut through her thinly veiled facade. Trying to recover, she mumbled, "Hypothetically."

"Yeah, yeah, I know. Anyway. Then, after you do it, you come down, right? A good coke high, instantly blown. A true fucking waste of greenbacks."

Nan just shook her head and found laughter erupting from her throat while tears of pain threatened her eyes. "The entire thing was a waste."

"Damn shame," Camille added, smiling broadly. "At least the shot could've been worth it. But, we're getting off the point. Point is, now you do this mess, and get sudden religion. You know how it is when you do a crash-and-burn from being real high? You swear on a stack of Bibles, to Jesus, Mary, and Joseph, that you'll *never*, ever, ever, touch the stuff again. Been there, seen it, done it. All right. So, now, you roll over and look at this bastard in the eyes and tell him to get the fuck out, and to never darken your doorstep again. Right? But it's too late, you've already slept with Count Dracula, and he feels like he can come by and take your shit at will, any night of the week. I'm surprised he didn't kick your ass in the process— cause you've got a mouth on you like me."

Tears streamed down Nan's face, and she didn't bother to wipe them away. To hear the horror recounted to her in such matter-of-fact terms was frightening. It was as if this child were her conscience, beating her to death with her own words. "You know an awful lot for your age," she whispered, trying to force Camille back out of the tiny space in her mind that she'd previously invited her roommate into. But, from the unwavering expression on the girl's face, Nan could tell that it was too late.

"Nan, like I said before. Been there. Seen it. Done it. There ain't no saints in this joint. It's just a matter of degree, is all. Nobody is in here that hasn't taken a walk on the dark side first."

Feeling a little relieved by the odd extension of comfort that Camille offered, she sat back and issued a silent invitation for the girl to continue.

"Okay," Camille said, straightening her posture and almost looking official. "The guy can hold this crap over your head. So you don't tell. Then he drops dead, or somebody offs him, whatever. It's irrelevant. The bastard dies. So, now, you have no intentions of going there with your sister. Not because you hate her, but because you love her. And because you are so sorry, that words can't even begin to explain it—shit happens. You want to run to her and tell her, because even though she pisses you off from time to time, she's still about the closest thing you have to a normal family, if there is such a thing. Makes sense to me."

Camille's words did make sense, maybe too much sense, but they only answered half of the question. Feeling a pull to something greater than herself, Nan let her own words rush forth again with force. "But then, last night . . . I don't know what came over me. I wanted to hurt Ginny, rip her to shreds, anything. She was so haughty, and pious, and judgmental. She looked at me like I was some pathetic creature that needed to get my act together, and I went right for her jugular. It was horrible," she sobbed, hiding her face in her hands. "So many years went by that I resented her. He was beating her, and she kept pretending he wasn't. She wouldn't do anything about it. I was afraid to, because then he'd tell on me. If she had just told any of us, then I could have had a reason to support her. I hated her for not telling, and for trapping me with silence again. My hands were tied!"

Undaunted by the sudden emotional outburst, Camille continued, her voice strong and authoritative. "Like I said, it makes sense."

"It does?" Nan looked up for a moment, and wiped away the tears in utter confusion.

"Hell, yeah."

"I'm not following? I could've kept this nightmare to myself, gotten the hell out of here in twenty-four hours, and now . . ."

"Look," Camille said standing and pacing, appearing totally impatient. "We're here because we mask our pain. Whatever caused you to do this to your sister in the first place didn't go away after the guy died. Whatever you resented about her before, whatever buttons she used to push, she was still pushing them, okay? The difference was, before you slept with her husband, you could argue with her and not feel guilty, but after you did that, then you had to eat crow and be humble, or feel like a piece of shit—since technically, you owed her at least that. And, probably, getting high numbed it up for you so you could tolerate her bullshit and let it ride. But after he died, and hell, after two days of drying out here, she gets in your face with the same old yang, and *kablooey*, you break, cuss her out, and try to wax the floor with her. Could be worse."

Nan was nearly speechless. "Could be worse?" she finally uttered, a chuckle strangely finding its way to her mouth as she wiped the tears from her cheeks. "Are you on drugs, now? Can I have some of what you've been sniffing this morning?"

They both laughed. "No, really. First of all, the guy could still be alive. Two, you could have killed him, and be sitting in the State Pen telling this story to Hard Copy. Three, your sister hated the bastard, too, and it's not like you broke up this deep love affair of all times. It's just one more thing to make her spit on his grave. Four, after you go before her prostrate, make it up to her . . . chant, beg, plead, kiss her ass, whatever, maybe she'll get over it. The other one, well, she'll have to play monkey in the middle for a little while, but sooner or later, she'll say, look, enough is enough—I've got my own life. She'll still speak to both of you, even if you two never patch it up again."

Shaking her head in utter amazement, Nan just stared at Camille. This young girl had taken the unspeakable and narrowed it down into bite-sized pieces so she could swallow the bitterness away. It was a gift, a blunt and very direct one, but a gift nonetheless. Still intrigued by the pixie sitting across the room from her, Nan posed another question, one designed to give her some insight to the source of this woman-child's wisdom.

"Camille, you said you've been there, seen it, done it. Have you ever done anything like this? Slept with your sister's husband?"

Camille laughed. "Hell no. I'm an only child, and I'm no skeezer. That shit was low-life, Nan." Obviously seeing the hurt shock on Nan's face, she sat down. "Oh, c'mon. Just playing with you, girl. No, really. I've done my share of trifling shit, too. Like the time I got blasted, screwed three different guys in the same day—the pool guy, my boyfriend, and this guy that does the lawn. Then continued to get high . . . man, I was basing then."

"Free basing cocaine?"

"Honey, I've done more drugs than a pharmacy. Best place to get 'em is in high school, good high schools— you know, where the people have the money to get decent shipments, uncut from Peru? Any ole way, my Mom calls up from some damned vacation somewhere, in a big, 'Oh, sweetie, how's everything' mood. Like she could give a shit. And I say, yeah, just did a pound of coke and had a couple of multiple orgasms, but other than that, things are boring." Camille fell back on the bed and howled with laughter.

Nan found herself joining in, giggling with the girl, albeit unable to hide her shock. "You did not!"

"Sure did. Talk about a goddamned confession, Nan. Shit, I was so high, and so pissed off, I busted myself! That's what landed me in this joint."

"And you hit your Mom?" Nan's laughter began to subside as the full horror of the girl's statement set in.

"The bitch is not my Mom. Well, she is biologically— sort of. But she never took the responsibility, and respect comes with that. She's a big kid herself. You've got to pay the cost to be the boss—and I don't mean just money."

"I hear you," Nan murmured. It was a reflex response, again, hitting very close to home.

"See, my Mom spends money to make up for the fact

that she's miserable with my Dad. He has his little flings, and she shops. Now, I get into family therapy, and they want to know why this and why that. At first, I'm cool. I'm not giving up any tapes, know what I mean? But then she starts this judgmental shit, as though her life were perfect. And one thing led to another. I say she's frigid, but so used to the money that she's not woman enough to leave a bogus situation. I call her a leech, and say that shopping gives her an orgasm . . . She slaps me, I slap her, Dad jumps up, threatens to beat my ass, he calls me a whore; I tell him he has whores in his stable younger than me . . . We all cry, everybody sits the fuck back down. Voilà! Family Therapy. Ain't it a trip?"

Both of them stared at each other for a few moments then burst out laughing simultaneously. "Oh, shit!" Nan screamed through peals of laughter. "I should've done that at sixteen years old. Maybe I wouldn't be so screwed up now!"

Still rolling on the bed, Camille choked out, "They woulda put you away, girlfriend! There was no such thing as child abuse back in your day—or therapy. They'd have kicked your skinny white ass and put you on the chain gang!"

The two women lay back on their beds, still laughing and wiping their eyes as occasional waves of giggles overcame them. "You know, we really are nuts. We belong here," Nan said, trying to catch her breath.

"We're lucky, though. Ninety percent of the world is crazy, but they don't get help. So they just keep right on being outta their freakin' minds. After we get out, Nan, we'll be the few, the proud, the Marines. Then we can walk around and look at them like they're nuts, and use group terms like it's a secret code . . . You should get manageability back into your life . . . Thank you for sharing . . . How do you really feel . . . And, what impact does this have on you . . . Hell, we'll have it down to a science."

Although Camille had been joking around when she made the statement, again, she had been correct. Out of the mouths of babes had come words of wisdom. As the girl popped off of the bed and shoved a tape into her boom box, Nan shook her head in wonderment. The sound of Queen Latifah filled their room, but this time it didn't bother her, even at nine o'clock in the morning. There was something upbeat, simple, refreshing about the youth that had become associated with the music. This morning she would laugh with Camille, move to the rhythm, and feel hope again.

One day at a time.

She had grabbed the phone on the first ring at least ten times during the morning, and she refused to do it again. Ginny would call her. Ginny had to call her, before she went out of her mind with worry. Forcing herself to concentrate, Allie went back to the stack of paperwork on her desk. There had to be a way to push from her mind the terrible picture of her small family breaking up and shattering into pieces.

This time when the phone rang, she waited a moment. On the third ring she picked up the receiver and took a deep breath.

"Hello, Women's Center. Allyson Barbera."

"Allie. Hi."

It was all she could do to keep from trembling as she listened to the sound of Ginny's voice.

"Al, are you there?"

"Yes, thank God you called," she finally managed. "Are you okay?"

Allie waited impatiently for her sister to respond. She had looked forward to this call all morning, thought of a dozen sensible things to say, and now that Ginny was on the line, she could only let the first thing that popped into her head fall from her mouth.

After a deep sigh, she heard her sister speak. "Yeah, I guess so. I'm not great, but I'm better than I had expected."

Allie hesitated again. What did that mean? She studied the tone of Ginny's voice for a moment before deciding to speak. Her sister seemed a little distant, yet very controlled and not totally devastated. Random questions tugged at her, creating a blur of confusion in her mind. "Gin, have you taken anything? Are you really all right."

Ginny's response was immediate. "Taken anything? No. Definitely not. After what we've been through with Nan?"

"Sorry, stupid question. I just feel so . . . helpless. Like I want to take this pain away, and I'm afraid of what you might be going through, and what you might do to yourself to stop hurting. I also feel so foolish and guilty."

"Guilty?" Ginny asked, her voice sounding as though she were trying to calm a frightened child. "Oh, Allie. Why?"

"Because, I didn't know . . . I would have helped, done

anything I could had I known what Evan was doing to you."

There was a silence that gripped both of them as they sat listening to the background static in the phone. Tears threatened the corners of Allie's eyes as she waited for her sister to speak, but she forced them away, refusing to cry at her job.

"Allyson. That was my nightmare. I know now that I have to take responsibility for my own silence. I'd be as wrong as Nan is if I shifted that blame off on you. No, I had a choice. Don't take this on, okay?"

A wave of relief flooded over her. Before Ginny said it, she hadn't realized that in some small way, she had needed absolution. "I'm still sorry," she whispered. "Sorry that you ever had to live such hell."

"I know. But I'm away from it now. I'm all right. I just needed a few hours to collect myself, to think about things."

"Do you ever think you can forgive Nan? I know it's a terrible question to ask, but I have to tell you that I wish we could all be together again. I wish none of it had ever happened."

After another long pause, Ginny answered her cautiously. "I wish it all never happened too, Al. And truthfully, I don't know if I can ever forgive her. I'll need more time to find the answer to that question."

"Yeah, I understand. But hearing all that last night about Nan. Ginny, we never knew . . ."

"I know," Ginny whispered. "It's all too horrible."

"We're a family," Allie whispered back. "Maybe you

could find a way to forgive her. It's just my own wishful thinking, I suppose. Pretty stupid, huh?"

"Allie, have you ever noticed that you always put yourself down? The way you feel, and what you hope for is who you are. It's valid. Nobody has to feel it but you. I did that for years, and I know what it does to your self esteem. Don't, okay? Just try to stop yourself and take a deep breath before you apologize, put yourself down, or jump in to help. That's a little trick I learned along the way, after Evan died."

Stunned, Allie found herself unable to respond. So many emotions were being unearthed, so many issues were being forced to the surface and out in the open, that she felt like a big beetle under a microscope. How long was everything going to feel like this, stay like this? What ever happened to just living and acting and doing without such scrutiny? Allowing a long, weary sigh to escape, Allie gave in. "Yeah, I do it a lot. Second nature, I guess. But, really, do you need anything? Do you want me to come over tonight?"

When she heard Ginny's soft laughter, the sound only made her more worried. Perhaps she had finally snapped. Her other sister was having a nervous breakdown!

"Ginny, I'll come now. Please, don't do anything until I get there."

"Allie, Allie, calm down," Ginny said between giggles. "I'm not losing it. You are hopeless, but I love you. No. The reason I'm laughing is because tonight won't be good."

"Why not?" She was still uneasy about the swift change

in her sister's mood, but somehow she detected that there was no immediate danger.

"Because, I have a dinner date."

"Wait," she said, standing up, "Did I hear you correctly? A date?"

"Yes," Ginny said shyly. "Matt Lewellyn."

A strange mixture of emotions poured over Allie. On the one hand, she had been adamant that Ginny date, go out, do anything but be alone. She had been worried about her sister, ready to gather the troops, ready to move mountains if they stood in her way. But Ginny was obviously fine. She had found her own way. Alone. An immediate sense of emptiness filled her, blocking her total joy for the good news. Nan was a case, but she had the professionals to help her—and now they weren't on speaking terms. Ginny, who was supposed to be devastated, wasn't. Plus, she had a romantic interest to carry her through this trauma, and sounded like an excited high school girl. But where did that leave her? Who would be there to pat her hand and offer her tissues as her marriage fell apart? Immediately, she was embarrassed and ashamed by the thought.

"Al, are you there?"

"Yes. Oh, Ginny, that's wonderful. I guess the shock was . . . well, just that. Shock. Matt Lewellyn. How about that."

"Are you okay, Al? You sound like you're about to cry."

Forcing a false laugh as tears splotched her blouse, Allie answered quickly. "Me, oh, you know me. I'm hopeless. I cry at happy occasions, sad ones, you name it. Well, listen. I've got to wipe my nose and get back to work. If you're all right, then I'm relieved. Call me tomorrow about the big date, okay?"

"I will, Al. Thanks a lot. Thanks for always being there."

Ginny's words stung as she swallowed down another wave of melancholy. Inherently, she knew that it wasn't Ginny's fault; it was just the timing. The rational side of her brain told her that she should be happy for her sister, and in her heart she was. Yet, guilt from even mentally wondering when her turn would come robbed her of their shared joy. She hated to feel this way, and was ashamed of herself for thinking such a thing. Maybe she was no better than Nan, and that horrible possibility made her hastily end their conversation.

"Gin, love you too. But I gotta go."

"I know. But I just wanted to let you know I was all right. Oh, also, I have a favor to ask."

For the first time in years, Allie hesitated. "What is it?"

"Boy, you are putting theory into practice immediately, with that deep breath stuff."

Allie forced another chuckle. "What is it, Gin?"

"On a very serious note. I have a client who has become a friend. Her husband is abusing her, and I'd like to get any literature or information I can about how she can get out of that situation. I never had the courage to do it myself. But there has to be an agency, a safe house, some legal steps, something . . . She has to know that she'll be safe, or she'll never take the first step to get out."

Allie felt punch drunk, like she was being barraged by a series of blows to the head from several different sources at once. "Jesus. Sure, I'll help. That's what we do at this agency. I'll send you some materials, and make some telephone inquiries, and call you back tomorrow. Meanwhile, I don't know . . . I can ask my director or the attorney that's on staff."

"Thanks, Al. I knew I could count on you."

Again, Ginny's words were a painful reminder of the emotions she was trying to tuck away. Everyone's issues were always paramount to her own. An immediate pang of guilt stabbed at her. Of course this woman's situation was more dire than hers. The people who came into her office had problems more urgent than hers. Nan's situation was more serious than her own. Ginny's had also been more dangerous than either hers or Nan's. Dave's job, and whether or not he'd be inconvenienced, was more important than her tiny efforts to launch a second career. And the kids? They always took first priority . . .

Straining against a new wave of tears, she said goodbye and hung up. Nausea swept through her with a rush of shame, followed by anger. She knew she had to pull it together, to just make it to the ladies room before another client walked into her office. Somehow she had to get rid of these ugly, conflicting emotions and solve other people's problems. That was her job. That was her life. Her lot in life. But the unanswered question clawed its way to the surface before she got halfway across the room. Who made it all right for her? Who soothed her? Who made sacrifices for her?

Anger nearly immobilized her and she covered her face with her hands, refusing to sob. She would not let this ugliness ruin the one positive thing in her life. She would not let her co-workers see her as anything other than professional. Not here!

"You okay?"

Allie could not take her hands down from her face when she heard the deep, male voice. Oh, God. Not now. Turning away from it before she lowered her hands, she took two very deep breaths and answered with her back facing him. "I . . . uh . . . I just need a few minutes. I'm okay."

She waited to hear footsteps leaving, prayed that they would leave.

"Is it business or personal that has you in tears? Look, we all get some client stuff in here that tears at your heart strings. You aren't a real social services veteran until somebody has made you cry, at least once."

The voice was soothing and gentle, and she appreciated the fact that the intruder had allowed her to save face. Rapidly wiping at her cheeks, she tried to stop the torrent and steady her voice. "It's just that . . . I'm so tired . . ." To her horror, her voice cracked at the end of the sentence, and she once more closed her eyes wishing for an instantaneous evaporation. She had to get out of here!

Immediately, she became aware of a presence directly behind her, then that presence reached out and held her shoulders. "Sick and tired of being sick and tired? I know. We all get that way sometimes. It'll be all right."

Allie felt her body melt into the warmth behind her, and the tenderness of the comfort it offered broke loose sobs in earnest. As Jason Levy turned her around, she couldn't think about propriety, professionalism, or co-workers. He seemed to have a way of suspending judgment and just feeling. Without question or censure, he let her ruin his shirt with lipstick and mascara as the tears came unceasingly. Only when she finally caught her breath did she become aware of the total mess she'd made.

Stepping back from him, shame washed over her again. "I'm so sorry," she said quietly, trying to rub off the makeup and feeling her bottom lip tremble from repressed tears.

"It was a cheap shirt, due for the cleaners anyway. Your crying jag just sealed its fate," he said smiling, and pulling her back to his shoulder. "Listen, Allie, I don't know what's wrong, but a client didn't do this. You don't have to tell me, but if you ever do need to talk, I'm here for you. Deal?"

Again unable to speak, she nodded and mumbled, "Yes," into his shirt.

"Okay, so now, how about if you go wash your face and get out of here for a few hours. If you want company, we'll go for coffee. If you need to be alone, I'll make up an excuse and you go home. Sound like a plan?"

Again, she nodded yes, before forcing herself to leave his embrace. "I think I should go home. Maybe we can have coffee another time?"

"Absolutely. Now, I'll go deal with our Dragon Lady director, and you get out of here before she can grill you. Is it your night to teach?"

"No, I only have classes to teach on Tuesday afternoons and Thursday nights."

"Good. Now, scoot."

Allie collected her purse as Jason Levy handed her a bunch of tissues. The walk down the corridor to the ladies room by the elevators seemed longer than usual. Everything felt strange. In those brief moments something had happened. Something had changed. As she opened the door to the ladies room and safely tucked herself away inside a stall, it hit her. Again, she had changed. She had undergone another metamorphosis. What was that going to do to her life, her marriage, her children . . . ? Nothing was in its original place in her mind. Everything that was once comforting and familiar seemed to be a million miles away. Especially Dave.

Dear God, what was she going to do?

Chapter 17

*E*xcitement coursed through her veins as she routed through her closet for something to wear. Ginny almost laughed at the irony of her first date with Matt. Then she had worn the classic black suit despite her sister's protests. Now she was looking forward to going out with him, searching her conservative wardrobe for something with a hint of sexiness to wear. It amazed her how much black she had in her closet, especially for someone who wasn't really mourning the dead.

Exasperated, she finally settled on a light apricot gabardine jacket with a sheer georgette skirt. Choosing pearl accessories, she had to admit that she hoped Matt would initiate a romantic encounter this evening. Dear God, she truly had become wanton after last night. She had told herself repeatedly that they had just been caught up in the moment, that he probably just felt sorry for her, and that once he saw her again, he'd be different. But those thoughts had been eclipsed by the warmth in his voice when he'd called to confirm during the day. He'd sounded excited, and almost a little shy, which endeared him to her even more.

Matt's call had shattered her concentration for the remainder of the afternoon and if she hadn't been so busy, she might have doodled his name on her blotter. "Stop it, stop it, stop it," she murmured to herself, hurrying into the bathroom to get ready. The last thing she wanted was to appear needy and desperate. If he didn't want her, she'd be crushed, and would need at least her dignity to fall back on.

The thought sobered her. Good Lord, what if he really didn't want her? What if he had some character flaw that he was hiding? Worse, what if he really had someone else? Someone he was serious about? What if she was just a diversion? Shuddering at the thoughts, she tried to shake off the self imposed torture. It was absurd. How could anyone be this insecure? She was so unused to being happy, that this seemed too good to be true. Determined to stop herself from anguishing over the questions, she showered and dressed, and returned to the mirror to apply her makeup.

Staring at her own reflection, Ginny smiled. Only twenty-four hours ago, she had stood in that same spot, trying to hide her tears and put on concealer. She had thought she was dying inside. Now she was smiling, trying to put on makeup to go out on a date. Perhaps that's the way it was. All a matter of perspective. Or maybe that's just the way her relationship with Matt was destined to unfold. First she had dreaded it, then had come to appreciate and enjoy it. This feeling sure beat the way things had gone with Evan, starting off great and ending in horror.

She would not think of that tonight. The subject was banished, dead and buried. Nan . . . ? She couldn't go down that path. Not now. Not tonight. Tonight was hers. No family problems. No betrayals. No heart-wrenching questions. What a difference a day made.

Starting at the sound of the bell, she applied her lipstick quickly and ran down the stairs. When she opened the door, Matt stood before her smiling as he handed her a bunch of fresh cut irises.

"You look wonderful," he said, brushing her mouth with a kiss.

His comment made her look away, and she led him into the living room after she accepted the bouquet. "These are beautiful, Matt. Irises . . ." she whispered, lowering her nose to take in their fragrance.

"And wine, for later . . ." he said, still smiling and producing a bottle of chablis. "I hope you have your dancing shoes on?"

"Dancing?" She was almost giddy with anticipation as she left him to find a vase and collect her purse.

"Yup," he called down the hall behind her. "Found this neat little restaurant called Layton's. We can dance there too."

"I've never been there," she said, adjusting the flowers and setting them on the table by the window. "I haven't danced the night away in so long. Well, not since that charity dinner. And it was many years before that."

"That's what we're gonna do, lady," he said with a laugh, opening the door when she was ready and ushering her to the car.

As they passed the boutiques on Main Street in Marlton, Ginny saw everything with a new perspective. Gaslights decorated each corner, and the shops all had old family names that looked like a quaint village from an era long ago. Bringing the car to a stop, Matt pulled up before a large white house that had been converted into a restaurant. "We're here."

"This is wonderful," she said, truly in awe. Waiting for Matt to come around and open her door, she nearly giggled. Never could she have imagined that she'd have an opportunity to restart her life this way.

They were greeted at the door by a tuxedoed maitre d', who immediately ushered them upstairs. "Who would have known this place had a second level," she said quietly as they followed their host. It was a dumb comment, but all of a sudden she felt nervous and lost for something witty to say. And the fact that Matt just smiled made her heart pound harder.

"I am showing you to one of our private dining rooms, Madame."

Ginny looked at Matt curiously. "A private dining room?"

"This night should be special," he said in a low voice that made her insides churn.

Once they were seated, she had a chance to take in the entire view. It had been too much to assimilate the beautiful glass enclosed porch, the stately Victorian decor, and the fine linen that graced each table. But once she sat down and drew a breath, it was as though her mind replayed everything in slow motion.

"Do you like it?" Matt asked, his expression full of anticipation.

"It's perfect," she answered, smiling and gazing at him affectionately. "You've really made this special. Thank you."

Matt almost seemed to blush and, again, her nephew's

image flashed before her, making her smile broaden. Even at his age, Matt had a boyish charm that affected her senses.

"Would you like some wine?" he offered, picking up the wine list and looking over the selections.

Somehow something had changed and charged the air between them. He seemed as nervous as she felt, and the easiness between them had vanished on this formal date. She took the wine list from him and laid it on the table.

"What's wrong?" he asked nervously, intently focusing on her expression.

"Oh, Matt. Nothing's wrong." She almost laughed. "But look at us. We're both so nervous. I mean, it's like we just met all over again. Don't worry. Nothing can ruin this evening."

Matt let his shoulders slump in obvious relief. "Man, Ginny. I'm glad you said something. I was so uptight about tonight. And that's crazy. I don't know why, but . . . I don't know."

They both smiled as their gazes met. "Maybe because we're anticipating after the date too much," she murmured and then laughed easily, helping him to relax even more.

"Maybe we should have done that first, then gone out to dinner," he said, joining her laughter and becoming comfortable. "Okay, so let's start again. How about wine?"

Somehow in that brief exchange, they had reset their old chemistry. Laughter and great conversation followed, easing any nervousness that they'd had. By the time their waiter joined them, their newfound easiness had been restored.

"My name's Scott," their waiter interrupted. "I'll be glad to serve you tonight."

Ginny smiled and looked at the handsome young man in his early twenties, who wore a tuxedo and his best table manners. "That'll be great, Scott, we're having a terrific time. I'm learning all about baskets of peas." She felt so light, so happy, so free, so touched by Matt's story, that she wanted everyone around her to feel the same way.

"Correction, we're trading baskets of peas," Matt joined in.

"I'm sorry?" their waiter questioned, clearly looking confused.

They both smiled and looked at the young man, sharing a secret understanding between them.

"So what's good today?" Matt asked.

Their waiter looked at them and smiled, his youth perhaps making him liberal in his questioning glances. "First date, huh? That's great. I love to serve people on their first big romantic date. Let me tell you our specialties . . ."

They laughed and looked at each other, almost ignoring Scott as he rattled off a series of entrees. "I guess it's pretty obvious, hmm?" Ginny said, not able to wipe the smile from her lips.

"It's obvious that you make me very happy," Matt answered, his voice dropping lower as he responded.

The way he looked at her, and the deep resonance of his voice, sent a tremor through her. It was also obvious that Scott had picked up on it, and the young man blushed as he closed the small portfolio.

"Maybe I should give you two a little time, and come back?"

"No, don't be silly," Ginny said, feeling immediately embarrassed. "We're starved, aren't we, Matt?"

"Definitely," he said, gazing at her intensely, causing a heat to creep up her legs.

Scott just looked away, and smiled. "I'll come back," he said still blushing, and heading for the door.

"You chased him away!" she fussed good naturedly, not looking at Matt when she spoke.

"I wish we were at your house, to tell you the truth," Matt whispered across the table, capturing one of her hands under his. "I haven't been able to stop thinking about it all day."

Unable to look up at him, she smiled down at the table, while the heat of his hand radiated an unbearable warmth up her arm. "Neither could I," she said softly, closing her eyes briefly. "But we should eat, shouldn't we?"

Matt chuckled. "I suppose we should. It would look really obvious if we just got up and left without even ordering a glass of wine."

Electricity coursed through them as they impatiently waited for Scott to return, and they both fought hard to dispel it with more light conversation. Once they placed their orders, and they were alone again, silence fell over them.

"This is really hard, isn't it?" she finally asked, unable to keep up the facade.

Matt just laughed. "In a manner of speaking."

Shocked and flattered, she shifted in her seat, accidentally brushing his knee. The contact singed her, and were it not for Scott's unobtrusive return with their wine, she might have suggested that they skip dinner. At least, now with wine and a salad before them, she could try to concentrate on the meal. And she had hoped he'd still want her? Lord! There was no mistaking it now.

"Want any dessert?" Matt said, pushing away his half eaten plate and gazing at her intensely.

"No. Everything was so good, and so filling . . . I couldn't," she said honestly, pushing her plate a few inches away from her.

As the silence wrapped around them again, she struggled for something to say. Matt's gaze held her with such longing that it was almost impossible to look at him and think at the same time. Drawing a deep breath, Ginny tried to steady her heartbeat. "Well, this was just wonderful." Stupid. Really stupid. But how do you tell a man, okay, we've eaten a great dinner at an exquisite restaurant, but now I'd like nothing more than to go home and make love to you? That was out of the question. "You said they had dancing here?" she asked, running out of reasonable conversation.

Seeming a little defeated, Matt smiled and nodded. "They sure do. Wanna go downstairs and cut up the rug?"

"Absolutely!" she said, standing immediately. Anything to calm her down and make the rational side of her brain work. She didn't want to seem desperate, or pushy, or worse . . . easy. God, this was so hard!

Leading her downstairs to the main ballroom, Matt immediately pulled her out onto the floor with him to a fast song. It was as though he needed a tension breaker as well, and he threw his entire body into the rhythm of the music. Ginny laughed and swayed and followed his movements, falling into an old dance step that she thought she'd long forgotten.

"C'mon, I thought you came to party, lady," he declared in a cheerful voice, not allowing her to leave the floor when the first song ended. He kept her up for two more

fast records, and they were both winded and laughing by
the time a slow song came on.

Pulling her into his arms, Matt murmured into her ear.
"One slow song before we go, okay? At least one."

His voice melted her, and she comfortably dissolved
into his arms as he moved her around the room to the
slow, easy ballad.

Nearly moaning aloud from the sensations exploding
within her, she rested her head on his shoulder and held
him tightly. "Just one song will be enough," she murmured, shame quickly escaping her.

She could feel him take a deep breath and exhale it
through his nose. "If we make it through this song . . ."

It seemed like an eternity for the music to stop, and
when the small band keyed up for another fast song, instinctively, she knew it was time to leave. Matt never said
a word. He just gently ushered her to the door, and handed
the valet his ticket.

"Wait, my purse!" she exclaimed suddenly, breaking
away from him to return upstairs. As she raced into the
tiny room, and tried to walk slowly back down the steps,
she felt like a clumsy teenager wearing her mother's high
heels. Why couldn't she have had her purse? It was perfect, then she messed it up by having to run off and get a
handbag! Thoughts crashed in on her. Matt was so
smooth, so sophisticated . . . What if the same thing happened in bed? What if as he's making a controlled, suave
approach, she did something silly to break the mood? Oh,
God. This was not as simple as relearning how to ride a
bike!

"Ready?" he asked, extending his hand.

No, she wasn't ready to be with a great man like him.

Hell no, she didn't have a clue as to what to do next. "I suppose so," she murmured, falsifying her terror.

"Good," he said, brushing her mouth and helping her into the car. "Did you have a good time?"

At least the man was kind, she thought, shaking her head yes. "Wonderful."

Again weighted silence stifled their conversation, hurling them into a void of inner thoughts and desires. As she turned the key to her front door, Ginny felt Matt's warmth emanate from his body as he stood behind her. It felt so good, so necessary now. "Want some tea, or some of the wine you brought?" Her mind careened into topics and crashed as it collided with each one. Everything was so awkward. "Am I rambling? This night is too important. I don't want to make any mistakes."

Matt didn't respond, but shook his head and held his palm out to her. When she placed her hand in his, he pulled her to him gently. "There are no mistakes that you can make. There's no right or wrong. There's only what two people want to do to make each other happy. Don't be nervous, Ginny. I promise it'll be okay."

Capturing her mouth in a gentle kiss, she knew the man had no way of understanding that in that moment he had also captured her heart. As she felt him deepen the kiss with pent-up desire, she returned his ardor, allowing her passion to consume her. "Let's go upstairs," she whispered. "I'm not afraid, anymore. Not with you."

Safe. After so many years she finally felt safe again, as she took his hand and led him toward the stairs.

* * *

Allie closed her eyes and fought desperately for sleep. She had arrived home early, lain in bed for hours, and forced herself to get up to greet Dave and the children when they came in. Initially she had fumbled for an excuse, a way to explain why she had come home before her usual time. Rather than setting herself up for the disappointment of Dave's misunderstanding, she had feigned illness and simply avoided the question. Her pretense had remained intact throughout dinner, and now that the kids were asleep and she could hear Dave's heavy, even breathing beside her, she could finally let down her guard.

Sleep . . . how she wished it would envelop her.

Again, dozens of questions besieged her. Yet, this time, she didn't attempt to banish them from her mind. For some odd reason, she had showered and slipped into the pretty ivory gown that Ginny had bought for her instead of donning her usual oversized cotton tee-shirt. Maybe she was trying to grasp at straws, to arouse her husband so that everything could go back to normal. The thought of any change in her family, her home, her marriage, was terrifying, and she needed something to cling to tonight.

Turning toward Dave, she molded her body to his form, shaping herself like a spoon behind him. Stroking his belly as he slept, she let his warmth include her until it wrapped around her like an additional blanket of comfort. How long had it been? Months. A pang of loneliness stabbed at her as she touched his body gently. This was what she needed. Human contact.

Closing her eyes, Allie let her head rest against Dave's back. Each tender caress that she issued felt as if she were being touched herself. She allowed her mind to imagine that Dave was responding to her, giving her the love and the attention that she craved. As each nerve ending in her body came alive, it radiated an intense heat within her, making her bolder. Nearly trembling, she grazed his neck with a gentle kiss, and trailed it across his shoulder blades. When he didn't respond, she took the lobe of his ear in her mouth and gently tugged, again imagining what that sensation might feel like had it been reciprocated.

Still getting no response, she whispered to him, "Dave, honey, are you asleep?"

His answer was merely a grunt.

Heightened desire soon replaced shame, and she tried again. This time, a little more aggressively. "Dave, Dave . . . I love you."

"Huh? What're you doing? Look, Al," he mumbled, "I've gotta get up early, okay?" His tone held obvious annoyance, and he moved away from her, breaking their body contact, and leaving a thin space of cool air between them.

Disappointment, humiliation, and anger rushed through her with a vengeance. Turning over onto her side and facing away from him, she tried to let the hurt neutralize itself just as she had so many times before. Why should she have expected tonight to be any different? Fighting against her own needs, she allowed silent tears to wet her pillow. If she just went to sleep, then busied herself the next day, it would be all right. These feelings would dissipate. She wouldn't have to crave being touched, crave being intimate, crave being loved. She could just . . . exist?

Unable to even continue the thought, an uncontrollable sob ripped through her and she threw back the covers, making a mad dash for the bathroom. As she slipped into the dark room, she didn't bother switching on the light, but chose to let the darkness envelop her. Sobs racked her body until she actually found herself rocking, seated on the edge of the tub, with her arms wrapped tightly around her. None of her practiced mental games worked as she tried to drive away the hurt. Her body still ached and resonated with the desire to be held. The pain of Dave's rejection slapped her as she continued to cry, refusing to even wipe her face as the tears fell.

After what seemed like a long while, a light tap on the door brought her to her feet. Sudden rage replaced the hurt, and she threw on the light and opened the door. Glimpsing herself in the mirror as she faced Dave, she saw an angry woman and in a flash remembered their Washington D.C. fiasco. Another bathroom. Another rejection. It stoked her fury.

"What is it?" she demanded, wiping her nose with the back of her hand.

Appearing confused, Dave ventured a step forward and entered the small space. "Is everything all right? What's wrong? You just jumped up, started crying, then ran into the bathroom. Is it this Nan stuff?"

Her expression narrowed to a glare as she considered how to respond. "No. Everything's not all right. And, no, this isn't about Nan, or Ginny, or the kids, or the job. This is about us, Dave."

When he shook his head and started to leave the room, she felt herself propelled to a state of near violence. "Look at me, Dave Barbera!" She no longer cared that her voice was escalating and might carry into the children's rooms. "Am I an undesirable woman? Am I!"

"Al, it's too late to start this. What'da ya want from

me? It's twelve-thirty at night. I've got an eight-thirty meeting in the morning, I—"

"Go to hell, Dave." she interrupted. "You keep worrying about your little meetings, and you keep giving your attention to the dynamic business women who don't bore you like your wife does. But guess what? I have options too."

Dave stopped his retreat from the bathroom, and turned to face her. "What's that supposed to mean?"

She saw a look of fear in his eyes that she'd never seen before. Strangely, his expression of doubt gave her confidence . . . power. This time, he'd hear her.

"Things haven't been right between us for a long time. But it was comfortable, expected, so we kept on pretending that it was okay. Then, I made the fatal mistake of surprising you down in Washington. It was the beginning of the end."

Dave sat down heavily on the closed toilet seat, as though the strength had suddenly drained from his body. "I know it's been a little . . . boring . . . status quo, between us. But, after all, we've been married for a lot of years, Al. Passion doesn't burn forever."

His voice seemed to be pleading with her, and she gripped the edge of the vanity behind her for control. This time he would hear her out, deal with her, validate her— or he'd get the hell out. Taking a deep breath, she pressed on, no longer caring about the consequences. "Do you know how it felt to watch my husband radiate around some other woman, then ignore me like I was a house plant just set by his table for decoration? Do you know how it felt to try your best to make yourself attractive, sexy, desirable, and to have the person you love most in the world turn his back on you?" Allie could feel the blood drain from her knuckles as she clutched the sink and waited for his answer.

"I've never cheated on you, Al. I swear to God. I mean, she's just a sales rep, and maybe I was flirting a little, but honestly . . . Allie, c'mon, I—"

"Stop it," she interrupted again, finding it hard to control the urge to slap him. "This is not about her. It's about me. You and me." Taking a deep breath, she tried to ignore the blood pounding in her ears. "We haven't made love in months. Months! You haven't once said how nice I looked when I tried to remake myself for this job. You never once told me how proud you were of me for doing one of the hardest things I've ever had to do in my life. Only under duress and threats will you pitch in to help our family reach a mutual goal. All of a sudden the children that we made together have become *my* children. Although I work as many hours outside of the home as you do, the house that we use and dirty together is still *my* responsibility. Therefore, I work two damned jobs, Dave— not one. We've had this conversation before, but you didn't hear me. Hear me now."

She pushed her hair away from her eyes and continued, knowing her marriage was on the line. "Have you any idea of the way it makes me feel to know that you respect other women who do what I do, desire other women who do what I do, but when it comes to me, you resent me, try to sabotage me, and then top it off by punishing me with your indifference. I thought you cared about me, even though you didn't find me exciting any more. I could deal with that. Cling to that. Your friendship made such treatment acceptable. But then I realized that I didn't even have your friendship—because a friend wouldn't rob an-other of his or her self esteem and revel in their failures. I almost hate you for that, Dave. And I never thought it would have ever come to this."

Dried tears streaked her face and she licked her lips, tasting the salt while she drew a deep breath. It had been said; the truth was out. Now there was no terror, only re-lief and a revived sense of personal power. As she watched the tears well up in Dave's eyes, she felt numb. For the first time, his pain did not touch her. She could not muster sympathy, or reach out to comfort him. Instead, she stood at the sink and stared at him, as though she were a ghost, removed from this plane and unable to cross the void to touch him.

"This family therapy . . . they told you this stuff, didn't they? I knew it was a bad idea."

"Don't you even give me enough credit for being able to see what's going on in my own home?" She was in-credulous. It was insult to injury, and now she'd fight back with every weapon available to her. It was her sur-vival or his.

"Well, what is it, then? Is there someone else?" he eventually managed, his voice wavering with repressed emotion.

"Yes."

The answer had flown from her mouth before her brain could screen it. Somehow, in that moment, she wanted him to feel the same sting of indifference that had robbed her of her dignity. The absolute humiliation and degrada-tion of being sexually and emotionally rejected by the per-son he loved. Dave could believe what he wanted to believe. It wasn't necessary for her to clarify whether or not she'd actually consummated the act of making love to another man. That wasn't the point at all. The real issue was that she wanted him to feel the insecurity of losing the one person in the world that he could always depend on, and to never, ever, ever, take her for granted again.

"Oh, Jesus. Do you love him, Allie?" Dave's voice wavered again and broke. Quiet tears of agony brimmed from the edges of his eyes and spilled down his cheeks.

"He makes me feel alive, valued, and wanted. He respects me, Dave."

Allie watched emotions rip through him as he sat staring at her. She felt too calm, as though she had transported herself to a strange place of peace.

Dave's voice had become barely a hoarse whisper. "When did it start?"

"The day you lost respect for me. Then we unraveled and unraveled until there was only a thin thread of us left. I didn't want this. I fought against it. I fought for us, but instead, you fought against me. So if this marriage is going to work . . . I don't know. All I can say is, you do what you feel you need to, and I'll do what I have to. I'm tired of trying to save it all by myself."

There was nothing more to say. Fatigue weighted her until she could barely stand. Without looking at her husband, Allie left the bathroom and climbed into bed, facing away from Dave's usual spot in it. Allowing her eyes to adjust to the darkness, she stared at the light coming from under the bathroom door. Closing her eyes when she heard Dave blowing his nose, she blocked the sound from her mind. Compassion eluded her as his muffled sigh broke through the quiet of the night. How many times had she cried herself to sleep? How many days had she walked around the house like a zombie, in too much agony to even speak? How many nights had she laid awake, trying to figure out where they went wrong?

Now it was his turn. And, for the first time in her life, it was her turn too.

Clutching a pen tightly in her hands, Nan said another prayer for the right words to pour forth onto the paper. There had to be a way to get through to Ginny. Even if her sister never spoke to her again, she felt compelled to at least attempt a reconciliation. Allie had been right. Ginny had always loved her, and she'd made a mess of their relationship.

Tears spilled onto the paper, blurring the first line, and she quickly wiped them back, drawing a deep breath for internal support. What would she say? The ninth step in the Twelve Step Program said to try to rectify any damage you've done to others through your addiction. But how could one repair irreparable damage?

It seemed like the only answer was to begin at the very beginning, and to take Ginny back through the memories of what had made them love each other before it all fell apart. In this letter, there'd be no excuses, no lies, no elaborate justifications. She'd tell her sister how much she loved her, how sorry she truly was, and recount all of the reasons she had come to resent her. But how could she be sure that Ginny would even open it, or read it through to the end and understand? She decided to leave that problem up to God, and turned it over to a power greater than herself as she began to write.

Stopping mid-sentence, she tried to visualize their

childhood. Surprisingly, she found happy moments interspersed with the terrible ones. Taking the high road, she
described a time when they were three little girls—a family. Without hesitation, her hand worked as though it were
an instrument detached from her body, and she began to
write down all of the things she admired in her sister.
Ginny was kind, but not a push-over. She was pretty. She
was smart. Probably the smartest of the three. She had a
quiet courage, and a keen intellect that knew when and
where it was safe to expose her intelligence. She was discreet, and could keep a friend's deepest, darkest secrets in
the strictest of confidence . . .

Nan's hand stopped abruptly on that last word. It was as
though a light bulb went off in her head. Secrets. Ginny
kept secrets, closing people out when maybe she should
have let them in. She had difficulty trusting, and could
make one feel like an outsider, even if they lived with her
every day. Allie was just the opposite. Her other sister
craved closeness, and took in every stray, ragged, pathetic
creature that landed on her door step. Considering the two
diametrically opposed personalities, Nan forced her mind
to analyze how they could all be so different and still be
from the same family. As her mind stumbled and bumped
into various childhood scenarios, another possibility occurred to her. Was Dr. Alberts right? Were they not all victims of victims?

New tears streamed down her face as the epiphany captured her. Of course! Ginny didn't trust, because in their
home, to trust meant to be hurt. Christ, their mother and
father were less than trustworthy. They were abusive alco-
holics. Her mother's lovers had committed unspeakable
acts against her. Who's to say they didn't attack Ginny or

Allie too? Guilt crept over her like a virus, until she found herself trembling. Remembering the doctor's words, she fought the nausea, and looked her personal demons square in the eyes. And poor Allie . . . Maybe she thought, or prayed, that if she was just nice enough, kind enough, sweet enough, the demons would leave her alone. That had been Allie's solution. Ginny's had been to hide. Hers had been to fight back and rebel. So, how could she have hated her sister for protecting her heart? Ginny had just chosen a different way to survive.

Picking up the pen again, she allowed her truth to spill across the page. She told Ginny how much she had needed her as a little girl. How angry she had been when she'd run away with Allie, because it had felt like another abandonment. She explained how Ginny's stiff-upper-lip way of handling things seemed like indifference, and only now could she understand just how terrified she had also been.

Almost faint with emotion, Nan kept writing. She wrote about how jealous she had been when Ginny married Evan. Although Allie married first, there was never any jealousy, because Dave was just a hard working Joe, someone average. But Evan—he had education, money, position, and prestige. He seemed to possess everything that would get Ginny out, and keep her out, of potential poverty. Robert, well, he was just a struggling professor, and Nan shut her eyes briefly as she recalled how much she'd hated marrying what seemed then to be a failure. It was so ugly. So small of her. She'd abused her own husband verbally, just because he couldn't measure up to her absurd standards.

Almost unable to continue, she steadied her hand.

Again, looking into the nightmares, she realized, for the first time, just how terrified she was of poverty. She had blamed Robert for not being more aggressive, more ambitious, and even though she made a lucrative salary, he didn't. That fear had bolted her to her past, and no matter how much she made, it was never enough to expunge the memories of the lights going out, the water being turned off, living through winters with only space heaters to provide warmth. Even though they had a house, the Sullivan females had lived like trailer park trash . . . and Ginny had escaped.

Unable to stop the flood of reality, she resumed writing. This time she focused on Evan. At first it started off as the thrill of being given attention by a handsome, powerful, fairly well off man. A man that had originally thought her sister was a better catch than she was. Nan cringed as she recalled reveling in Evan's charismatic presence. It had never crossed her mind to sleep with him. She was merely content with the way he always gave her more attention than Ginny, and the way he could make her sister cower in public. It was terrible, but she had actually liked to watch him humiliate the untouchable Ginny Sullivan. Soon their relationship escalated. She and Evan would always sit together at family dinners, always have little inside jokes, always shared the same perspective on current events and politics. He made her feel special, in a way that Robert couldn't, simply because she never really respected Robert, even though she loved him. Attention coming from a powerful man seemed to validate her, regardless of her initial choice for a husband.

Nan's insides hurt. There was no turning away from the truth of who she'd become. There was no place to run away and hide. And no drugs to cloud her memory. A life-time of fear had made her tear down the blind alley which had become her life, and now she had to pick her way through the rubbish and garbage to get out. Returning her thoughts to the Evan nightmare, she acknowledged just how easily she'd been manipulated. Evan obviously worked her like he worked the throngs of people at fund raising events. That fact was inescapable. Her own neediness and low self esteem had been her trap.

She let out a deep sigh of disgust, and continued to write down the horror of it all. In excruciating detail, she explained how the situation had evolved over two years, and not something that had happened in an instant of insanity. First the attention, then the shared perspectives, having someone who seemed to understand her, someone with whom to share her secrets about Robert. Someone who one night gave her cocaine when she was crying and wanting out of her marriage. Someone who listened while she tried to reconcile loving a man but not respecting his earning capacity. Someone who seemed strong, wanted her more than he wanted her greatest vexation in life, her sister. Someone who had a secret double life of drug usage and philandering to share with her. For once, a secret that she had and Ginny did not.

Then it all came crashing down around her. Evan had told her that the only reason he'd had sex with her was to hurt her cold sister. That he'd never marry a woman of her caliber, because he'd end up killing her. She remembered leaving the hotel room feeling lower than she'd felt since she was fifteen years old and had initiated revenge sex with her mother's boyfriend. It was a dirty, unclean filth that cloaked her as she found her way to her car in the parking lot, stricken by the physical shock of Evan's near rape. Her thrilling secret became a nightmare of guilt and lies, numbed from existence by drugs. Robert's true worth and strength, now recognizable, only became a torment to her soul.

She had slept with the devil, and he had her. As her hand flew across the pages, she told her sister when she finally found out that Ginny was being abused by Evan. It had been a full year after the incident between them in the hotel that she realized he was beating Ginny. Knowledge had compelled her to confront Evan only weeks before his death. She had planned to expose the whole ugly thing to protect Ginny. But then he attacked her, bruising two ribs. She had known fear. Powerlessness. Terror.

From that point on, her world had changed. She had taken the beating as though she deserved it. In her mind, she did. Then, to tell after Evan was gone would have only hurt Ginny even more. She had been so angry. At Ginny. At Evan. At Robert. At herself. Even Allie . . . No one could stop the torture. Nobody confessed.

Secrets.

Robert didn't see through the pain and magically intervene. She hated herself for her own weakness and fear of the consequences if she told. She hated her sister for covering up her own nightmare, and for the fact that they couldn't possibly begin the dialogue of healing without her confession. Ginny's refusal to talk about the horror meant that she had been trapped in silence with her. And just like before, Allie couldn't have handled the situation. It was like a horrible rerun of the old movie from her childhood. Forced silence, terror, powerlessness, and wishing to God that somebody stronger than yourself would find out and stop it. And Evan, like her parents, had died and escaped it all! Damn them.

Ending the sixteen page letter, Nan closed her eyes and again prayed for divine intervention. Somehow, Ginny had to understand. Somehow, there had to be a way to get her family back. Evan had taken so much; she wouldn't allow him this. Folding the letter carefully, she addressed and stamped it, wondering how much of it her sister would read. Taking out a clean new sheet of notebook paper, Nan began the next letter.

Dear Robert . . .

Chapter 18

"Y ou what?" Allie gripped the phone tightly and stared at the cubicle wall before her, trying to fathom what her sister was telling her.

"Yes. Last night, I wrote to everybody that I've hurt, and mailed the letters this morning. You'll get a letter, too. I started with only the intention of writing to Ginny. I have to try to patch this up with her. But, in doing so, I've realized just how much pain I was in and how that has ruined almost every relationship I've had and cared about."

Allie was speechless. She'd never heard Nan so close to tears in her life, and even though she had been determined to keep their conversation brief, something had changed.

"Look, Al. This isn't my typical bull. I know I've cried wolf a lot of times in the past . . . but please believe me when I tell you I'm sorry. Not just for the Ginny thing, but I've messed up so much . . ."

Allie's mind grappled for an answer as Nan's voice dissolved into sobs of anguish. For the first time, she didn't know what to say. She couldn't pretend that everything would be okay. How did she know how Ginny would react? How did she know what Nan's boss would do when she returned to work? Who the hell knew if Robert would ever forgive and accept her? And the drugs? What in God's name could she do about that? This time, Nan had crossed an abyss of trouble that was too deep for anyone, except herself, to bridge.

"I love you, Nan," was the only thing her mind could carve out to say. It was the only truth that she could give her sister now.

"Thank you for not hating me," Nan sniffled. "I've called Joe Carter, and I talked to him from Dr. Alberts' office for a long time."

"What did he say?"

"He was very supportive, and asked if I needed anything. He said he'd let me come back . . . I asked him to put Tony on the line, too."

"What!"

"I had to, Allie. I've treated people like shit. I apologized and thanked him for busting me."

"Jesus. What did he say?"

"He was quiet. Seemed skeptical. But he was decent about it. We'll never be friends again, but at least I can sleep at night knowing that I apologized."

Dumbstruck, Allie stared at the blotter on her desk until her brain could function again. "Are you coming home today?"

"No. I've decided to stay and finish out the program. I didn't know I had so many skeletons buried out there, so I figured I'd better stay and get well before I do any more damage."

Nodding, even though Nan couldn't see her, she wholeheartedly agreed. "I think it's the right thing, Nan. I'm relieved, to tell you the truth. Especially . . . well, I just think you should."

"Yeah. I'm pretty messed up right now, huh? Besides, I'm not sure what I'd do next."

Alarm coursed through Allie's veins. "You're not thinking of hurting yourself, are you?"

"No. No. I just meant that I don't know how to pick up the pieces in my life, and have no idea how I'd function at work."

"Oh," Allie said, releasing an audible sigh. "Well, you've got plenty of time to figure that out."

"Yeah, I guess so. But how are you, Al? I know this has taken a terrible toll on you. I'm sorry."

"I'm doing okay. And Ginny's doing as well as can be expected. I think she's handling this well, given the circumstances."

Allie heard a pause as Nan took a deep breath.

"I didn't ask because I was afraid to. Not because I don't care. I love her too, Al. I just hope she reads my letter and can understand."

Before she could censor herself, she had jumped in, feeling the need to help the healing process, the one that she had prayed so hard for all along. "Look, I'm getting together some information for Ginny about a client of hers that's being abused. When I take it to her, I'll see what I can do."

"Wait. Stop. Run that by me again. One of Ginny's clients is getting abused? God, it must be like a terrible flashback for her."

"It is. I think that's why she's gotten so involved—it's almost like a catharsis for her, to help somebody."

"Well, how did she find out about it? Of all people to have to rake through that muck and mire again . . . Damn. Not Gin."

Losing patience, Allie interjected quickly. "Listen, Nan, sometimes you have to do something for others, even if there's no immediate personal benefit. That's just how Ginny feels about this. To tell her to sit by and watch without at least attempting to help this woman is too much like what everyone did to her. So forget it."

"That's not what I was implying, Allie. Please, I know that's how I used to be, but give me a chance before you jump to conclusions. I'm in no position to say this now, but maybe I could help. You know?"

Unused to her sister's new behavior, Allie had to fight hard to reset all of the old triggers between them. This was so new, so different, and they felt so out of sync. Finally understanding the heartfelt offer, Allie declined it, knowing that Nan was in no condition, but had extended the help out of a genuine interest in repairing the family rift. "Nan, that's kind of you. Really," she began cautiously, "but your own recovery is paramount at the moment. I really don't see—"

"You never even gave me a chance, Allie. True, I'm not able to take this on now, and that's not what I'm suggesting. But I might be able to make a phone call and get the woman a decent job after she leaves the guy, or something. Or, if I knew where the son of a bitch that's beating her works, I might be able to drop a dime to a Vice President or two, and get him fired. Who knows."

Allie laughed. "Nan, you've changed, but there are some things about you that I hope never change."

Nan joined her laughter and something fragile between them realigned itself, bringing back the old bond in locked step. "Maybe you can help her get a job. But we can't do anything without Ginny's okay. Understood?"

"If she'll have my help, I'll do whatever I can from here." Again, her sister sounded different, unsure, even nervous. This was definitely not the old Nan.

"It'll take a little while, Nan. You'll probably be out before the woman leaves the safe house, and that's providing she goes immediately. But maybe Ginny can find out where her skills used to be, if she has a degree or not, stuff like that in general conversation that won't frighten her. That way, you can start to make inquiries about openings. Okay?"

"Sounds like a good, solid, discreet plan—but do you think Ginny will accept my help?"

"I think Ginny will accept it on behalf of the victim. At least that's how I'll try to approach her with it."

There was a moment of companionable silence on the phone before Nan spoke. "Allie, you've been patching us up all of your life. I promise, after this, you won't have to any more. I love you. Thanks."

Allie closed her eyes. She prayed that Nan was telling the truth, that this would be the last time she'd have to be the go-between for her sisters. The truth was, she might not have the wherewithal in the future to do it. Ginny was obviously getting on with her life, and dating a great man. Nan was cleaning up her act, and at least still had a job. And she might be disintegrating her own life with a divorce and an affair . . .

"I've got to go, Al. My time's up. I'll call you tomorrow, okay?"

"Yeah, okay," she said distantly. "I've got a million things to do to pull this info together for Ginny. I've compiled and checked out three good safe houses this morning, and spoken to the directors who can take a client immediately. A friend of mine on staff here is an attorney, and he's looking into the legal options as we speak. But everything is on hold until Ginny talks to the woman and gets her okay. Hopefully I'll have some news in a couple of days. In the meantime, take care of yourself, all right?"

"I promise. Bye, Sis."

"Nan?"

"Yeah?"

"I love you, and I'm proud of you."

Nan didn't respond for a moment. Allie could tell that her sister was struggling with her emotions in the silence, and she listened to the dead air, fighting against her own, until Nan spoke.

"Thanks, Allyson Sullivan Barbera. I'm proud of you too."

When Nan hung up, Allie just stared at the phone. Would her sister be proud of her if she wasn't there for any of them anymore? Would she be proud of her if she just walked out on Dave? Would she be proud to know her if she started a wild affair with a co-worker?

Shaking off the feelings of dread, Allie stood and collected her papers. She had a project, a mission, something more important than herself to take her mind off her worries. It had always worked before, yet her mental subterfuge seemed to be more difficult to master when she heard the sound of Jason Levy's voice booming down the hall from his office. Steadying herself, she entered the corridor. There was work to do.

Ginny went over the papers in her hands as though preparing for an exam. She wanted to know every possible answer to any question that Joan Caldwell could ask. It was paramount that she sound like an authority, because she knew full well that Joan would interpret any hesitation on her part as a flaw in the plan. A simple flaw would be translated into the word impossible, and fear would keep the woman paralyzed and trapped forever. Therefore, the discussion about Joan Caldwell's move, safety, legal options, and possible future, had to go smoothly.

Allie had grilled her like a drill sergeant, until even the telephone numbers to the safe houses were burned in her brain. If Joan said yes, she'd take Joan to her office, they'd call one of the numbers and give Allie's name. Then they'd go by the school and get Joan's daughter. After that, she'd drive them to the refuge site. Joan Caldwell would then give her the key to her home, and she'd go back and instruct the movers on what to take and where to store it. She'd be responsible for keeping their excess clothes and children's toys in her basement. The immediate goal was to get the woman out. Furniture, clothes, toys, could all be replaced or haggled about in court. There was no amount of money or material possessions that could replace the loss of life or limb.

The plan was airtight, and she and Allie had hugged on it as Allie had left. Despite her current feelings about Nan, her suggestion had been a godsend, because the next rational question Joan Caldwell had to address was how to support herself temporarily until the courts acted on her behalf. If she suggested welfare, even though that was an option, she knew Joan Caldwell would firmly shut the door in her face. She would have done the same.

Refusing to allow her mind to rake through the past, Ginny concentrated on the traffic in front of her. Fear gripped her as she drove slowly up the Caldwells' long drive, searching the terrain for any sign of Joan's husband. She sat for a few moments, breathing deeply to calm her nerves. What if he'd stayed home today? She had to think of a quick reason for stopping by. She was their realtor. She could just say that she had stopped by to see how the house was coming along. Right? Right. Okay.

As she opened her car door, she was surprised to see the large oak doors of the house eerily creak open. Standing partially concealed behind it was the shadow of a woman whom she knew to be her friend. When she mounted the stairs, Joan Caldwell quickly ushered her in.

"I knew you would come, Ginny," she said near tears. "I'm scared to death. He had a huge fight with a new young client that he's trying to recruit. His secretary told me when I called to see if he'd be home for dinner tonight." Joan's gaze darted around the room like a frightened bird looking for an exit. "He'll be home in a few hours, and when he gets like this . . . Oh, God, help me . . ."

Sobs stopped Joan's torrent of words, and Ginny embraced her quickly. "Listen, I have a safe place for you where he can't find you. Get your purse and keys and let's go."

"But I can't hide from him forever, and Sarah's in school."

"No. You can't hide forever. You won't have to hide forever. But you have to get out now to avoid another beating. You and your child don't deserve to live like this. Nobody does. We'll go get Sarah now before the school buses load up, then we'll call the safe house from my office, and I'll take you there."

"But, I don't have any clothes . . . Her school . . . Her dolls . . . What about money?"

Pulling Joan forward as she grabbed her purse from the foyer table, Ginny ushered her out of the door, not even bothering to lock it behind them. "Dolls can be replaced more easily than teeth or ribs. I'll come back and collect her things, and get some clothes for you. You'll have time once you're safe to make a list. We'll write a note to the school at my office and give it to the principal, explaining that a relative is ill and Sarah will have to go with the family for a few weeks. I can ask them to send her assignments to me, then I'll re-route them to you. When you make a list of things you want out of the house, let me know where safe deposit boxes are, keys to them, jewelry, and anything of sentimental value. The big stuff, let the courts distribute that in your property settlement."

The terror in Joan's eyes was like that of a hunted animal. She merely nodded as she slipped into the passenger seat, and Ginny tore out of the driveway as though she were behind the wheel of a getaway car.

"Do you have your checkbook with you?"

"I'm not allowed to write any checks without Richard's permission."

Fury burned Ginny's insides until she feared she might explode. "Do you have them with you?"

"Yes, I think so," Joan said timidly, rifling through her purse and producing the small leather case.

"We're making one pit stop. The bank."

"The bank?"

"Yes, the bank, Joan. Take everything, except a hundred dollars. In a cashier's check."

Joan's eyes widened, and she gasped as a new wave of fear overtook her. "I can't do that. What will he use for money? How will he pay the mortgage?"

Swerving to miss a slow-moving vehicle, Ginny had to control her urge to scream. "If you can't take the money for yourself, then take it for your child. Think of it as money that he owes you for the pain and suffering. Think of it as your payment for the battery claim you rightfully have against him. Think of it as anything that makes you feel better, but never as something you are taking from him. This is your survival, Joan!"

Joan Caldwell seemed to soak in the words as they rushed forth from her mouth. Through her tears, an odd expression transformed itself on her face, leaving a trace of a sad smile. "For Sarah and me . . . I'm really doing this, aren't I, Ginny?"

"Yes," Ginny said quietly. "For you and your child who won't have to grow up thinking that this is normal. Heaven forbid that she allows a man to abuse her, because it's what she saw her own Mom take."

Again, Joan's expression changed, but this time it hardened. "Never!" she shrieked, almost scaring Ginny with the force of her voice. "Never would I allow my daughter to go through this hell! Never!"

"Then you have to stop it now by example, Joan. Words aren't enough. Trust me."

Both women looked at each other as a silent understanding passed between them.

"He banks at Chemical."

A smile found its way to Ginny's mouth. "Do you think you've got enough in checking to cover you for a month or so?"

Joan shrugged her shoulders. "It's one of those accounts that's a savings plan, and you can write up to ten checks off of it per month. I haven't done the bills yet, because of the settlement expenses, but the last time I looked there was eighty thousand in there."

Ginny just stared at the woman, unable to keep her jaw from hanging as she watched her calmly search for a pen. "Eighty thousand dollars?" She quickly turned her attention back to the traffic.

"More or less." Joan shrugged, taking out her pen and filling out a blank check. "It's for my child. And even the smallest animal in the forest will fight for its young. Right?"

There were no words to be said, and Ginny just kept her eyes on the road for the remainder of their drive. As they accomplished each task, each stop placing them closer to their goal, she couldn't help but reflect on her own inaction years ago. A knot of anxiety and shame settled in the pit of her stomach, and questions crashed in on her, leaving a headache in their wake.

After all of the worry, her little prepared speech had

been unnecessary, and perhaps it was divine will that she didn't have to sell Joan Caldwell on the idea of leaving. Maybe God knew that she didn't have the answers, and thus provided a catalyst for their escape. Maybe He knew that had Joan waffled, she might have abandoned the mission entirely, since it was too close a look at her own life choices. And the one thing that they both thought would be the most difficult, explaining to Sarah, hadn't been what they expected at all. The child had simply hugged Joan and made her mother promise not to go back to get beaten up any more.

"We're here," Ginny said in a quiet voice, interrupting her own thoughts.

Joan and Sarah looked around at the beautiful landscaping that flanked a small house tucked away from the road. As Ginny brought the car up to the front drive, she marveled at the neat little home herself. This was not what she had expected. Not what she had seen on the six o'clock news. Not the nightmare her mind had pictured, and thus kept her from attempting to find a refuge years ago. It was plain, but not barren . . . utilitarian. Most of all, it was safe and clean.

As they approached, Sarah spotted children on swings in the backyard, and immediately pleaded to run off and join them. But, still uneasy, Joan put her off until they got settled. Nervous energy surrounded them as they waited for the director to come down to admit them, having been asked to have a seat on the porch furniture by a large, surly security guard.

Turning to Joan, Ginny squeezed her hand for reassurance. "Joan, no one can get the number or address here.

They aren't listed in the phone book. You have to go through a known agency or the police to get admitted here. That's why we have to wait. I could be Richard's girlfriend or secretary if I just walked in off the street. They wouldn't give me any information until I showed proper I.D. Only an agency social worker can find out where you are, and my sister, Allie, is the caseworker who has your file. The only reason I'm allowed to bring you is because I have agency clearance under the circumstances. The director is probably on the phone now with Allie giving her a physical description of me."

She could feel Joan relax a little as the muscles in her hand lost some of the earlier tension.

"This is almost like the witness protection program," Joan said, marveling and still looking around cautiously.

"You're safe now. Just remember that," she said again, still holding Joan's hand to offer support.

When the porch door opened, both women breathed a sigh of relief as a tall woman in her early forties approached with a kind expression on her face.

Extending her hand, she smiled. "Welcome to our safe house. I know there's a lot of questions and concerns for you all, but I assure you, your safety is our primary goal. My name is Mary Whitherspoon. I'm the director."

Once the formal introductions were made, Ginny was surprised to find that she was asked to leave so quickly.

"I know you're concerned," Ms. Whitherspoon said in a pleasant, yet firm voice. "But we have to get them acclimated, fed, and let them settle in. The sooner they start feeling comfortable, the sooner they can begin to get some of the rest and recovery that they need."

It made sense and, in truth, Ginny felt a need to be alone herself now. So many emotions had barraged her that it was almost impossible to think. What made it worse was that she still had a few things to do for Joan before the day was over. Conceding graciously, both friends hugged each other while trying not to cry.

"I'll call you in a few days, okay, Ginny?"

"Okay. And I'll take care of everything else. You'll see."

"Ginny," Joan called down to her from the porch as she descended the stairs. "I don't know how I can ever repay you. You've saved our lives."

Holding up her hand to stop Joan's words, she smiled. "Joan, it's my basket of peas. Remind me to tell you the story one day."

Appearing confused, but accepting her answer, Joan and Sarah waved as she got into her car.

"We'll take good care of her. We'll handle future employment prospecting, make any out-of-state family calls that can be trusted, etcetera," the director shouted over the start of Ginny's engine.

Waving again as she pulled off, she forced her mind to go blank for a portion of the drive. Time. She needed time. There was just too much to think about, and so much to do. She'd have to swing by her house, call Allie and give her the mission-accomplished report, call some movers, and try to get a same day van, this late in the afternoon . . . Damn! It was four o'clock. No way in hell could she get back home and get anybody to send a van out at this time! She never expected Joan to move this fast.

A fatal flaw in the plan unraveled before her eyes. Cursing at herself, she slapped the steering wheel several times and screamed into the unoccupied space in the car. "Damn, damn damn!" How could she have been so stupid! How could she have let Joan down like this? She'd have to haul the stuff herself. It was the only way.

Pressing her foot down to the floor, she revved her speed up to eighty miles an hour, praying the whole way home that a State Trooper wouldn't be in hot pursuit behind her. Screeching into a Seven-Eleven lot, she jumped out of the car, ran inside the store, purchased two large boxes of green garbage bags, and hopped back into the car. Almost crashing into her own garage door, she left the car running as she ran into the house, snatched the phone, and called Allie.

"Al, you there?"

"Ginny—"

"We did it, she's safe, her kid's safe, but I gotta get back into the house before Caldwell comes home. *We forgot to line up the freakin' movers!*"

"What are you going to do, Ginny? You're not going in there yourself? Not this close to when Caldwell is due home!"

"I have no choice. I promised her. I'm gonna stuff as much as I can of her things and Sarah's special little toys into garbage bags, then I'm outta there."

"No! You can't! Are you mad? The man is violent, you don't know what he might do. He could shoot you and say he thought you were burglarizing his home, and not a court in the world would—"

"I know, but this isn't up for discussion. He'd torch her

mother's family album. He's just the type to be so cruel, knowing she couldn't replace those photos since her mother is dead. He'd take her jewelry and sell it, he'd—"

"Ginny, listen to yourself! You've done enough already! This isn't about you and Evan!"

Without thinking, her hand had slammed down the receiver. Arguing with Allie was wasting valuable time. Grabbing another box of garbage bags from under her sink, she was out of the house in a shot. The entire ten-minute drive to the Caldwells' seemed like a blur, as flashes of her own horror increased her speed.

Her hands were still shaking as she opened the unlocked door, dropping the boxes of trash bags and cursing, while entering the home like a clumsy bandit. Mentally ticking off the list of items, she went for the photos first, then raced to Sarah's room to get the bunny, the dolls, the must-have blanket. Then she tore into the master bedroom. Spinning around on the rug, she tried to remember what Joan had said. Her stash of safe deposit box keys, bonds, stocks, papers in the armoire, or was it the vanity, under her panties? Jesus!

Hauling four huge bags out, she had the essentials. In one swift move, she stashed and locked the items in her trunk, and went back in. Just one more load. Coats? China? What the hell was a priority when you had Hefty three-ply bags as your substitute for a van? Personal effects . . . high school year books, the stuff money couldn't buy. But in this Ponderosa, where in God's name would Joan have stashed it?

Breathing heavily as she went to the study, she flung open the large mahogany doors and stood, perplexed, in the middle of the floor. She didn't know what to take, what was important . . . Without the time to sort through all the personal things, Ginny started dumping papers and ledgers into the huge plastic bag. Let Joan do it when she was settled. Suddenly, a loud crash made her spin around and, to her horror, she was facing an enraged, drunken Richard Caldwell.

"Where's my wife!"

Ginny's voice caught in her throat as she backed into the room, her gaze quickly darting from object to object, searching for something to use as protection if needed. "She went to the store, and—"

"I'll bet the hell she did! My bank called and said that sneaky little bitch withdrew eighty thousand dollars from my account and wanted to know if I was aware of the transaction. And here you stand in my home with garbage bags in your hands, helping that whore clean me out, looking like a common thief! What did she tell you? That I slapped her around a little, so that justifies everything? Is that it? Huh, did she?"

Rage amplified by fear sent adrenaline through her veins. "Yes!" she screamed, hoping to back up her would-be attacker. "She told me everything, and she's safe now. I'm leaving. Get out of my way. Men like you repulse me."

Hurrying past him, her arm was jerked back as he turned her around to face him. "Bitch, you're not going anywhere until you tell me where she is."

As he raised his hand to slap her face, something snapped. This time, she didn't recoil. This time, she didn't cry. This time, she saw Evan as the blow landed and stung her face.

This time, she'd kill him.

A red haze of rage came over her eyes. Her hands were not her own, and her strength felt like it suddenly doubled as she hurled herself against him, kicking, screaming, punching . . . until her body lifted and she heard voices.

"Ginny, Ginny, he's out! Let the man go—you're strangling him to death!"

Reason slowly crept its way back to her mind, and she saw Dave bent over Caldwell, and realized that Matt had been the strong arms that lifted her off of Caldwell's lifeless form.

For an instant renewed panic tore through her, until she heard Caldwell cough, gasp, and throw up on the rug next to where he was laying.

"That crazy bitch tried to kill me! I'll sue her, you hear me! I'll take her down!" Caldwell gasped, as he struggled to get up.

Ushering her under her elbows, Matt took one side and Dave took the other. "C'mon, Gin, it's okay. Let's go."

Anger still quaked in her body, and she fought against Matt and Dave. "That bastard hit me. He slapped my face, and I tried to kick the living shit out of him. That'll teach you to hit a woman!" she screamed, twisting away from their hold and rushing at Caldwell.

When he recoiled, she stopped mid-step as the irony suddenly assailed her. He was afraid of her. Her! From within Ginny's depths, laughter ignited her soul until she had to wipe her eyes at the spectacle. Here Matt and Dave had obviously come to save her. Richard had come to beat her. And she was completely capable of addressing both issues.

"If I hadn't hit my head on the way down, I'd have kicked your skinny ass!" Caldwell yelled, still gasping, but remaining safely out of her reach.

Apparently, adrenaline was also still running high in Dave and Matt, and both men advanced in Caldwell's direction, shielding her despite her hysteria. From some male reservoir of chivalry, her would-be heroes decided they would not be outdone today.

Posturing angrily, Matt threatened their nemesis with his fist raised. "If she hadn't already punched you out, you slime ball, I would have."

"Yeah," Dave echoed, grabbing up the Hefty garbage bag. "And if you ever lay a hand on my sister-in-law—"

"Or dare to even speak to her again," Matt added emphatically. "We'll be back to see you. Court or no court!"

Then scooping her up under her elbows as though she were weightless, Matt and Dave hustled her out of the house. To her shock, there was a white paneled body van from Dave's company in the driveway, and two more guys sitting on the back lift.

Looking at Matt, then to Dave, then toward the truck, again mirth found its way into the melee. Chuckling, Ginny just shook her head. "When Allie sends out an S.O.S. to call in the troops, she doesn't mess around."

Still obviously upset, Matt ushered her to her car. "I'll take Ginny home so you guys can get back to the job."

Running his hands through his hair, Dave shook his head. "Hell, after this, I'm going home for a couple of beers. Why don't you come over? Allie's there, and I'm sure she wants the instant play by play." Giving her a sheepish grin, Dave added with a chuckle, "You pack quite a wallop, little lady."

She gave Matt's arm a gentle squeeze and moved over to Dave, offering him a big hug, then returned to Matt to give him a kiss. "Thanks, guys. I'm kinda glad you showed up. I sure could've used you twenty minutes ago, though. But, it's too late now and he's home, so we can't take anything else."

"It was dangerous, Ginny. I can't believe you did this," Matt fussed as he ushered her into the car. "Let's get out of here before the cops come, or something."

"Right behind you," Dave yelled, motoring up the van and putting the truck into gear. "What a helluva day!"

Ginny leaned her head back against the leather and sighed. How right Dave was. It had been one hell of a day.

Evan Harrison was finally dead and buried.

Chapter 19

Allie paced nervously in front of the window as she waited for her posse to return. As soon as she saw Ginny's car pull up, followed by Dave's white company van, she bolted out the front door.

"Is everybody all right?" she asked as she quickly assessed Ginny's disheveled appearance.

To her amazement, a round of laughter followed the question as Matt helped Ginny from the car.

"You should have seen her, Al. Your sister packs a serious one-two punch!" Dave joined Allie's side and gave her an affectionate squeeze. "Thanks, fellas, want a beer?" he asked, waving in the two guys from the van.

"No, gotta get home to the wife," one of the men called back, pulling away from the curb. "See you at the job tomorrow, Barbera."

"Then I owe you guys one," Dave called back, looping his arm around her waist as he waved goodbye.

Although Dave's actions surprised her, at this point she was too confused and too curious to really register it.

"What are you talking about? Come inside. I don't want the neighbors to think we just robbed somebody."

"Well, that's close to the truth," Matt said smiling mischievously, and opened Ginny's trunk to show it stuffed with large green garbage bags. "Here's her loot."

As everyone poured into the house, Allie noted that her sister had been extremely quiet through all of the commotion outside. Finally able to sidle up to her, she touched Ginny's arm. "Are you okay? I hope you aren't mad that I sent the guys, but I was worried."

Shaking her head, Ginny sat down at the kitchen table. "You were right, Allie. It got a lot uglier than I imagined. He attacked me, and—"

"What? Oh, my God! We'll call the police. This is an outrage! Do you need to go to the hospital? Jesus, I—"

"Calm down, Al," Dave said gently, still smiling as he touched her shoulder. "This little lady here stood her ground, and stood it well."

Confusion tore through Allie's brain, and she searched each face in the room for an explanation.

"You tell her, champ. This was your TKO."

Matt's comment made Ginny laugh and, for the first time since the ragtag parcel of bandits returned home, Allie relaxed.

"Remember when we were kids, Allie, and I used to have a really bad temper?"

"Yeah, you and Nan were terrors. They used to gang up on me, and . . ." She stopped, looking at her sister after accidentally mentioning Nan's name, but quickly sanctioning herself. "You go ahead."

Allowing the slip up to pass, Ginny continued. "And you know how I would always try to avoid a street fight, and would almost beg the bigger kids not to pick on me."

"Yeah, but I don't see what—"

"And how I had a long fuse, but once it got burning, I would sort of lose it?"

"Jesus, you didn't?"

"Afraid I did."

Absolute shock stopped the barrage of questions that she had stored up in her brain since the men left. As she stared at her sister, a giggle found its way to her lips, capturing her in a belly laugh, and forcing her to collapse in a chair beside Ginny. *"What the hell happened?"*

Joining in her laughter, they gave her the entire instant replay, albeit in snatches from each person's perspective. Allie's head quickly turned from one face in the room to the next, until they were all nearly rolling on the floor as Dave imitated Richard Caldwell gasping in a high-pitched voice.

Wiping the moisture from her eyes, Allie finally stood and put a pot of hot water on the stove.

"What, are you kidding? Tea, after a prizefight? No way," Dave said, still in high spirits, pulling a six-pack from the fridge and handing beers all around. Again, to her amazement, Ginny accepted one, popped the can, and took a sip as Dave handed her a glass from the cabinet.

"And what makes it so great, Allie, is that your sister cleaned him out."

Allie stared at Matt. "Cleaned him out?"

Pushing back in his seat, Matt precariously balanced on two legs of the chair while using his hand that held a beer to motion outside. "First, she got Joan to hit his bank account for eighty thou, then she rolled back in there like a one-woman S.W.A.T. team, and singlehandedly collected photo albums, mementos, kids clothes, some of Joan's favorite clothes, shoes, handbags, all of Joan's jewelry, safe deposit box keys, bonds, stock certificates, important papers, and, drum roll please . . . her most pretty lingerie! She was going back in for more when she got busted."

"Eighty thousand dollars?" Allie just stared at her sister, feeling the muscle in her jaw begin to slacken. "Eighty thousand? You have got to be kidding me? Ginny!"

"A helluva haul for one sting operation!" Dave chimed in, popping open another brew. "Hell, they should have her working for that show COPS. You know how they bust in, whip it to the bad guys, and confiscate everything. Holy Cow!"

Allie couldn't stop laughing, but the loud merriment in the kitchen didn't keep her from noticing Ginny's unnatural quiet. Placing an arm around her sister's shoulders, and watching the men to be sure that her actions went unseen, she whispered to her softly, "You're not so okay, are you?"

Ginny just shook her head and Allie watched as tears began to form in her sister's eyes.

"Where are the kids?" Ginny whispered back after a moment. "I never want them to see this."

Allie clutched Ginny's hand under the table and gave it a light squeeze. "I sent them down the block to their friend's house. They were glad to get to stay up later and have pizza for dinner. I didn't want them to hear about this either."

"I am so embarrassed. I never lose it like that. Never. I could have killed the man. It frightened me."

"Scared him, too! Bet he's . . ." Matt's words trailed off when he glimpsed Ginny's face, and Dave stopped talking and looked at her as well. "What's wrong?" Matt asked, now sounding worried. "You look like you're about to cry."

Two big tears formed in her sister's eyes, and Allie hastily grabbed a napkin from the holder on the table and handed it to Ginny.

"You okay, kiddo?" Dave said, sobered, and looking worried. "Anything hurt? Should we take her to the hospital, Al?"

Shaking her head no, Ginny wiped her nose with the napkin. "I don't know what came over me. All of a sudden I just felt so blue, and so embarrassed. I haven't had a catfight since I was a kid. I don't condone violence as a way to handle things. If we had more time, maybe it wouldn't have been necessary to fight violence with violence. And if Meghan and Pat ever found out . . . I'd just die. I detest this."

Allie hugged her sister, and let her bury her face in her shoulder for a moment as she sought to regain her composure. "It's all right, honey. Look, the kids won't find out, and nobody thinks any less of you for what happened . . . Shh, Shh . . . She just needs a minute, guys."

Both men looked around nervously, appearing totally overwhelmed and at a loss. Finally Matt spoke softly, obviously trying to interject something that would help Ginny regain her spirits. "Emotional letdown, is all."

Ginny peeked her head up, and wiped her now red nose again as Allie pushed another napkin into her hands, taking the wet one away and tossing it in the trash. "Emotional letdown?"

"Yup," Dave added softly. "Happens after every big fight, huh, Matt?"

Matt nodded in concurrence. "It's physical, really. Happens in sports, the fights . . . war, too. Guys come back all amped up after winning a big victory. They pass around the brewski's, champagne, whatever. Everybody cheers the conquering heroes. Then, the quiet sets in and all of a sudden you realize just how close you came to getting killed. It sends a shudder of reality down your spine, which sobers you up real quick. Then you just want to bawl."

Allie stared at them. It was absolutely amazing. Here her sister was crying her eyes out, and probably scared to death of the consequences of her actions, and all the fellas could do was talk about post-game depression—like it was postpartum, or something. Incredulous, Allie shook her head, and stared at them like they were Martians. "Is that all you guys could think of to say to her? She doesn't care about the chemical reasons for feeling like this. She just needed a shoulder for a minute, to pull it together again. Hell, this whole thing had to be like an Evan flashback except this time she stood up for herself. That alone, not to mention being scared about what will happen next, is enough to make anybody weep. Post-game trauma . . . gimme a break."

Again, the guys looked down at the floor, appearing totally bewildered after being so duly chastised. Ginny squeezed her hand under the table, in unspoken appreciation.

Dave sat down nervously, and laced his fingers around a half-empty beer can. Obviously searching for words, he spoke hesitantly. "We really ought to figure out what to do next. I guess Allie's right."

Agreeing, Matt nodded. "This isn't the end of it. Not

with a guy like Caldwell. We have to have a plan B, just in case he tries to pull something."

"That's what I'm worried about," Allie said in a serious voice. "People like that hate to lose, and he'll just take it out on Joan."

Looking at Ginny's stricken face, she immediately wished that she could bite back her words.

"He'll kill her," Ginny said quietly. "And we can't protect her forever. Dear God. What have we done?"

A pall fell over the once merry group, and Matt and Dave looked at each other uneasily. "Aren't there laws to protect women from this kind of thing? I mean, can't the police protect her, now that everything's out in the open?"

"Laws?" Ginny scoffed with a hollow laugh. "Dave, you watch all of those shows . . . America's Most Wanted, COPS, 911 . . . How many of the people they're tracking down are lovers, ex-husbands, etcetera, that were finally successful in killing the woman?"

"Jesus," Matt whispered, running his hands through his hair.

Allie looked at the men seated in the room directly. "That's why I have a job. I try to get victims into hiding, provide safety, and the attorney I work with tries to get bench warrants, child support, and the like." Ignoring the questioning look on her husband's face, she made her point with conviction. "Most women don't leave with eighty thousand dollars cash and the support of their friends. They go into homeless shelters with their children, or they go on welfare. Meanwhile, if the guy is only stalking them, in most states, the law can't intervene until there's been an incident."

She watched as the information sank in, and her sister

nodded sadly, backing up her claim. "That's why I was so afraid to leave Evan. He swore he'd kill me, and he had the law on his side. He was the D.A. after all."

Allie surveyed the faces in the room, and her focus settled on Dave's stricken expression. For the first time since the family therapy session, it occurred to her that he didn't know about Evan.

"I guess that's why Nan was scared of him, too," Ginny continued softly, obviously assuming that everyone in the room was aware of what had taken place.

"Look, we're panicking," Matt finally interrupted, standing and pacing with nervous energy. "I say that we find a way to bring him down. Hard."

Everyone's focus turned to Matt, and stayed there as they waited with bated breath for his next comment.

"This guy is a sports agent. Right?" Looking around to see if he had the group's attention, Matt continued, fidgeting with refrigerator magnets as he circled the small kitchen island. "He offered DeWayne Henderson a bogus contract, tried to get him to sign it, but he didn't."

"I'm not following," Dave interjected. "That's not enough to put Caldwell away."

"Well, we could get Joan to file spousal abuse charges, that's one thing," Allie added, remembering what Jason Levy had told her.

"But that takes time, assuming that Joan is willing to go through with it, and she's already frightened enough. Maybe she'd do that later . . ." Ginny interrupted, totally dismissing the concept.

"Listen," Matt said firmly. "This guy also offered Henderson cocaine." Ignoring the harmonized gasp that broke out at the table, Matt continued, formulating the plan as he paced. "We could set him up. Have him busted for possession. Especially with all of the brouhaha around drugs in sports, they'll throw the book at him. With a few well-placed calls to some of my friends in the press, his face and name will be plastered all over the Delaware Valley—if not ESPN, then nationally. That should raise the visibility on this character. There won't be a squad car in the area that wouldn't recognize him. After all, men read the sports page."

Quickly picking up on Matt's proposal, Allie embellished his suggestion with her own. "Combine that with spousal abuse charges, and witnessed assault and battery of a local, very well-loved realtor . . . He wouldn't be able to jay walk after he gets out of the joint and on parole."

"Would serve him right," Dave said loudly, banging his fist on the table for emphasis. "Can you imagine what they'll do to an arrogant, pompous ass like that in jail? Jesus, he'll really get what's coming to him, and more."

"At least this way, Joan will have a few years to get herself together before having to face him," Matt said. "She'll get a no contest divorce, and can call her price in front of the judge. Then, when the guy gets out, if he gets within a hundred yards of her, he'll be in parole violation. Not to mention which, he'll go bankrupt in the process. She has all of his quickly available cash now—possession is nine-tenths of the law and, if memory serves me correctly, he just bought a million dollar property. The greedy bastard is probably in debt up to the wazoo, and I can't imagine that his clients would stay with him while he's in the joint. Nobody would give a convicted felon their money or contracts to manage, especially after the kid's story breaks—not unless he becomes Don King, or something." Matt smirked and sat down, appearing satisfied.

Although renewed confidence temporarily allayed her fears, again Allie took note of how quiet her sister had been throughout the discussion. "Gin, you've been awfully quiet. What do you think?"

Ginny didn't respond immediately, but the tension in her body said more than words. Running her fingers through her hair, she attempted to speak, then shook her head.

"Please, Ginny? Say something," Allie begged, looking at Dave and Matt for support.

Ginny drew a deep breath and expelled it heavily. "If this were a television show, I'd say, great, let's go for it. But it's not. This is real life, gang, and I'm not so sure that we all understand that. There are a lot of things that could go wrong. Like what if Caldwell is wary now, and wouldn't take the bait? Or what if, through some fluke, DeWayne Henderson gets erroneously implicated, and his reputation gets tarnished? We could destroy an innocent rookie's career behind some madcap scheme to bring Caldwell down. And, how do we go about getting cocaine? *Cocaine*? Are you all crazy!" Ginny's voice had suddenly escalated, and she stood quickly, walking away from the table with her arms wrapped around herself. "What if somebody gets hurt? And we haven't even discussed any of this with Joan. What if she doesn't want to file charges? What if she doesn't want to deal with the humiliation of her husband's picture plastered across the newspapers. Her last name is Caldwell too, you know? And she has a little girl to consider."

Silence gripped the small group, and Allie felt her

shoulders slump in defeat. "Ginny's right, guys. It's too dangerous, and there's too many what-ifs. I think we better take the conventional approach, and let the authorities handle it from here. We can help by being witnesses if it comes to that, by supporting Joan emotionally and physically, and helping her get a job so she can begin to rebuild her life. But the high drama is over. Agreed?"

Allie waited, glaring at the men seated before her until they issued a series of disgruntled confirmations. "Good," she said softly, finally allowing the tension to ease out of her shoulders with weary relief. "Look, it's been a long day. How about if I make up the extra bedroom, Gin, and you can stay the night? You shouldn't be alone after this."

Dave looked from Ginny to Matt and smiled sheepishly, giving Matt a little wink. "Nah, Al. She'll have to get used to being home soon. She can't hide out here forever."

Appalled at her husband's callousness, she almost blurted out an objection, until she caught Matt's gaze.

"Dave's right. I'll stay with her," he said shyly, looking to Ginny for her approval.

Blinking, and trying to force away a smile, Allie looked at her sister, noticing a slight blush come over Ginny's face.

"Thanks, Allie, but the guys are right. I'll be okay."

As they all filed toward the front door, Allie gave Ginny's side an inconspicuous pinch. "You're sure?"

Returning the poke, Ginny reached over to hug her, "Yes. Very sure."

Allie stood on the steps with Dave until Ginny's car pulled off. Turning to Dave, she gave him a spontaneous hug, and was surprised to have it returned so hard.

"Thanks for everything today. For leaving work so fast and getting the van. I really appreciate it."

"C'mon, let's go inside," he said quietly, leading her up the stairs.

Following him, her mind sorted through the mixture of emotions that now assailed her. Watching Dave climb the stairs before her while still holding her hand, she realized just how much she appreciated the man walking in front of her. She was proud of him. He had put aside their differences to come to the aid of her sister, and she admired the way he took control of that situation. No matter what, Dave could be counted on, and as they crossed the threshold of their bedroom, he turned her around and looked at her intensely.

"Allie," he said in a soft voice, inches from her face in the dim light. "I had no idea that you were grappling with all of this stuff. Evan beating Ginny and Nan? Jesus."

"Yes," she said quietly. "I've felt so lonely without you to talk to at the kitchen table when the kids went to sleep. I wanted you to know what was going on at work too, the good stuff we do there . . . Everything. But, I felt so shut out."

Hugging her tightly, he murmured into her hair. "Oh, God, Allie. I'm so sorry. I never meant for this to happen to us. I don't know . . . I guess I was scared. When I saw what happened in that Caldwell house, and heard all of the ugly things Ginny said about the law and her life, I looked across the table at you and prayed to God that would never happen in my family, or to our children. I never had an appreciation for what you did before. But now, I think I understand a little bit. You're doing such good for people in terrible need . . . women, and children.

I'm ashamed to admit that maybe I was just jealous that we didn't have you all to ourselves anymore. I'm so proud of you, honey," he said, kissing her neck and squeezing her harder. "Really. I am."

His words and simple admission were like balm on an open wound. Suddenly her little family seemed more precious than anything in the whole world. It had been so long since she felt this way, totally at peace, totally secure, totally loved. Emotions swept through her, burning her and bonding her in Dave's embrace. His kiss began as a gentle brush against her lips, then slowly became a fervent request for greater intimacy. Allie clung to his shoulders as his hands slid down her body, rekindling a dying desire for the man that she soon remembered how to love.

"You're so beautiful, Allie. Inside and out," he said hoarsely, moving her toward the bed. "I'm a lucky man."

Reaching out her hand, she joined him, blanketing them with long-forgotten warmth. "I missed you so much," she whispered, swallowing down tears of joy.

"Promise me we won't break up," he murmured, emotion catching in his throat. "I don't know what I'd ever do if you left me. I'm so sorry for shutting you out."

Returning his kiss, she gently stroked the tears away from his cheeks, "You never will, Dave. I love you, too . . . I never stopped."

Ginny allowed the steam to curl up from her coffee cup and infuse her nostrils with the strong familiar aroma of morning. Closing her eyes as the warmth livened her senses, a feeling of well-being enveloped her. She had spent the night with a man, and awakened in the morning protected by his embrace. Opening her eyes, she peered out of the window from her comfortable spot in the cushioned winged-back chair. Spring was in full bloom in her yard, and for the first time in years, she would be a part of the wondrous season.

Lush blossoms from the trees cascaded a delicate scent in through the window. The sun was brilliant and golden, casting a glow to the grass, birds, and yard plants . . . How long had it been since she'd taken in and appreciated nature's beauty? A gentle breeze kissed her face, and she smiled, remembering Matt's soft caress the night before.

"You look comfortable," Matt said in an easy voice, crossing the room to give her a peck. "I saw the postman when I went out to the car to bring in the bags, and I brought in your mail."

Ginny smiled lazily and stretched. "I guess we'd better get started and sort through Joan's things. I don't want to shove a bunch of trash bags at her. We could at least organize it into boxes for her before delivering it."

Matt placed the mail on the small table beside her and sat down on the window seat. "Yeah, no matter what, it's going to be emotionally rough for her for a while. I'm sure she'll appreciate it." Heaving himself up again, he looked at her and smiled. "You sure look pretty in the morning."

His comment made her blush and look down, not knowing how to answer. His presence still felt so new, so different . . . yet it seemed like they had known each other for years.

"Got any boxes?" he said moving toward the door. "I'd better keep focused on our mission, or you may not get much done today."

"In the basement," she said, suppressing a giggle, picking up the mail as he left the room.

Sorting through the bills and catalogs, she separated the junk mail from the important correspondence. As she rifled through the remaining letters, she spotted an odd-shaped, ivory-colored envelope on expensive bond. Curiosity halted her, and she opened it immediately. A sly smile erupted into a low chuckle as she read the words out loud, "You are cordially invited to a housewarming of the Caldwells' new home . . ."

"You have got to be kidding me?" Matt stood in the archway of the living room with three large boxes in his hands.

"He probably had his secretary in New York send them out, and hadn't had the opportunity to tell her about his little altercation yesterday. They were probably already in the mail when it happened."

Matt laughed, setting the boxes down next to the bags. "Well, that'll be a real eye-opener for his guests when they find out that Joan Caldwell is gone and her whereabouts are unknown. And I bet he invited all of his top clients to show off his fancy new house. Serves him right."

Ginny didn't answer. Her gaze had caught another piece of correspondence that had stopped her heart. She could tell by the familiar script on the front that it was a letter from Nan.

"Is everything all right?" Matt asked, becoming wary as he advanced toward her.

"It's from my sister, Nan."

Giving her another light kiss, he squatted in front of her and covered her clasped hands with his own. "Why don't you read it? Even if you can never forgive her, at least that might help you let it go."

Matt's words sank in slowly, and she held the letter tightly and shut her eyes. "Why can't all this just be over? Why can't she just go on and live her life and let me live mine?"

"Because, no matter what, you're still family," he said softly, brushing her mouth as he stood. "I'm going to take this load into the kitchen and begin packing. Why don't you take some time to read her letter and, if you want, we can talk when you're done."

"I guess I have to hear her out sooner or later," she said. "I'd rather get it over with and put it behind me as soon as possible."

When Matt had left the room, she let her fingernail slide under the sealed edge, carefully opening Nan's thick letter. Taking a deep breath, she allowed her sister's words to enter her brain and to settle in her heart. Each sentence pulled her to a new place of understanding, wringing her of emotion, until the feelings spilled down her cheeks, blotting the paper. Ginny sat for a long while, holding the letter in her hand and staring out the window. There had been so many good times interspersed with the bad times. Each of them in their own crazy, dysfunctional way had tried to cope and survive . . .

"Ginny! Get in here! Quick!"

Matt's yell startled her and she bolted toward the sound of his voice. "What is it? You scared the life out of me!"

"Good Lord, woman. Do you know what you got your hands on?"

Still confused, Ginny knelt down next to Matt and peered at the two large ledger books he held in his hands.

"Where did you get this?"

Touching the books, her mind scrambled to sort out the insane events of the prior evening. "I think I pulled these from the cupboard in the study when I took her high school yearbook. I thought they were photo albums. I really just grabbed whatever I could."

"Well these ain't yearbooks, hon," he said in a triumphant laugh. "You got the keys to the kingdom!"

Shaking her head, she ran her fingers through her hair. "Please speak in plain English, Matt. What the devil are you talking about?"

"You got his books, kiddo. That slimeball was keeping two sets of books. One details what his clients' investments are supposed to be. The other is what he's skimmed from each of them, so if he needs to backtrack and cover his trails, he can. The second set tells just how much interest he's robbed his clients of, and where he's banking it."

"Why would he do that?" Ginny asked perplexed.

"Greed."

"That's not what I meant," she said impatiently, standing to work out the kink in her legs. "I know he's a greedy little man, but I mean about the second set of records."

"Because," Matt answered, sighing with his own growing impatience, "if he ever got caught, he'd probably claim that he invested their money for them and had a record of where it was kept. However, the one problem he'll have is, all the investments were done through his own personal accounts, not in their names or in his business' name. Look—this is all under Richard M. Caldwell."

Ginny was nearly speechless as she perused the documents that Matt held before her. "Look at this, Matt. He's stolen at least fifty thousand dollars from each client and transferred it to his own accounts. But the way he stole it was so sneaky! He just didn't give them their full dividends or interest on their investments. And look," she added, flipping pages furiously, "He stole it in small, unnoticeable increments. A thousand dollars here . . . twenty-five hundred there . . ."

"I believe the word is fraud, or embezzlement. Stole is such a common phrase."

Ginny looked up at Matt who was smiling, noticing a mischievous glint in his eyes. "Oh, no. What are you thinking?"

Shrugging his shoulders and placing the ledgers in an empty box, Matt chuckled. "You are *so* suspicious, Virginia Harrison. Just because the press and his clients would love to get hold of this . . ."

"Don't even think it. I thought we said no more master plans. We just box this stuff, tell Joan what's in there, and we've done our civic duty for a friend."

Eyeing Matt cautiously, she was not relieved to notice that he hadn't stopped smiling. There was a twinkle in his gaze that made her wonder if he'd truly dropped the subject. If he had appeared a little more defeated, she'd be able to relax. "Seriously, Matt. No more heroics."

"Whatever you say, Gin."

Frustration gripped her. "I really mean it," she said again, issuing a warning glare.

"Are we having our first fight, my dear?" he asked, pulling her into his arms and kissing her neck hard. "You know what an adrenaline junky I am . . ."

Even though his attentions were sending delicious shivers through her, she squirmed out of his embrace. "I'm serious," she protested, unsuccessfully stifling another giggle. "We've intervened enough, and have to stop this craziness."

When his shoulders finally slumped, she breathed a sigh of relief. Although he looked so forlorn as he went back to packing that she immediately wanted to rush over and give him a hug. "C'mon, Matt. It's not that bad. People like Caldwell eventually get what's coming to them. Believe me, I know. I've seen it played out too many times in my life."

Shrugging again, he didn't respond to her attempts to cheer him. "Yeah, yeah, yeah, I know. But it would just be so perfect."

As she stared at him, his expression reminded her of Pat's boyish grin when he tried to coax her into something he wanted badly. Smiling at Matt, she gave him an affectionate hug, and joined him beside a box. "Listen, it's not that bad. We've got Joan and her daughter safely tucked away. She has all of his available cash . . . She'll be divorced, or whatever she wants to do, and knows that she has good friends. Caldwell knows that he can't go around bullying everybody—at least not his wife—any more. So what else is there?"

"To keep him from robbing people blind, and to run him out of town on a rail."

Unable to censure herself, Ginny laughed. "I hate the guy, too."

Matt just glowered at her, and continued sorting Joan's belongings. "But what if DeWayne Henderson and I weren't friends? Maybe he would have gotten hold of that kid and ruined him. How many people have to get hurt before somebody puts a stop to this character?"

Matt had sat back on his haunches, and was looking at her directly. For the moment, she didn't have an answer to his question. All she knew was, enough was enough. They had helped a friend in need, proven their point, and now it was time to give it up.

"I rest my case," he said, becoming peevish, and returning to the task when she couldn't come up with a rebuttal to his position.

Silence strangled them as they worked side by side, completing the task and sealing the boxes. "How's Nan?" he finally asked, breaking the unbearable mood.

His question made her stop and focus on the issue that she'd buried when the fracas broke out in her kitchen. "She's getting better," she said tentatively, monitoring Matt's expression. "She said a lot of things that made me think."

Matt stopped what he was doing, and stared at her. "Do you want to go and see her?"

Ginny considered his comment, because that's just what she'd wanted to do. Each word had begun to repair her damaged heart, and at least made her know that she'd meant something to Nan. The part of this whole ugly nightmare that had haunted her the most was the feeling that Nan hated her. As she read the letter, it had become obvious that wasn't the issue at all. Nan was just an angry, confused, terrified individual in pain, lashing out at the people closest to her.

After a long while she answered Matt's question. "Yes. I suppose I should."

"That's not what I asked you, Ginny. I asked you if you *wanted* to go see your sister."

She returned his sobering question with a sad smile.

"Yes, I suppose I do. We have a lot of fences to mend . . . A lot of healing to do. I'm not so sure if isn't too late, though."

Crossing the room, Matt encircled her with his arms. "It's never too late if both people are willing to try. As long as you're both still alive, there's time."

Again, his arms provided a haven, and his tender nature made even the most frightening things seem less challenging. It was so odd how this gentle soul had come into her existence, bringing with him a breath of life and freedom from her past exile. In that instant, she knew she could face anything with Matt by her side. He didn't co-opt or threaten her personal power. He simply added to it in his own quiet way, harmoniously blending his strength with her own.

"Would you go with me?" she said softly, snuggling into his warmth.

"I'd go anywhere with you, Virginia Harrison. Anywhere."

Chapter 20

S he was grateful that Matt hadn't assailed her with questions during the entire car ride home from the hospital. Instinctively, he seemed to know that she had too much to sort out, without having to immediately analyze everything. Just as she had expected, he'd been quietly supportive, issuing her a hug when she returned to the car, and only asking how it went. He had even accepted her one-word answer, and had allowed her to ride undisturbed and absorbed in her thoughts. It had been painful and exhausting, but it had been done.

When they crossed the threshold of her home, he walked back toward the kitchen with her. "Want some tea?"

"Thanks," she said, still absorbed in her thoughts as she pressed the playback button on her answering machine. Listening intently, she recognized Joan Caldwell's voice, and was relieved at her message which explained that she and Sarah were fine and adjusting well to their temporary environment. The next message was from Allie, and the wry tone of implied curiosity in her sister's voice made her smirk.

"She wants to know how we're getting along," she said over her shoulder, laughing at Allie's innuendoes.

"Tell her we're doing fine," he said, smiling as he rummaged for a couple of mugs.

"I will, if Nan doesn't beat me to the punch."

"It went that well?" Matt took a seat and expectantly watched her until she sat down.

"Yeah, it really did, Matt. We hugged . . . and cried, and we didn't linger on the ugliness. I just told her that I received her letter, and that it took me back to a special time in our lives that I'd forgotten."

"That's a great start, Gin. I'm glad for you guys. Maybe I'll even get to meet the infamous Nan one day."

Ginny laughed. "You two would really get along well. She has a devious mind, just like you."

"Me?" he said, feigning surprise.

"Yes, you. When I told Nan about the whole Caldwell situation, she had the same reaction that you did. First she screamed and got really angry—you should have seen her. That Sullivan temper . . . Then I could see the wheels turning in her mind, and that's when I decided to get out of there before she cooked up something insane."

"What could be so insane about putting that sleaze bucket away?"

"Oh, no," Ginny said with a groan, and standing to get the tea kettle. "We're not starting that again."

"But, Gin—"

Putting up her hand, she cut him off. "Saved by the bell," she exclaimed with a giggle as the phone rang. "You'll have to table it."

Relieved to delay the long standing debate of Caldwell's future, Ginny answered the phone.

"Hello," she said cheerfully.

"Hi, Gin," Allie said almost yelling with excitement. "I just talked to Nan. She called me and told me that *Matt* drove you to the hospital. She also told me that you two have made a first start at reconciling. Oh, this is so great!"

She had to laugh at her sister's voice, which practically exploded with enthusiasm.

"*Soooo* . . ." Allie said, giggling, her voice laden with anticipation.

"Soooo . . ." Ginny said back, winking at Matt and laughing harder.

"Oh, you're making me crazy," Allie exclaimed.

"You're making *me* crazy, Allie. So Matt says hi," she added, trying to let her sister know that part of the discussion would have to wait until later.

"Oh, my God! He's still there?"

"Yes," she said, now fighting back laughter. "So what else did Nan say?" It was a weak ruse, but she didn't want Matt to think they were discussing him. It would seem so tacky.

Shifting gears quickly and picking up on her cue, Allie rushed to fill her in on Nan. "She said you guys found two sets of Caldwell's books, and I agree with her idea. You should bring that bloodsucker down."

"No!"

"She agrees with me, doesn't she?" Matt interjected with a hopeful voice.

"He agrees with us, doesn't he, Gin?"

Feeling outnumbered, Ginny squared her shoulders. "All of you are crazy. First of all, how could we let Nan pose as DeWayne Henderson's agent and go to this party? Absolutely not. You want her to distribute copies of the ledgers to all of his clients while she gets the kid out of the room because of a contrived argument? Then, the *pièce de resistance*, call the cops and claim that there's drugs in the house to have the guy busted? Total complete insanity. No."

"Nan is a genius!" Matt yelled, standing and pacing toward the phone. "Tell Allie that it would be perfect."

"I'll do no such thing," she said covering the receiver with her hand.

"I heard that and it's a great idea, Gin. Why not? Nobody'll get hurt. Not with all those witnesses around. What could happen?"

"Hey, guys. We agreed," she said sternly, ignoring the click that momentarily interrupted Allie's voice. "Look, Al, I gotta go. I've got another call. Buzz you back later, okay?"

"Okay," Allie said through another click. "But promise to call me later?"

"I promise. Now, hang up."

"Okay, okay, I'm gone. Tell Matt bye," Allie said, still sounding upbeat.

Not even bothering to say goodbye, Ginny pushed the button down and let it up with frustration, giving Matt a little shove to move him out of her space. Eyeing him with a playful glare, she acknowledged the next call as Matt drummed his fingers on her answering machine.

Immediately, her blood ran cold when she recognized the sinister voice on the other end of the line.

"It's not over, bitch."

Shoving Matt out of the way, she pushed the record button on her answering machine and ignored Matt's confused expression.

"I'll kill you and Joan both, but not before I cause you some serious pain. You shouldn't have fucked with me, Mrs. Harrison. Truly. And that stupid jock boyfriend and brother-in-law of yours . . . Doesn't he have kids? I'll ruin the lot of you. I have connections. Trust me."

As the call disconnected, Ginny couldn't stop her body from shaking. The thought of all the people in her life being threatened chilled her to the core.

"Jesus," Matt said quietly. "This guy is sicker than I thought."

"It's never going to end, is it?" Tears formed in her eyes as the reality of the situation settled in her brain. "What can we do?"

"We do what we have to do, Ginny. We bring this bastard down, like I said before. Hard." Putting his arm around her, Matt looked at her intensely. "Call Nan back. Call Allie back. We go to plan B."

Hesitantly reaching for the phone, Ginny punched in the number of the hospital. Although all of her instincts went against it, another part of her was determined to fight back. She refused to be trapped again by terror. No longer would she be held hostage by fear. No. This time she'd fight back as though her family's lives and her own life depended on it.

Because this time, maybe it did.

"Now, you remember how this goes down?" Nan looked at her protégé and nearly chuckled. "Aw, c'mon, Henderson, you'll do fine."

"I hope you know what you're doing, Ms. Sullivan,"

DeWayne Henderson said uneasily as they got out of the car.

"Do I look like I don't know what I'm doing?" Nan preened as she smoothed her red backless cocktail-length sheath and stepped out of the vehicle to join his side. "And it's Nan. We should be on a first-name basis if we're close to signing a deal together," she said, giving the tall, handsome young man at her side an affectionate poke. "I do my best work under fire," she added with pride. "I'll slice this SOB's throat, and he won't even know that he's been cut till he sees the blood on his oriental rug."

Issuing an appreciative look that stirred her, DeWayne flashed a set of brilliant white teeth. "That smooth, huh?"

Returning a lethally sexy gaze, Nan let her voice drop an octave. "That smooth, kid. Just watch me work."

As they entered the Caldwell home, Nan couldn't help but marvel at the sumptuous environs. She had seen wealth before, but even to her this was impressive. "See how he's lining his pockets," she said in a conspiratorial whisper. "Joan should get all of this and more. Bastard."

When Richard Caldwell approached, she had to fight with herself to keep her gaze from narrowing into a glare. Taking a deep breath, she whispered to the young man beside her again. "We're on."

"Richard," she said in an affected voice, almost nauseating herself. "I've heard *so* much about you. I'd like you to meet my newest client, DeWayne Henderson. Although I'm sure no formal introductions are necessary. You two have already met, haven't you?"

Reveling in Richard Caldwell's glare, she turned to DeWayne and laced her arm around his waist.

"I didn't realize that you'd already made a decision,"

Caldwell said suspiciously, barely shaking the young man's hand.

"Not quite, but we're close," DeWayne said awkwardly, looking down.

Nan nearly cringed. Geez, the kid couldn't even lie straight. He must be awful at poker, she thought, turning a magnetic smile toward Caldwell. "We're still negotiating and ironing out a few little details," she purred, rubbing the kid's side suggestively to further provoke Caldwell. "But after tonight, I'm sure we'll come to terms."

"I'm sure," Richard Caldwell said, offering no attempt to conceal his annoyance. "You obviously possess a strategic advantage. However, he'll soon learn that he doesn't have to pay for it at your rates. It's not over till it's over. I know you've heard that one before."

"Touché!" Nan laughed, throwing her head back and clapping her hands. "By the way, I'm Nancy Lynch. Shall we join the other guests, or are we banished to your foyer for bad behavior?"

"Please, come in," Caldwell said grudgingly, leading them back to the central gathering. "Would you like some champagne?"

"Perhaps later," Nan remarked, surveying the room of dignitaries with a shark's precision, and swallowing down the sudden urge for a drink. "First I'd like to mingle. Is your wife here?"

Bullseye. She had him. As Caldwell stuttered a series of unacceptable excuses, she floated away from his side and joined in with a throng of men who were hotly disputing an issue.

". . . I knew that the Nike campaign was going to be a hit when they first proposed to use Jordan. But now, the rest of them are only following, and not as successfully," one man emphatically protested.

"That's bullshit and you know it, George! The soft drinks were the first to capitalize on celebrities. And now that Jordan's retired, his marquee value is way down."

"Just look at the ratings on those Shaq Attack commercials. Never seen anything like it." Another voice came into the fray.

"I heard the Shaq thing is going well, but that's irrelevant. Look at what the beer industry did with the no-name Taste Great—Less Filling campaign. Now that was a low-budget attention grabber, which got a healthy return on investment," a third contender interjected.

"Perhaps a combination of comedy and super stardom works best, gentlemen," Nan said demurely, edging her way into the center of the group. "Take DeWayne Henderson, for example. He's new, he's hot as a firecracker, and has a marquee that will grow with his batting average."

"The lady certainly has a point," one of the men said, raising his champagne glass to her.

"And who might I ask are you?" another asked rudely, turning on Nan for daring to join their conversation.

"Just Henderson's new agent, and an advertising pro extraordinaire," she said calmly, smiling at the group.

"Well, you are most certainly extraordinary," one of the men said with unconcealed lust. "We hadn't realized that Richard had lost Henderson so quickly."

Nan shrugged, giving them a shy look. "Shit happens," she said for effect, as she purposely stunned the group for a few seconds before they broke out into a round of chuckles and guffaws.

"Well, I'll be damned," the man to her left said, obviously admiring her coup, if not her curves. "I bet old Richard had a shit fit when he heard that one. He's been promising us a look at the rookie that nobody can sign."

"Well, as you noticed, gentlemen, he's right over there. Richard is trying to steal him from me as we speak, but I'm not the least concerned."

"You're not?" another man asked in pure shock. "You'd better watch out. Richard plays hardball."

Nan chuckled, and took the man's champagne glass from him, unable to resist the libation any longer. Taking a sip, she swallowed it slowly, and issued a provocative pout. "So do I. That's why I'm not worried. And when it comes to balls, gentlemen, the only thing harder than mine is kryptonite."

Again they stared at her for a few moments, then broke into a round of hearty laughs. On that note, she decided to move the plan into the next phase, and get the hell out of there. She hated assholes like this and, to make matters worse, she felt like Cinderella on leave from the hospital with an eleven o'clock curfew.

"What I'd really like is a beer right about now," she said holding the little group in thrall. "You'd be surprised at how thirsty all of this is making me."

"I'd be glad to get you a beer," one man said, nearly bumping into another guest as he hurried to find a butler.

"Tell me, Miss . . ."

"Ms. Lynch. Nan Lynch," she corrected, still smiling at an older man in the group.

"How did you come to know DeWayne Henderson?"

"If I told you that, then I'd be giving away my best trade secrets, now wouldn't I?" She smiled prettily, still sipping on the half-filled glass. "Let's just say that I had to do a lot of research to get the information I needed to win him over."

"Such as?" The man who went to fetch her beer asked as he rejoined the small circle.

Even though she had only taken a few sips from his glass, her head was beginning to spin. She had cleaned out her system, and the bubbly was invading her mind like an instant shot of morphine. She had come too far to blow it now, so her only option was to get this whole ruse over with as quickly as possible.

"Such as, I needed to know what Caldwell offered his other clients, how he handled their business, et cetera. Then I offered the kid more."

She could see them trying to figure out her cryptic statement and knew that their curiosity had the best of them. Now all she had to do was to get Caldwell out of the room so that she could hand over the papers. "Would you boys excuse me?" she said in a confident tone, trying not to let her words slur. "I can't let Richard monopolize all of DeWayne's time, now can I?"

"Well I do hope you'll join us again before the evening is out. You have us all mystified," the eldest man in the group said politely, opening the circle so she could leave.

"I promise you'll see me later," she said over her shoulder as she moved toward DeWayne. "Don't leave without talking to me."

Needing a moment to steady herself, she stopped by the piano and held on for dear life. Jesus, what was happening to her? As she tried to clear her vision and figure out how to walk a straight line toward DeWayne and Caldwell in high heels, her gaze stopped abruptly at the door.

Christ in heaven! It was Joe Carter, Tony Amato, and

their clients from the auto dealership! *Please*, she prayed almost out loud, *please God, don't do this to me.*

Experience had taught her to meet any problem head on. Squaring her shoulders, she walked right up to Joe Carter. Kissing his cheek, she whispered in his ear. "I'll explain later, Joe. This is important. This is for Ginny and Allie, and you can't mention their names."

"What?" Joe demanded with annoyance. "What the hell is this, Nan? What happened to the hospital? Are you moonlighting now? Is this how you repay me and the firm after all of these years?"

Panic turned the blood in her veins to ice water, and she looked from Joe to Tony to the buffoon who owned the dealership. Not now! Christ, not now!

"We've already met," Bob Jegnes said angrily, leaving them at the door.

"Nan," Tony said quietly, extending his hand.

As she shook it, a pang stabbed her in her heart. "Tony, I told you I was sorry. Please, don't blow it for me here."

"At the very least, you should know I'm a gentleman," he said to her curtly, distancing himself and stepping back a pace. "What happened went down because you forced my hand. There's no reason to discuss it here."

Relief washed over her as she nervously looked at Joe Carter.

"No. There's no reason to discuss anything, Nan. You stand before me with a drink in your hand, recruiting potential clients for another firm . . . No. There's nothing to say here. We're through."

Nan closed her eyes for a brief moment as her career flashed before her. "Joe, I signed DeWayne Henderson to the firm for you. I know we're not in sports management, but it's a new direction that I wanted to try on you when I got out. It's a perfect blend to manage the athletes and manage the advertising portfolios . . . I was just trying to be helpful."

She stood stock still, watching Joe Carter recalibrate himself. Why had she lied? What the hell was she going to do when the kid signed with a bonafide agent? Her lie had gained momentum before she had a chance to think of something plausible to say. But her back was against the wall and to have an altercation now would blow everything. Once again, she'd have to clean up behind the elephants later. Giving Joe's arm a little squeeze, she looked at him directly, pleading with her eyes as Caldwell approached. "Later, Joe. I owe you one. Make that two. Okay?"

Joe took a deep breath as Richard joined their circle. "Have you two met? It seems like Ms. Lynch knows all of my favorite business associates."

Joe and Tony looked at Nan, and she held her breath. "We've met during a few contract negotiations. She's one of the best," Joe said calmly, stonewalling Caldwell as her shoulders slumped with relief.

"Joe and his new associate are worthy adversaries, Richard. I've been honored to be in their presence. But now, I must find my protégé. Have you seen DeWayne?"

Using Joe and Tony as decoys, she left them with Caldwell, growing more confident as she walked away that they'd keep her identity a secret. With no small measure of satisfaction, she appreciated the way Tony assessed her, and smiled when she paid him the cryptic compliment. He was a good sport. He knew all was fair in love and . . . Nan stopped her thoughts abruptly. She couldn't afford to go back to that old way of thinking, not after the progress she'd made. After this sting, she was out of the cutthroat way of doing business. She pressed through the small gatherings of people to find DeWayne. Hell, if this was her last performance, she'd make it a grand finale and enjoy every moment of it!

Finally sidling up to DeWayne, she tugged at his sleeve, nearly yanking him away from his conversational group. "Sorry, we don't have much time," she said nervously, ushering him to a window. "Look, we've got to get Caldwell out of here and distribute this stuff. We gotta have a fight. Now."

"Shit," he whispered back fervently. "This is the part of this whole cockamamie idea that I hate."

"I know, I know. You don't know how I wish we didn't have to do the fight thing. Hell, my boss is here and he thinks I'm freakin' moonlighting on him. You gotta get him away from Caldwell before something slips. Like he's known me before, and I'm not an agent, or he knows Matt or Ginny . . . Jesus."

"Okay, okay. What do I say?"

Losing patience, Nan nearly groaned. "We've been over this a hundred times. I say 'no.' Loudly. You say, 'Why not.' Loudly. Then I say, 'Because it's unprofessional.' Loudly. Then you say, 'Hell girl, we ain't even signed yet. I bet Caldwell can take care of it if you can't.' Even louder. Then you walk over to him and ask to speak to him privately. He'll join you, and we're on. Got it?"

Nan ignored the young man's pained expression. "No!" she screamed, not giving the kid a chance to rehearse.

"Oh, shit," he said under his breath, then responded correctly, "Why not!"

As the mock altercation ensued, Nan allowed the level of their voices to escalate. The startled expressions on De-Wayne's face almost made her want to laugh, but each time she looked at Joe and Tony, the feeling subsided instantly. Before DeWayne could even get Caldwell's name out, Richard was walking in their direction, thoroughly baited.

"Is everything all right?" he asked with a sly grin.

"Eat shit, Richard," she said before she could catch herself.

"Client troubles?"

"I'm tired of this bitch telling me what to do. I want to talk to you, man to man," DeWayne shouted angrily, totally in character now.

Nan actually groaned. The kid was overplaying it, and ruining her credibility when she went back in to give the rest of the clients the paperwork. Issuing DeWayne a lethal look, she searched the faces of the other guests. She'd have to do damage control now, that was obvious.

"Why don't we go into my study," Caldwell suggested, pulling DeWayne's elbow. "Let's not talk business in a crowded room."

"Yeah, I'm outta here," DeWayne said following Caldwell, but not before giving her a little wink.

She nearly heaved with anxiety as they left the room, and her fear that Richard might have seen the wink terrorized her. With little time to worry about it now, she joined the most influential part of the group, motioning Joe Carter and Tony Amato to join her.

"We warned you that Richard played hardball," one of the men said as she closed the circle.

"And you're right," she answered flippantly, ignoring Joe and Tony's strange expressions.

"Listen up, guys. Henderson isn't pissed off. He just had to get Caldwell out of the room so we could talk shop. Now I know this is unorthodox, but—"

"But, you're using the same slimy tactics that almost got your ass fired from McKinley, Carter and Brown when you mishandled my account!" Bob Jegnes said with a sneer, joining the group and taking a gulp from his glass.

"Fuck off," she nearly yelled, causing a hush to fall over the group. "Listen, the reason the kid will *never* sign with Richard Caldwell is because he steals from his clients."

Quickly handing xeroxed copies of the ledger pages around, she recounted the incidents of embezzlement. "Fifty-two thousand from you, Mr. Gribonni. Twenty-eight thousand from you, Mr. Ponzio . . ." she went on, giving each client a tally as she handed out the sheets. "Now, that's hardball, gentlemen. And you've just been balled, but good."

As each man in the circle looked down at the pages, she could see stark rage envelop their faces.

"Young lady, do you have hard proof? How do we know that this isn't some fraudulent scheme to make us leave Caldwell's firm?" questioned one man.

"Quite right. I've been with Richard for years. I know his wife, and—" another began as she cut him off.

"—And did you know that he beat Joan? Well, just check it out, and you'll see divorce papers going in soon that say she's been abused for years. Look, don't take my word for it, call the investment houses directly and see how much they cut in a check to Caldwell. Then go over your statements carefully and see how much has been deposited. You should pay special attention to interest payments. After you do that, then you challenge me. Besides, I have access to the actual ledgers if your attorneys need to subpoena them for court, since copies won't be admissible evidence."

"I'll be a son-of-a-bitch!" the most skeptical client said, looking at the page in his hand as he spoke. "I'll bury that bastard in court. And if the court doesn't get him, trust me, I'll, I'll . . . deal with him!"

Nan watched the eldest client in the group intently, since he had barely uttered a word since this all began. "I trust that Joan is okay? She's been like a daughter to me."

"Yes, she is okay," Nan said quietly, becoming nervous from the tone of the man's voice.

"Good. She may be a widow soon, and I would want to be sure that her assets aren't a part of this dispute," he said evenly, his glare never wavering.

"I understand," Nan remarked cautiously, edging toward the door. "Listen, there are also drugs on the premises, and the press and the police should be here shortly. I think it would be advisable if we wrapped up this party."

A collective rumble of agreement followed her suggestion, but the eldest man's voice stopped the exodus to the door. "Ms. Lynch. I like your style. You look out for your client's best interests, and that's a rare and admirable trait to find these days. What firm do you represent again?"

Casting her gaze to Joe and Tony, she smiled broadly. "I'm proud to still represent McKinley, Carter and Brown."

Merely nodding, the older man walked toward the door, leading the group behind him.

"Aren't you coming, Nan? We have a *whole lot* of catching up to do," Joe said with a wide grin.

"No, you fellas get out of here," she said, shaking her head. "I've got to get my partner in crime out of Caldwell's study before the crapola hits the fan. I'll call you over the weekend."

"You sure you're gonna be all right?" Tony asked tentatively.

"Yeah, Tony. Thanks for asking, though. It's generous of you," she said, touched that he cared. "That kid in there is big enough to stop a Mack truck if Caldwell tries anything. I'll be fine. And I've got to be back in rehab by eleven. After I flunk the urine analysis for that couple of sips of champagne, I'll be in for the duration and not hard to find."

As the other guests filed out, Nan raced toward the study, then stopped abruptly, searching the premises for a phone. She had to call Matt, who was waiting at the diner on Rt. 130, and the local police. Then she still had to stash the drugs. Ripping through the empty rooms, she realized her heart was pounding inside her chest. What if the cops came and *she* was the one in possession? What if she didn't get out fast enough with the kid? Caldwell would try to ruin him for sure.

Finally seeing the mobile unit on the kitchen counter, she dialed Matt first. "Is Mr. Lewellyn in there? This is his wife, there's been an emergency."

"Nan, there you are," Richard said in a too-calm voice. "Did you steal all of my clients yet?"

"No, but I'd like to," she said, nervously laughing, and

hoping that he hadn't gone into the living room first. "Where's DeWayne?"

"Probably rejoined the other guests. I told you, it wasn't over till it was over, Nan. And he's mine, now."

"You did say that, didn't you, Rich—"

"Nan, you there?" Matt yelled anxiously into her ear, as she continued to smile at Caldwell.

"Yes, darling, I'm here. We're just about to leave, and I'd appreciate it if you made that other business call for me. Would you be a dear?"

"Scolari from the *Daily News* is with me. But something's wrong. I can tell," Matt insisted. "Get out of there."

"I'll try to. Now be a dear and put my mind at ease. Make the call, honey."

"To the police?"

"That's right."

Hanging up the phone quickly she walked down the hall with Caldwell. "This champagne is running right through me, Richard. Do you have a powder room I can duck into before I rejoin the throng?"

Appearing quite satisfied with his coup, Richard pointed out the facilities as he walked ahead of her. "Don't be too long, Nan. Who knows what else you might lose tonight."

Caldwell's comment chilled her as she ducked into the bathroom. Opening her purse quickly, she pulled out the remainder of the cocaine that she had stashed in her apartment, and wiped her prints from the plastic bag with some toilet tissue. As she turned the bag over and over in the tissue to clean it, she almost had to close her eyes to fight the craving that burned her insides. She broke out into a sweat as she stared at the powder. Needing it . . . Wanting it . . . Hating it . . . Hurriedly, she slipped it under the sink in the vanity and emerged from the room, bumping into Caldwell in the process.

"Where is everybody?" he demanded, grabbing her arm tightly and hustling her into the living room. "I said, where the fuck did everybody go?"

"Get your hands off me," she said indignantly, shoving him away. "How the hell should I know? And where is DeWayne?"

"Your bodyguard went out to bring your car around, which will be long enough for me to wring your scrawny neck if you tried anything funny with my clients." Grabbing her by the throat, he pushed her back against the sofa, making her shin collide with the coffee table on the way down. "Who the hell do you think you are to come into my home and try to rob me of a lifetime of work? You bitches are all alike!"

Fear numbed the pain and propelled her to a standing position. Trapped between the coffee table and sofa on one side, and Caldwell on the other, she considered her options. When he reached for her hair, she screamed, and threw a punch at her nemesis that didn't connect.

"Let her go, man." A deep bass voice called over Richard's shoulder. "If you want a fight, at least do it man to man."

Caldwell turned and looked at DeWayne, then pushed her away from him. "You stupid punk. You're so pussy whipped that you can't even do business like a man. Go ahead. Get the fuck out of my house."

Even though DeWayne looked like he wanted to kill, he helped Nan to the door quickly and into the car. As they pulled out of the drive, she finally let herself relax, especially as they passed an Eyewitness News van in hot pursuit behind a squad car heading toward the Caldwells'.

"You okay, lady?" DeWayne asked, still sounding worried.

"I'm better now," she chuckled, rubbing her bruised shin. "What a lunatic."

"Yeah, I should have never left you. I was just trying to move our getaway car in front of the house."

"Hey." Nan laughed again, slapping his shoulder. "You done good, kid. If the pros don't work out, you could always make it in the movies. Boy! When you finally got warmed up, you were red hot!"

They both laughed as they made their way to Allie's house. "This whole thing has been a trip," DeWayne chuckled, pulling up into Allie's driveway.

"DeWayne, my entire life has been one hell of a trip!"

Ginny almost fainted when she saw Nan's rumpled condition. Anxiety had kept her and Allie pacing in front of the window all evening as they waited for Nan and DeWayne. Had it not been for Dave's constant insistence that they sit down, she might have levitated from her seat.

"Dear God . . . He hit you?"

"Yeah, yeah, yeah. But it was worth it," Nan said, swaggering in triumphantly. "We buried his ass, ladies. And the best part of all," she said obviously hesitating for effect, "I may have brought over some of his accounts to McKinley, Carter and Brown! The old girl still has the Midas Touch!"

"What?" Allie whispered, sitting down at the table heavily.

"Guess who showed up while we were in mid-performance? Joe fucking Carter, and Tony Amato!"

Ginny screamed. "No! Oh, my God, no!"

"I almost died," Nan said while laughing and accepting an iced tea from Dave.

"No beer. House rules," he said softly.

"Not even for an award-winning performance? I'm already burned for the champagne at the party."

"*Nan,*" they all said in harmony.

"Tell us what happened," Ginny demanded, bringing them back to the point at hand.

"Boy, such party poopers," Nan continued, taking a sip of iced tea. "It was my best ever! And the kid, he was *fantastic*!"

As they all listened intently to Nan and DeWayne's detailed description of Caldwell's downfall, she could barely wait for Matt to get there.

"You know you're going to have to go through this again when Matt comes," Ginny said.

When they finally heard Matt's car pull into the driveway, everyone bolted from the kitchen as though it were on fire. Ginny couldn't help but laugh harder as they all barreled through the door and down the steps.

"Put on the news! Put on the news!" Matt yelled as he raced up the stairs to greet them.

Like an excited gang of children, they all bumped into each other, doing clumsy about-faces, and herded into the living room. Dave reached the set first, and popped on the T.V. "What channel?"

"I dunno," Matt gasped out of breath. "They were all there."

Silence fell over them as a flash bulletin came on. They all broke out in cheers. One would have thought that they had just won the world series when Richard Caldwell was taken from his home in handcuffs. Matt was slapping Dave and DeWayne high fives, Nan had entered the fray, giving each a big hug and yelling, "Way to go, champs!" Ginny grabbed Allie and spun her around in circles until they were both dizzy with laughter. They could barely hear the news report as everyone yelled, hooted, and hollered out comments.

Flipping to another station, Dave caught the tail end of a repeat report. "Hold it down, hold it down," he yelled over the fracas. "We gotta find out what they're charging him on."

". . . Alleged spousal abuse, fraud, embezzlement, drug charges . . ." The television anchor's voice droned on.

"Drug charges?" Ginny asked, turning to Nan in the now quiet room. "He had drugs in the house?"

Nan smirked. "After I left them there," she said sheepishly, batting her eye lashes for effect.

"You didn't!" Allie exclaimed, her mouth open wide enough to catch flies.

"All in a day's work," Nan laughed, falling back on the sofa. Catching Ginny's glare, she pouted. "Aw, c'mon, Gin. I had it left over in the apartment when I went home to change, and I didn't want to spoil the environment by flushing a toxic chemical into the eco-system. And if I threw it in the trash, some small child might pick it. Drugs. A mind is a terrible thing to waste."

"Nan, weren't you supposed to be back at the hospital by eleven?" Allie cut in, growing concerned.

"Hell, this is just like the old days. You know my credo—once your ass is in a sling, you might as well have fun in the hammock!"

Despite herself, Ginny had to laugh. "Nan, you are incorrigible!"

"She's brilliant," Dave said, giving her a hug. "All of you ladies make the best double agents I've ever seen!"

"Hell hath no fury like a woman scorned," DeWayne added in. "After seeing this shit, I'm gonna just say no!"

They all laughed again, as Matt pulled Ginny into his arms. "But I can never say no to this lady," he said giving her an affectionate kiss. "I've waited too long to find her."

Ginny returned his kiss and looked down, feeling suddenly shy and embarrassed. She had never been so openly affectionate with a man in her life, but it felt good.

"Now you aren't going to start crying again," Matt said, giving her another peck. "But, then if it'll mean I'll have to stay the night again . . ."

"Oooooo," Nan giggled, elbowing her. "A lot sure happened while I was gone, huh?"

Ginny found herself giggling as she slapped away Nan's hand and tried to get out of Matt's embrace. "Thank you, Nan. You were wonderful."

"You're pretty terrific yourself," her sister answered. "Now what about this man? A jock, huh?"

"Ex-jock," she said while Matt pulled her back into his arms.

"You don't have to be shy," he said, issuing a wanton smile. "We could make it legal, you know?"

"What?" Ginny's mind refused to work.

"If you'll have me?" he murmured, looking at her deeply, and leaning in to kiss her again.

"Oh, my God," Allie screamed, hugging both of them. "Yes! Yes! I'm sure she will!"

"Allie, let the woman answer her own proposal," Nan laughed, looping her arm through Matt's.

"You're outnumbered again, kiddo," he said affectionately. "What do you say, Gin?"

Emotions caved in on her, and the room became blurry from tears. "I have waited so long . . ." she began, her voice wavering. "I don't know, what if—"

"What if we spend the rest of our lives together? Me, you and this whole big crazy family of yours—"

"I can see why he says I'm crazy," Nan interrupted, and jabbed her elbow into her older sister's side. "But you're okay, Allie."

"Shut up, Nan," Allie commanded. "He's proposing. Go ahead, Matt. You were at what if . . ."

Matt rolled his gaze toward the ceiling and Ginny bit the inside of her cheek to stop the laughter.

"What if we get one of Bummer's big-footed, floppy-eared puppies and make a home together? What if we laugh, and cry, and make up for all of the missed years? What if we love and grow old together, and put the past behind us? What if we just follow our gut, take a risk, and trust that this could work? There's a lot of what-if's, Ginny. Consider each one before you answer me."

All laughter disappeared with his words. Ginny stared at the warm, gentle man who had become more than a lover. He had become her friend, someone she could depend on, a part of her rag tag little bunch of crazy people she called family. Suddenly, the risk didn't seem so great.

Her fears about what could go wrong felt like they were a million miles away.

Somehow, God had smiled on her and given her a second chance. Her winter of isolation and pain had ended, blooming forth a new life, with new wonders ahead. Touching Matt's face, she looked deeply into his eyes, no longer afraid of what she might see.

"What if I said yes?" she murmured, sealing her answer with a kiss, and allowing her heart to fully open amid the sounds of cheers.

Epilogue

Ginny peered out of the window, trying to pray the clouds away. It had been sunny all week and, now, for some unfair reason, today of all days had become overcast.

"You look beautiful," Allie said, positively glowing as she looked at her with affection. "Why such a long face on your big day? No last minute change of heart, I hope?"

Ginny just shook her head and sat down heavily on the bed, trying not to rumple her ivory crepe dress. Allie sat down next to her and adjusted one of her sheer, chiffon sleeves. "Matt loves you, Ginny. It'll be good this time."

Giving her sister's hand a light squeeze she looked at Allie, feeling lucky that she had such a dear friend with her to share this special day. "It's not Matt, or really being afraid that it won't work. It feels so right this time . . . I'm almost afraid to admit being so silly, but I just wanted everything to be perfect this time. It's the weather . . . Oh, I just don't know."

Allie smoothed a stray wisp of hair away from her face and adjusted the flowers in her hair while smiling with tenderness. "Ginny, even if it hurricaned, nothing could make this day less than perfect."

Both sisters turned toward the door as Nan popped in smiling. "Ready, ladies?"

"Ready," Allie announced, standing and pulling Ginny to her feet. "We have a wedding to attend."

When she stood, Nan gasped. "Oh, Ginny. You look positively beautiful. You're radiant." Tears began to form in Nan's eyes and she quickly brushed them away. "You deserve this, Sis," she said in a quiet voice. "Thanks for letting me share your day with you."

Ginny left Allie's side and walked over to Nan, looping her arm about her waist. "I wouldn't have it any other way. I'm glad you're here, Nan. You're my sister."

This time tears fell from Nan's cheeks in earnest, and she tried to dab them away. "I know it'll never be the same between us again, but I just wish . . ."

"Shh . . ." Ginny whispered, pulling her sister into a tight embrace. "I never told you the story about a basket of peas."

Nan forced a chuckle, and stood back a bit to look at her. "What? You're going to tell us a story about peas? Now? On your wedding day?" She shook her head. "This is a crazy family."

Ginny only smiled. "Matt told it to me, and I think you should hear the story. It was the season of harvest, when the fields were ripe and full, and ready to yield their bounty after hard work and a long winter. Each man had his assigned rows in the field of peas, and would only be paid for full baskets they delivered to the buyers—who stood by their trucks at the end of the field. As the day of harvest drew to a close, they had to finish their rows before the sun went down and the buyers left with their loads. This meant that the last pickers would probably miss the trucks if they didn't finish in time."

Allie stood by quietly, and Ginny continued, ignoring the perplexed expression on Nan's face.

"One picker had been working hard in the field since early morning, trying to gather as much as he could, but he was falling behind the others. Soon, it became evident that he wouldn't finish in time, and he began to panic. As he picked up his pace, and tried desperately to catch up, his work became sloppy. He tried his best to meet the deadline before the trucks pulled away. Fear and anger made him work feverishly, but he knew there wasn't any way he could finish. Almost ready to pass out, the man noticed another worker standing in the opposite end of his row, picking his peas, and putting them into his own basket. But there was no time to stop and argue, no time to fight about his territory. So he just kept picking, until the two met in the middle of the row. When they did, the poor man was ready to fight, and he angrily challenged the poacher. The poacher simply smiled, and dumped his full load into the poor man's basket. He then told the man, 'Now it's your turn. Someday, give someone a basket of peas when they need it.'"

Both of her sisters stared at her, then gave her a hug.

"Thank you for my basket," Nan said, fighting her emotions.

"Thank you for mine, too," Ginny whispered back, hugging both Allie and Nan. "Al, you forced me to go on a date with Matt. You knew how tired and terrified I was, but you made me do it anyway. Nan, you forced me to face my deepest nightmare head on. If we hadn't had that big fight, it may have never surfaced and come out in the open. Then you taught me how to let things go, and how to really bury the past."

Allie touched her cheek, tearing as she looked at her. "You made me go to Washington, and that unearthed some real issues that had to be handled with Dave. If I hadn't, I might have lost him forever."

"I had to learn to take responsibility for my actions, Gin. Maybe that's why I was so angry at you. You were the only one who wouldn't let me off the hook," Nan added quietly, walking over to the window and looking down to the yard. "Robert and I are in counseling now. I don't know what's going to happen, but we're trying."

"You ready, Aunt Gin?"

All three women drew an audible breath when Pat entered the room. He looked so mature and handsome in his suit that Ginny almost couldn't believe that her nephew had grown up on her during one short summer.

"Look at you," she said, holding him out from her and turning him around. His sandy brown hair was immaculately cut, and there was just a trace of peach fuzz above his upper lip. She marveled at his height, which was now taller than her own. "You've grown up on me, Pat. Where's that little boy who used to sit in my lap?"

Nan squeezed Allie's shoulders, and walked over to her nephew. "Just look at him. You'll make a perfect escort for your Aunt Ginny. Are you ready to give her away?"

Looking down at his shoes with embarrassment, Pat shrugged. "I guess so. Whenever she's ready."

"Aunt Ginny! You're beautiful!" Meghan exclaimed, barreling into the room and hugging her around the waist tightly. "Oh, Mommy, she looks like a princess!"

Bending down to kiss the child's merry, upturned face, Ginny brushed the profusion of Shirley Temple curls away from Meghan's cheeks. "You're the one that looks like a princess," she said, turning Meghan around and making her blush. "You look so pretty."

Meghan did a little pirouette and giggled. "Me'n Mommy picked it out special for your wedding."

"It's perfect," Nan chimed in. "You and Aunt Gin will be the belles of the ball."

"Allie, you must be so proud," Ginny said, still looking at Pat and Meghan. Her sister's smile said it all.

"Then, let's stop crying and go get married!" Nan laughed, dabbing her eyes carefully and bringing harmonized joy to the room. "Let's get this show on the road."

Lacing her arm through Pat's, Ginny descended the stairs and stood expectantly at the back screen door. Allowing Meghan, Allie, and Nan to walk out first, she glimpsed Matt. He stood waiting for her next to Dave and DeWayne, shifting his weight from foot to foot. When he spotted her, his previously nervous expression softened, and his gaze fell upon her with such anticipation that she felt like a brand new bride again. Through his eyes, she became a young girl on her first wedding day, with her entire life before her.

As the wedding march began, Pat held open the door for her, then rejoined her side. Before allowing him to proceed, she stopped him for a moment to steady herself and to breathe in the wondrous moment. The yard was lush and full of dazzling green foliage, and her most cherished friends had come to witness the beginning of her new life. Dave, Joan and Sarah, her staff and friends from the real estate company, Nan's husband, Robert, De-

Wayne, Matt's family, co-workers, best friends, old team-mates . . . Allie had been right. It was perfect. Nothing could ruin this day, especially not a few little clouds. God was indeed smiling on her.

Stepping carefully down the deck stairs and onto the short walkway, she soaked in the smiles and well wishes coming from those dearest to her as she neared the small podium of flowers. Finally, as Pat delivered her next to Matt, he took her hand and gave it a gentle squeeze of re-assurance. Then, as though the angels were beaming, a light breeze moved the clouds, allowing the sun to bathe them in gold.

Surely it was a sign from God.

Her season of winter had ended.

Now, for all of them, it was finally time to reap.

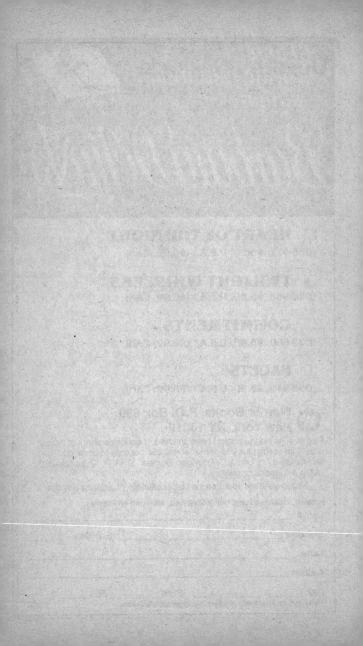